DEAR JULIA —
I HOPE YOU ENJOY THE
RIDE TO GRITTY CITY BANG!
BANG!
IT'S A BLOODY YARN ABOUT
A LOT OF IMPERFECT PEOPLE

SHOE
TOWN

WE'RE REALLY GOOD
(BEING REALLY BAD.
WHEN YOU FINISH SHOE TOWN
CALL ME @ 314-496-5653
AND I'LL INK UP A COPY
OF MY NEW BOOK DOUBLE
WHAMMY FOR YOU!

Kirk

SHOE TOWN
A tale of law enforcement in St. Louis
back in the day of the Irish Enterprises
by T. J. Birkenmeier
Copyright: March 23, 2007

United States Copyright Office
Registration: June 20, 2007 - TXu-358-348

Writers Guild Of America West
Intellectual Property Registration
Number: 1220039
Effective Date: 08.08.07

ISBN: 1-4392-6500-3
ISBN-13: 9781439265000

For my pal Julia Toscano
Viva Volpi! Viva Armando! w
04.20.2011 Viva Lorenza!

There's NOTHING like a fresh
made Volpi sandwich!

SHOE T WN

**A TALE OF LAW ENFORCEMENT
IN THE DAYS OF
THE IRISH ENTERPRISES**

T. J. Birkenmeier

Dedicated To My Best Friend
Francis Gregory "Greg" Slack
who lives, eats, breathes, sleeps,
and revels in his Irishness

And to my friend and distinguished
author, Richard P. Henrick who said,
"Write it!"

Wednesday, August 13, 2031

The telephone rang for what seemed like the millionth time when Mac finally yelled across the newsroom.

"God damn it Harry! Will you *pleeeease* pick up that phone!"

"Harry waved back and called, "I'm on deadline...you get it."

"You're on deadline! What the fuck do you think I'm on... *vacation?*"

She was sarcastic, annoyed and wondering, *where the fuck is everybody?*

The whole newsroom was empty except for her and Harry "Psycho" Ward the Sports Anchor.

WebKSDK's top-rated news reporter was far north of pissed off and more than a little clipped in her speech when she picked up. "Newsroom, McGauley."

The ensuing 2 seconds of silence seemed like an hour to her.

"C'mon speak up God damn it! I haven't got all fucking day," she snapped.

A soft voice with precise pronunciation began, "This is Sister Loretta from the Little Sisters of St. Joseph of Carondolet. I'm trying to reach Mary McGauley, the Webcaster."

Mary Katherine "Mac" McGauley suddenly felt a full body shudder and her 13-years of Catholic education instinctively kicked-in and her voice automatically shifted into the respectful tone that had been drummed into her by the Madames of the Sacred Heart at Oak Hill and Villa Duchesne.

She stammered awkwardly, "I'm afraid this is *she*.

Oh Sister, please I'm so sorry…I had no idea that I was going to be talking to a nun…I'm very sorry."

"Please, don't worry about it…no offense is taken."

"Yes, but I'm still horribly embarrassed and very, very sorry.

Sister, how can I help you?"

"Our Mother Superior, Sister Agnes would like to invite you to come visit her as soon as possible, at your convenience, about an important news story."

"An important news story? I wouldn't expect to find one of those in a Convent; do you have any idea what it's about?

"No, I'm afraid not. Mother Agnes just asked me to call you and give you the message and to see if we could set up a time for you to visit her here. I'm afraid that's all I know."

Mary McGauley rifled through the stack of paper on her desk to uncover her iWebster and clicked it to open her calendar, "I'm open all day Friday, the day after tomorrow… would that work?"

"That would be fine, Mother Agnes has nothing on her calendar after Mass at 5:00 a.m., should I put you down for 6:30 a.m.?"

McGauley laughed, "Oh, Sister, that's a little early for me... would 10 o'clock work?"

"I'm sure that will be fine. I'll put it on Mother's calendar. Do you need directions?"

"Are you still on Gravois?"

"Yes, we are on Gravois just west of Grand...if you're coming out Gravois from downtown, you'll pass the old Southside National Bank building on the corner of Grand and Gravois and the convent is about 4 blocks west on the right, between Spring and Gustine. You can't miss it. We have 17-acres right in the middle of South St. Louis. Mother's office is in our main building, Cabrini Hall, the old red brick 4-story building. Just come up the driveway and park right out front."

"Tell me Sister, is the Convent still running a home for unwed mothers?"

"Yes, that was our only mission here for many years. Although in recent times we've also become a haven for other troubled young ladies who have been abused or are in drug re-hab."

"Does this news story have something to do with that?"

"I can see why you're such a good reporter Miss McGauley, but I really don't have any inkling as to why Mother wants to see you. But I will tell you this, Mother said these exact words, it is *'about an important news story.'*

"I've been here 17-years and I have never heard Mother utter the words, *'important news story'* before...so, that may tell you something."

"Well, Sister it tells me something and it tells me nothing. But it has piqued my interest. Please tell Mother Agnes that I'll see her at 10:00 am sharp the day after tomorrow. And Sister, please forgive my language, I'm truly sorry."

"Please, don't go on about it. Apology is accepted Miss McGauley, good bye."

"Good bye Sister." Flushed and red-faced Mac hung up her phone and reverting to her normal *alpha female* newsroom speak yelled, "Harry you asshole I'm gonna cut your fucking balls off."

———◆———

Friday, August 15, 2031

The pea gravel in the convent driveway crunched under the wide profile radial tires as she drove past the neatly trimmed, oak-lined lawn that spread out before the imposing structure.

The Convent of The Little Sisters of St. Joseph of Carondolet was erected in 1882.

The main 4-story red brick building was typical of the many sturdy dark red brick structures of the era. In recent years its century-old slate roof had been replaced by new polymer resin shingles and solar panels. Other than that, the outside of the building looked pretty much the same as the day it was built.

Mac parked her Lexus, stepped out and took a deep breath. Nuns still intimidated her. *Well, here we go. I hope I don't run into Sister Loretta.*

She wondered, should I apologize in person or just let the whole thing go? I'm sure there's a Catholic nun rule that I've forgotten that would tell me how to handle it.

Nuns had a rule for everything from patent leather shoes to eye-liner and petting.

The large old door with its lead-lined frosted glass panes opened with surprising ease. Mac entered and crossed the highly polished oak-floored foyer and stopped at the reception desk. As she approached, a short stocky Sister swiveled around in her chair, her well tuned ears cued by the sound of high heels crossing the slightly creaking floor.

"Good Morning Miss McGauley, I recognize you from your Webcast. I'm Sister Ruth, Sister Loretta told me you would be here at 10:00 and that I should take directly up to Mother's office."

"Thank you Sister." Mac breathed a sigh of relief at not having to face Sister Loretta after treating her to an unexpected litany of newsroom profanity. Profanity...that's a funny old-fashioned word, you don't hear much anymore, she thought.

"I'm a big fan of yours. I think your job must be so fascinating. And, I have to confess that I'm a crime junkie. My Dad was a policeman and if you grew up in a police family you never really get it out of your system," Sister Ruth confided.

"How long have you been in the Order?"

"I will celebrate my 35th year this January. It doesn't seem that long."

The two talked casually as they moved down the long hall and past a group of uniformed girls cleaning and vacuuming the rooms that flanked both sides of the main hall which was decorated with large gilt framed oil paintings of the Holy Family and archbishops and cardinals of the Archdiocese of St. Louis dating back to the early 1800's.

"Morning housekeeping, all these rooms are set up like living rooms or family rooms where our girls can have visitors on Saturday and Sunday. We try to make it feel as much like a normal home as possible."

"I see, it looks very nice. Do all the women here wear uniforms?"

"Yes, and we keep make-up and personal accessories to a minimum. It just prevents a lot of problems and intramural female competition. A lot of these young women became pregnant because they had deep self-esteem issues. For many of them, being seen as attractive to a man and having a baby became their way of seeking acceptance, fulfillment as a woman and an affirmation of their own self worth."

"We try to teach them that self worth really has little to do with how you look, or whether you are a mother or not...what counts is who you are inside. Many of these women will go on to raise their own child. Others will give it up for adoption. Sad to say, but some of them have been here before. We turn no woman away, ever. We believe that any life choice is better than the decision to end an unborn's life."

"Are you Catholic?" the nun asked.

"Yes, *Irish* Catholic...emphasis on *Irish*."

"Ahhh...that's the best kind of Catholic, under this habit is one Margaret Mary Brennan.

But don't tell Mother Agnes, that I said that, she's Italian – a *Cusamano* – and they have an entirely different opinion on that topic, as you might imagine" Sister Ruth smiled.

"Well here we are." Sister Ruth knocked on the thick mahogany door.

"Please come in," a deep voice beckoned from within.

Sister Ruth opened the door and as Mac crossed the threshold, she found herself inside a large dark walnut paneled room filled with Jacobean bookcases flanking a large desk. It was like stepping into an 1890's office preserved in a time capsule.

From out of the arc of light softly glowing from the Tiffany-style lamp on the corner of the desk, she saw a large and imposing woman well over 6 feet tall briskly crossing the large oriental rug to greet her.

"I'm Mother Agnes, thank you for coming Miss McGauley.

"Please let's sit over here by the window where it's a little brighter. I like to work in very low light at my desk. Sister Ruth won't confirm it, but I have heard a rumor that the staff and the residents call me *'Mother Mole.'*

"Is that true Sister?"

"I have no comment," Sister Ruth replied.

"Miss McGauley, you're an investigative reporter, perhaps you can help me get to the bottom of it?"

"Is that the 'important news story' that you called me about?"

Mother Agnes laughed softly, "Hardly my dear...*hardly.*

"Sister Ruth will you be kind enough to bring us some refreshments at 10:30. Miss McGauley and I will finish our meeting by then. Please close the door on your way out."

Sister Ruth smiled and withdrew. As the door clicked soundly behind her, Mac and Mother Agnes settled into two deep leather chairs on either side of a wide and low coffee table in front of the Chesterfield leather couch tucked neatly beneath the heavily draped window.

"Thank you for coming over so quickly," Mother Agnes began.

"Well Mother Agnes, I must confess that it's not every day that someone on the crime beat gets a call from a convent about what's been described as 'an important news story.' So I'm more than curious. What's this all about?

"It's about this."

Mother Agnes opened the drawer in the coffee table and placed a large manila envelope on the coffee table. The envelope was mottled brown and discolored with age. It was tied tightly and crimped in by a dried out twine. A smaller age-yellowed envelope was on top of the package held in place below the crisscrossed strings.

"What is it?"

"I have no idea."

Mac paused and wondered *what kind of mind game is this?*

"Sister, excuse me, but you called me out here about *an important news story* and now you tell me its all about this old package and when I ask you what it is, you say you 'have no idea.' What's that all about?

"I'm just following instructions."

"Okay, I'll take the bait, instructions from whom?"

"From Mother Mary Elise, she was my predecessor here."

"I see, and what did she tell you?"

"She told me that this package had been entrusted to our care way back when Mother Elizabeth was in charge."

"And when was that?"

"1931."

"1931? Mother Agnes, this is Friday, August 15, 2031!

"If this is an important news story, why have the Sisters been passing it along like a baton for 100 years?"

"We were keeping a solemn promise to the man who brought it to us. He asked us to safeguard it for 100-years and then to call the man who is leading newspaper crime reporter in St. Louis and give it to him.

"As you can imagine, that presented me with a bit of a dilemma, since there is no longer a daily newspaper in St. Louis and the leading crime reporter isn't a man, it's you. I guess the gentleman who entrusted the package to Mother Elizabeth didn't have a very good crystal ball," Mother Agnes speculated.

"So this is for me?"

"Yes and *only for you.* The instructions are quite explicit about that and now that I've turned it over to your hands, the promise has been kept," Sister Agnes rocked back and rested her crossed arms over the cardboard-stiff front of her habit.

"So you really have no idea what's in here," McGauley asked skeptically.

"That's true."

"What about the man who brought it here...who was he?" she bored in, digging for details.

"I don't know. Mother Elizabeth was the only one who knew his name. But, I suspect that the answers you seek are probably inside this envelope and the package. My guess is that whoever he was, he must have been someone important.

"Mother Elizabeth by all accounts was a very austere woman of the highest ethics and morals, she certainly would not have agreed to be part of some charade or foolishness," Mother Agnes said as she leaned in and tapped the package with her finger.

"We've had 12 Mother Superiors here since 1931 and every one of them has faithfully protected this and transferred the package and the instructions to her successor."

"Didn't curiosity drive you crazy?" Mac asked as she picked up the package.

I know it would have made me completely spatial."

The knock on the door announced the arrival of Sister Ruth.

"Come in Sister.

'Miss McGauley would you like some iced tea? It's Orange Spice Pekoe and quite good?"

"It sounds great. So, should we have a look at what's inside?"

"*Oh no!*" Mother Agnes placed the palm of her had down quickly on top of the package.

"The instructions were very particular about that. You and *only you* are to open it and I'd prefer that you take it with you and open it in privacy.

"Sister Ruth," Mother Agnes put an edge in her voice, "Thank you for bringing the tea. You may go now."

Sister Ruth turned quickly and silently glided out of the room closing the door behind her with a soft click.

"Sister Ruth is very dear and very curious and more than a little bit chatty. She says more than her prayers. If you know what I mean."

"Not exactly the soul of discretion?"

As they said in *Pulp Fiction*, "Correctamundo."

McGauley was surprised by the reference to Tarantino's 20th century crime classic.

"You've seen *Pulp Fiction?*"

"It's one of my all time favorites...I especially like the scene when Samuel L. Jackson retrieves his wallet in the restaurant hold-up scene. One of the girls in our recreational therapy class made one like it as a gift for me. It was kind of an odd tribute, but a tribute nonetheless."

With that Mother Agnes whipped a wallet out of a concealed pocket in her habit's sleeve and tossed it on the coffee table.

It was a small thin wallet with clumsy plastic stitching looping up the sides. The big letters emblazoned on it were not skillfully burned into the leather. The two-lined inscription read,

Mother Agnes
Bad Motherfucker.

McGauley coughed and shot iced tea through her nose and mouth when she tried to suppress a laugh.

"Oh my God, I'm sorry I've made a mess," she blurted

"I'm surprised it shocked you," Mother Agnes said as she daubed up the sprayed tea droplets off the coffee table.

"Miss McGauley, surely you know that we don't deal with little angels, *magna cum laude* college graduates from Smith or VP debutantes here. And, since I am the one who has to maintain order and discipline, the nickname is not wholly undeserved.

"I actually took the inscription as sort of a left-handed compliment...besides; Sister Loretta told me you were also quite conversant with the saltier side of The King's English.

The two exchanged pleasantries and played the game of St. Louis Catholic genealogy for the next 10 minutes when Mother Agnes glanced at her wristwatch.

"I'm going to have to take my leave since I have a counseling meeting with the staff that I need to prepare for, do you mind?"

"Of course not, I'm anxious to get home and see what's inside your gift."

"I think you'll be able to handle whatever's in there," Mother Agnes rose, handed over the package and extended her hand. "Thank you for coming and good luck with wherever this journey takes you."

Mac didn't remember much about the drive back to her home. Her mind was busy mulling back over the events of the morning and she was so fixated on thoughts about the package laying on the seat beside her that she drove right past her Kingshighway exit.

"God damn it."

She regained her focus and swung off Highway 40 at the St. Louis Zoo exit and cut back through Forest Park to Union Boulevard, then north a few blocks to Waterman, then east to Lake Avenue. Her home was on Lake, right across the street from Central West End's famous *The New City School.*

The once marginal area of the Central West End was very fashionable now and legions of young professionals were living in the rehabbed city homes, stylish condos and renovated apartments. Her building was built in the late 1920's and she loved her updated condo with its classic millwork, marble fireplace, large dining room and its kitchen with butler's pantry. The bay-windowed living room was also quite spacious and she had 2 large bedrooms, one that served as her home office and library.

As her key threw the latch, *El Diablo Rojo*, her Abyssinian, began to purr loudly and prance dance in a circle, his tail erect and wildly twitching with excitement.

"Well look who's glad to see me. C'mere baby, c'mere. Atta boy. C'mere baby boy. Who's my baby?"

She picked up her red devil and moved toward a heavily cushioned chair in the bay window alcove.

"Let me show you what I have."

McGauley curled up in the chair and released the cat, which scampered up the arm and sat on the back of the chair just behind her head. She looked out the window and the street was quiet. She slid the letter out from underneath the strings and opened it. The dry paper flaked a bit as she broke the seal.

Inside was a time faded, but legibly typewritten letter on the letterhead of **THE ST. LOUIS STAR.** *The St. Louis Star???*...I've heard of *The Globe Democrat* and *The Post Dispatch* but this is a new one on me, she thought, *I'll Yahoogle it later.*

She slipped on her half-glasses and began reading.

THE ST. LOUIS STAR
905 Chestnut Street
St. Louis, Missouri

Dear Sir,

I don't know who you are, but if you are now holding my journal and notes, I know you are the leading newspaper reporter in St. Louis in the year 2031. I know this because I have sealed my journal and entrusted it to care of the Little Sisters of St. Joseph of Carondolet with explicit instructions that it be held for 100 years and then given to the most prominent crime reporter in St. Louis.

At the time I'm writing this letter, it is August 12, 1931.

St. Louis is in my time, as the saying goes is, *"First in booze, first in shoes and last in the National League,"* although, with all the legal breweries now closed, the first statement is at least temporarily no longer applicable. We'll have wait and see what the upcoming 1932 election brings; the second statement is very true and as for the third assertion, at least so far this year, the Cardinals are faring much better than the Browns. So maybe the latter is subject to change. As for myself, I'm hoping for a Cardinals -Athletics World Series. We'll see.

Now to the case in point, as a newspaperman, you know that all murders are worth reporting and some deserve more telling than others. The murder story chronicled in my journal has largely been told and many of the facts have been widely reported in the press to date.

But there is much more to the story than meets the eye and the final chapter and every detail contained in my journal and notes has never been publicly reported. Nor will they be in my lifetime, or indeed in the lifetimes of those who were intimately involved. I have made that journalistic judgment for reasons that will become clear.

I will go to my grave wondering if it is the right decision. Only the light of history, looking back on my present as the past from your professional reporting perspective can make that assessment.

So, if you are reading this, all of the participants - including me - are now long dead and gone. St. Louis will have moved on too. I wonder what my city will be like as you read this. I wonder if my decision to sit on the story and leave the true facts surrounding the murder "unresolved" will have made any difference for better or for worse.

You'll have to be the judge of that. At least now in 2031, the story in its entirety can be told without causing any further harm or pain. After you read the contents, if you think it's worth the full telling, you'll know what to do.

Sincerely yours,

Fred Kirtschner

Frederick L. Kirstchner
Police Reporter,
Central District,
12th and Clark Streets
St. Louis Star
Home Address:
4536 McPherson Avenue,
St. Louis, Missouri

———————

Mac pulled on the brittle 100-year old twine and it easily snapped in her fingers. She unwrapped the package and inside were five items.

On top, were three old publication-issued reporters' notebooks imprinted with the masthead of *The St. Louis Star.* Each was dog-eared and well worn from hard use.

The first notebook was labeled: *March-April, 1931*; the second, *May-June, 1931* and the third; *July-August, 1931.* Below them was a larger accordion file folder containing a bound document about 2¾ of an inch thick. The document was labeled:

The Journal of F. L. Kirtschner
RE: The Tower Grove Park Murders.

It was composed on the old onion skin style paper, the kind once used to make a carbon copy of typewritten text.

The third item was a large ledger style scrapbook and it was filled with ancient age-yellowed newspaper stories clipped from various St. Louis newspapers of the era:

The St. Louis Post-Dispatch, St. Louis Globe Democrat, The St. Louis Times, The St. Louis Star and *Il Pensiero*, the Italian language newspaper.

Many of the stories from the *St. Louis Star* were by-lined by Frederick L. Kirstchner.

The reporter's first notebook also contained a neatly typed note inserted inside its cover, obviously intended for the ultimate recipient of the package.

This is the key to my reporter's notes and Journal sources:
EW - Eyewitness, I saw it myself
1H - Firsthand, I got information from an eyewitness or participant
2H - Secondhand, a reliable recounting of an event from an informed and trusted source or from a paid snitch
HS - Hearsay, gossip, squadroom lore or street snitches
OF - Official Files from the City Morgue, Police Department, Fire Department, Park Commissioner, Circuit Courts, Coroner's Office and et cetera.

I have made every attempt to accurately record all of the events surrounding the so-called Tower Grove Park Murders. My Journal is as near to a complete chronological compilation of events that I could reconstruct from my notes, other news stories, and from personal interviews with dozens of participants in the events and with other pertinent sources who had special access to or knowledge of the events.

You can be sure that what I have written here is the truth behind the murders.

As you read my Journal, it will become clear to you that there is much more to this story than was ever reported in the pages of the newspapers of the day.

FLK

Mac looked up at her Italianate coved ceiling and addressed the ghost of the departed reporter, "Well Fred, you certainly have this girl's attention. I hope you won't mind if I put on a pot of coffee. It looks like we might be here for quite awhile."

FLK Notebook: March-April 1931

Events of Monday night of 3/16 and early Tuesday morning of 3/17 with Det. J. Culhane *et al* at Tower Grove Park crime scene

KIRTSCHNER'S JOURNAL ENTRY: EW

I remember the night the murder call came in. It was about twenty-five after midnight; I was loafing on the bench in the detective bureau on the second floor of the Central District Station at 12th and Clark.

It had been a pretty slow evening and most of the second shift detectives were catching up on paperwork or reading the latest play-by-play stories about the Browns and the Cardinals."

The desk sergeant's phone rang and Emil Schumacher put down his greasy fried brain sandwich and picked up. "Detective bureau, Sergeant Schumacher."

Dick Carter, the night radio room dispatcher was on the other end.

"Hey Kraut, we've got a homicide called in from the 7th District.

Major O'Connell is requesting immediate investigative help. He asked me to call the detective bureau. He also told me he was calling Harrigan himself. So you'd better get some of your best boys to hot foot it out there or there'll be hell to pay."

"Where's the scene?"

"It's in the far end of Tower Grove Park. On one of those little lover's lanes over on the Arsenal Street side in the southwest end. A local beat officer went over to tell the lovebirds to go get a room, when he discovered the mayhem.

"If I was you, I'd go in past the bandstand on the west side of Vandeventer. You can't miss it...apparently the whole station house and half the neighborhood is already over there."

"Lemme get Culhane. Hey Joe, c'mere!" Schumacher called.

"You've got to hurry out to Tower Grove Park, here's the location." He handed him the notes he'd just scrawled down. "There's been a homicide and Jeremiah's already calling Harrigan. So it must be something pretty damn big," Schumacher speculated.

Joe Culhane grabbed his coat and said, "Schu' get on the horn and call the *Welcoming Committee*, tell 'em I'll pick'em up on the 18th street side in 5-minutes. And, then call Major O'Connell and tell him we've already left. I don't want him getting Harrigan all over my ass."

Culhane waved at me and called, "Wake up Sleeping Ugly...c'mon Freddy me boy, we got a killing to attend and since you're the only reporter stupid enough to be working this late, you're invited. Who knows laddy, it could be a big break for you."

I said, "And, afterwards I suppose I can buy breakfast for you and the rest of the boys too."

"Freddy, darling, tell me...am I that transparent?"

"Joe you are a fuckin' pane of glass," I replied.

A few minutes later, the unmarked Ford sedan pulled up at the 18th Street Terminal exit on the east side of Union Station where Mickey Finnegan and Luigi "Louie" Columbo, two members of the *Welcoming Committee* quickly piled into the back seat.

The other members, Eamon "Finn" O'Meara and Sean Corrigan came around the front of the car and leaned in close to the driver's side window.

"Call us if you need us, Joe, but I think it's best for me and Sean to stay here and make sure none of Capone's wops try to slip in. The last train from Springfield is due in any time," O'Meara said.

"Right you are, but we've got fly now...O'Connell has called Harrigan himself."

With that, Joe Culhane floored the car and sped off into the night, moving over the rain slicked street west on Market toward Grand Avenue. As he raced along, he was briefing the two detectives leaning forward in the backseat straining to hear over the siren's wail.

Back under the railroad station canopy, O'Meara looked at Corrigan and asked, "Sweet Jesus, Sean, who went and got themselves killed? The Mayor?"

FLK Notebook: March-April 1931

Went with JC and members of WC to TG Park. CH present – big to do - two victims – helluva mess in J O'C's backyard

KIRTSCHNER'S JOURNAL ENTRY:
EW/1H/2H/HS

A little background about *who's who* and *what's what* is in order dear reader. So let me explain who all of the involved parties are, why they are relevant.

Major Jeremiah O'Connell is the Precinct Commander of the 7th District, located on the corner Grand Avenue at Magnolia, just across the street from the far east end of Tower Grove Park. The 7th headquarters with its mounted police stable, and its famous a horse head bust looking down from over the entry way, is almost directly across Grand from the old main entrance to Henry Shaw's Estate.

Jeremiah is a rising star in the department. For a killing to happen in his neighborhood is very bad, because many of St. Louis' finest families live in the mansions on Hawthorne, Longfellow and Flora Places and in the graciously elegant town homes on the Sycamore-lined streets like Halliday, Cleveland and Shenandoah that surround the private streets in the Compton Heights neighborhood.

Prominent bankers, manufacturing executives, former beer barons, coal and ice company owners, lawyers and politicians all call the fashionable 16th ward home. Jeremiah knows all too well that these are the very people who will have a big say in who the next Chief of Police will be.

Neighborhood residents to the west of Compton Heights, also include the colorful cigar-chomping Chief of Detectives of the City Of St. Louis, Charles Michael *"Iron Charlie"* Harrigan. Harrigan and his wife Sarah, occupied a tidy two-story brick home on McKree Avenue, just east of the bustling 39th Street shopping district,

Harrigan and O'Connell have been friends going all the way back to their boyhood school days at old St. Malachy's and both are purported to be very prominent figures in The Ancient Order of Hibernians, the powerful Irish Political and Social Club.

In my opinion, Harrigan is the most powerful and most feared law enforcement officer in St. Louis. For O'Connell to call Harrigan directly for help at anytime, let alone well after midnight, has to mean that something terrible has happened.

The Welcoming Committee is a special hand-picked squad reporting directly to Harrigan. Their primary beat is St. Louis' Union Station. They have one assignment and that is to intercept any crime figures that might be arriving in St. Louis to set up shop and to persuade them by any means necessary to immediately return to whence they came.

With Al Capone's trial reaching a climax in Chicago, a lot of Capone's hoods have been seeking greener pastures in St. Louis and southern Illinois far away from the pressures brought on their Chicago bootlegging, gambling and prostitution operations by Elliot Ness and his so-called "Untouchables."

"Iron Charlie" was bound and determined that, "No Wop bastards from Chicago, New Orleans or points east are going to set up shop in my town."

Harrigan was not a man to make idle threats or leave his promises unkept.

The Welcoming Committee members are Sgt. Joseph Patrick Culhane and detectives, Mickey Finnegan, Sean Corrigan, "Finn" O'Meara and Luigi "Louie" Columbo, who speaks fluent Italian, including 2 obscure dialects of Sicilian.

They mostly wear plain clothes, but on occasion they have been known to wear a Railway Expressman's or a Missouri-Pacific or Frisco railroad conductor's uniform. They operate out of a converted Railway Express mail office inside Union Station.

It wasn't bad duty...it was warm and dry...and there was always plenty of action with unsavory arriving passengers, and during the lull between trains, plenty of other opportunities also existed with the *Fred Harvey* waitresses.

Louie, who was blessed with an abundant mane of dark wavy black hair, chocolate brown eyes, light olive skin and Valentino-style good looks, was famous for banging many a willing *Harvey Girl* on the canvas mail sacks in the freight office's backroom.

He called it "Working his Italian magic!"

The Irish cops on his squad called it, "Louie's Dago *Romeo* bullshit."

FLK Notebook: March-April 1931

Harrigan in foul mood
Follow up with cops – J. Clancy and Les (?) Batavia – 1st on scene
- Finnegan found something fishy???
- JC/CH knows what
- who called it in? - Slavboda ??

KIRTSCHNER'S JOURNAL ENTRY: EW/1H/2H

The crowd of cops and neighborhood people shivering in pajamas covered with overcoats or robes parted like The Red Sea as the formidable man in the Hamburg and double-breasted camel's hair topcoat exited his LaSalle in a blue cloud of Cuban cigar smoke.

"Sergeant!" Harrigan yelled at the fat 3-striper as he crossed the police line and moved into the crime scene.

Harrigan was firing questions with each step

"What have we got here Jerry?"

"Jeremiah told me there were two stiffs, is that right?"

"Has anybody made their identity?"

"Where are *my* fucking men?" Harrigan looked around, clearly annoyed.

"Who called it in?"

"Has anybody fucked with anything?"

"Have you called the coroner? I'll want Pat Taylor himself to handle this."

"C'mon man talk to me!"

Sergeant Jerry Clancy was puffing from trying to keep stride with the fast-moving, fast-talking Harrigan, as he began his rolling report.

"Well Chief, we have a dubble mordor. A man and a woman. Both shot in the backseat of the Caddy. Officer Batavia called it in. He's right over here. He's vomited a lot…I guess it was too much for him walking in on all that gore and all," Clancy reported.

"Lemme see what's in the Caddy," Harrigan leaned down and peered inside the open back door.

"Holy Christ! What a massacre."

The inside of the Cadillac's backseat and headliner was soaked in the blood of the two entangled corpses. Brains and tissue were splattered everywhere.

"His pants are down around his ankles," Harrigan observed.

"Yes Chief, and if you look closer," Clancy shined his flash light on what was left of the woman's head as it rested in a pool of blood in the male victim's lap, "I'll direct your attention to his cock."

"Holy Mother of God, it's bit half off!"

"It looks like the young lady was sucking him off when she got shot. The impact that created that hole in her head probably made her jaw bite down," Clancy guessed.

"What's that smell? Jesus Christ..." Harrigan pulled his handkerchief out of his pocket and covered his nose and mouth.

"He lost his bowels too, Chief. He literally had the shit shot out of him," Clancy commented as he shined his light onto the watery shit streaks running down the dead man's bare legs. "What a way to die...coming and going."

"Shine your light on his face," Harrigan ordered.

The stark white light from the flashlight revealed a male victim with multiple gunshot wounds to his face and chest. It was hard to tell exactly how many times he had been hit because of the tissue loss, swelling disfigurement and the brains and the blood that were splattered everywhere.

"Think it's a professional job?" Clancy asked.

"Where is her purse, his coat and his wallet?" Harrigan asked. "Did anybody remove them?"

"Look here Clancy, he's sporting a pair of very pricey patent leather and brushed suede dress shoes and he's wearing fancy pin-striped slacks. These two were out on the town or at some house party or at some speakeasy. Where's his jacket? And, where's her purse...ever know a woman to go out without her purse?" he continued.

"Somethin' smells besides the victim's shit. Get Officer Batavia over here."

"Hello Chief, I see you beat us here," Joe Culhane said as we walked up.

"Nice of you gentlemen to make it to the party.

I hope this isn't too much of an inconvenience.

Who's that asshole? Harrigan asked sarcastically as pointed at me.

"That's Fred Kirtschner from the *Star*...he's jake Chief."

"Tell him to get back and keep out of the way or I'll toss his ass in the tank."

"Better step back Fred," Joe winked, "I'll fill you in on everything. Don't worry."

Patrolman Lester Batavia and Clancy approached Harrigan.

"Officer tell me exactly what happened. Leave nothing out. Joe, pull a pad and write it all down - word for word." Harrigan barked to Joe Culhane.

The still shaken Batavia nervously began his narrative, "Chief sir, I was on my beat. I always come through this end of the park to use the callbox on the corner. As I pulled up to the curb I was approached by a lady and her husband who live across Arsenal street. They told me that they saw flashes of light and heard a lot of shots as they were unlocking the door to their house.

"I got back in the car and drove into the park. As I came down here I saw this big Cadillac parked in this side lane over by the gazebo in the picnic area. At first I thought it was just another couple of lovers makin' a little whoopee. We run love birds out of here all the time.

"But when I pulled around the turn in the lane and flashed my spot on the car, I noticed that the backdoor on the far side of the Caddy was wide open. And the windows weren't steamed up a'tall. Steamy windows is a sure sign of hot 'n heavy sex goin' on inside, ya'know.

"I got out of the car and walked up calling for the occupants to *'pull 'em up, put 'em on and tuck 'em in'* – but there was none of the usual hurly-burly of activity that usually happens when you catch a fella with his pants off and a girl with her tits out.

"So I wondered if someone had passed out from drinkin' bad hootch...I've run into that before too." Batavia paused and controlled the gagging urge to vomit as he looked past Harrigan into the car.

"I'm sorry sir, I was not ready for what was waiting inside. I have never seen anything like that before. It made me puke. I threw up right over there."

Harrigan pressed him, "Officer did you touch anything? Or, remove anything?

"No sir, I could tell that they were both dead…so I drove back to the callbox and called it in. Then I came right back here and waited for assistance."

"How long were you gone?"

"No more than 3 minutes."

"Was anyone here when you came back?"

"No Chief, the crowd only came out to see what was going on when the other squad cars arrived. The sirens woke everyone up I think," Batavia added.

"Did you look in the front seat?"

"Yes sir, before I left to make the call, I opened the driver's door to make sure there were no more victims in front."

"Was there a suit coat, a purse or any other items up there?"

"No sir, the front seat was empty."

"Thank you officer, I'll expect a full report tomorrow…why don't you report back to the watch commander and tell him that Chief Harrigan told you to sign out and go home."

"Thank you sir, I appreciate that."

Mickey Finnegan walked around from the back of the car, "Chief I think you need to see what's in here."

Harrigan, Finnegan and Culhane peered into the Cadillac's rear luggage box.

"Well, well, well, what have we here?

"Now what in the world do you suppose a rich swell is doing with two cases of nigger whiskey in his trunk?

I'd've taken him for a better class of drinker." Harrigan observed.

Then he pulled Culhane aside and whispered, "Joe, you'd better call *The King* and ask him what he knows about this whiskey."

"When do you want me to call him?" Joe asked.

"How about *right now*? He's still open all night isn't he?"

"Sure...but, you know how he..."

"But what? Call him now...or better yet, go see him now. You do know where to find your big brother now don't you?" Harrigan growled.

"Is there anything else you want me to do here Chief?

"Do you have a wooden ear Joseph?"

"No sir, I heard you perfectly."

"Then why are you still standing here?"

Culhane turned and quickly walked toward his car and grabbed me as he passed, "C'mon newsboy I can use some company." I was eager to tag along to get all the details.

"Finnegan!" Harrigan bellowed, "Get a man down to the department of motor vehicles first thing in the morning and look up the license and tax registration on this Caddy. It's a custom-built 1930 Cadillac Madame X V-16 with Fleetwood coachwork. Plate number, PLD-1764"

Harrigan knew his cars, "This beauty had to cost eight grand...maybe ten.

Just look at the paint job will'ya...ebony black over dark claret with pale cream pin-striping stem to stern and brass inlayed mahogany running boards.

"Mmmm mmm mmm." Harrigan muttered in admiration as his hand traced the graceful flowing outline of the large clam shell fender in front of the right side-mounted spare, "This kind of car usually comes with a chauffer. There can't be more than 5 of them in the state. And I'm betting the dead stiff in the back seat used to be one of the big money swells."

"Finnegan, when it gets to be better light, take a squad of men and check the entire park and the streets, sewers and alleys in the neighborhood – ten blocks deep on all sides. We're lookin' for a purse, suit jacket and probably the wallet that was once inside it. Keep me posted, I'm going to stop by the 7th to see Jeremiah and then I'm going home to get some sleep. In the mornin' I'll swing by the morgue to see if we can get a make on the stiffs. Call me there as soon as you have the vehicle owner's information. And, tell all the rest of the boys to be in my office at 10:30 tomorrow morning. We've got lots of work to do. Get to it.

"People can't go around St. Louis shooting and murdering citizens in public parks on the eve of St. Patrick's Day, that kind of bullshit cannot be put up with," Harrigan muttered and lit a fresh cigar as he walked across the wet grass in the cool March moonlight.

And so it began…

Mary McGauley rubbed her eyes and got up to brew another pot of double-strength Starbuck's French Roast Espresso. She had a long night of reading ahead.

The Newspaper Clipping File

Newspaper Clipping – *St. Louis Star,*
                                    March 17, 1931

DOUBLE MURDER IN TOWER GROVE PARK

Frederick L. Kirtschner
Of The Star Staff

The southwest end of Tower Grove Park near Arsenal and Kingshighway was the scene of a grisly double homicide last night. Patrolman Lester C. Batavia of the 7th District was alerted that gunshots had been fired in the park by Mr. and Mrs. Ted Sloboda of 5520 Arsenal Street.

The Slobodas had returned home from bowling and as they were entering their home, they heard a series of gun shots fired from the park. Officer Batavia investigated the scene and found a male and female victim apparently shot to death in the back seat of a late model Cadillac.

A police news embargo was put on the crime scene and details are not as yet forthcoming. Major Jeremiah O'Connell, commander of the 7th District referred all questions to Chief of Detectives Charles Harrigan. He did comment that crime in the 7th District is extremely rare and that the murder has the appearance of a robbery at first examination.

FLK Notebook: March-April 1931

Check on incident at Union Station on 3/17 – last train???
Dust up with hoods?
Redcap/Clarence Merrill/shoeshiner wheelchair Willy/Sheila
Finlay-Harvey girl what went down with O'Meara/Corrigan –
scuttlebutt/Schu?

KIRTSCHNER'S JOURNAL ENTRY: 1H/2H/HS

The last train from Springfield, Illinois pulled in to Union
Station right on time. at 1:55 a.m. and Sean and Eamon were
waiting.

The Land Of Lincoln was just one of the scores of trains
that arrived in St. Louis everyday. In 1930 alone, trains from
St. Louis carried over 25 million tons of freight to the west, and
32 million to the east. More than 50,000 passengers passed
through Union Station everyday. The city was a rich trade

center and always had been since Pierre Laclede and Auguste Chouteau settled it in 1764. Of course, in those days, it was the Mississippi and the Missouri rivers that were the commercial highways. They carried the fur traders' canoes loaded with traps and Indian trade goods up river in the early Spring, and returned riding low in the water with beaver pelts in the late Fall a year or two later.

The keel boats, paddle wheelers and sternwheeler riverboats with their cargoes of cotton, cattle and gamblers came later in the mid-1800's and flourished here until Grant sent his ironclads south and blockaded Vicksburg to cut the Confederacy in half. After the Civil War, the golden age of the riverboats gave way to the railroads: Sante Fe, Union Pacific, Missouri-Pacific, St. Louis-San Francisco - or the *Frisco* line for short - all operated out of the massive and magnificent Union Station that had been built in 1893 just a few years before the St. Louis World's Fair and Olympic Games of 1904.

In 1904 the entire world responded to the invitation *Meet Me In St. Louis*, but tonight the last train in was carrying a far less desirable complement of passengers. The night train was the cheapest ticket from Chicago, since it stopped in Peoria and Springfield to take on mail before it meandered down to St. Louis. It was a long and tedious ride and the few passenger cars were old and the food service was almost laughable. *The Land Of Lincoln* was a favorite train for thugs trying to slip into St. Louis, at least that was true in the days before *The Welcoming Committee*.

Finn O'Meara and Sean Corrigan watched the disembarking passengers from a small window overlooking the station platforms. The observation window, originally designed for hotel bellmen was located in the Grand Gallery on the second story of Union Station, just across the lobby from the elegant Terminal Hotel. As they checked the arriving passengers, two familiar faces emerged from the last car.

"Look here Sean…here come Vincent and Ernesto Caruso."

Hours of studying mug shots of known Capone associates had just paid off.

O'Meara called over the old Negro Red Cap they often used as a come on.

"Clarence, you see those two? Tell them that some luggage was damaged on the way here and ask them if they'll come to the Railway Express office and see if any of it belongs to them."

"Yessir, I'll bring 'em right on down."

A few moments later as the brothers from Chicago approached the baggage car, and Clarence greeted them, "Gentlemen, I'm awful sorry but some luggage from Chicago got itself damaged on the way down here and we've taken it on down to the Railway Express office. Can you all come with me and see if any if it is yours?

"Sunovabitch, it better not be my stuff." Ernesto cursed.

"Or mine either 'Sambo'," Vinnie slurred.

"Oh sirs please don't worry, if there is a damage claim it will be paid promptly, the railroads is mighty good about that. Are you staying in the Terminal Hotel? I can help you up with your bags."

"Never mind where we're staying, just take us to our fucking luggage."

"It's right inside here," Clarence said as he politely opened the door marked *Railway Express Baggage.*

As Clarence closed the door behind them, Vincent and Ernesto heard O'Meara's voice as he stepped forward out of the shadows into the light.

"Welcome to St. Louis gentlemen, I'm sorry to be the one, who has to tell you that your stay will be so short."

"Who the fuck are you? And what the fuck you talking about?" Vinnie snarled.

"Well my *Eye*-talian friends, Chief of Detectives Charles Michael Harrigan himself has sent me here to make sure that you two fine gentlemen are on the very next train back to The Windy City."

O'Meara held up his badge for the two to see, "I'm detective Eamon O'Meara. And the officer behind you tapping that "Irish Exclamation Point" in the palm of his hand is my associate in law enforcement, detective Sean Corrigan.

"If you gentlemen aren't familiar with an 'Irish Exclamation Point,' it's also called a Billy club, a nightstick or 12-inches of persuasion."

"You fucking Irish cops don't scare us. We fuck the wives and daughters of Irish cops in Chicago," Vinnie smirked.

"You do now, *do you*? D'ya mind if I ask you a question? Are you two insulting Wop assholes Cubs or White Sox fans?"

"What's it to you? You Mick prick," Vinnie glared.

"Yeah...what's it to you?" Ernesto chimed in.

"Oh listen Finn, another county's heard from," Sean observed.

"Well we're just curious...you see I'm a Cardinals fan and Sean here, well he's a Brownie lover. And we'd just like to know what your baseball persuasion is.

"You see, Sean likes to kick the shit out of National League Wops and I prefer stomping on the little bitty greasy balls of American League Dagos.

"You don't scare us." Vinnie huffed and squared up his chest.

"Oh, lads, you are *torribly* confused about our intentions, we're not here to scare you...*we're here to hurt you.*"

With that, Sean delivered a roundhouse swing with his steel-filled Billy club to the side of Vinnie's head – the bone shattering impact caught him just below his ear. O'Meara whirled and clocked Ernesto square across the face full force with the 2-foot long steel-banded oak stake from a nearby baggage cart.

Both men dropped to the ground like bags of concrete, as the two Irish coppers weighed in with the billy, blackjacks and the brass knuckles pulled from their coat pockets.

"Who did you say you were fookin' in Chicago you stoopid wop bastard?

You won't be fookin' anybody's wife or sister when were done fookin' with you!" O'Meara shouted as he pounded and kicked the stunned Vinnie.

The beating went on for nearly ten minutes until the cops' arms were numb from wailing on the unwelcome visitors.

Then the two cops dragged the barely conscious, swollen pulpy purply-faced hoods over to the baggage room's pea-green tiled wall and sat them upright.

"It's time to do the flip. Heads up is uppers…Tails up is downers.

Okay?" Corrigan asked.

"Okay by me," Finn shrugged.

The first coin flipped lazily into the air and clinked on to the floor, clattered about a bit and then settled to stillness… Heads came up.

"Uppers it is."

O'Meara lifted up the first hood's head by his hair and steadied it against the wall. Corrigan took two practice taps to line up his swing and then knocked out all of Ernesto's upper front teeth with two sharp wraps from his Billy.

Finn O'Meara flipped the second coin in the air and against all odds, it landed straight upright in a seam between the concrete slabs in the floor. O'Meara glanced almost sorrowfully down at Vinnie, "Oh Vincent, this is not your lucky day. It's both Heads and Tails."

Corrigan rained down a series of vicious blows splaying Vinnie's lips and nose wide open. Bits of his bloody gums and shattered teeth spewed across the baggage room floor. It was all over in less than 20-minutes.

The half-dead semi-conscious men were stuffed headfirst into two large canvas Federal mail sacks. Only their shoeless feet protruded and comically twitched from the tightly-pulled drawstring ends.

O'Meara and Corrigan tossed the two sacks and their groaning contents onto a baggage cart and rolled it down toward the mail car that was loading up for the run back to Chicago.

"Hey, hey, hey...what's all this? Look I don't need any trouble," Cap Mueller, the mail handler waved his hands in protest.

"Calm down Cap, it's just two bags of shit, being sent to Mr. Al Capone in Chicago, Special Delivery from Chief of Detectives, Charles Michael Harrigan himself. I promise you, these two wop bastards won't be any trouble at all," O'Meara laughed as he stuffed one of *'Iron Charlie's* calling cards into the postal worker's shirt pocket.

"C'mon Sean, it's late, let's take the Caruso's unclaimed luggage down to the evidence room and see what swag the Lord has provided. On the way, what say we go get us a slinger? I've worked up quite an appetite. How about you?"

As Clarence rode the cross town Hodiamont streetcar home that night he sat with a paper grocery sack on his lap that held two highly polished pairs of nearly new Allen Edmunds' shoes. A gold-plated alligator-banded Elgin inscribed, *To Vincent with luck from Alphonse Capone* graced his arm. He thought, *"Them Irish cops is so nice."*

KIRTSCHNER'S JOURNAL ENTRY:
EW/1H/2H/HS

In St. Louis, it is all connected.

The "Irish Enterprises" in the city are known as the 4P's - police, politics, public transportation and prohibited beverages, with an occasional foray into the unspoken fifth P, prostitution.

Hizzoner Victor Miller is the Mayor, but make no mistake, it is the Irish who run the city. And foremost among them is *The King of Kerry*. He is the power in back of all the "Irish Enterprises," and the man who runs the bootlegging, gambling and political shenanigans.

He derives his moniker and his power base from deep roots in the old and once impoverished Irish northside enclave called Kerry Patch, which until quite recently, was the stomping grounds of Egan's Rats and the deadly Cuckoo Gang.

But today, the "Irish Enterprises," more respectable and better organized are run out of *The Celtic Room* at Grand and Dodier, just across the street from the main gate of Sportsman's Park, the home of both the St. Louis Browns and The St. Louis Cardinals.

The Celtic Room to all casual passers-by looks like an ordinary neighborhood restaurant.

But behind its first floor dining room with its oil painting of St. Patrick, lies a catacomb of private dining dens and backrooms dedicated to gambling, the enjoyment of fine Irish whiskey and the pleasurable company of ladies of questionable character and unquestioned talents.

Admittance to the gated rear parking area off the alley was regulated by The King's driver, the one-armed and well-armed Matt Hellman. The walled parking lot regularly conceals the cars of prominent St. Louis businessmen, politicians, judges and out of town celebrities and athletes. Actors playing at the Muny Opera, the Fox Theatre, Lowe's Orpheum or The American often find their way into *The Celtic Room's* inner recesses. Even the great *Bambino*, Babe Ruth himself has slept off more than one all-night session of food, booze and fornication frolics in one of the upstairs suite's bedrooms.

Babe was even quoted in the *New York Herald Tribune's* sports pages as saying,

"You can't get a steak in New York as great as the steaks they serve up at The Celtic Room in St. Louis. I eat there whenever I'm in that town to beat the Browns!"

High quality liquor or the so-called "White Whiskey" from Boston's Kennedy connections flows through *The King of Kerry's* northside warehouses. Every Saturday night at 11:30 pm, just like clockwork, tarp-covered stake trucks from his Fitzsimmons Cartage company drive right through the open doors on the Vista Street side of the Public Service Corporation's 39th Street streetcar barns, just as easy as you please.

Once inside the drivers transfer the quality hootch onto out-of-service streetcars in the maintenance building. The borrowed streetcars, run by *The King's* hand-picked motormen, deliver the forbidden fruit in the wee hours of Sunday morning. The motormen run a lively cash 'n carry trade dropping off individual bottles of Jameson's, Dewar's and Canadian Club in the pre-dawn hours at dozens of corner streetcar stops all across St. Louis to otherwise law abiding citizens. The motormen also deliver 'unbroken cases' to waiting Paddy Wagons for neighborhood redistribution through the District precinct houses or the local Engine Companies of the St. Louis Fire Department.

"Black Whiskey," the cheaper inferior goods from the whiskey cookers in Tennessee and Arkansas also run through *The King of Kerry* and his associate, Fred Washington, who is known rather appropriately as *"The Big Nigger."* At 6'3" and 230 lbs, Fred is a muscled mountain of a man. His powerful physique is capped by a handsome freckled *café au lait* complexioned face that could flash the warmest smile or the most threatening glower with equal ease. *The King of Kerry* had taken Fred under his wing when he was just a kid of 17 and brought him into the "Irish enterprises" for the express purpose of *"tending to the fun loving impulses of Negroes."*

Backed by the muscle and money of *The King of Kerry*, Fred Washington built a lucrative trade in the colored neighborhoods and personally benefited from it, not only financially, but socially and physically as well. He was a welcome figure in *The Celtic Room's* high stakes poker and crap games, and his legendary sexual prowess was frequently demonstrated on many a white woman's appreciative ass in the upstairs suites.

Fred Washington was *"the personal pet"* of *The King of Kerry*. He even accompanied him on trips to New York, Chicago, Havana, Cuba and on *The King's* annual pilgrimage to The Kentucky Derby. Every one knew that if anyone fucked with

Fred, they were fucking with *The King* himself. And that was career-ending move.

At the very center of the "Irish Enterprises," in a $250 custom-tailored suit with his trademark fresh yellow rosebud *boutonnière* and starched breast pocket handkerchief embroidered with an Irish Harp and a lone Kelly green shamrock, sits the ruddy-complexioned, red-haired *King of Kerry*. By Christian name, Thomas Edward Culhane; and first cousin of Chief Of Detectives, Charles Michael Harrigan and brother of Detective Joseph Patrick Culhane.

He is also the lifelong friend of Major Jeremiah O'Connell, and a fellow Immaculate Conception parishioner of Coroner Pat Taylor and Robert Emmett Hannegan, the esteemed Chairman of the Democratic Party of Missouri and the chief local supporter of the national party's Repeal candidate, Franklin Delano Roosevelt and the other Missouri Repeal slate candidates.

Because his fingers find their way into a lot of legal and illegal pies, sooner or later, *The King of Kerry* touches everything and everyone. City aldermen, judges, prosecuting attorneys, coal and ice deliverymen, boilermakers, prostitutes, bootleggers, parish priests, streetcar motormen, widows, beat cops, police Lieutenants, Captains, Majors and Colonels benefit from his favors - and all respect his power.

One hand washes the other, as the saying goes.

All of St. Louis swirls about him like a hurricane around its eye. Yet, at age 49, he truly is a man apart. A widower, he lives with his two children, Harry and Rosemary and his unmarried sister Mary Clare, who tends the children and keeps his home and hearth. His 17 room mansion sits in the very midst of the City's movers and shakers in the castle at 34 Hawthorne Place. His elegant and imposing 4-story *Egyptian Revival* mansion is complete with a library, map room, music conservatory and ballroom. The mansion's double wide, curved driveway flows gracefully beneath an expansive *la porte cochere* with a domed leaded-glass roof and then into an ivy-covered brick walled inner courtyard defined on two sides by a rose garden and a 6-car garage with full servants' quarters above. The high-walled courtyard and the large garage were necessary precautions to protect nocturnal visitors from the prying eyes of curious neighbors, for despite his many diverse legal and illegal activities, he desires to remain quite a private person. *"Privacy is always preferable to publicity in my line of work,"* he had been heard to say.

The March night Joe Culhane and I drove up Grand Avenue from Tower Grove Park to *The Celtic Room* to ask his brother about the "black whiskey" in the Caddy's boot proved to be the first gossamer strand in a web that will ultimately reach from the depth of bloody murders in that secluded lover's lane to touch and influence the very heights of wealth and national political power.

Like I said, *"In St. Louis, it is all connected."*

———◆———

The yellow-edged pages of the old reporter's journal unfolded a chronicle of cryptic connections that began to form the backdrop tapestry for the story. At first, the pattern was unclear and constantly changing, the seemingly unrelated images partially reflecting off each other like spinning images in a mirrored kaleidoscope. Mac poured another cup of Starbucks and re-focused her heavily caffeinated brain on the task before her.

———◆———

FLK Notebook: March-April 1931

Rode with JC to Celt. Rm
JC likes to seem important – talks a lot –not discreet
Maybe good source???
Kof K meeting/TEC/whiskey questions??
best to forget all

KIRTSCHNER'S JOURNAL ENTRY:
EW/1H/2H/HS

As we sped north on Grand Avenue to meet with *The King of Kerry*, the Chief of Detectives went to the 7th Precinct to meet with Major O'Connell while the bullet shattered bodies were collected from the park and sent to the city morgue. By the time the corpses arrived there, Coroner Taylor, who had been rousted from his peaceful sleep by the 7th District Night Watch Commander, was waiting to begin the autopsies.

The City Morgue occupies a virtually windowless 3-story building on Clark Street. Its pale gray stone exterior is the same as the Central District Police Headquarters, which is right next door at 12th and Clark. Just to the north, St. Louis' impressive City Hall, designed to replicate the *Maison de Ville* or City Hall of Paris, France, extends for a full block to the corner of 12th and Market Street. A small dimly lit sign reading, **MORGUE** hanging over the oxidized front door identifies the grim business that's transacted inside. The interior of the Morgue is dark and ominous on even the sunniest day. Low lights, narrow twisting stairwells and dimly-lit hallways set a fitting mood. The place reeks of death, despair and depression. On the lowest level you'll find the autopsy and refrigeration rooms. One flight up is the office of Pat Taylor, the Coroner. The short, fat, balding Taylor is not a forensic physician, or even a mortician, but a citywide elected official; and like O'Connell and Harrigan, he is a resident of the 16th ward, a member of Fr. Jimmy Johnson's Immaculate Conception Parish and by all accounts, a high muckety muck in the Ancient Order Of Hibernians.

Halfway across town in the 7th District stationhouse, Jeremiah O'Connell was clearly agitated. "Jesus Christ, Charlie, I can't have citizens getting murdered in the middle of the ward's finest park right under the noses of me and my men. Jesus Christ! " O'Connell cursed.

"Settle down Jeremiah, we're all over this one. I promise you, no mud and no blood is gonna get splashed on your reputation. I understand what's at stake here. Trust me on that. Let me run the interference for you. This is now a detective bureau matter. I'll be the lightening rod. Nobody's gonna go fuckin' around with me. I'll handle it all, Harrigan reassured.

"Hav'ya got any whiskey?"

"You know that it's illegal?" O'Connell laughed.

"Well then do you have a Gaelic cough remedies?" Harrigan rephrased his question.

"Just so happens that I have a bottle of Erin's finest phlegm cutter right here," O'Connell pulled a bottle of Jameson's and two shot glasses from his lower desk drawer.

"Tell me Charlie, d'ya think it's a gang or a Mafia job?" O'Connell asked as he poured two shots full up.

"I'm not a hunnert percent certain. But, my nose tells me it's not a Wop job.

Or one by one of the old Egan's Rats or any other of the other usual gang morons. But, I'm withholding my final opinion until we establish the stiffs positive identities and start rousting the deceased's' family, friends and enemies...*in that order.*

"All I know for sure is this. The lad with the lead ventilated face is a gentleman of *fine*-nancial consequence. His shoes alone cost a-month's pay and his suit is $300.00 if it cost a dime." Harrigan noted.

"Wrong place at the wrong time?" O'Connell wondered.

"Well, if ever there was a wrong place and a wrong time this was certainly it. At least the poor dumb, dearly departed was getting his cock sucked when the lead started flying."

"Jealous husband? Boyfriend? Lovers triangle?" Jeremiah wondered aloud.

"Mebbe, but my nose and my gut is telling me that there's more to it than that? There was some petty thievery – I noticed that her purse and some of his jewelry and top coat has gone missing. They left his watch, but took a ring and a stick pin... there was a tiny hole in his tie...from a missing stick pin, but the beat cop was sure the items were not there when he came upon 'em."

"Was it a stick up that turned into a murder?"

"No, I don't think so. It looks more like some greedy asshole grabbed up a few souvenirs...no professional killer would bother with loot or trinkets, and no self-respecting stick up man would shoot 'em up in the middle of the park in the middle of the night in the middle of a blow job. It just doesn't add up.

"Let's call it a night lad. I'm going home to get some sleep and I'll meet with my boys tomorrow, by then we'll have the Coroner's preliminary report and the records from the Department of Motor Vehicles. With any luck at all, somebody will call in and report a missing person. I'm guessing that by end of first shift tomorrow, the circumstances will start to coalesce and we'll know how to organize the investigation. I'll put my best men on it." Harrigan promised.

"What time will you be convening the squad?" O'Connell asked.

"We'll be meeting around 10:30 tomorrow in my office. But I don't want you sittin' in, you need to keep arm's length on this one. I'll ring you up afterwards and we can meet for a late lunch at Beffa's and I'll fill you in on what we know by then. *Fair enough?*"

Harrigan squeezed O'Connell's shoulder reassuringly. "Don't worry about anything; I'm on top of this one...to the bitter fuckin' end wherever that may lead me."

Maj. O'Connell looked up at the clock in the 7th's Watch Room, "Happy St. Patrick's Day, Charles Michael."

"And, *Erin Go Braugh!* to you too, Jeremiah. Kiss Kathleen for me when you get home willya?"

The two shook hands, and as both departed, they wondered what troubles have been loosed from Pandora's box earlier on St. Patrick's Day eve.

Only time and lots of detectives' shoe leather would tell.

———

KIRTSCHNER'S JOURNAL ENTRY: EW

When we pulled in to the brick-paved alley behind *The Celtic Room*, Joe flashed the Ford's headlights against two tall wooden yard gates. In an instant, a one-armed man emerged from the gangway and said, "Leave the keys Joe. I'll park it in the third garage down, Judge Wendell just pulled out."

"Thanks Matt, where's himself?"

"I think he's up in the Galway room, *but if he isn't there...*"

Joe, interrupted, "he's probably upstairs banging Mamie."

Matt Hellman smiled knowingly, as he switched places with Joe and drove the car into the garage just up the alley. In order to protect the privacy of his clientele and their comings and goings, *The King* rents all the garages on both sides of the alley behind *The Celtic Room*.

"C'mon newsboy, but keep your mouth shut. Don't be in a hurry to start talking and let him know how stupid you are."

We walked up the dark narrow gangway and into a one-time backyard that was paved to now serve as an off street parking lot. It held about 8 cars at most, and as I was to learn, it was very prestigious to park here. *The King* reserved these spaces for himself and his very best clients, friends and associates.

"Well he's here for sure," Joe commented, as he tapped the hood ornament on the dark grey Pierce-Arrow roadster that was parked in the yard. I noted that it was the only car parked in an open truck delivery lane allowing unimpeded access to both Grand Avenue and the alley behind. I judged that *The King* did not like to deal with anything or anyone being in his way should he decide to leave the premises in haste.

We walked up a short flight of stairs and across a wide concrete porch. We passed the kitchen entrance and there were still cooks working even at this late hour. At the end of the porch was an unmarked steel door. Joe pressed the doorbell. A small door slid open and a man asked, "What's your business?"

"I've come to City Hall to have my ass painted green," Joe replied as he flashed his detective's badge. The door unbolted and swung in. "Sorry Joe, I didn't recognize you; my eyes aren't what they used to be."

"Go back to sleep you old fart, I know the way."

Joe led me up a long flight of carpeted stairs and at the second floor landing, we turned right through another door and into a long hallway filled with cigar and cigarette smoke that was wafting through the transoms from rooms on both sides of the hall.

As we walked along, I read the brass plaques on the doors; *Tipperary, Dungarven, Killarney, Cork, Blarney, Dublin* and *Galway.*

"This is it," Joe knocked a rhythmic rap on the door, turned the highly-polished ornate brass knob and entered. I followed him into a room that hung heavy with cigar smoke and the curious smell of whiskey, beer and cheap perfume. A card game was in progress and many of the players turned to greet Joe.

"Hey Joe, what brings you out so late?"

"Who's your skinny-ass pal there?"

"Want a scotch high? Mamie, get Joe a Dewar's water high, willya?"

Joe laughed and replied to each man as he made his way around the table to greet his brother. Thomas Edward Culhane rose to his full 6'2" height and vigorously embraced his little brother. The one-time hod carrier, boilermaker and World War I Marine veteran liked to hug the air out of his baby brother. "Joseph Patrick, good to see you brother. I thought you might have been mad at me or had a bone to pick with me since you've been so scarce of late."

"No Tom, I've just been real busy fightin' the bootleg whiskey crime wave that's sweeping our fair city."

The King roared, "Well, I hope you are being real fuckin' successful at arrestin' every mother lovin' one of my unscrupulous competitors."

"I didn't know you had any competitors? I'm shocked." Joe fired back.

"You're right in one respect, Joseph, I have no *worthy* competitors...just petty a bunch of petty pickpockets lacking the Irish gift for epic larceny," Tom Culhane quipped

That exchange brought a big round of laughter and side banter from the card players.

One heavyset man elbowed the player on his left, "Judge, tell Joe he'd better not look in your cellar or in the Prosecuting Attorney's either, he might find a one-man crime wave down there."

"C'mon Joe, sit down, have a drink and we'll deal you and your friend in on the next hand," *The King* gestured.

Joe answered with, "Our cousin of the *House of Harrigan* sent me here. We have a situation that's come up that requires your immediate attention. Can we talk in your office?"

Tom looked annoyed at Joe's indiscreet public announcement. He paused and took a final look at his hand. Then his mood turned suddenly ugly, "Joe, whatever the fuck is on your mind, it'll have to wait, can't you see I'm in the middle of this hand."

"Yeah Tom, you've been raised three hundred and the bet's to you," the lawyer pointed out.

"Thank you for that enlightenment Counselor Lawley, here's your three hundred and fifteen hundred more. How big are your balls now, William me boy?" *The King* inquired.

"I'm out."

"Me too."

"Are you trying to buy the pot, Tom?" the courthouse denizen asked.

The King flashed a wide smile, "It'll cost you $1500 to find out."

The remaining player tossed his cards onto the table,

"All I have is three 5's...the pot's yours."

The King laughed and mucked his cards into the discard pile.

"Ahhh, c'mon Tom, for Christ's sake don't kill me with suspense, would my hand have been good enough to win... or were you bluffing?"

Culhane stood up and as he adjusted his silk repp tie, said,

"Those my friend, are questions that will have to remain *for the ages*."

"Mame be kind enough to collect my winnings will you, Joseph and his friend and I have need of few words in privacy. Get Eddy to make us both a big 3-egg breakfast and bring it up to the apartment. I'll meet you there in...*in, ah,* Joe how long will the matter at hand take?"

"No more than an hour."

"An hour it is then Mame darlin'"

Tom Culhane put on his suit coat and led us out of the *Galway* and down the hall past the other sporting rooms and through a pair of doors with elaborate etched glass inset panels. The flight of stairs behind them led up to the 3rd floor office ante room. He turned on the table light and then unlocked the door to his private office.

"Make yourselves comfortable boys, pour yourselves a drink if you like. You'll find everything you like behind the bar."

"How much was in that last pot?" Joe asked.

"I'm guessing 7 to 8 grand give or take a few hundred.

"Jesus, you must've had a helluva hand."

The King laughed, "I had a hand like a fuckin' foot, a pair of deuces, Jack of diamonds, three of clubs and a nine of hearts.

"And you raised $1500 with that mess?" Joe shook his head.

"When you walked in, I was about to fold, but you were the perfect distraction. If you, my own brother couldn't pull me away from the table on an urgent police matter, well then I must have been holding the winning cards, eh?

"Joe my dear boy, don't'cha know by now that you don't win poker with cards, you win poker with balls. It's just like real life."

Joe sank deeply into one of the two leather chairs in front of the Edwardian desk, "Well Tom, you always did have a big set."

"The prize bull of the County Clare, I am," Tom laughed has he clenched his balls, "if you don't believe me, go ahead and ask Mamie about the racket these babies make when they're slappin' away playin' *McNamara's Band* on her sweet freckled ass."

"I'll take your word for it." Joe smiled. "Now, cut the clownin' and get serious for a minute Tom and let me tell you why I'm here."

As Joe Culhane walked his brother through all of the evening's grisly events, I found my mind drifting and my eyes wandering around the office. The paneled walls looked like mahogany or maybe cherry. I was never good at telling fine woods apart. Bookcases were built into the wall behind his desk and I could see that he possessed a wide and diverse appetite for books. The shelves were filled with the works of Irish poets and essayists along with classics, political biographies of British and American leaders and popular sports titles of the day. They were not neatly arrayed either, but stacked oddly with pieces of paper protruding from their well-turned pages. I could see that many of the note papers or bookmarks had handwritten notes on them. I wondered what notations and ideas *The King* had scribbled down as he read. Amid the disarrayed stacks of books stood two small statues, one I recognized as the Blessed Virgin Mary, the other I assumed was St. Patrick.

On the far wall was a neatly arranged collection of framed pictures. A boy's soccer team. Altar boys standing around a priest. A wedding party photo. There was a large shadow box with military medals, a photograph of group of soldiers and an official looking certificate mounted inside it. Various other individual photos of friends and family and people obviously meaningful in some way to *The King's* life completed the gallery. His desk is illuminated by a low rectangular Tiffany-style *art nouveau* lamp. A large cigar box with the monogram TEC and an inlaid ivory ring of shamrocks on the lid sits to one side of the lamp and an impressively gilded pen and inkwell set flanks the lamp on the other. If you were to show a photograph of this office to any one, they might guess it to be the office of a successful businessman, a banker, attorney or perhaps an academic professor. It had an almost reverent air about it. But, it is also an eclectic dichotomy of rough and tumble bootstrap success and traditional time-honored elegance. I thought, it fits the demeanor and deportment of its lone occupant very well, very well indeed.

My mind had drifted totally away from the conversation until Tom Culhane yelled, "What the fuck do you mean, *he's a reporter!*"

Culhane leapt from his chair, rounded the corner of his desk and grabbed his brother by the coat and jerked him up like a spineless rag doll out of the chair where he had been lolling.

"Joseph, my dear stupid, idiot brother, do you really have shit for brains? What in the name of Christ made you think it was a smart idea to bring a newspaper man into my place of business? Have you lost your last bit of sanity and judgment man?"

Joe stammered in utter shock and tried to answer, but the furious *King* continued his breathless tirade as he moved across the room and slammed Joe full force into the wall. The jarring impact rattled the entire room; pictures fell off the wall and crashed down onto the hardwood floor that bordered the oriental rug.

"You have got to be the dumbest moron ever to call himself a Culhane."

"But Tom, he's okay...*I swear,*" Joe pled.

"Okay? Okay? You say. Okay? I'll decide what's Okay."

Joe tried to speak, but Tom clapped his hand across his mouth.

"Shut the fuck up - not another word." Tom Culhane was flushed with anger.

I decided that I needed to be elsewhere fast and began to move toward the door, when Tom turned suddenly and came toward me.

"C'mere you little mutherfooker…don't you try to run from me."

I stood frozen in my tracks as Tom Culhane hit me square in the chest with both palms wide open, I flew backwards off my feet and landed in a heap against the wall. I tried to breathe and struggled to get up, but he had knocked all the air out of me. I felt his shoe heel jam down hard pinning my shoulder and when I looked up, he was glaring straight down at me. "Now you listen to me, if you ever want to draw breath again, you forget that you ever came here. If so many people hadn't already seen you here in the company of this numbskull brother of mine, I'd just put a .38 into your brain and call it a day."

I could feel the spray from *The King's* mouth on my face, he was spitting and fuming.

"Hell, maybe I ought to just shoot your sorry ass and be done with it." I saw him reach behind his back to return with a small revolver pulled out of his back belt holster. He cocked it and took dead aim at my forehead.

"Tom, for the love of Christ," Joe yelled. "Don't kill him He's okay I swear. Don't kill him. Please Tom, remember, Harrigan knows he came here with me to see you…you know he won't look the other way if you kill him.

"Look he's already pissed his pants…he's scared enough. Let him up. Please Tom, I'm beggin' you don't shoot him." Joe's pleading must have had an effect.

I felt a sudden sharp pain in my side, then another. *The King* had delivered two hard swift kicks to my ribs. Then he leaned down and almost whispered.

"Mark my words Mr. Newspaperman, if I ever see you here again. If I ever hear that you spoke to anyone about you ever being here. If I ever read so much as one word in your goddam newspaper that even so much as alludes to anything I do…and I mean *anything* - and that goes for wiping my ass and clipping my toenails...if, I read one fucking word the next sound you hear will be..."

I instinctively jumped in panic, the pointblank sound of the gunshot practically deafened me and the bullet sent wood splinters flying into my cheek as the .38 round tore a hole in the baseboard less than two-inches from my head.

"Now, get this asshole outta here and tell Matt to get somebody up here to mop up his piss," Culhane shouted.

"What'll I tell Harrigan?" Joe asked as he lifted me up and moved toward the door.

"First of all let's get what you *don't tell him* straight. Don't tell him you're a fuckin' idiot that brings newspaper reporters to *The Celtic Room*. That would make him question your intelligence, judgment and your sanity. And, I need your eyes and ears in the middle of the Bureau of Detectives, not shovelin' up horseshit in the 7th District stables. Are you with me?"

Joe nodded as *The King* continued, "Tell our beloved cousin that I will get *The Big Nigger* to find out how the black whiskey got in to the Caddy's trunk. Tell him that I will call him when I have the information and that he should leave that matter entirely to me. Now repeat what I've said word for word."

As I stood in the ante room aching and reeking from my own piss, Joe dutifully repeated *The King's* message, not once, but three times.

"Now get the fuck outta here before I change my mind," Tom Culhane slammed his office door and Joe helped me limp down the stairs and out into the alley. "Wait here, I'll go get the car, and while I'm doing that, you peel off your wet trousers and shorts, I'll give you a blanket to sit on and we'll throw the mess in the trunk. I don't want to be smelling your piss all week."

On the ride back, I sat silently and mulled over the events of the evening. As we pulled up in the alley behind my home,

Joe said, "Fred, I'm awful sorry about the '*to do*.' I had no idea he would fly off the handle like that."

"Don't worry about it Joe, but let's keep the whole sorry episode just between you and me, okay? I don't need the story about me wetting my pants to get around." I asked. "Can you open the trunk? I'll leave my pants in the garage and retrieve 'em later."

"Sure thing. And Fred, bear in mind what he told you. He means what he says."

"Then you think he *isn't* bluffing this time?" I asked.

"I've known himself, man and boy, for 40-years since the day I was born. He only bluffs at poker. Trust me on that.

"Now go on in and get some sleep, you'll still have the inside track on the story – but, for God's sake whatever you do, don't make any mention of the black whiskey. If The King gets wind of that from the street or from your paper, I won't be able to keep the next gunshot on the outside of your head," Joe shaped his hand like a pistol, pointed his finger at me and as he pretended to pull the trigger he winked. "Keep your lip buttoned and no harm will come your way. I promise."

I walked on the flagstone path in my yard, and up the back porch steps and through the kitchen door, I felt a weird sensation. It was an eerie combination of brutal personal humiliation and comic opera silliness. Wearing a Fedora, shirt and tie, socks, shoes and suit coat with a horse blanket wrapped around my cold bare ass visually reinforced the quixotic sensation. I hoped the neighbors were all still sound asleep, and that my embarrassing entry had gone unobserved. I checked my watch. It was 5:45 a.m.

I closed the kitchen door, slid the chain bolt into the lock and latched it. I felt suddenly relieved as I leaned against the kitchen wall. My ribs ached with every breath, the echo of the gunshot was still ringing in my head, and the smell and taste of gunpowder was in my nostrils and mouth.

I went upstairs and into the bathroom. I found a pair of tweezers in the medicine cabinet and used them to pull the remaining small splinters out of my cheek.

I looked at my bruised face in the mirror and thought, *I'm glad to be home...glad to be alive.*

.

KIRTSCHNER'S JOURNAL ENTRY: 1H.2H/HS

At exactly 10:27 a.m. on March 17, 1931, Chief of Detectives Charles Harrigan pulled into his reserved spot in the Police Academy Garage which adjoined Central District Police Headquarters.

"G'morning Chief," the Desk Sergeant greeted him as he passed by on his way to the stairway that led up to the Detective Bureau on the 2nd floor.

Harrigan waved in acknowledgement and took the stairs two-at-a-time. He was in a hurry to see what developments had taken place.

Inside the Bureau's dayroom, 19 detectives, the entire bureau, were swapping gossip and swilling Old Judge coffee. As the hand on the wall clock clicked to 10:30 a.m., the door swung open and Harrigan entered. Everyone immediately stood up and the room went as silent as a tomb.

"Be seated gentlemen," Harrigan said as he took the podium.

"Good morning Chief," the assembled men spoke almost in unison.

"Good morning...*good*? *That*, gentlemen, *remains to be seen*. Is the Coroner's report here yet? Finnegan, where's Finnegan?

"He's on his way sir, he called from the 7th to say he is getting the last reports from the squad that did the alley and park sweeps. And here is the Coroner's Report." Finn O'Meara handed a manila folio to him.

"Finn, what's this I hear about an incident at Union Station late last night? I had a call from the railway postmaster early this morning. It seems one of his men gave him my calling card and said that I had personally authorized a Special Delivery to one Mr. Alphonse Capo-*knee* of Chicago What do you know about that?" Harrigan queried.

"We did have a little run in – *just a minor scrape*, with two upstanding gentlemen from Chicago, but after we talked with them, and gave them *'The Key to the City,'* they decided to return home. I think they might have even hopped a late mail train back to the Windy City."

"Hmmm...I heard they weren't so upstanding or even capable of standing up a'tall when they left," Harrigan injected.

"I hope no repercussions will be caused," Finn said sheepishly.

"Repercussions! That's a lovely $10-dollar word, did you learn it from one of the *Harvey Girls* who's workin' her way through college?

"Listen to me Finn, there is already helluva lot of repercussions!" Harrigan bellowed, "When you send Special Delivery mail to Chicago in a United States Government mail sack, you have to be sure that there is enough postage on it. Or, it'll come back to the sender. Now, since I don't want the mail comin' back here to my return address, here's what has to happen. Right after this meeting, I want you to deliver the *'postage payment'* to the railway postmaster. You'll find a case of 100-proof *'stamps'* in the trunk of my car. See that you don't spill any on the way to deliver it." Harrigan laughed and said, "Nice job Finn, tell Sean I also approved of his dentistry."

The room erupted in laughter, but fell silent again when Harrigan raised both hands in the air. "You can all have a good laugh about Finn and Sean's shenanigans later, but let's get down to the serious business at hand. Last night we had two citizens murdered right in the middle of one St. Louis' finest neighborhoods. That will not be tolerated in my town, on my watch. Are we all clear on that?

"Clear sir!"

"Good." Harrigan rattled off his instructions, "Now here are your marchin' orders. I want you to roust every snitch, shylock, bookmaker, pimp and pawn broker in town. Put the word out to the all Jews on Washington Avenue and Sixth Street too. Tell 'em all to keep an eye out for any funny business, like the pawning of fancy men's jewelry; cufflinks, tie-pins, rings and the like. And I also want to know about any unusual people tossing around cash that they shouldn't have in frivolous ways."

"Joe Culhane and *The Welcoming Committee* will handle the sporting houses, and I'll personally handle the gang bosses and the bootleggers. It's a durty job, but somebody has to do it," Harrigan grinned.

"Look gentlemen in all seriousness, I want results and I want them fast. These shootings took place in my neighborhood, within blocks of the 7th District, and within earshot of more Compton Heights millionaires than you can shake a stick at. So, pull out all the stops. Call in every favor…and dole out a few if you have to…but, let's find out who killed these two fine citzens."

"Any questions?" Harrigan asked.

"Yes sir, do we have any identification on the man and woman other that the physical description sheet from the coroner?" The questioner read from the sheet in his hand, "White male 25-30, 155 lbs. 5'10" tall, no scars or distinguishing marks and White female 18-25, 108 lbs., 5' 0" tall, with crescent birthmark on left inner thigh, isn't a lot to go on."

"Good points and a good question, Larry, but at this time we do not have any more information. As soon as we do know more, we'll be filling you in. I do expect the car registration information at any time, they're looking it up this morning. Hopefully, at this very moment."

"Has anyone called in to report on a missing person or on the car?" a detective asked.

"Not a so much as a peep as yet." Harrigan added, "I'm kinda surprised by that to tell you the truth, but maybe the deceased gentleman was *'out of town on business'* if you get my drift."

"We'll have a 10:30 a.m. briefing on this every day until the matter is concluded. Get your dailies in to Sergeant Bortle every day by 4:00 pm., he'll have a daily recap for me by end of shift. If there's nothing else gentlemen, may I suggest that you get off your collective *arses* and get moving."

As the dayroom emptied out, Mickey Finnegan, who had been up all night running the neighborhood sweeps came in.

"You're looking a little scruffy Mick me boy, what did you find?" Harrigan asked.

The bleary-eyed Finnegan made his report that the early morning treasure hunt of the park's trash cans, grounds and the surrounding neighborhood alleys, ash pits and sewers turned up a lot of curious junk, including one drunken husband, two cases of homemade wine and a brand new bowling ball, but no ladies purse, man's suit jacket or wallet were found. If the shooter had grabbed the goods, he had not tossed them nearby.

"Do it again" Harrigan calmly instructed.

"*Dooo it again?* Sweet Jesus, tell me you're kiddin' Chief," the worn out Finnegan was incredulous.

"Yes Mickey, **do it again**. I'll call Jeremiah and tell him to get you a fresh set of men by 1:00 o'clock. Then have 'em do it again. Fresh eyes and fresh minds may find fresh things. And, the stuff may have been tossed *after* the first sweep was made.

"Do you see the wisdom now?"

Finnegan nodded and left with his ass dragging behind him.

Harrigan rang up Jeremiah. "Jerry, meet me at Beffa's and I'll buy you a corned beef and cabbage lunch and we can go over the coroner's report together. There's something here that doesn't make any sense to me. I'll explain when I see you.

"Great, I'll meet you there," Jeremiah replied.

"Oh hold on, Jerry! By the way, Mickey Finnegan is heading back to the 7th to round up another dozen or so men to re-sweep the park and the alleys. You might want to call the 3rd District to see if Crawford can spare a few men to help him. Invoke my name if you have to, Crawford can be an asshole sometimes.

"See you at Beffa's...noon straight up." Harrigan hung up and sat down at one of the gray metal dayroom tables and opened the coroner's report.

He wanted to take another look at the woman's right hand. When he found the photo, he noted that her right hand hung limp at her side and she was wearing a diamond ring and a gold signet on its thin frail fingers. Both of her rings were in plain sight. It would have been easy to take 'em off her dainty little hand. Did the killer simply miss them?

He flipped back through the grisly photographs, until he reached the close-up shot of the man's left hand. Harrigan used a pocket magnifying glass to confirm his observations from last evening. The photo clearly showed that the man's ring finger was swollen and bruised-blue. As Harrigan read through the coroner's autopsy notes, the report confirmed that the man's left ring finger was broken and its knuckle had been violently torn and dislocated by pulling and twisting.

It appeared that the deceased male's wedding ring was missing and someone had brutally mangled his finger in a big hurry to get it. Yet, the killer had inexplicably left behind items that were much easier to remove: a fine watch on the man's wrist and two valuable rings on the female's fingers remained undisturbed.

Harrigan wondered, *Why?*

———

FLK Notebook: March-April 1931

Rode with JC to Celt. Rm
JC likes to feel important – talks a lot – indiscreet
Maybe good source???
K of K meeting/TEC/whiskey questions??
best to forget all

KIRTSCHNER'S JOURNAL ENTRY: 1H/2H

Beffa's was a strange hangout. It was a restaurant without
an outdoor sign. The unmarked entrance was hidden inside
the basement of an office building near the Civil Courts
Building. It was a family affair, run by Papa Joe Beffa who
worked the steam table plating up hot vegetables, salads,
soups and their famous turtle chili. Greg and Robbie Beffa,
his sons worked the carving stations slicing the ham, roast
beef, corned beef and hot pastrami. Every sandwich was piled

high on white, rye or crusty Italian bread and came with a deviled egg and slice of kosher dill pickle Angelina Beffa, the mother cooked in the back and her daughter Lorenza worked the cash box.

Beffa's had no posted prices. It had no menu or menu board. It had no cash register. It had no table service. It had no airs or pretenses. What it did have was a cadre of powerful and prominent customers. Lorenza knew everyone by name and by sight. She knew who to charge, what to charge them and who not to charge at all - and the price of a lunch could vary from free to 35 cents. Beffa's had no airs about it. It was the great food and the generous slices stacked high by Greg and Robbie that made it a popular lunch spot for the city's politicians, lawyers, aldermen, bankers, rag merchants and police officers above the rank of Sergeant.

Many a deal was made in Beffa's dining room over hot homemade potato salad, and sandwiches overflowing with layers of meat. It was a man's joint. No women ever frequented the place. It was a place to talk politics and argue sports and maybe lay off a bet or too.

On St. Patrick's Day, everybody at Beffa's wore green even though their ancestry was of Italo-Swiss origin. A garland of paper cut-out shamrocks hung above the corner table that was perpetually reserved exclusively for the use of Charles Michael Harrigan and his invited guests.

Maj. O'Connell arrived about five 'til noon and took a seat at the table. As the cuckoo clock above the bar struck 12, *Iron Charlie* cleared the side door. He crossed the room shaking hands and slapping backs until he reached his table.

"Been here long?

"Five minutes, but I'm starved, let's grab a tray and get in line."

Jeremiah and Harrigan picked up their trays and set-ups and joined the procession past the steam tables.

Joe Beffa called down the line when he spotted them, "Two St. Patrick's Day Specials for the Major and the Chief of Detectives."

"With extra boiled carrots and potatoes and horseradish," Harrigan sang back.

"Hi Chief how are you?" Robbie hollered as he sliced away at huge slab of corned beef.

"Tip top, laddy. Tip top! And you? Are you married yet? Or still breaking young girls' hearts?

Robbie laughed, "I'm on a tight leash...."

"You and every other horny dog in town. Now don't be stingy with the meat portion," Harrigan joked.

When they reached the end of the line, Lorenza smiled and said, "Happy St. Patrick's Day, please accept the compliments of the house."

"Thank you Lorenza," Harrigan leaned over and whispered, "And tell Joe and Mama that we truly appreciate it."

"Wave at me if you want seconds," Lorenza reminded him.

As he arrived back at the table with his heavily laden tray, O'Connell intoned,

"Good Lord Charlie, will you look at the size of this sandwich. It could feed half the force."

"You gonna eat that pickle? If you're not toss it over here. I can't get enough of these pickles...damn they're good. Old lady Beffa makes them down in the cellar in a crock." Harrigan spread a spoonful of Meyer's fresh horseradish on the top slice of rye bread and dove into the sandwich. The first bite completely cleared his sinuses, welled up his eyes and sent tears streaming down his cheeks. "Ummmm, this is wonderful...*wonderful*"

"Any word on the victims' identities or the car registration?"

"Nothing yet, Jeremiah. But the registration department promised us the paperwork by the end of the day tomorrow. They have to get it from the State DMV in Jefferson City."

"I'd add three days to any date they give you, that department is the most fucked up mess in City Hall. And the State is even worse," Jeremiah shook his head.

"And so far, nobody's called in to report a missing woman or man either...were they both orphans?

"It just takes time, sometimes to pull all the pieces together. But, believe you me, the pieces always do come together. The world is not a perfect place and this is not a perfect crime," Harrigan noted.

"What troubles you about the case so far?" O'Connell asked.

"Let me read some of the coroner's notes to you. And see if the same things jump out at you."

———◆———

PRELIMINARY POLICE SUMMARY
CORONER'S REPORT
CITY OF ST. LOUIS

DATE: March 17, 1931
TIME: 03:45 a.m.
AUTOPSY OFFICERS: Stephen Stevens, MD, Elaine Buder, RN
ATTEST: Patrick C. Taylor, Coroner

NARRATIVE FINDINGS:

Two Caucasian victims were found in the backseat of a Cadillac car in Tower Grove Park. Autopsy estimates time of death between 11:30 pm and 12:10 a.m.

Causes of death were gunshot wounds.

VICTIM ONE: John Doe
White male, 25-30 years of age, 155 lbs. 5'10" tall, no scars or distinguishing marks.

Blonde hair, brown eyes. Blonde moustache.

The male victim was hit by a total of twelve (12) shots, any of which could have been fatal. Five (5) .32 caliber rounds were recovered from the anterior lobe of the victim's brain and four (4) .32 caliber rounds were recovered from the soft tissue inside the mouth and posterior sections of the skull. Three (3) .25 caliber rounds were recovered from the chest. Two (2) of the .25 caliber bullets had penetrated the heart the third shattered a rib and lodged in the lung.

In addition to the gunshot wounds, the male victim's left hand ring finger was severely distended and radically fractured. The knuckle had been violently torn and dislocated by probable violent pulling and twisting.

VICTIM TWO: Jane Doe

White female, 18-25 years of age, 108 lbs., 5' 0" tall, with crescent birthmark ¾ " by 2" on left inner thigh. Blonde hair (dyed) natural hair color: brunette, green eyes.

Red manicured finger nails and toe nails.

The female victim was hit by a total of one (1) fatal shot. One (1).32 caliber round was recovered from the remains of the right posterior lobe of the victim's brain. The braincase suffered severe trauma and approximately 25% of the right posterior skull above the ear was removed by the impact force of the shot.

RECOVERED AT THE SCENE:

Two (2) additional .25 rounds were recovered from the backseat's upholstery proximate to the site of the male victim's head.

ITEMS RECOVERED FROM VICTIMS:

Female Victim: Two (2) rings were recovered from the female victim's right hand. One ring appears to be a diamond ring approximately 1 ct in size, the other is a gold signet ring with monogram *MKE* and an 18k gold stamp inside the band. Date is engraved on obverse side of top, *05/02/11.*

A pearl necklace was recovered from the backseat floor of the car. It appears to be costume jewelry in nature and the strand appears to have broken in the course of rough play since the lock and hasp are still intact.

Male Victim: One (1) man's Elgin watch with black lizard band was recovered from his left wrist. The cufflinks from his French-cuff shirt were missing as was a stick pin. A hole from a stickpin was found in his tie, which was recovered from the passenger side floor in the front seat of the car.

The male's belt buckle is solid sterling silver and engraved with the monogram *PLD,* a maker's mark, *Tiffany, New York* is on the obverse side. The belt appears to be made from the same type of black lizard skin as the watchband.

His shoes appear to be custom made as no manufacturer's codes were within.

FINAL AUTOPSY TEST ANALYSIS AND ANTICIPATED REPORT COMPLETION DATE: April 1, 1931

———◆———

"So there you have it. Do the math Jeremiah, fifteen total shots are fired. That's a lot of lead. Ten shots came from a "six shot" .32 and 5 from a .25. The male victim takes 12 hits with two near misses. She takes one hit only." Harrigan counts the shots on his fingers.

"And your point is?"

"Well, I have a few points.

"First off, every .32 I know of holds 6 rounds. So how'd our shooter get off 10 rounds? Did he reload? Or, was he shooting with a .32 in both hands and when the first one was empty he switched to a .25 to finish the job with the last five shots? Who was this guy? Tom Mix?"

"You have a theory, I can tell. What do you think happened," O'Connell leaned in.

"I think we have two shooters. That's what I think. And here's the way I believe it went down. Our two shooters followed the lovebirds to the park in their own car, it wasn't a waiting ambush. They kept out of sight in the dark while things heated up in the front seat of the Caddy. When the love action moved to the back seat, they moved in for the kill.

"I think the girl took the first shot from the .32.

"Willya just look at this photo, judging from her position, she never even looked up or knew what hit her. She was kneeling down between the front and back seats and probably had her little head down bobbin' away in his lap giving him a blow job when the top of her skull and half her brains went flying. In an involuntary reflex reaction, her mouth went shut and her teeth bit the poor bastard's cock half off. Will you just look at it?"

O'Connell grimaced and put his sandwich down as Harrigan rolled on unfazed by the gore.

"Then I think our shooter fired the next five shots from the .32 pointblank into the male victim's face. That emptied the first shooter's gun.

"That's when the second shooter stepped in and put three .25s into the man's chest, the second shooter must have lost his nerve when he saw the man's face all blown off and his last two shots missed the victim's head entirely and went into the back seat.

"Next, I think the first shooter, now fully reloaded, steps back in to make sure the job was done and put the final four shots into the man's face and mouth.

"The shot to hit ratio is 12:1, male:female, make it 14:1, if you count the two missed shots aimed at the man's head. The girl was just the door prize here, somebody wanted this guy really dead and I mean dead with a capital D-E-A-D," Harrigan tapped his knuckles on the report.

"What about robbery as a motive?"

"I was born at night, Jeremiah...but not *last night*." Harrigan continued. "If this was a random robbery, I'll kiss your big Irish ass in the middle of 12th and Market at high noon. Look at this photograph, the girl's wearing two valuable rings right in plain sight.

"I reckon that the .32 shooter went in after the man's wedding ring and he had one helluva time getting it off. Look here, that would explain all the blood and brains splattered around by a flopping head on a corpse that's having its finger practically pulled off. He finally got the ring off, he also took the man's cufflinks and grabbed for the girl's pearl necklace, but it broke off. I also speculate while he was doing that, his .25 shooting partner grabbed the man's suit coat and the girl's purse off the front seat. By now they've made a lot of noise and their hearts have to be beating a mile a minute. So they run off into the deep dark park, get into their car, keep the lights out and take off in the moonlight."

"So what was the motive, if it wasn't robbery? A gang killing?"

"I don't think so. Contract gunmen are professionals. They shoot as few shots as possible. They don't like to make a lot of noise. Many prefer a knife or an ice pick. They kill fast and silently and move on. And they don't take any souvenirs, that's for sure. They never want to have any evidence that can connect them to the deed. They make their money from the hire, the last thing a professional would do is waste time practically pulling the finger off a dead man. If they wanted his ring, they'd just shoot it off or quietly cut the finger off. The less muss and fuss the better. No, I don't think it was a contract killing or a random robbery that went bad." Harrigan washed down the last bite of his sandwich with a cold *Bevo* malt beverage. "I can't wait 'til Prohibition is repealed and real beer will be back legally at lunch."

"Well if it isn't this or that, what is the motive? And, who are the shooters?" O'Connell wondered aloud.

"That's precisely what I aim to find out, Jeremiah. I think the wedding ring is the key to the mystery. Ask yourself this, 'What could be so important about a man's wedding ring that you'd take the time and risk to try to steal it after you just fired 15 shots in the middle of the night in a nice quiet neighborhood park?' Could it be the gold? Did the ring have a diamond or ruby in it? Or, was it important to someone for sentimental reasons?'

"When I know why somebody pumped 12 rounds into a citizen's skull to get a wedding ring and some other minor trinkets and cash, you'll be the second to know.

"How about a piece of pie? The lemon pie here is very tart," Harrigan asked.

"No Charlie, I think I'll pass, seeing the photograph of his half bit off cock sorta ruined my appetite."

"I guess bratwurst is going off your diet too." Harrigan laughed and shook his head, "I also heard that Batavia, the copper who found 'em, has given up brain sandwiches! Bless us and save us Mrs. O'Davis." He made the sign of the cross, got up and walked out laughing with his arm on Jeremiah's shoulder. "What's this force coming to?"

"Will I see you at the Hibernian tonight?" O'Connell asked.

"Wouldn't be any where else on St. Patrick's Day. Be sure to join us at my table for a spirited conversation and a few spirited libations, it will take your mind off the day's bullshit."

Harrigan stepped out into the warmth of the mid-afternoon sun, "*Ahhh*, look at this day will you Jeremiah, it's a grand and glorious day to be shooting Protestants."

"See you tonight, Charles Michael."

"Til tonight at the Hibernian!" Harrigan waved back at O'Connell as he drove away.

KIRTSCHNER'S JOURNAL ENTRY: 1H/2H/HS

The Hibernian Hall dominated the corner of 14th and Cass, it was a garishly impressive 4-story tribute to the industrious nature of three generations of St. Louis' Irish. Inside is a first floor library, reading room, billiard and card room, the second floor presented three dining rooms, the basement held a swimming pool and steam room; private meeting and gaming rooms filled the top floor and a Grand Hall Gymnasium that could seat up to 500 was built off the back of the central hall foyer.

The Grand Hall never looked grander than on St. Patrick's Day when the members of the Ancient Order Of Hibernians assembled in mass with their ladies for a gala evening of fellowship and revelry in the joy of all things Irish. The enclave convened promptly at 6:45 pm with the Piper's Procession, eight pipers leading in the Hibernian honor guard carrying a golden Celtic cross atop a tall staff, flanked by the flags of the United States and The Irish Republic. Immediately behind came a contingent of priests led by the popular Monsignor James "Jimmy" Johnston, the chaplain of the Order, the head of Fr. Dempsey's Charities and pastor of Immaculate Conception parish.

Then in rank order, the Hibernian's 4-abreast processed in, led by their officers wearing traditional dress blouses, kilts and garter. Unlike the Scottish clans, the Irish wore no tartans, only solid color kilts to differentiate their clans.

The multitude this evening numbered nearly 400 and represented the cream of St. Louis' Irish society including alderman, businessmen and lawyers, doctors, trade union leaders, police and fire department officers, college professors, funeral directors and the "black sheep contingent," the most prominent members of the "Irish enterprises," led by none other than *The King of Kerry.*

As the audience and officers filed into their seats, the Sergeant-At-Arms took the podium and gaveled the assembly to order. He greeted the throng and referred them to the program of events to be found on their chairs. The General Assembly is from 7:00 to 7:30 pm, with invocation by Monsignor Johnston, Dinner from 7:30 to 9:00 pm in the three dining rooms and library, followed by a concert performance and dancing in the Grand Hall commencing at 9:30 pm.

At the end of his remarks, he said, "Please give a warm welcome to Monsignor Jimmy Johnston, and remember that the proceeds from midnight's 50-50 Pot of Gold drawing goes to support the fine work of Father Dempsey's Charities. Buy a lot of raffle tickets and *Help Father Jim carry on for Father Tim.*"

Monsignor Johnston began, "In the name of the Father and of the Son and of the Holy Ghost." He prayed the Our Father, Hail Mary and Glory Be To The Father, and then he asked the audience to be seated.

"What a fine day for the Irish…it is St. Patrick's Day!" He applauded and the audience followed his enthusiastic lead. "This is a time for joy, remembrance and faith. Joy in the Irish heritage, blood and spirit that we share, remembrance in the hard roads we've traveled together and faith. Faith in the day that's coming when all Irish will be able to reap the fruits of religious freedom and economic prosperity, not only here in *Sint* Louis, but in all of Ireland too…from Dublin to Galway, and from Belfast to Brittas Bay!"

The audience rose to its feet and clapped wildly at his reference to the dream of a united Ireland, north and south.

"Tonight, let us celebrate and take well-deserved pride in all of our accomplishments. Embrace your kinsmen, dance with your wives and all the fair colleens present and sing the songs of home and hearth and heritage. It's St. Patrick's Day and it's a grand and glorious day to be Irish. God Bless you all! *Erin Go Bragh!* "

As the current Hibernian President, Robert Emmett Hannegan rose to take the podium from Monsignor Johnston, Thomas Edward Culhane whispered, "There's nothing like a right-to-the-point invocation. Jimmy knows how to get a party rollin'" Charles Michael Harrigan, who was seated to his immediate right nodded in agreement.

The King of Kerry and Harrigan were seated directly behind the podium in the Order's officer's chairs. *The King* sat in the chair of Immediate Past President and Harrigan in the 1st Vice president's chair. It was tradition for the Hibernian hierarchy to address themselves in private and in public by their first and middle names; Robert Emmett, Thomas Edward, Charles Michael, Joseph Patrick and so forth. It was a bit of pretension left over from the traditions of the immigrants from the old sod, who thought it added dignity and decorum to the Order's proceedings and a level of respectful; recognition to its leaders in the community.

"By the way Charles Michael, I have a little St. Patrick's Day present for you," Culhane tapped atop his coat's inside pocket, "Let's adjourn to the Officer's Room before we go in for dinner. I think you'll find it interesting."

Robert Emmett made a few remarks, thanked Monsignor Johnston, adjourned the opening ceremony and invited everyone to join him for dinner. As the crowd rose and exited the Grand Hall, Harrigan and Culhane slipped through a hidden seam in the stage curtain and walked across the backstage to a hallway that led down one flight of stairs to the *Officer's Room*.

It was a comfortable room appointed with banners and photographs from the Hibernian's history. Harrigan went directly to the bar and filled two Waterford tumblers with ice and poured three knuckles of Jameson over it. "Have a drink on me cousin darlin.' Let's sit a spell so I can enjoy the presentation of my gift to you," with that he handed an envelope to the Chief of Detectives.

"What is it?" Harrigan asked as he bit the end off a fresh cigar and lit up.

"It's the name of the gentleman who met a very untimely demise in his Cadillac last night in Tower Grove Park." Culhane said coolly.

"How did you come by it?" Harrigan asked, "I've been waiting for a make on the license plate registration all day so I could find out who the owner is...and they said it would take at least two days to find out from the State."

"Charles Michael, I didn't mess around with any of that rigmarole down at City Hall or in Jefferson City trying to find the person the plate's registered to. I just called your Evidence Room and asked the impound officer to read me the stencil numbers off the two cases of black whiskey that Joe said you found in the Caddy's luggage box. I thought I'd better not tarry in making the call since liquor – *good and bad* - has a way of escaping from the impound cage."

"And the impound officer gave those numbers to you? On whose authority?"

Harrigan was incensed.

"On no less authority than your very own, Charles Michael. To his credit, he did try to follow proper police procedures, until I told him that I was you and that. *'I'd reach down his fuckin' throat and grab him by the asshole if he didn't get me the numbers.'* I must've been quite convincing in my eloquence because he coughed 'em right up," Culhane laughed.

"Well I'll be damned. But how can you track down the car and the owner from the numbers on the whiskey cases?"

"By the genius of Isadore Cohen."

"You mean your little Jew clerk tracked down the owner of the car from just the numbers stenciled on the two cases?"

"Exactly right. Izzy can track down a single drop of whiskey from the number on a case. When I gave the numbers to Iz it took him all of 15 minutes to tell me where *The Big Nigger* sold the whiskey, when he sold it, who he sold it to, how much he made on the deal, how much I made on the deal and when we might expect a re-order. It's all very fucking scientific the way he does it.

"I plan to set up beer and liquor distributorships across the country when the Volstead Act is repealed. The inventory procedures Izzy's developed will make it easy for us to get a jump on the other contenders, who are generally speaking, very sloppy businessmen and a bunch of fucking morons who can't find their cock with both hands and a Handlan lamp.

"I do love my little Jew. And, he loves to show off his skills in bookkeeping too.

He even impressed Sammy Bronfman when we went up to Canada to make our trade arrangements last summer. Didn't take little Isadore any time at all to tell me who bought the whiskey. Aren't you curious?" Culhane asked as he pointed to the still unopened envelope in Harrigan's hand.

Harrigan opened the envelope to find a neatly typed message on plain paper.

Information as requested:

Two cases of goods numbered **09-87675-31** and **09-87676-31** were sold to negro Bee Henderson on March 15, 1931 by FW. The goods were delivered to the 43 Washington Terrace rear on that date.

Bee Henderson is the chauffer for Mr. Pierre L. Devereaux, who resides at the address. Mr. Devereaux owns a 1930 Cadillac with the license number PLD-1764.

Cash payment and next order information is left in an envelope in that car's trunk and the negro goods are placed inside the trunk by *The Grand Leader* deliveryman in our employ.

Delivery is made every 2 weeks. Bee Henderson is the negro goods neighborhood distributor to the colored valets, chauffeurs and maids working on Washington Terrace, Portland Place, Westminster Place and the apartments on Union Boulevard and Waterman Avenue.

It is part of a piggy-back order of white and black goods delivered to the same Washington Terrace address. The white goods part of the order is for "EOR" and sold by the house account Mr. Devereaux opened.

Those goods are stacked in a box in the rear of the garage. The "EOR order" is placed every 3 months. Let me know if you need more.

IC

"Well I'll be damned, you use *Grand Leader* department store vans to deliver the hootch?" Harrigan was clearly surprised.

"We only use 'em in the most exclusive neighborhoods. It arouses no interest from the neighbors, and the vans have to be out and about every day anyway, might as well use their gas and save ours, keeps the overhead down," Culhane smiled

"I'd say little Izzy is worth whatever you're paying him. I'm impressed.

Maybe you should be the Chief of Detectives," Harrigan joked.

"Oh no, not me...my side of the law is more fun and far more profitable."

"Why do I know this name, *Pierre Devereaux?*" Harrigan struggled to pull it up from his memory.

"Well, let me close the loop for you Charles Michael. Does the name *Pierre Laclede* ring a bell? Pierre Laclede Devereaux is descended from one of the two founders of St. Louis. *Pierre Laclede* and Auguste Choteau. Guess which one?"

"Pierre Laclede," Harrigan conjectured on the obvious.

"You are a quick learner," Culhane laughed "And get this, the license plate is PLD-1764...because St. Louis was founded in 1764.

"And it gets better, the late Pierre or *"Pete the Prick"* as we called him, is what polite society calls a 'playboy.' Me, I call him a whore-mongering, rich asshole with a perpetual hard-on. He'd fuck a drape if it would hold still. He is a regular in the 'speaks' near 'The Hill', out on the Rock Road and over on the Eastside. He's also been a frequent guest at *The Celtic Room* when Judge Thomas brings his lawyer buddies in.

"Is he a lawyer?" Harrigan asked.

"No, he's an executive in his father-in-law's business. He married very well you see.

Care to guess who he's married to?" Culhane arched his eyebrow.

"You're a Niagara Falls of information cousin, don't stop now."

"Well, he's married to a former member of the Court of Love and Beauty, The Veiled Prophet's Special Maid Of Honor, Ada Elizabeth Robertson. That's *Robertson* as in Edmund O. Robertson, the President of Continental Shoe. And, the dear departed son-in-law is the exalted Executive Vice President of the same venerable family enterprise. Rumor has it that he worked his way up to the top by going down on the daughter."

"Edmund O. Robertson, he's the biggest Prohibitionist in the state. Wait a minute, do you mean to tell me that the Edmund O. Robertson is EOR? And that he buys his liquor through his son-in-law Devereaux. Well, that's an interesting development," Harrigan was adding things up fast.

"That's the conclusion the circumstances seem to lead to. Looks like old EOR is either a fucking hypocrite or a person, who just opposes the consumption of distilled spirits by people other than himself," Culhane mused.

"*Holy Mother of Christ*...this is going to create a big *to do* when it's made public. It's gonna cause a real stink downtown," Harrigan took a big drink that drained his glass.

"I don't suppose you know who killed him and the girl? Or why? Even knowing who she is would be a big help."

"I can make some discreet inquiries, if you like," Culhane replied, "but I can assure you, it wasn't any of my boys. We would never shoot a well-heeled cash customer, even if he was a bit of a pain in the ass from time to time.

"C'mon Charles Michael, enough business for one night. But, let me know if I can be of further assistance to you at anytime dear cousin. That's what blood is for you know."

"Thomas Edward, I'm deeply indebted to you."

Culhane winked, "*I know.*"

The King drank up; pocketed a half pack of abandoned *Old Gold* off the bar and left to rejoin the evening's festivities.

Harrigan had his information on the car's murdered owner, but at least for tonight, he decided to sit on the news. He needed time to sort out what to do next.

FLK Notebook: March-April 1931

SES deal – ok'd with GAP/AD $350

KIRTSCHNER'S JOURNAL ENTRY: EW

"Hey, Schu, it's like a ghost town in here. Where is everybody" I asked? It was only 7:00 pm and the squad room was empty except for Emil Schumacher, the night desk Sergeant.

"Whaddya doin' here Freddy? Don'tcha know, all the muckety-mucks are at the St. Patrick's Day shindig and all of the lowly peons are either goofin' off or running down leads for tomorrow's murder meeting with the Chief? He's like a man possessed on this thing," Schumacher observed, "Say, what happened to your face?"

"I walked into a door. Well, I hope they get some news in the case soon, my editor was none to pleased with the story I filed, especially since I was the only reporter on the scene while the bodies were still there," I added.

"Fill me in willya, what did it look like when you got there?"

"Well, to be truthful Schu, I didn't even get to see the bodies, Harrigan was pretty angry when Joe brought me past the police line, he even threatened to lock me up if I didn't get back. So, the story I filed was based solely on what I gleaned from Joe and the boys down at the 7th. I plan to interview Batavia, the officer that was first on the scene as soon as he's back on duty. O'Connell gave him a couple of days off, apparently he was really shaken up by the crime scene. Harrigan has got the lid on this case very tight," I said.

"Tight is right all right…but, in all fairness to the Chief, he still doesn't have the information back from the state on the license registration. I know, because he was calling the day Sergeant every five minutes all day today to see if anything had come in. I was left instructions to call him at any hour if the information came in.

"And, so far nobody has reported a missing man or woman that fit the description of the John and Jane Doe. That is really odd, especially since it got written up in the papers and was all on all the hourly news on KMOX today. You'd think somebody might wonder if one of the two stiffs belonged to them.

I was bemoaning the fact that no photos had been made available to the press, "I hear the victims were literally shot to pieces, but I haven't been able to get my hands on the crime scene photos or the photos from the coroner's autopsy."

When Schu injected, "You haven't seen the crime scene photos?"

"No, my contact over in the morgue said that there's an investigative news embargo on them."

"Would it help you write your stories Fred, if you could lay an eye on them?"

"Schu, don't play with me, of course it would help, but if Harrigan's embargoed the pictures, there's no way any reporter is going to see 'em before he wants 'em seen."

"If, and I'm saying, *if* there was a way to lay your eyes on them for say, oh, five or so minutes, what would that be worth to the *Star?*"

"It could be worth, lemme see," I counted out the money in my pocket, "Five dollars and fifty three cents now and another $20 tomorrow, if my editor likes the story I can write based on an informed source. Why do you ask?"

"So $25 bucks is all you think its worth?" Schu seemed disappointed, "Risking the wrath of *Iron Charlie* Harrigan ought to be worth more than that it seems to me."

I put on my glasses and stared straight into Schu's eyes, "If you were, and I'm saying, *if you were* accepting bids on the value of letting a reporter peek at those photos, what would you think a fair price would be?" I waited in silence as Schu mulled over the question.

Finally he answered, "Well let's consider the facts, first of all the nature of the crime is horrible and bloody and that sells newspapers." Schu ticked off the points with his fat stubby fingers, "Second, there is a high probability that the victim's were not united in the bands of holy matrimony, and a sex scandal sells papers. Third, considering that the dead man was driving a car that only a pharaoh of some sort could afford. That's a 3-bagger in any league; bloody murder, sex and big money. Are you with me so far?"

I nodded in agreement and marveled at the perception of the man who was widely regarded as a near Neanderthal by the other inhabitants of the squad room. I was seeing a whole other side to Schu.

"Now, let's consider one more thing…something that I'm told on good authority always sells newspapers. I think you call it a *scoop*, some inside source that can give you information that the other newspapers don't have. *Am I right?*" Shu knew the answer before he even asked the question.

"Schu, in light of what you've just said, let me repeat my question, If you were, and I'm saying, *if you were* accepting bids on the value of letting a reporter peek at those photos, what would you think a fair price would be?"

"I think it would be $50 a week until the case was solved, maybe more if the case took on a spectacular nature through some development that we can't possibly predict," his eyes narrowed to see what my reaction would be.

"If, and I'm saying, *if* that could be arranged, what assurance's would the paper have that the informed source would not be filtering the information to other papers as well?"

"$100 a week would totally guarantee that that circumstance would never occur. I think that's what you call an exclusive scoop, am I right?"

Okay, if I could get my editor's to agree to that outrageous price...*and by the way, at 5 cents a copy, we'd have to sell 2000 extra papers just to break even*...how might this be arranged?"

"Well, to protect everyone's interests, I would think that discretion must be the rule of the day. That means, no direct face-to-face handoffs, but a way of dropping off cash and picking up information with a go-between who knows nuthin' from nuthin'," Schu had obviously been thinking about this for some time.

I asked, "Such as?"

"Ummm, *such as*, a system where a newspaperman might drop off an envelope with a #1 on it. Inside is $50 in $5 bills. And when he drops it off he picks up an envelope with a #2 on it, and inside is the information from the informed source. All the go-between knows is the numbers on the envelopes, as to what's inside, it's a mystery," Schu spelled all it out.

"And, where might such an exchange take place?"

Schu replied, "Well maybe at a spot like the O.T. Hodge's Chili Parlor over on Olive.

A place where the go between might be someone like a cook. In the wee hours of the morning, Hodge's is a place that might work out just fine. If and I'm saying, *if, I was accepting the bids.*"

"I'd need something to persuade my editor, a sample that would convince him I had a source, would be very helpful in making my case"

"Would a peek at the crime scene photos help?" Shu asked wryly. "If a lad was really a go-getter, there might even be a way for a photo to leak out for a front page splash, but that of course would be worth another $100."

"Jesus, Schu...this sounds like it's getting awfully expensive, I'm not sure."

"Lean over here," he instructed.

On his desk was an official envelope from the Coroner's Office stamped:

Attn: Charles Harrigan.

"Even the Chief of Detectives has not seen these as yet; he got one set of crime scene photos early this morning. This second envelope came over just after I came on my shift. I'm the only one who has looked at the contents. The note inside says the lab found another roll of film after the first batch was developed. I think that there is a distinct possibility that this envelope could become lost in the interdepartmental mail for a few days before it reaches Harrigan,"

Schu opened the envelope and looked inside, his fat fingers ruffling through the contents until he found the photo he was looking for. "Here's just one example of what could be coming the way of a real go-getter," he said as he slid out a photo.

It was awful, it was a shot taken through the open door of the Cadillac with the two victims literally blown to pieces.

Their faces were unrecognizable. The female's head, or what was left of it, was buried in his blood soaked lap, her face obscured by the angle and all the blood. The male's face was shot into a bloody pulp. I gagged as I looked at the gore.

"Oh my God, we could never print this, it's far too brutal an image," I said.

"True, but you could write a *very accurate description* based on seeing it. There are also 11 other photos in here, some of them are fit to print, pictures of the car, the cops working the scene. You know what I mean," Schu added.

"What would it cost if, and I'm only saying, *if* this entire envelope got lost for a day before it reappeared, and during that day, the contents got copied. What might that be worth?"

"That's a big risk. I don't think any clear thinking informed source would even consider it for less that $250," he said without so much as batting and eye.

"Let me make a call." I left the squad room and went down the hall to the bank of pay phones. I closed the wooden sliding door and dialed Arnold Dexter, my editor. When I got Arnie on the phone, I walked him through the 'opportunity' and the logic behind compensating an informed source for letting us make copies of the photos and for being a continuing stream of inside information. He only asked me one question.

"Are you willing to risk your entire career on this? If it doesn't pan out to be worthwhile, you will be fired. Is that clear Fred?

"Sir, I think this is the biggest story in town, and I think it will only get bigger. If it means putting my job on the line to get this kind of jump on the *Globe-Democrat* and the *Post-Dispatch,* then I'll risk it."

"Hold on."

I waited on the line for about three minutes while Dexter went away. Finally a voice came on the line. "Kirtschner, this is Gordon Alcott."

"Yes sir." Jesus, it was the old man himself, Gordon P. Alcott, the Managing Editor. He had never spoken to me before, I didn't think he even knew my name.

"Dext tells me that he trusts your instincts in this matter and that you're willing to put your job on the line. Is that right?"

Yes sir."

"The *St. Louis Star* does not throw money around willy-nilly, so I asking you only once, is this a good use of our money?"

"Yes sir, I've seen one of the photos and I'm sure that the information source is rock solid and that the dope he will give us will pay off."

"It better young man or you'll not only be fired from here, but I'll personally see to it that you never work in another newspaper anywhere in the world, including Borneo and Belleville. *Is that clear?*"

"Yes sir."

"You're sure you want to proceed?"

"Yes sir."

"All right tell your source we have a deal. Get over here and Dext will have $350 in cash waiting for you. I hope for your sake young man that your nose for news is working overtime. Good bye."

I went back into the empty squad room and told Schu that I was going back to the paper to pick up $350 in cash. I confirmed our *"ifs, ands and buts"* understanding. I wanted to be sure that we're singing off the same page in the hymnal. This was not the kind of thing one would put in writing.

"I knew you were a go-getter Fred, now why don't you *go get the money?'* Schu smiled.

We agreed to all the terms and steps and the wheels were put in motion. Later that night, I delivered an envelope marked #1 to the night cook at O. T. Hodge's Chili Parlor.

In return he handed me the envelope marked #2, containing the photographs.

I now had 24 hours to have copies made and to return them via the same system.

With the envelope tucked under my arm, I raced back to the *Star's* photo department to have them start the copying process. They would have to re-photograph each photograph in the envelope and create a new inter-neg. We'd loose some sharpness and reproduction quality, since we were not making prints directly from an original negative. But, for our purposes that would be just fine.

I went up to the photography department on the 3rd floor behind the composing room where Arnold Dexter was waiting. He and I inspected the contents and then we handed the package directly over to Danny Lundstrom. Arnold Dexter insisted on me babysitting the entire process, and when the work was completed, I took our photograph print set and the inter-negs to Dexter's office. By staying with Danny while he completed the entire process, we could be absolutely sure that only one inter-neg was made and one set of photographs was made from them into 8 x 10 glossies. The entire set of prints with inter-negs would be kept under lock and key in Dexter's office.

When I delivered the goods to Dexter's office, he called in Mr. Alcott and two other assistant editors. Together we reviewed each of the photos. There were 12 shots in all. This included six interior shots of the victims from various angles, two shots showed the front seat of the car, one from left and one from right side. There were two photos of the car with police standing around and talking, Harrigan was even in one of the shots, but his back was turned to the camera. Finally, there were two shots of the backseat interior after the bodies had been removed. The editorial team was simultaneously thrilled and appalled by what they saw, thrilled as newspapermen on the hunt for a big story and appalled as human beings at the sight of the carnage inside the car.

"Listen up gentlemen," Alcott somewhat solemnly intoned. "It seems that our associate Mr. Kirtschner has fallen into an outhouse and come up smelling like a proverbial rose.

I want you to support him on this story with any resource he needs inside, but this is *his story*. He has the lead on it, and he'll be meeting with Dext and me on a daily basis to keep us informed on what's what and who's who.

Alcott continued, "Now that I've seen the photos, I think Fred's assessment on the scale of this story is fundamentally correct. It is definitely *big* and it may even be *epic* in the annals of St. Louis. Starting the day after tomorrow, I want it on the front page above the fold in every edition with a 24 pt headline, with a jump story from Page One to two additional sidebar stories in Main News. That will lead us into big weekend sales. I want it like that every day until this case is solved. Gentlemen, this is a great opportunity for us to take the lead in circulation, if we do it right.

"And, while we're pushing circulation, it will also give us a chance to really work our craft as reporters and to keep on this story and *own it*. Mr. Kirstchner has developed a great *–and somewhat expensive–* informed source, let's work him to death and make him earn every farthing," Alcott stressed.

I was feeling absolutely on *Cloud Ten*. The Managing Editor was singing my praises in front of men many years my senior. And, he was also taking a personal interest in *my* story. He even called me, *Mr. Kirtschner*. All I could think was this could be my big break. The feeling made me both excited and anxious... but, I felt like this could be the story that would make my bones as a reporter, and that chance was worth taking almost any risk.

After the meeting broke up, I went back to my Underwood and started pounding out the copy for the first expansive front page story to describe the horrors contained in the photographs.

The headline writers were busy banging out a series of banner headlines and leads for future sidebars to cover any eventuality that might occur in the case. Alcott wanted us to 'own' the story and he was putting his best team on it. We were to anticipate any twists and turns that may come from our source and to be ready to jump on it. There was even talk of putting out an early Bulldog edition EXTRA, if we had a breaking story.

Headline ideas and sidebar leads flowed in by the score and were winnowed down to the best contenders and held for later publication.

Bloody Massacre In Tower Grove
Mystery Couple Slain
Unidentified Couple Murdered
Lover's Lane Bloodbath
Neighborhood Shocked By Brutal Slayings
Police Puzzled Town Horrified
Killers Identity Remains Mystery
Gang Killing Or Revenge Murders
Victim's Identity Shocks City

The story by-lined by me would break in the next edition, and the graphic detail of crime scene will give us a big reporting edge. The one area I had to be very careful about was never to even hint at the contents of the trunk, much less confide in my colleagues about the ride I took to *The Celtic Room* with Joe Culhane.

Those details would remain strictly secret and permanently off the record. If news about bootleg whiskey was going to appear in print, it wasn't going to be in my paper under my byline. I didn't need to tempt fate with *The King of Kerry*. One shot two inches from my head was one shot too many.

To keep our end of the devil's bargain, I personally put all 12 of the original prints into another envelope and marked it with #1, sealed it and then, I hand delivered it back to the night cook at O. T. Hodge's at the appointed time. I wondered what the public reaction would be to my first front page story. I would not have to wait long.

———◆———

KIRTSCHNER'S JOURNAL ENTRY: 1H/2H/HS

Mary Clare Culhane waved her lace handkerchief to catch her brother's eye as he made his way through the crowd of cronies, well-wishers and mooches. Mary Clare was The Kings' official companion at all public events. Mamie O'Halloran, who was always good enough for pursuits of the fornicational nature, was not an appropriate companion in the public eye. Her lack of manners and colorful 'mouth' were not suitable in the company of polite society known as the 'lace curtain' Irish.

Mary Clare, Tom's sister on the other hand was the very modicum of decorum.

Mary Clare was always properly and very respectfully attired from her hat down to her white buttoned gloves and modest dresses. After Tom's wife died, she became the person who cared for her nephew and niece, Harry and Rosemary, as well as the mistress of the castle, what everyone called The King's Hawthorne Place manse.

"Where have you been Thomas Edward?" she greeted him as took his seat at the table, "Joe and Stella and I thought you might have gotten lost. The salad course is already been served"

Joe Culhane spoke up, "Not likely lost, more likely found by somebody needin' a five or a favor."

"I just had a kind word with our cousin, Charles Michael of law enforcement fame. You know him Joseph Patrick, I believe he's the lad who keeps you off the street and out of saloons in the gainful employment of the city," Tom joked.

"Tom let me get the waiter to bring you a salad," Stella volunteered.

"Don't trouble yourself about it Stella, the only thing green that I'm interested in is printed by the Treasury Department,"

"Well, let's all enjoy ourselves shall we, Mary Clare encouraged, "I don't want you men taking up all evening talking about business."

"Then how about sports, then?" Joe proposed. "I hear the *St. Louis Stars* are making a run for the championship in the Negro Leagues. I wish we had that *Cool Papa* Bell playin' for the Browns, or even the Cardinals."

"Joe, do you really think a monkey could play at that level?'

"No doubts in my mind, these boys are every bit as good as the white major leaguers.

I've seen 'em play at games with Fred Washington," Joe averred.

"Ahhh, you're daft. Talent or no talent, you'd have to paint a lot more than their black asses white to make that happen," *The King* quipped, "We'll probably see an Irish Catholic President of the United States before we'll see a coon playing in the Major Leagues. The white players'd take no part in it, especially the likes of the *Bambino* or that crazy fucker, Ty Cobb. It'll never happen in our lifetimes. God made them black and us white for some good reason, but what the reason is escapes me at the moment. What's for dinner, as if I don't know?" he asked.

Almost on cue, a waiter set down a large plate with a huge sizzling New York strip flanked by a twice baked potato and fresh asparagus with Hollandaise sauce.

"Direct from the aging locker at *The Celtic Room*," Joe assumed, "with your compliments?"

"*Where else?* Dig in everyone, enjoy," Tom encouraged his guests.

Three tables away, Major Jeremiah O'Connell was toying with his food.

"What's wrong Jeremiah, you're not eating...is something eating you," Harrigan asked.

"It's the park murders, they're preying on my mind," O'Connell replied.

"He hasn't slept a wink since it happened," his wife Kathleen chimed in, "he's been unable to eat or sleep."

"Why don'tcha relax tonight Jeremiah and let all your cares pass away?

Take Kathleen for a whirl around the dance floor and enjoy the company of your friends, tomorrow, maybe we'll get together at the *Pelican* for lunch and talk over some turtle soup, Harrigan suggested, "I'll have good news to share with you by then, for sure."

"You sound confident, whaddya know?"

"This isn't the time or the place, trust me on that Jeremiah. I need a little time to make some verifications," Harrigan replied, "Go dance, for Christ's sake willya? Go on now, Kathleen get him out on the floor! Whirling around with your beautiful wife will take your mind off the cares and woes of this vale of tears. Go on now...dance with your girl."

Harrigan glanced across the aisle at Tom Culhane and winked. Little did they know where the twisting trail of evidence would lead them in the weeks ahead. They had no idea. Not even an inkling.

KIRTSCHNER'S JOURNAL ENTRY: 1H/2H/HS

Robert Emmett Hannegan crossed the dining room making his way toward *The King's* table. He had a nattily dressed man at his side and both appeared to be on some sort of a mission. Hannegan was the powerful chairman of the Democratic Party in Missouri and a leading supporter of Franklin Delano Roosevelt and any other politician who was in favor of Repeal.

Hannegan put his hand on the man's shoulder and said, "Thomas Edward, I'd like you to meet Judge Harry Truman, the Presiding Judge of the Jackson County Court. Mr. Truman is a rising star in Missouri politics. Harry meet Thomas Edward Culhane."

Tom rose from his seat and reached out to shake hands with the dapper man from western Missouri. "Pleased to meet you Mr. Culhane," Truman shook his hand firmly.

"Call me Tom, why don'tcha?" Culhane continued, "If you're from Jackson County way, you might know a friend of mine over in that neck of the woods, who bumps around in political circles from time to time, he's named Tom too. Fine people those Toms, right Robert Emmett?"

Hannegan just grinned.

"Would it be Tom Pendergast by any chance?" Truman posed..

"It would," *The King* replied, "Tom Pendergast and I have had the occasion to do some business together, every blue moon or so. Will you give him my best when you see him?"

"I certainly will," Truman replied.

"The reason I wanted you to meet Harry is because we have plans to help advance his career in Missouri politics. I was wondering if we could come by your office in the next day or so and have a little powwow to get the two of you acquainted," Hannegan asked.

"Why don'tcha drop around my home instead, say at 3:30 p.m. tomorrow. We can spend some time getting to know each other over a late lunch and a beverage or two. But, Harry, I'll tell you one thing, if you're a friend of Tom Pendergast's, that already means you're a friend of mine," Culhane winked.

"That's very kind of you sir, I look forward to spending some time with you and listening to your ideas about what needs to be done here in Missouri."

"Listen to my ideas??" Culhane laughed, "Now why would you want to listen to my ideas?"

"I'm interested in what we should be doing to make Missouri a better state, and there's no reason for modesty, Mr. Culhane. I know that you have a lot of political influence both here and in Jefferson City, Truman said.

"I thought I told you to call me *'Tom'*," Culhane arched his left eyebrow in mock disapproval, "My son's name is Harry too, so naturally I have a kind and warm, fatherly feeling for all Harrys. Let's just make a little deal, no matter how important you think I am or how important you might become, let's just agree that whenever we talk or meet it'll just be, Tom and Harry."

"Thank you sir, I mean…Tom. I look forward to seeing you tomorrow, I've taken you away from your guests long enough," Truman reached out to shake hands.

As Culhane gripped Truman's hand, he pulled him in close and whispered in his ear, "Harry, are you carrying a gun?'

Truman instinctively recoiled in shock, "Why no."

Culhane laughed, "Harry darlin' if you're goin' into Missouri politics, and are gonna be hanging around with the likes of Robert Emmett, you might want to consider making an investment in Mr. Smith-Wesson. It's sometimes good to have an eloquent little friend who can speak six times."

"Sounds like prudent advice," Truman laughed.

Hannegan shook his head, "Don't listen to him Harry. Thomas Edward, what am I going to be doin' with you?"

Culhane pointed his finger at Truman, "Remember what Al Capo*knee* said, *'You can get a lot further in life with a kind word and a gun, than with a kind word alone.'* Now Harry, I don't agree with that Wop bastard on many things…but," Culhane opened his coat to reveal a .38 in his shoulder holster, "he's right as rain on that particular topic."

"Tom, I'm glad to see you take your own advice. Perhaps I should have my suit retailored to accommodate a traveling companion like your own," Truman gestured to his coat's inside pocket.

"I've heard that you have connections in haberdashery circles, so suit yourself Harry, suit yourself," Culhane patted Truman on the shoulder and sat back down at the table.

"How did you know about that?" Truman was obviously surprised by *The King's* reference to Truman & Jacobson, his ill-fated men's clothing store on West 12th street in Kansas City."

The King looked up at Truman and smiled, "I once bought a pair of socks, a tie and a fine Hamburg hat from you Harry, and I never forget a face or a name. And if you're going to be *'throwin' your hat in the ring,'* I'd suggest that you develop that talent too."

"I'll remember that. See you tomorrow *Tom*," as Truman and Hannegan walked away, Truman wondered, *how could he possibly remember me?* Truman & Jacobson went bankrupt in 1922.

———

Rainy Lazy Saturday: August 16, 2031

Her Bose clock radio came to life and *The Star Spangled Banner* blared from the bedroom abruptly waking Mac. "Oh man, don't tell me its Saturday already," she moaned as she got up from the chair and straightened her coiled body. She could feel her neck, back, knees and ankles cracking as she stood up and stretched. She padded down the hall and into the bathroom.

"Welcome to the KMOX Trading Station, where you can call in and offer items for sale, sorry, no real estate, guns, weapons, ammunition, knives or sporting event tickets. Sorry, no dealers, retailers, private party sales only," the announcer droned on with the litany of rules that governed the long running morning show.

That show has been on every Saturday morning since I was a kid, she thought. Some things in St. Louis never change. CBS affiliate, KMOX with its 50,000 red hot watts was still *The Voice Of St. Louis*. It was the undisputed leader in local broadcast radio and always had been except for a few years back in the '02 to '10 era when KTRS, The Big 550 had briefly dethroned it, by luring away the broadcast rights for the St. Louis Cardinals, Rams and Blues.

Looking in the mirror she said, "Jesus, girl you need to get to the spa. Your eyes look like they have meatballs under them." She rubbed her eyes and grimaced to stretch her face back to life. Impressions of the chair's corduroy pillow were still evident in her right cheek. "Oh that's a cute look." She turned on the shower to the full hot setting, stepped back out and closed the mirrored shower door, letting the steam build up inside. She stripped off her clothes and underwear and stared at her body in the full length mirror. She turned slowly to look at her back reflecting in the vanity mirror. She flexed up on her toes to tighten her butt, thighs and shapely calves. "Not too bad for 32," she though as she leaned over to touch her toes, At least my boobs don't touch my knees yet."

Mac took a long, hot, soapy sudsy shower with *Ruban d'Orange* body wash by *l'Occitane*. The steamy shower and the piquant citrus aroma filled the bathroom. She loved her long, hot showers, and she loved the luxury of fine bath products, expensive little extravagances that she indulged and delighted in.

Toweling off, she quickly wrapped her mop of wet auburn hair in a terry turban and put on her floor length robe from *The Four Seasons Papaguya Peninsula*, a souvenir from her adventure travel eco-trip to Costa Rica the year before. She tied its thick belt in a lazy looping knot and made her barefoot way down the hall to the kitchen. The pot of coffee had been left on the warming plate all night and the kitchen had the smell of half-burnt coffee.

"Shit, I don't think I'll drink another cup of coffee until next month." When she saw the empty coffee packs on the sink, she realized that she had consumed 3 full pots during her all-day into the night journal reading session.

She sat down at the table and clicked on her computer to check the day's forecast and see what the headlines were. She wouldn't work again until Monday, so she had the weekend for R&R. *El Diablo Rojo,* her Abyssinian red devil jumped up on the table and began nuzzling her. "Hi baby, how's my baby... *awwww*," Mac purred, "...somebody loves me. You are so sweet, you're such a good kitty," then she scolded, "Rojo did you let me fall asleep out there? I can't curl up in a chair like you, I need to be in my bed."

She scanned the morning headlines as the Trading Post announcer continued to provide background noise from the bedroom. The shower had made her feel clean, but not very refreshed. The last thing she remembered was looking at the mantle clock and seeing 2:13 a.m. The computer clock now said it was 7:45 a.m. She yawned and contemplated crawling under the covers and crashing for the rest of the day, but her curiosity got the better of her. She *Yahoogled, St. Louis Star* and discovered that the venerable afternoon daily had become the *St. Louis Star-Times* in 1932 and survived until 1951, when Elzey M. Roberts, the owner lost his patience with union demands and relentlessly rising costs and in a surprisingly secret move decided to sell it to his downtown afternoon rival, Joseph Pulitzer's *St. Louis Post Dispatch.* The on-line account from the archives of TIME magazine proved to be very enlightening.

The P-D Takes Over Star-Times Monday June 25, 1951

Managing Editor Norman Isaacs of the *St. Louis Star-Times* hurried down to his office ahead of nearly everyone else one morning last week. As his staffers drifted in, he called them into his office to break the surprising news he had heard only the afternoon before. Then he sat down and wrote the news for Page One, took the story to the composing room himself. Composing Room Superintendent Earl Barker read it and gasped: the *Star-Times* had been sold to the rival *Post-Dispatch* (circ. 290,052), would publish no more after that afternoon's press run.

Post-Dispatch Publisher Joseph Pulitzer had bought the *Star-Times's* name, linotypes, presses, newsprint and circulation (179,803) to gain a monopoly in the afternoon field, leave St. Louis with only one other daily newspaper, the thriving morning *Globe-Democrat* (circ. 282,611). Reported price: between $3,500,000 and $8,000,000. The downtown five-story *Star-Times* building was not included in the deal; neither was the paper's ABC radio outlet, KXOK, or its FM affiliate. *Star-Times* Publisher Elzey Roberts had sold out because "material costs have risen faster than the increased revenues necessary to meet them."

The city room grapevine had carried no warnings of the sale. From outward appearances the Star's position had not been precarious. It had made money since 1932, despite rising costs, had carved out its own niche in St. Louis. Its small but spring-legged editorial staff took an underdog's delight in occasionally beating the P-D on stories. Like the Post-Dispatch, it generally followed a Fair Deal line, and like the Post-Dispatch, it had its unpredictable lapses, e.g., both supported Dewey in '48.

Publisher Roberts himself, more a business office man than a journalist, had seemed determined to stay in business. He had inherited control of the old *Star* from his father, John C. Roberts, one of the founders of International Shoe Co., had combined the *Star* with the *St. Louis Times* in 1932. A few months ago he began planning to enter the Saturday-Sunday field next October; he had just hired the Nation's Washington correspondent, Willard Shelton, as his chief editorial writer. A new copy-desk man was on the way from Binghamton, N.Y., and another had just reported for duty.

What prompted Roberts to get together with Pulitzer three weeks ago was the fact that newsprint was going up $10 a ton (TIME, June 18). Roberts' plan for the new Saturday-Sunday edition—aimed, newsmen suspected, at bluffing the morning *Globe-Democrat* into merging production facilities with the *Star-Times* —was not working out. Said Roberts:

"As a businessman, I've given 36 years of my life to this business. But I'll be 60 next March, and I don't intend to go broke gracefully." The outlook for almost 600 Star employees, including 100 editorial staffers, was dark. Some of them grumbled that Roberts should have found a buyer who would keep the paper going. The P-D promised to hire "some, but not many"; the rest would leave with severance pay.

"Hmmm...I wonder what happened to Kirtschner. But, he might have been retired by '51," she mused, fetching a jug of *Tropicana Lots 'O Pulp* from the refrigerator, she took a long gulping chug right out of the bottle and retrieved the reporter's Journal from the living room floor where it had fallen from her lap.

"Okay, Freddy, let's keep going and see where this sleigh ride takes us," she said half aloud, as she returned to the kitchen and popped a *Kellogg's Raspberry Strudel Puff* in to the microwave. Mac sat down at the kitchen table, snuggled her robe tighter, opened the journal and found the page that she was reading when the arms of Morpheus had embraced her.

KIRTSCHNER'S JOURNAL ENTRY: 1H/2H/HS

A slightly hung over Harrigan called the Saturday morning March 18th briefing to order at 10:30 a.m. on the dot. "Mickey, what have you got for me after the second sweep of the park and the neighborhoods?"

"Chief, we came up with nothin', absolutely nothin' and believe you me, we looked in every can in the park, in every bird's nest, up every squirrel's ass, and down every sewer on every corner and in every alley and in every ash pit in a ten block radius. There was nothin' to be found, I'm sorry to report," Finnegan started to sit down.

"Don't get too comfortable Mickey, you need to get right back out there and expand the search by another 5-block radius," Iron Charlie ordered.

Under his breath, Finnegan softly cursed, *"Fookin' asshole."*

"What was that?" Harrigan snapped.

"I said *'Fine sir, I'll go"* And with that Finnegan was up and out the door like a shot.

"Finn, what's up with the car registration? Any word from Jeff City?"

"I called 'em no less than ten times yesterday Chief and they say they're still looking," Finn reported. Harrigan shook his head in disgust.

"Now as for the rest of you, what have you found out by rousting the vermin?"

Each member of the squad made a detailed report on their activities rousting hoods, squeezing the neighborhood rats and spreading around the news about the murder and Harrigan's determination to find the responsible parties.

"It's a little early to be expecting much. Nobody's shootin' his mouth off about the deed. And, so far nobody's throwing any cash around in the houses or speaks. It's real quiet out there, nobody seems to know a thing. Even the bartenders and working girls haven't heard so much as a rustle. Maybe the shooter left town," Columbo theorized.

Harrigan listened attentively and when the last man had his say, he began, "Now listen to me all of you. And listen with both ears and your asshole. I have a theory about these murders; I think we have not one, but two shooters. I also think that when the identity of the couple comes to light the shit will really hit the fan over in the Mayor's office. And, then the Chief's Strickland's phone upstairs is going to jump about 3 feet off his desk and then, gentlemen, a bonfire will be lit under my ass and in Jeremiah's personnel file.

"Then, guess what happens next? An even bigger bonfire, you might even say a five alarm fucking inferno will be lit under each one of your asses by me. Now lads, let's not let that happen, because, believe me on all that's holy, if my ass gets warm, your asses will be incinerated. Am I clear on that point? Harrigan asked.

"Now, get out of my sight and get out there on the streets and squeeze everybody's balls until either their eyes, entrails or evidence pops out. And, if you know what's good for you, don't come back tomorrow with, 'nuthin' to report," Harrigan looked ominously around the room, "Why are you still here?"

As the dayroom emptied, Harrigan went into his office and rang up Jeremiah. "We need to talk privately as soon as possible, I'm going to call *The King* and see if we can meet at the castle and talk things over. If I can set it up, can you be there?"

"Tell me when and I'll be there," Jeremiah replied.

"I'm calling him now, I'll be back in touch." Harrigan hung up and immediately dialed *The King* at his home. Harrigan figured he'd just be rising about 11:30 a.m., especially on the day after St. Patrick's Day gala at The Hibernian Hall.

The phone rang only twice when Mary Clare answered. "Mary Clare, it's me, Charles Michael is Thomas Edward up and about?"

"Oh yes, he's just having coffee and reading the morning *Globe*, let me get him," she said.

"Hello Charles, to what do I owe the pleasure of this call," Tom Culhane inquired.

"Cousin, we need to have a meeting of the minds on the matter of *"Pete the Prick,"* just as soon as possible. Because of the necessity for privacy, I'd like to impose on your hospitality and suggest we meet at the castle and I'll bring, Joe and Jeremiah and I think you should have the *Big Nigger* there. We need to talk before the stiff's identity hits the papers and the Mayor and the ever lovin' Chief of Police fly up my butt. Can that be arranged?"

The King did not hesitate, "Come here with Joe and Jeremiah and park in back, the fewer and the plainer the cars the better. I'll call Fred and make sure he's here. Come right away as I have guests coming at half past three this afternoon."

At 12:45, one black Plymouth pulled into the driveway of the castle at 34 Hawthorne Place and parked next to Fred Washington's *Buick* sedan in the rear brick-paved courtyard, well out of the prying eyes of neighbors.

Within a few moments, Major Jeremiah O'Connell, Chief of Detectives Charles Harrigan and Detective Joe Culhane emerged and entered the rear of the house. Mary Clare greeted them, "Tom and Fred are waiting for you in the Map Room."

She escorted them down the hallway and into a large mahogany paneled room with its cross-mitered beamed ceilings. As the men entered, Mary Clare eased the pocket doors out of the in-wall recesses and silently closed them sequestering the occupants inside.

Tom Culhane gestured for the arrivals to sit down in the chairs around a low ebony map table that had an inlaid ivory compass on its highly polished top. The map table's side had five wide and shallow drawers with campaign chest-style brass pulls. Culhane was in shirtsleeves and suspenders and Fred Washington in a double breasted steel grey suit sat in an upholstered chair on the opposite side of the table. A large Mercator-projection of the world was on the wall behind them. The other walls had walnut panels that slide open to reveal the maps of Europe and Africa, North and South America and Asia-Pacific. Culhane had always been interested in geography even as a boy, and now his wealth allowed him the time and money to indulge his wanderlust.

"Charles Michael, you called this meeting, you have the floor," Culhane pronounced.

As the guests settled into their seats, Harrigan wasted no time cutting to the chase, "Gentlemen, here's the way I see it. At any moment, the State morons in Jeff City will send the car registration to me through proper channels. Once that happens, the male stiff's identity will be known. That said, last night, a 'little birdie' told me that the car was registered to Pierre Laclede Devereaux. Right now, me and the 'little birdie' and now you four are the only one's who know that fact. Harrigan looked around the room, "I wish I had a more delicate way of saying this, but when that news goes public, the Mayor will hit the fan, just like the piece of shit that he is," Harrigan paused.

Jeremiah asked. "How sure are you of your information?"

"I'd bet my balls on its accuracy. Here's what we know. The two cases of black whiskey we found in the Caddy's trunk were sold to a negro named Bee Henderson on March 15th by our friend Fred Washington, Fred, thanks for being here today. The goods were delivered to the 43 Washington Terrace rear on that date. Bee Henderson is the chauffer and valet for one Mr. Pierre Laclede Devereaux, who resides at the address. Mr. Devereaux also owns a 1930 Cadillac Madame X with the license number PLD-1764.

"Fred confirms that black whiskey delivery is made every 2 weeks. Bee Henderson is the neighborhood distributor to the other colored valets, chauffeurs and maids working on Washington Terrace, Portland Place, Westminster Place and the apartments on Union Boulevard and Waterman Avenue.

"Fred's conjecture is that Bee uses his boss's car to deliver the black goods, which explains how the whiskey walked into the trunk. But, Bee's order is also part of a much bigger order of white goods delivered to the same Washington Terrace address. The white goods part of the order is for an "EOR" and sold to the house account the late Mr. Devereaux opened about 2-years ago with our gracious host today. Those white goods are stacked in a storage box in the rear of the garage. The 'EOR' order is replenished about every 2-3 months.

"So, what's the connection? O'Connell asked.

"Hold on Jeremiah, I'm coming to that. It seems that the late Pierre is known as what polite society calls a 'playboy.' But, in plain language, *'Pierre or Pete the Prick'* is a whore-mongering, rich asshole with a perpetual hard-on. He is a regular in the 'speaks' near 'The Hill', the houses out on the Rock Road and over on the Eastside. He's also been known to even frequent *The Celtic Room.*

"He does? *I'm shocked.* What's he do for a living to be able to afford coming to my high class place," Culhane bit his lip to suppress a laugh.

"He's an executive in his father-in-law's business. He married very well you see.

Care to guess who he's married to?" Harrigan asked.

"Do tell," Culhane spoke up, only half concealing a smile at Harrigan's reenactment of his own performance the night before at *The Hibernian,* "You're a veritable flood of information cousin, don't stop now, I'm enthralled."

"Well, he's married to Ada Elizabeth Robertson. That's *Robertson* as in Edmund O. Robertson, the President of Continental Shoe. And, the dear departed son-in-law is the exalted Executive Vice President of the same venerable family enterprise. We also surmise that Edmund O. Robertson is 'EOR', Harrigan stopped, "Are you with me so far?"

"Wait a minute," Jeremiah suddenly had an epiphany, "All of you know all this already, except me."

"*And me,*" Joe Culhane chimed in, "I'm not sure what's going on here?".

The King, Fred and Harrigan burst into laughter. Harrigan, still laughing, pointed at Jeremiah, "I was wondering when you'd figure out that you were sitting in the nest of 'the little birdie."

"And the black crow," Fred Washington laughed.

"C'mon men, this is serious business, don't be joking with me about it," O'Connell was clearly irritated.

"As usual, you're absolutely right Jeremiah, but I couldn't resist the chance to pull your leg.

"Well, what do you propose?" O'Connell leaned forward and put his arms on the legs of his razor-creased uniform slacks.

"Let me give you my thoughts and then let's talk about it," Harrigan began, "first of all, I think this whole thing stinks to high heaven. It's been over 30 hours since we found the victims, yet so far, no concerned widow has called to report a missing husband. Further, the job had to have at least two shooters because of the number of rounds fired. I did the math for Jeremiah yesterday day at lunch, recall?" Jeremiah nodded. "Alright then, I also think the shooters were amateurs. A pro would never fire that many shots, pick that location or dilly-dally around to make off with souvenirs. It just doesn't add up to a gang shooting, a shooting over a debt or a botched robbery."

"So where's that leave us? Who did it and what was the motive," Joe asked.

"Those Joseph Patrick are the seminal questions. Let me give you a theory, Harrigan paused, "I think the murder of 'unlucky Pierre' was of an extremely personal nature for several reasons. Not the least of which is the number of shots that were pumped into his body. Second, consider the circumstances, who might want to see a philandering husband shot while he was havin' his skin flute played? And, finally why would a killer, who has just fired enough rounds to re-enact the battle of the *Chateau-Thierry*, stop and take the time to twist a ring off the finger of dear Pierre with such force as to dislocate the knuckle and break his finger?"

Harrigan got up and walked over to the window. "I think Jeremiah and I need to make a call on the widow Devereaux, just as soon as I have an official confirmation on the car registration. I' don't want to get ahead of myself here and go calling on one of St. Louis' most influential families until I have proof from Jefferson City to corroborate what "the little birdie" told me." He winked at *The King* who was sitting quietly with his fingers knitted together resting on his stomach.

"How long 'til you get it?" Jeremiah asked.

"I'm expecting it any minute now. As soon as we have it, I'll call the Chief and bring him up to date and he can call the Mayor and give him a heads up. Then, we'll pay a visit to 43 Washington Terrace and break the news to Mrs. Devereaux. Any other thoughts?"

"I think I can be helpful here, Mr. Charles," Fred Washington spoke first.

"In what way?" Harrigan asked.

"Well sir, I can nose around with the colored folks in the household and in the neighborhood, if there is anything strange goin' on in that house, they'll know about it."

"Why's that?' Joe asked.

The Big Nigger grinned from ear to ear, "Well, most rich white folks think their colored help is ignorant or just plain stupid. They also treat them like they're invisible. It's like they are a piece of furniture or a family pet that's just around. So, it's not unusual for the colored help to hear all the goin's on between the white folks. Trust me, if somebody's fucking somebody else's wife or husband, they'll know it. If somebody is a drunk they'll know it. If a business is doing something crooked. They'll know it. There isn't much that escapes the attention of the colored help, and you'd be surprised that they can even understand and speak The King's English. A lot of that subservient *"Yassa'M'am'* and *"Nossah Boss"* is just an act. If you tell me what your suspicions are, I can nose around quietly and get information that you'd never get out of them otherwise."

"Don't be too sure about that," Joe chimed in, "I've seen the Chief make a levee stone sing."

"That maybe true, and I've heard tales of Mr. Charles' formidable persuasive talents, but there's no reason to go scaring or hurting any common folk who are just trying to get by in the world. I don't think they're your shooters. Do you, *Mr. Charles?*" Fred directed his question to Harrigan.

"No Fred, I think you're right. And, when you call me, *Mr. Charles* is that out of respect or part of some subservient colored act?"

The Big Nigger laughed,"Out of complete respect Mr. Charles. Ask Mr. Tom, if you don't believe me."

Harrigan laughed, "All right then, *Mr. Fred*, I'd be pleased if you would be kind enough to assist me in my investigation as you have suggested, use your own means and methods. Thomas Edward, would it be alright if *Mr. Fred* gave his information directly to me instead of filtering it through you first?"

The King had been characteristically quiet and attentive. He was taking it all in, finally he spoke, "That would be fine with me, we have no secrets – *at least in this matter.* Fred, call in anything you find out directly to Charles Michael, if something comes up that concerns our business, also let me know about it. In the meantime, I'll see what I can find out about Pierre's prostitutional proclivities through my connections," Tom said.

"I was going to ask you to do just that, thanks for offering your help," Harrigan replied.

"One hand washes the other," *The King* smiled, "Gentlemen, I'm going to have to break this off as Robert Emmett is bringing 'a man of political promise' around at half past three and I need to make some preparations to properly receive them."

"Thank you for your hospitality and help, we really appreciate it," O'Connell said as he shook hands with *The King* and Fred.

"What are friends for? Remember, prosperity makes friends, but adversity proves them." Culhane said, as he walked the three to the back entrance and bid them farewell. "Have a great day gentlemen."

Culhane and Fred lingered for a few moments. "Fred, check everything with me first, then I'll tell you what to pass on to our police friends."

"I planned to do that anyway, Mr. Tom," Fred picked up his hat, "And here is the week's sales report."

"How'd we do?" *The King* asked.

"Izzy says we could do better, $23,000 from my runs. I'm up about $2500 from last year this time...but, it could be better...should be up $5,000. We've got some new competitors working out of furniture store over on Union and Natural Bridge," Fred said.

"Brenahanny's?"

"That's the one."

"Why that low life motherfuckin' cocksucker! Make a note, we need to take you and me and five of our best movers and go pay a visit to Dennis Brenahanny one day next week when he opens up," Culhane instructed, "Good-bye Fred." Culhane walked down the hall and went into his library and closed the pocket doors, he had some checks to write.

As Fred Washington powered his big *Buick* out on to Grand Avenue, Robert E. Hannegan and his passenger from Kansas City turned in to Hawthorne Place. As they passed each other, Fred waved and Hannegan acknowledged him.

"Who's the nigger?" Truman asked.

"That Harry is *The Big Nigger*, Fredrick Washington by name. He's a very close – and I mean, *very close* - associate of our friend Mr. Culhane. Well here we are." Hannegan pulled his *Packard* up under the *la porte cochere* and the two men got out and walked up the three polished pink granite steps to the double glass doors. As Hannegan reached out to ring the bell, the door opened and Mary Clare greeted them. "Welcome gentlemen, Robert Emmett, good to see you as always, and you must be Judge Truman, I'm Mary Clare Culhane. Please follow me, Thomas Edward is in his library waiting for you."

"Pleased to meet you Mrs. Culhane," Truman said.

"Oh, I'm not Mrs. Culhane. Tom is widowed. I'm his sister."

"I'm sorry, I just assumed," Judge Truman was a bit embarrassed.

"Don't worry, it happens all the time," Mary Clare knocked and opened the library pocket doors, Thomas Edward, your guests are here."

"Come in gentlemen, come in," Culhane warmly greeted and shook hands with his distinguished guests, "Mary Clare, please ring us when lunch is ready, let's eat in the arboretum, it's nice and sunny in there at this time of the afternoon.

"Harry, will you join me and Robert Emmett in a whiskey?"

"Bourbon on the rocks please," Truman replied.

"One 12-year old bonded bourbon and two Irish whiskey's coming right up," Culhane filled the heavy cut crystal glasses with ice and poured from two Waterford decanters. "Whiskey neat or on ice is a man's drink Harry. That's a good sign for someone with political ambitions. C'mon sit here and tell me all about yourself."

Culhane, now dressed in the rest of his 3-piece navy blue pin-striped suit and sporting a red foulard tie, sat down in the leather chair behind his ornate Louis XIV desk. "Do you recognize this tie, Harry?" Culhane unbuttoned his vest and turned the tie over to reveal the back label. It read, *Truman & Jacobson, Kansas City, Missouri.*

"Well I'll be damned," Truman smiled.

"I dug it out of my closet in your honor, Harry. I always liked the way this tie could take a knot. And, I didn't want you to think I was bullshittin' you about me being a former customer," Culhane laughed as he rebuttoned his vest, "Shall we get down to business?"

Robert Hannegan began, "First of all, thanks for seeing us today…"

"Robert, I'm on a really tight schedule, so let's dispense with all the formalities and pleasantries and get right to the nut cutting," Culhane directed.

"Well, to your point then. We're here on behalf of the Missouri Democratic Party to see if we might persuade you to help on two important issues. We need money to help FDR get elected in the upcoming Presidential election and we need more money to help Judge Truman get ready for the future. We need to get started now. The plan is to get FDR into the White House in '32, and then once we've got some momentum rolling to get together a slate of like-minded candidates to run in the '34 Senatorial elections.

There is a possibility that Judge Truman might be just the man to fill that role here in Missouri, if he has the right backing. That's the way the Party sees it and that's the way I see it," Hannegan went mute and waited.

Culhane sat back in his chair and crossed his hands over his chest. He looked at Hannegan and then at Truman. Then he leaned forward and almost sneered, "What the fuck is in it for me?"

Hannegan started to speak, but Judge Truman reached over and put his hand on his arm and said, "Let me see if I can answer that one, Robert."

Culhane eased back in his chair and waited quietly for Truman to begin. Truman removed his glasses, breathed on to the lenses and wiped them clean with a handkerchief from his breast pocket.

"Hmmm, an effective technique to compose his thoughts," Culhane thought.

Truman began, "Tom you and I are both common men from simple family backgrounds. We both served in the Great War, I was a Captain of artillery and I've heard about your exploits with the Indianhead Division's First Marine Brigade. So we've both seen some mighty bad stuff in our time, but nothing as bad as the human despair and misery that has been gripping the families of our country since 1929. Now, I believe that President Hoover is a good man with a fine mind and honorable heart. But, in plain language, I don't think he has the grit and gristle that this country needs to lead it out of this Depression. I think Franklin Delano Roosevelt is the man we need. He'll be a great leader..."

"He's nothin' but a fuckin' cripple," Culhane snapped.

Truman instantly shot up straight and erect, "That may be sir, but he's got a bigger set of balls than you'll ever have, you son-of-bitch, let's go Robert, this conversation is over," he spun on his heel and started to leave when he heard Hannegan and Culhane erupt in laughter.

"Hold on Harry, Tom was just testing your mettle," Hannegan said as he raced after and grabbed the fuming Truman by the arm. "C'mon on back Harry, calm down and sit down.

"You see what I meant Thomas Edward? I told you that Harry had quite a temper; don't let his glasses, easy demeanor or polite manners fool you. If we were goin' into a perilous fight, we'd want Harry Truman to be with us."

Culhane smiled and said, "Harry, I'm awful sorry I got you all riled up, it's just a bad habit of mine, fucking with people's minds. I talked with Tom Pendergast early this morning and he told me that you had a mind of your own and a helluva lot of personal integrity and loyalty. Tom also said those traits could make you a bit of a pain in the ass, but he still admired you for it.

"I just wanted to be sure he was right. *Here.*" Culhane casual as you please, tossed two envelopes across the desk, one to Hannegan and one to Truman.

Culhane had written three initials on each envelope, FDR on one and HST on the other. Hannagan opened his first, and the check inside was made out to the Missouri Democratic Party with a ledger note; *FDR war chest*, the amount was $175,000. Truman opened his and it was made out to the Missouri Democratic Party with the ledger note; *HST war chest*, the amount was $25,000.

The room was silent for a very long moment.

Then Truman stood up and reached across the desk to shake Culhane's hand, "Tom this is more than generous. I'm glad I passed your test." Truman smiled warmly.

"So am I Harry! So am I!" Hannagan went from speechless to euphoric, "Thomas Edward, thank you very much," Hannegan could hardly believe his eyes, this was the largest single contribution he had ever raised for FDR. "I don't know how to begin to thank you."

"You can thank me by winning and by getting FDR to repeal the Volstead Act and by getting America up off it's backside and back on it's feet working at decent jobs with decent wages again. That's how you can *'Thank* me." Culhane pointed his finger at the two of them, "Now it's up to you to deliver."

Down the hall, Mary Clare pressed the button that rang the bell on his desk. Culhane stood up and said, "Let's go get some lunch. I hope you're hungry and I hope you like chicken salad. Mary Clare makes the best in the world with capers and a little dry mustard in the mayonnaise to give it a bite."

The King's arboretum on the back of the house was filled with lush tropical plants. It was a brightly lit and a completely pleasant setting for the long leisurely lunch that followed. As it turned out, Culhane had no other plans for the day, even his 'tight schedule' and curt manner were part of the earlier ruse. Over the course of the next two hours, Tom, Harry and Robert solved 90% of America's problems. A warm and abiding friendship began to develop between the former Captain of Artillery and the Marine Corps Sergeant, who had merited two Purple Hearts and a French *Croix de Guerre*.

When Truman and Hannagan were getting into the car to leave, Culhane handed Harry a small package, "Here's a little gift to help you remember today. Keep it around to remind you to always stand up for what you believe in, no matter what the consequences may be. It might come in handy, *who knows*. Good bye Harry. Have a safe trip back to the cow town. And, remember me to Big Tom."

As Hannegan drove him back to Union Station to catch the evening train to Kansas City, Truman asked, "Why would Culhane be so eager to see Repeal happen. Wouldn't that put him out of business?"

"No Harry, it would put him into the legitimate liquor distribution business. Tom is no fool, he's watching what's happening to Capone in Chicago and he has no desire to see that happen to him. The sooner he can become legitimate the better.

"By the way Harry, you made quite an impression on him today, and that is not an easy thing to do. I could tell. He likes men that have strong beliefs, integrity, loyalty and courage. Or, as he likes to say, *'brass balls'*."

Truman made his goodbyes at the station and settled into his seat and as the west bound train pulled out of Union Station, he unwrapped the small package that *The King Of Kerry* had given him. Inside was a small wooden desk sign about two inches high and six inches long, as Truman turned it over he saw a small brass plaque bearing the message:

The Buck Stops Here.

KIRTSCHNER'S JOURNAL ENTRY: EW/1H/HS

The phone on my desk rang. "Hello, Fred Kirtschner here."

"Your order at Hodges is ready." The phone clicked as the caller hung up.

I grabbed my hat and raced over to the drop. I went up the alley and into the kitchen from the back door. "Got an order for me?"

"Sure do, tub of chili, 10 cents, need any crackers or bread," the cook asked

I shook my head *"No"* and handed him the money and took the brown paper sack from him. It was hot and I burned my hand carrying it. I stopped halfway down the alley, and looked in the bag, inside I found a carton of chili and a small envelope. I set the bag on a window sill and quickly unfolded the note and read the hand written message.

Car registered to Pierre Laclede Devereaux.
43 Washington Terrace, St. Louis.

I could not believe my eyes, "Holy shit wait until Gordon Alcott and Dexter see this." I stuffed the paper in my pocket and ran down the alley, leaving the steaming bag of chili sitting amidst the pigeon shit on the rear window sill.

Back in the Detective Bureau, Harrigan had returned and was going though his mail when Emil Schumacher knocked on his door.

"What is it Schu?" he asked half annoyed with the intrusion.

"The registration report from Jeff City came in."

"Well, Jesus Christ man, give it to me!" Harrigan jumped out of his seat.

Missouri Department Of Motor Vehicle Registration

Vehicle Type: 1930 Cadillac
License Number: PLD-1764
Registered Owner: Pierre L. Devereaux
Address: 43 Washington Terrace
      St. Louis, Missouri
Phone Number: CAbanne 3456

Harrigan now had the official confirmation he needed. He pulled on his coat and headed out into the elevator bank, but decided to take the stairs to save time. He bounded up four flights to reach the top floor and the Office of Colonel Gordon C. Strickland, The Chief of Police of the City of St. Louis.

Harrigan briefed Chief Strickland and then they called Mayor Victor Miller and gave him the news. The phone conference lasted nearly an hour as Miller expressed his concerns and the Chief of Police and the Chief of Detectives outlined how they planned to proceed. The Mayor was appreciative of the forewarning, since it would give him time to prepare for the outrage and the outcry from the city's elite and the onslaught of newspaper and radio reporters. It wasn't going to be pretty, but at least he wouldn't be blindsided.

Strickland agreed with Harrigan's strategy and authorized him and Major O'Connell to immediately visit Mrs. Devereaux to inform her of her husband's death. Harrigan called Jeremiah from the Chief's office and told him that he was leaving immediately and coming by the 7th to pick him up.

Back at the *Star*, I was meeting behind closed doors with Alcott and Dexter.

"Fred are you sure this is true?" Alcott pressed, "We've got to be 150% sure.

I want you to call your source and find out where he got this information.

Holy Mother of God this is big news, if it's true."

I called the Central District Detective's Bureau and Dexter and Alcott leaned in close to the receiver so they could hear the conversation. The phone rang three times and was picked up. The voice on the other end said, "Detective Bureau, Sergeant Schumacher speaking."

"I got the chili. *How do you know?*"

Schumacher never missed a beat, "Yes, Major O'Connell, the report from the Missouri Department of Motor Vehicles came in just about 3 hours ago. Yes sir, I gave it to Chief Harrigan as soon as he returned. No, sir, no one else has seen it as yet. Although I think he's upstairs discussing it with the Chief Strickland right now. Thank you sir. Yes sir, I'll tell him that." The phone hung up.

"That's good enough for me! Dext, call the linotype room and tell the typesetters to get ready to reset and re-plate Page One, call the press room and tell 'em to hold the shift over for a special edition," Alcott looked me in the eye and put his hand on my shoulder. "Get back to your desk Fred and write the story of your life and have it on my desk in 20 minutes. Get going man!"

"Dext, I'm going to call Elzey and let him know about this, he'll be floored. Continental Shoe is the arch rival, no pun intended, of his own family's International Shoe Company. Jesus, this is gonna be a big story and we've got an exclusive. Let's get a move on man!" Alcott was flushed with excitement as he called the the *Star's* publisher on his private home line. The phone rang only once in the well-appointed den at 55 Washington Terrace, when it was answered by a deep and refined voice, "Hello, this is Mr. Roberts."

"Elzey, are you sitting down?" Alcott asked.

———◆———

KIRTSCHNER'S JOURNAL ENTRY: 1H/2H/HS

"How do you want to play it? O'Connell asked as Harrigan's LaSalle sped north on Kingshighway toward Lindell Boulevard.

"I think a combination of the finest of sympathetic condolences and firm resolve to solve the case, is the order of the day. You break the news to Mrs. Devereaux and we'll see how she reacts. Frankly, Jeremiah, I hope all my instincts are wrong about this. Why don't you handle the sympathetic condolences and I'll handle the firm resolve part of the equation," Harrigan said as he turned left to take the park cut-through to Lindell. He caught the light and shifted into 4th as he moved into the westbound curb lane ready to make a right onto Union.

The LaSalle roared through the private gate's entrance clock tower and west down the divided and tree-lined boulevard. Washington Terrace was one of St. Louis's most exclusive neighborhoods. Unlike the *nouveaux riche* of Compton Heights, the gentry of the Central West End's private places constituted the old money social elite of St. Louis. Bankers whose ancestors lent the money to fur traders, businessmen, the likes of whom bought Colonel Lindbergh his *Spirit of St. Louis* and the shoe barons lived quietly in the stately mansions that lined both sides of the boulevard that ran the length of five regular city blocks

Harrigan slowed down, reading the house numbers. "There it is #43. Are you ready, Jeremiah?" The police officers walked up the wide sidewalk that lead to the polished granite steps and up to the expansive marble railed front porch, which ran the full length of the front of the 3-story French Imperial style mansion. The entrance featured 8-foot tall Tiffany sidelights flanking two large bronze doors with polished brass lion-headed ringed knockers. The Tiffany glass in the window arching above the doors featured the number 43.

Harrigan rang the doorbell. He waited impatiently for a few seconds then rang it again.

The door slowly opened and a diminutive colored woman in a black and grey maid's uniform asked, "May I say who is calling, gentlemen?"

O'Connell handed his card to the maid and said, "Is Mrs. Devereaux here?"

"Yes Major, please come with me into the parlor and I'll let her know that you're here."

The maid deposited the officers in the parlor and left to announce them.

"Will you get a load if the size of this room? O'Connell marveled, "It's 10 times the size of our living room, dining room and kitchen combined.

"Major O'Connell," a lovely female voice spoke, "I'm Ada Devereaux, what brings you calling? It's a little late in the day and a little early in the year to be soliciting support for *The Policemen's Charity Ball*, isn't it?"

Ada Devereaux was a stunningly beautiful woman in her late 20's, at 5'9" she was tall for the times. She was almost statuesque with a wonderful figure and a distinguished mane of white blonde hair coiffed in the latest vogue-style. Her suntanned skin was creamy and flawless and her clothes were tailored to accent her well proportioned body. The modest skirt that ended just below her knees revealed a pair of long slender legs that led to a trim ankles and feet in soft low heeled shoes, obviously of very fine quality.

"Mrs. Devereaux, I'm Major Jeremiah O'Connell, commander of the 7th District and this is Chief Of Detectives Charles Harrigan."

"The "Iron Charlie," *the* Charles Harrigan I've read so much about? I'm impressed," Ada smiled.

"Don't believe everything you read in the papers," Harrigan modestly responded.

"Mrs. Devereaux, I'm afraid we're here on a very serious matter. Perhaps we'd better sit down and talk a bit," Jeremiah continued, "Do you know where Mr. Devereaux is?"

"Why yes, Pierre's in New York meeting with Macy's or Gimbel's this week. Why do you ask?" Ada looked confused by the question, "What does your visit have to do with Pierre?"

"Night before last, we found Mr. Devereaux's car in Tower Grove Park. Did he lend it to anyone while he was away? O' Connell inquired.

"I don't think that's very likely, only Pierre and Bee, our driver, ever use the Cadillac. Pierre had it specially built, appointed and custom painted just for him, there is not another Cadillac in the world like it. So, I don't think he would have loaned the car to anyone. Maybe it was stolen from the company lot downtown. Pierre often leaves the car at the office and takes a cab over to Union Station to catch the train.

"What was it doing in Tower Grove Park?" she seemed puzzled.

Jeremiah said, "We cannot be absolutely sure of what I'm about to tell you, until a positive identification can be made..."

"What do you mean positive identification?...identification of the car? That will be easy. There is no other car like it," Ada assured him.

"No M'am, we're absolutely sure that the car we found is your husband's. But in the back seat of the car we found a man's body." Jeremiah paused to see what reaction the news would have on her.

Ada sank back in the couch and looked deflated like someone had just let the air out of her. She looked at Harrigan and then back at O'Connell. Her blue eyes welled up with tears and her lips and hands began to tremble.

"And you think the dead man is *Pierre?*"

"We're not sure, do you have a telephone number where we might reach him in New York? A phone call to him would be very helpful to our investigation and it could quickly put your mind at ease, "O'Connell was masterful at tact and diplomacy.

"Yes, he always stays at the New York Athletic Club on Central Park South at Columbus Circle, I have the number in my book," she wiped her eyes and regained some composure. "Let me get it. We can call from the study."

O'Connell and Harrigan accompanied her to the study where she retrieved the leather bound phone book with the initials PLD and looked up the number, " Here it is," she said.

"Please call it if you don't mind," O'Connell asked.

Ada sat at the desk and dialed the Operator. "Operator I need to place a long distance call to New York City, the number is TUxedo 9000. "Yes, I'll hold. You say you found a man's body, was he tall, with a blond moustache and wavy blonde hair? Oh, yes Operator. It's ringing now. Hello, this is Mrs. Pierre Devereaux calling from St. Louis, Missouri can you please connect me with my husband. Yes, he is a guest staying with you this week. His arrangements are always made by the Missouri Athletic Club in St. Louis. Yes, I'll hold.

Ada turned to Jeremiah and repeated her question, "Was the man you found tall with a blond moustache and wavy blonde hair? Before he could answer, the Guest Desk Manager at the NYAC came back on the line, "Oh, yes, I see. Can you please check again? You're sure. Positively sure? Yes, I see." Ada hung up the phone and began sobbing softly, "He's not there. Oh Pierre…oh sweet Jesus no no no…it can't be Pierre…"

O'Connell moved to comfort her, "Charles can you call the maid to get her some water and aspirin too?"

Tears and mascara streaked down her face, she was completely inconsolable, sobbing and trembling from head to toe.

"Mrs. Devereaux there is still a possibility that the man we found is not your husband. Is there anyone I can call who can make a positive identification down at the morgue.

"I can do it," she said through her sobs.

"I think it is best that you don't in your present state. Is there anyone else, a male family member perhaps?" He suggested.

"I can call Daddy."

"Let me call him, can I have his number."

"Yes its PArkview 6543. His name is Edmund. Daddy will come right away" she sobbed.

"Let's get your 'help' to get you settled upstairs in bed and I'll call him straight away," Jeremiah assured her. When the maid came back with Harrigan, she gave her some aspirin and she took Mrs. Devereaux upstairs to lie down.

"Well whaddya think?" Harrigan asked.

"She seems genuinely shocked and in a state of grief," Jeremiah commented, "Let's call EOR and see how he takes the news." O'Connell dialed the phone and waited, finally after a series of long rings, someone picked up.

"Hello."

"Yes, this is Major Jeremiah O'Connell of the St. Louis Police Department; I'm trying to reach a Mr. Edmund O. Robertson. Is he in by any chance?"

"This is Edmund Robertson, how can I help you, are my truck drivers blocking the alley again?"

"No sir, I'm at your daughter's home and we have a situation that requires your immediate attention."

"Is Ada all right, what's happened," he asked excitedly.

"Yes sir, she's fine, but we found Mr. Devereaux's Cadillac night before last in Tower Grove Park and Mrs. Deveraeaux called New York to try to reach him but he isn't there."

"Does this have something to do with the shooting in the park that I heard about on the radio today?"

"Yes sir, I'm afraid it does. We've kept a tight investigative embargo on all the details of the case until we've been able to run down and verify some information like the car's registration."

"Are you sure it's Pierre's car?"

"Yes sir."

Robertson continued, "Was Pierre involved in the shooting, I mean is he the *victim?*"

"That's what we're hoping you can tell us. We need a positive identification of the man's body and we don't think it's in any fit state for Mrs. Devereaux to see it," Jeremiah said.

"How bad is the condition, I'm a veteran, you can tell me," Robertson braced himself for the news.

"It's bad sir, that's all I can really say. Can you come to your daughter's home right away?"

"Yes of course, let me collect my wife and her sister and we'll be there in…30…make it 20 minutes. Goodbye Captain."

"It's *Major*," the rank correction was too late, EOR had already hung up.

"Look at the time willya, it's getting on toward seven o'clock. Where the hell does time go?" Harrigan wondered.

Twenty minutes later, a long black Pierce Arrow touring car pulled into the driveway.

Mr. Robertson his wife and Ada's younger unmarried sister, Edith hurriedly alighted from the car and made their way into the house through the side entrance.

"Mr. Robertson, I'm Major O'Connell and this is Chief of Detectives Charles..."

"I know who he is, his picture's right here in the paper that's being hawked on every corner," the red-faced Robertson was clearly very angry. "Is this your idea of an investigative news embargo? No one has even identified the victim's body yet... so, how do you explain this headline? Answer me that Mr. Chief of Detectives. My family's reputation is being dragged through the mud and somebody's going to pay!" Robertson brushed them aside and ran up the stairs behind his wife and daughter.

O'Connell and Harrigan looked down at the **EXTRA EDITION** of the *Star.* On the front page was a three column photo of the back of Harrigan with Mickey Finnegan and Joe Culhane looking into the trunk of the car. A large inset file photo of Harrigan with an accompanying cutline read.

Chief of Detectives Charles M. Harrigan and unidentified officers examine the trunk of the car confirmed as belonging to Continental Shoe Company executive, Pierre Laclede Devereaux.

The 24-point banner headline read:
Tower Grove Park Murder Victim May Be Socially Prominent Shoe Executive

Below it, the smaller eyebrow headline read:

Female Victim's Identity Remains A Mystery

Harrigan exploded into a cursing rage that would have made a Marine drill Sergeant blush. He grabbed Jeremiah by the arm, "I'm going straight back to the station house right now. You ride with Mr. Robertson down to the morgue and see if you can get a positive ID. I'm going to find the son-of-a-bitch that leaked this information and that photograph.

Harrigan snatched up the paper and stormed out the front door. He got into his LaSalle, and made an immediate U-turn, he didn't bother going to the end of the block to turn around, he drove over the curb and across the boulevard's grass median and through the flower beds.

On the other side of the street, *Star* publisher Elzey Roberts was walking his dog. When Harrigan sped past him, Roberts recognized him and mused. "I'll bet he just heard about his front page picture in the Extra." Elzey continued to walk his Labrador, *Duke* down the street watching the Devereaux house as he passed by. "Hmmm...looks like EOR's over there, but I don't think it's for a caviar and champagne celebration tonight. It's so sad to see such a good family go so bad." Elzey Roberts, smiled wryly, took a long slow draw on his pipe and walked on.

As Harrigan's car careened out on to south bound Union Boulevard, he hit the siren and turned on the bullet-shaped flashing spotlights on both sides of the front doors. He shoved a cigar into his mouth, bit off the end, rolled down the window and spat it out. After he closed the window he lit up with the trench lighter pulled from his coat pocket and reached over on the front seat to retrieve the wadded up newspaper he had tossed in. "Who wrote this fucking thing." His eyes focused tightly as he read the byline:

Frederick L. Kirstchner of the Star Staff.

Harrigan sped due east straight down Lindell Boulevard and then two bocks east of Grand, Lindell merged into Washington. He pushed the LaSalle to speeds well past 50 mph weaving in and out of traffic. In the distance he could see the lighted sign *Star* atop the newspaper's building.

"Oh Freddy boy, Freddy boy, you're fucking with fire when you're fucking with me,"

Harrigan yelled at the top of his lungs inside the smoke-filled car.

———

Newspaper Clipping – *St. Louis Star*,
March 18, 1931

EXTRA BULLDOG EDITION
Tower Grove Park Murder Victim May Be Socially Prominent Shoe Executive

Frederick L. Kirtschner
Of The Star Staff

Informed sources to the *Star* have confirmed that the car, in which the Tower Grove Park murder victims were found on the evening of March 16th, is registered to prominent St. Louisan Pierre Laclede Devereaux. Mr. Devereaux is the executive vice president of Continental Shoe Company and the son-in-law of its president Edmund O. Robertson

Major Jeremiah O'Connell, commander of the 7th District could not be reached to confirm the information obtained by this reporter. All inquiries were referred us to Chief of Detectives Charles M. Harrigan who is heading the investigation. Chief Harrigan was also unavailable for comment. However, the *Star* was successful in obtaining a photograph taken at the crime scene. The Missouri license plate visible in the photograph clearly shows that the number is PLD 1764. We are currently awaiting official confirmation from the Missouri Department Of Motor Vehicles on the registration. *Star* sources in Jefferson City have reported that the official DMV records when released through police channels will confirm that the custom-built 1930 Cadillac 'Madame X' with coachwork by Fleetwood will be registered to Mr. Devereaux.

Female Victim's Identity Remains Shrouded In Mystery

As to the identities of the male and female victims found in the car, no official report has been released from the Coroner's Office or from the office of the Chief of Detectives. Speculation is rampant that the male victim may be Mr. Devereaux. *Star* sources confirm these suppositions. However, as the *Star* goes to press, neither the family nor the police have confirmed this widely held conjecture. The female victim also found in the car has not been identified.

Photo Cutline:
Chief of Detectives Charles M. Harrigan and unidentified officers examine the trunk of the car confirmed by exclusive *Star* sources as belonging to Continental Shoe Company executive, Pierre Laclede Devereaux.

KIRTSCHNER'S JOURNAL ENTRY: 1H/2H/EW

"Tom have you seen the *Star?*" Joe Culhane called to ask his brother.

"Yes, Joseph good of you to call, but, I've already seen it. It looks like that little shot I put in the baseboard next to your newspaper boy's head the other night had the desired educational effect," *The King* noted.

"Whaddya mean? I thought you'd be hoppin mad."

"On the contrary, I'm quite pleased. Look little brother, there was no way the story was going to stay bottled up, but if you'll get somebody to read the entire article to you very slowly, you'll discover that there is no mention of my black whiskey anywhere, even though the front page picture shows Harrigan, Finnegan and your sorry ass staring into the trunk where it was found. I'd say that Mr. Kirtschner had a very convenient and well-timed case of Irish amnesia. As long as his recollections stay that way, he'll have no beef with me. See that that good word gets passed along to him at the earliest opportunity. Is there anything else, Joseph?"

"No, I was just calling to..."

"Goodbye then," *The King* hung up and rolled over and put his ruddy freckled hand on the warm naked belly of Mamie O'Halloran, "Now where we're we?"

"I think we were right here," Mame guided his hand up from her belly to feel the erect peanut-size nipples crowning her glorious 36DD tits.

"Ahhh, yes it's all coming back to me," *The King* pulled her close and they resumed their carnal recreations in the love nest above *The Celtic Room*.

About 25 blocks to the south and east, the elevator doors on the 5th floor of the *Star* burst open as Charles Harrigan came raging into the newsroom. "Where's that asshole Kirtschner?" he bellowed bringing the entire newsroom to a dead stop. He watched as the reporters looked at him and then turned their heads in the same direction. There I was, standing at my desk with every eye in the newsroom on me. "I'll shoot you if you run, you scrawny son-of-a-bitch," Harrigan shouted as he brushed past several reporters and bore down on me.

As Harrigan closed to within 10 feet of me, the equally formidable figure of Gordon P. Alcott stepped directly into his path, "Welcome to the *Star* Mr. Harrigan, to what do we owe the honor of this unannounced visit?"

"I want to know where that son-of-a-bitch got his information. And, I want to know now, not five minutes from now." Harrigan was pointing wildly at me and yelling right in Alcott's face.

"Now, I'm only going to say this once Mr. Harrigan," Alcott stepped up closing the distance between them to less than inches, and in his soft measured refined voice, Alcott said, "So listen very carefully. Nobody comes into my newsroom, not the Chief of Detectives or God Almighty Himself and makes threats to me or my reporters." By now, Arnold Dexter had reached Alcott's side. "If you want to have a talk in a civilized tone of voice, I suggest that you accompany me quietly to my office. If you don't and continue to create a ruckus, tomorrow's lead story will have a picture of you being dragged out of here in cuffs by your own cops. Try me, if you think I'm kidding," Gordon Philpott Alcott stared the devil right in the eye, and the devil blinked.

"All right then, Harrigan composed himself and said, "Let's continue this conversation in the privacy of your office, as you suggest."

"A very sensible decision Mr. Harrigan, please follow me. Dext bring Fred along in about 10 minutes and tell him to have no fear. This way Mr. Harrigan." Alcott led him through the newsroom and into the corner conference room that connected to both the Managing Editor's and the Publisher's Offices on opposite ends.

"Would you like something to settle your nerves," Alcott produced a bottle of whiskey from the credenza in the conference room.

"I could run you in for having that," Harrigan smiled.

"Right and you could run Chief Strickland in too; I had a nip with him in his office last week. He keeps a quart of scotch in his lower left desk drawer," Alcott volunteered.

"I know where he keeps it," Harrigan grumbled.

"Now look Charles, I can understand why you might be a little upset," Alcott began.

"A *little upset*. A little upset," Harrigan began to build up a head of steam again.

"Have a drink and listen to me for a minute. You have a problem and we both have an opportunity,"

"I'm listening, and this is good whiskey."

"I get it from your cousin Tom, *The King of Kerry*, he's a bootlegger you know," Alcott added.

Harrigan coughed as the whiskey went down the wrong pipe. "Need some water?"

Harrigan waved to indicate that he was fine. But he kept coughing as he tried to clear his throat.

"Here's your problem. You've got an unsolved, high profile, volatile-as-hell crime on your hands and here's our mutual opportunity. I can win a circulation battle with the PD. The *Star* can help you control the *favorable* way the story develops in the public eye, if you'll play ball with us. Just let us have the inside track on all the information and we'll make sure that you and Chief Strickland and Major O'Connell all end up looking like the heroes you really are. This is the kind of story that can help make more than one man's career. Especially ambitious men that have their eyes on greener uplands, shall we say."

"Where's my *quid pro quo?*" Harrigan asked.

"A cop that quotes Latin, I'm impressed," Alcott said.

"Jesuits," Harrigan replied.

"The *quid pro quo* is, we give up the *Star's* snitch in your department after the crime is solved. In the meantime our snitch stays in place, to keep you honest and to make sure we really are getting the inside track. Do we have a deal or not?" Alcott came right to the point.

"Done," Harrigan extended his hand and Alcott shook it.

A few seconds later, Arnold Dexter and I came into the room. I was scared shitless.

"Arnold, Fred, Chief of Detectives Harrigan and I have just had a wonderful *tête-à-tête* and have arrived at a mutually beneficial understanding. From know on, Fred will call Chief Harrigan after all the squad's morning briefings for a little private update. The Chief has agreed to help the *Star* on both an *"on-the-record"* and *"off-the-record* basis to continue the fine journalistic coverage that Fred has begun. Gentlemen let's all shake hands and have a little glass of old John Barleycorn to toast our new working arrangement."

Ten minutes later, Harrigan, Alcott, Dexter and me emerged from the conference room all smiles, laughing and joking as we walked through the stunned newsroom to the elevator bank.

"Have a nice day Mr. Harrigan."

"And, you fine gentlemen have one too," Harrigan stepped alone into the empty elevator and smiled and waved goodbye to me as the doors closed.

Harrigan's demeanor and entire countenance completely changed from bright and sunny to malevolent once the doors shut, his image in the burnished brass doors glared back the distorted reflection of a very angry man who had been temporarily bested, but not beaten by any means. "Freddy boy, your day will come. Mark my words," Harrigan swore.

As we walked back to Alcott's office, I asked, "What did you say to him in there? What kind of deal did you make? You didn't give up my source did you?

"Relax son, your source is safe and we have the inside track, the rest is, shall we say, a 'managerial trade secret.' By the by Fred, the old man told me to sweeten your pay envelope this week and to give you some 'walking around money' to help with your contact and informant development work, it seems the boss thinks you have a real knack for it.

"And I've been meaning to ask, how did you bang up your face?"

"Walked into a door," I said.

Alcott looked incredulous.

"Three times," I added.

Alcott laughed, "Watch out Fred, the world is not a perfect place, there are a lot of doors out there that might walk into you."

KIRTSCHNER'S JOURNAL ENTRY: 1H/2H/OF

About 25 minutes passed until Edmund Robertson reappeared in the parlor where O'Connell was patiently waiting.

"How is your daughter," Jeremiah inquired.

"She's terribly distressed, I called our doctor and he is on his way here. I believe he'll give her a sedative to help her sleep. Her mother and sister are trying to console her. I told her not to give up hope. It might not be Pierre's body after all, and we can't be certain until I return from the morgue. Should we get about this ugly business?" Robertson seemed emotionally drained by the events thus far.

"Yes sir, Chief Harrigan left in the car I came in, if it's all right with you, we can ride down together," Jeremiah suggested.

"Yes, that will be fine, shall we go?"

The ride down to the morgue was unusually quiet, Mr. Robertson had a reputation as being one of the shoe industry's leading executives having personally built Continental Shoe from a cobbled together alliance of small manufacturers in the early '20's into a combine that is one of the nation's leading shoe manufacturer's and specialty retailers with a line of factory-distributed workman's shoes and hospital-distributed nurses shoes.

At 53, he was vibrant and in excellent physical shape from working out and swimming 100 laps daily at the Racquet Club, St. Louis' most exclusive all-male preserve and the place where Col. Lindbergh received the $25,000 check to buy the *Spirit of St. Louis* and finance the first non-stop New York to Paris transatlantic flight. The Princeton-educated Edmund Oscar Robertson had been a leading St. Louisan for more than 25-years. He returned to St. Louis in 1919, having served as a combat infantry Captain in the AEF's Rainbow Division commanded by General Douglas McArthur. Today, he sits on the boards of the American Legion, which he helped found in Paris on St. Patrick's Day, March 17, 1919. He was also instrumental in bringing the Legion's First National Caucus to St. Louis just over a month later on May 9, 1919. EOR currently serves on the board of Southside National Bank with Adolphus Busch III, and on the boards of Barnes Hospital, Ralston-Purina, Carter Carburetor, Culver Manufacturing and many civic, charitable and social organizations. By all accounts, he is a man who loves his family, his country, his business and his city, in that order.

As Robertson pulled into the small lot next to the morgue, Jeremiah asked, "Are you sure you're feeling up to this right now? If you like, we can wait until tomorrow."

"No, if there is only one thing that I have learned in my life it is this, there is no better time to face the unpleasant than *immediately*, the longer you put off dealing with an unpleasant situation, the worse it becomes. Let's get it over with," Robertson said.

Once inside, Jeremiah led the venerable executive down to the lower level where Pat Taylor, the coroner, was waiting outside the autopsy room. "Coroner Taylor, this is Mr. Edmund Robertson, he's going to be viewing the victims to see if he can identify them," O'Connell said.

"Before we go in, Mr. Robertson," Pat Taylor looked him in the eye, "Do you have any kind of heart weakness or any nervous condition?"

"No, I'm in perfect physical and mental condition," Robertson replied.

"Well, I want to prepare you for what you're going to see. Let me ask you to read this preliminary report before we go in. Would you mind taking a seat here on the bench and reading over this document. It is the Preliminary Police Summary, It is not the complete autopsy report or the summary of official findings of this office. We are still working with the bodies and anticipate that all final work should be accomplished by end of day tomorrow. Do you have any questions?' Taylor asked as he handed him the document.

"Let me read it over and if I have any questions or require any clarifications, we can go over them before I go in for the identification. Is that acceptable?"

"That'll be fine Mr. Robertson, Major O'Connell will wait over here by the door, take all the time you need sir, and join us when you are ready to go in," the Coroner said.

PRELIMINARY POLICE SUMMARY
CORONER'S REPORT
CITY OF ST. LOUIS

DATE: March 17, 1931
Revised: March 18, 1931
Revised 2: March 18, 1931
TIME: 03:45 a.m.
Revision Time: 2:30 p.m
Revision Time 2: 5:00 p.m..

AUTOPSY OFFICERS: Stephen Stevens, MD, Elaine Buder, RN
ATTEST: Patrick C. Taylor, Coroner

NARRATIVE FINDINGS:

Two Caucasian victims were found in the backseat of a Cadillac car in Tower Grove Park. Autopsy estimates time of death between 11:00 pm and 12:10 a.m. 03/16-17, 1931 Causes of death were multiple gunshot wounds.

VICTIM ONE: John Doe
White male, 30-35 years of age, 155 lbs. 5'10" tall, no scars or distinguishing marks.

Blonde hair, brown eyes. Blonde moustache.

The male victim was hit by a total of twelve (12) shots, any of which could have been fatal. Five (5).32 caliber rounds were recovered from the anterior lobe of the victim's brain and four (4) .32 caliber rounds were recovered from the soft tissue inside the mouth and posterior sections of the skull. Three (3) .25 caliber rounds were recovered from the chest. Two (2) of the .25 caliber bullets had penetrated the heart the third shattered a rib and lodged in the lung.

In addition to the gunshot wounds, the male victim's left hand ring finger was severely distended and radially fractured. The knuckle had been violently torn and dislocated by probable violent pulling and twisting.

The male victim's penis was severely bitten and partially detached. His bowels had been completely evacuated by shock from sustained trauma.

VICTIM TWO: Jane Doe

White female, 18-25 years of age, 108 lbs., 5' 2" tall, with crescent birthmark ¾ " by 2" on left inner thigh. Blonde hair (dyed) natural hair color: brunette, green eyes.

Red manicured finger nails and toe nails.

The female victim was hit by a total of one (1) fatal shot. One (1).32 caliber round was recovered from the remains of the right posterior lobe of the victim's brain. The braincase suffered severe trauma and approximately 25% of the right posterior skull above the ear was removed by the impact force of the shot.

Traces of semen were found in her throat along with blood and brain fluid.

RECOVERED AT THE SCENE:

Two (2) additional .25 rounds were recovered from the backseat's upholstery in an area proximate to the site of the male victim's head.

ITEMS RECOVERED FROM VICTIMS:

Female Victim: Two (2) rings were recovered from the female victim's right hand. One ring appears to be a diamond ring approximately 1ct in size, the other is a gold signet ring with monogram MKE and an 18k gold mark inside the band. Date is engraved on obverse side of top, *05/02/11.*

A pearl necklace was recovered from the backseat floor of the car. It appears to be costume in nature and the strand appears to have broken in the course of rough play since the lock and hasp was still intact.

Male Victim: One (1) man's Elgin watch with black lizard band was recovered from his left wrist. The cufflinks from his French-cuff shirt were missing as was a stick pin. A hole from a stickpin was found in his tie, which was recovered from the passenger side floor in the front seat of the car.

The male's belt buckle is solid sterling silver and engraved with the monogram *PLD,* a maker's mark, *Tiffany, New York* is on the obverse side. The belt appears to be made from the same type of black lizard skin as the watchband.

His shoes appear to be custom made as no manufacturer's codes were within.

**FINAL AUTOPSY TEST ANALYSIS AND
ANTICIPATED REPORT COMPLETION DATE:**
April 1, 1931

———◆———

It took Robertson less than 2-minutes to read the report. He rose from the bench and came over to the door marked, **AUTOPSY LAB** and said, "Gentlemen I'm ready."

The three walked inside the cold room and up to the first of two examining tables. The heavy medicinal and chemical odors caused Robertson to place a handkerchief over his mouth and nose. "It takes some getting used to the smells in here," Taylor commented, "Are you ready?"

Roberson nodded and Taylor pulled the sheet back to mid-chest to reveal what was left of the male victim's face. Robertson tensed and steeled himself at the sight of the shot away face. "Take the sheet all the way off," Roberson requested.

Taylor obliged. Robertson stepped up and looked at the nude body from top to toe. "Can you lift his left shoulder please" Robertson asked. Taylor slipped his gloved hands under the victim's body and rolled the shoulder up so Robertson could get a good view.

Robertson leaned in close and touched three moles in succession on the victim's left shoulder and said, "It's *Orion's Belt*, it's Pierre."

Taylor re-covered the body and the three moved to the next table. Taylor pulled back the sheet to reveal the face of what was once a lovely young woman. Her face looked strangely peaceful, as the examiners had closed her mouth and eyes during the examination. Yet, just beyond the middle of her skull, one could see the severe damage caused when the brain case was blown off.

"Do you need to see more," Taylor asked?

"No, I have never seen this unfortunate woman before. I'm quite sure." With that Robertson turned and walked out of the room. O'Connell followed as Taylor remained behind to return the bodies to the refrigeration room.

Robertson returned to the bench, sat down and put his head in his hands and began to weep. Jeremiah went down the hall and returned in a few moments with a glass of water, a spoon and a tin of *Bromo Seltzer*. Pat Taylor had rejoined the group too.

"Here, take some Bromo it'll help settle your stomach," Jeremiah said.

"Just the water please, I'll be fine." Robertson seemed dazed and distant, like his mind was somewhere else. He stared off into space for some time, occasionally sipping the water.

Finally, Jeremiah spoke, "Sir, we'll have to ask you to come upstairs and complete some formal paperwork, are you able?"

"Yes, of course," EOR seemed to be coming back to the present reality and the shock of the grim sights were fading at least temporarily. "When can we have the body?"

"In a day or two at the most," Taylor replied.

"As a professional, who would you recommend as the mortician? The face needs a lot of reconstruction," Robertson noted.

"Well, sir, there is no one who can make the corpse fit for an open casket viewing. Frankly, I'd suggest a cremation and a Memorial Service. We could send the body directly to Valhalla, they can handle the entire process," Taylor stated.

"Of course, what was I thinking? It's my daughter's decision, naturally, but I'll give her your recommendation and support it. There is no way, I'll permit Ada to see him like this. Can we suppress the details in the Coroner's report? She can't know about all of this filth," Robertson's mood was turning to anger and his instincts to protect his family were kicking in fast.

"Let's go up to Mr. Taylor's office and talk about all those things. There are ways that we can have documents sealed, but not before the criminal investigation is complete, there might well be a Grand Jury that will need to see the report before they can hand down an indictment in the matter. This is a capital murder case, and even a man in your position and with your influence and resources can't circumvent the legal procedures in a case like this," Jeremiah counseled as they walked up the stairs.

O'Connell could tell that EOR was listening, but he could not tell if he was acquiescing.

"What did you mean by your comment, *Orion's Belt*, I didn't understand that?" Jeremiah confessed.

"Pierre and I play squash at the Racquet Club every Wednesday. After the game we have a steam, eucalyptus rubdown, shower and then lunch. I've sat next to him in the steam room a hundred times and I always thought that the three moles on his left shoulder looked like the star constellation called *Orion's Belt*. When I saw them tonight, I knew it was him for sure," Robertson stated.

"This is a hard question, but were you surprised by the presence of the woman?"

"No, not at all, I've been looking the other way for several years. Pierre was a philanderer from the beginning. I warned Ada about his reputation even before they married. I wanted her to break off the engagement. But, she is a strong-willed woman, and she'd have none of it. She knew that Pierre was a cad, but she loved him anyway and always forgave his infidelities. I tried to get her to divorce him, but, to no avail. Ada always said, 'Pierre loves me and his dalliances mean absolutely nothing to him. He's French, he can't help himself.' There was no changing her mind, she is a very strong-willed woman."

"But, he worked for you?"

"Yes, Pierre was an able enough executive and having him in the office almost everyday let me keep an eye on him, at least as much as that was possible. I hoped he would grow up and grow out of his wayward ways, especially if they would start a family. To be candid, our relationship in the company also assured that my daughter continued to live the life she deserved. It was an economic accommodation that assured their social positions," EOR said.

"Any idea who might have killed him?" O'Connell queried.

"No. Am I suspected?" Robertson asked.

"At this point we don't know who to suspect, that's why I asked the question," Jeremiah replied, "We haven't got much to go on and any insights that you or any member of your family or business associates might have as to motive, would be most welcome."

Pat Taylor who had been preparing the paperwork said, "Here is the statement of positive identification by a relative. It authorizes us to release the body and will serve as an exhibit in our final report. I left the space blank regarding where to deliver the remains. Once you decide, call my office and we'll fill that in. If you'll sign here, sir. We'll be all done."

Robertson signed his name in a large flourish across the bottom of the document.

"Thank you Mr. Robertson, and please accept my sympathies on your loss and troubles," Taylor said.

"I'll walk out with you," Jeremiah said, "Would you let your daughter know that I'll be coming around after the funeral to see if we can get a detailed description of the personal items that were taken from Mr. Devereaux; his stick-pin, wedding ring and cufflinks were missing."

"Do you need a lift back to your district," EOR asked.

"No, but thanks for the offer, I'm going down the street to Central District to see if anything has developed. Thanks for your help tonight. We'll find the killer. Be assured of that."

"Goodnight Major, and good luck."

Robertson turned right, out on to Clark eastbound, then left and north on 12th to Market Street where Jeremiah lost sight of his Pierce Arrow when it turned left and headed west.

"What was that son-of-a bitch thinking fooling around with her again," EOR wondered as he drove back to his daughter's home. "I thought I put an end to that affair when I asked Adolphus to fire that bitch." EOR had been far less than truthful about the identity of 'Jane Doe."

Jeremiah slowly walked up the stairs to the second floor to see if 'Iron Charlie' was still in his office and to check on the daily reports. It had been a long, hard day. Maybe tomorrow would be better.

Newspaper Clipping – *St. Louis Globe-Democrat*, March 20, 1931

A Cup Of Joe with Joe

Your morning coffee column with Joe Leonard

Persuasion is crime prevention – Chief of Detectives Charles M. Harrigan's new crime initiative at Union Station is already paying big dividends. Scuttlebutt from the sages at Wheelchair Willy's shoe shine stand and from around the *Fred Harvey* stools has it that last St. Patrick's Day eve, two known criminal associates of Chicago mobster Al Capone reportedly we're intercepted arriving at Union Station by Chief Harrigan's special crime detail. The two thugs from *The Windy City* ended up heading right back to Chicago after a brief meeting with Harrigan's elite squad. Chief Harrigan commented, "Persuasion is a good form of crime prevention. Our goal is to point out the disadvantages of setting up a crime league in our city. And to see that criminals return home immediately with the message that St. Louis is closed to criminal enterprises."

Morning Joe says, "More free donuts and coffee from *Fred Harvey* and the lovely *Harvey Girls* for our hardworking St. Louis policemen, Eamon O'Meara and Sean Corrigan!"

———◆———

KIRTSCHNER'S JOURNAL ENTRY: 1H/2H/HS

The briefing of Saturday, March 21st began at the appointed time of 10:30 a.m.

"Well, by now, you've all seen yesterday's *Star* Extra, and today's front page. So, the story's coming out faster than I'd like, but there's not much more I can tell you, except that the murdered male was in fact, Pierre Laclede Devereaux. His body was positively identified last evening and it will be confirmed officially by the coroner later this morning. As for the female victim, she remains a 'Jane Doe' at this point.

"All right, enough of that, let's get down to the business at hand." Harrigan's opening question had a ring of *déjà vu.* "Finnegan, what have you turned up? And, for the love of God, please don't say, 'nuthin'."

"Well Chief, late last night one of O'Connell's boys turned up parts of two guns in a commercial trash dump behind the *Navy Brands* plant out on Southwest Avenue. "Here they are,"

Finnegan said as he untied and unfolded an oily white cloth on the table in front of him. Harrigan came over and the other detectives crowded all round.

Finnegan continued, "As you can see, this junk is what's left of a .32 and a .25 just like the shooter or shooters used." He pointed to the marks on the base of the butts with a pencil, "And, you can see here that the serial numbers have been completely filed off and as you can also see from the stains on the apron they were tied up in, the guns have been oil-wiped clean and the barrels were cracked and smashed almost flat and the grips all busted up with something heavy, like maybe a sledge hammer. My guess is these are the guns that were used, and person or persons unknown went to a lot of trouble to make it impossible to trace them, "Finnegan looked up at Harrigan, "That's it Chief."

Harrigan looked at the circle of detectives and said, "Does any one see anything differently?" The detectives crowded in closer, looking at the guns and the broken off parts, some pushed them around on the apron looking for who knows what?

"Chief, that's all there is, do you want me to put 'em in the evidence room or send off 'em to that new laboratory that Hoover's opened up at the FBI, *or what?*" Finnegan was wondering where the *'Nice job Mickey'* was.

"Jesus *Haitch* Christ, do I have to do all the thinking and detective work around here?" Harrigan asked the group, "Are you all fucking blind?' He waited for a response, but none came. Finally in utter exasperation he pointed to the oil stained apron, "Sometimes the obvious is the most elusive. What's this?"

"It's the apron they was wrapped up in Chief, that's what I told you," Finnegan protested.

"Yes, dear Mickey, it's an apron. But what kind of apron?"

"I dunno, it's a white one, an apron's an apron, ain't it?"

Harrigan exhaled deeply, "Look at it. It's long and white, so it's probably either a butcher's or baker's apron or maybe a waiter's. And what's this?" Harrigan pointed to a mark on the backside hem.

"It's a number," Finnegan replied.

"No, that's a laundry mark," Finn O'Meara spoke up.

"At last, we have illumination! Now think it through lads. This was found in a trash dump behind *Navy Brands* plant. Right? And is *Navy Brands* a bakery, butcher shop or a restaurant?"

Tired of waiting for the answer, Harrigan shouted, "No, it is NOT!

It is an industrial paint and sealants company. So what's that tell you?"

"Sit down all of you and let me walk you through a hypothesis," Harrigan audibly sighed.

"What's a *hypothething*?" Finnegan asked O'Meara.

"Mickey, please just sit there and listen in blessed silence, and if he gets stuck, Finn you can draw him a picture." The entire squad laughed, except for Mickey who didn't appreciate being made a fool of. Harrigan continued, "Let's assume that our shooters did not stop on their way home from the murder to clean the guns, smash them to bits and wrap them up in an apron right outside the *Navy Brands* plant in full view of God's creation. That seems like a reasonable assumption. So that means the cleaning and the smashing up took place somewhere else, like maybe in a garage or in the cellar of a house where nobody would be aware of it. That seems like a reasonable assumption too. Are you all with me so far?"

"Yes Chief," the group replied almost in unison.

"Okay, so let's put ourselves into the minds of the killers. We get home, we've just shot the living hell out of two souls and we're nervous as hell. We want to get rid of the guns, so we go down in the cellar or out in the garage, and we start by filing off all the serial numbers, then we the break the guns down in to their component parts and clean up all the parts with heavy oil to remove all the gunpowder residue and finger prints, next we get a handy sledge hammer and smash the livin' shit out of the parts.

"Then we geniuses grab a handy item to wrap up all the pieces in. Finally, in the next day or so, when no one will be around to see us, we toss the whole magilla into the trash dump behind the *Navy Brands* plant.

"Now what can we surmise from that scenario?" Harrigan asked.

Harrigan sighed, "Don't get a fucking headache straining your little brains, let me keep thinking for you. Here's what I surmise.

"*One*, the killers live within a mile or two, at most, of the *Navy Brands* plant. Why? Because if I was going to ditch the guns and I was smart, I'd throw them in the fucking Mississippi River, or better yet in the Missouri river 35 miles west of town. But, if I was a lazy dumbshit, I'd throw them into someplace nearby that was soon going to be taken someplace else, like trash dump that gets picked up every few days. And, I'd do it in a trash dump that I knew about, either near my home or my job.

"*Two*, after I got done bustin' up the cannons, I'd wrap 'em up in some handy item, I think that's the way I put it earlier, 'some handy item.' Newspaper wouldn't do because the oil would all leak through. So I pick up and use an apron that just happens to be down in the cellar, in my garage or maybe in my car trunk.

"*Three*, if I have a white apron in my possession and if I live within a mile or two of the *Navy Brands* plant, I probably work in the area at a bakery, a butcher shop or a restaurant.

"*Four*, when I look at the apron, I don't see any faded blood stains. Do you? No matter how much bleach you put into a butcher's apron, you can never get all the blood stains completely out. Next time you're in a butcher shop look at the aprons, they all have kind of pale pink cast to'em. So, I'm ruling out butcher shops. *At least for the time being.*

"*Five*, the *Navy Brands* plant is on Southwest Avenue near Kingshighway right by Southwest Bank, literally on the southwest edge of 'The Hill' where a lot of Luigi Columbo's Pisano pals live."

"And where many fine family neighborhood *ristorante's* are," Columbo hastened to add.

"Point well taken. Louie, you may have a promising career in law enforcement yet," Harrigan continued, "Let's hypothesize further, if you wanted to throw something in a trash dump, and you wanted to do it when nobody was around to see you do it, wouldn't the dark of night be an ideal time to do that? Now ask yourselves, who gets off work or goes to work while it's dark? Waiters get off in the dark and bakers go to work in the dark."

"*Six*, the commercial laundry mark means that our killers probably brought this apron home from their place of employment. It looks worn around the edges, so it's not brand new. The laundry mark is faded, but still legible. It usually identifies a customer and the laundry itself, that's how the commercial linen laundry business works.

"*Seven*, if I'm big enough to afford a commercial laundry's linen service, I'm probably not a Mom and Pop restaurant or bakery. Money's too dear for them. Mama washes the aprons and the table cloths and the napkins or the bakers' aprons herself. So, if you geniuses were running the investigation, what would you do next?" Harrigan crossed his arms and sat on the edge of the table next to the podium. "C'mon prove I have some detectives in here before I put every one of you back on the street walking a beat."

Finn O'Meara raised his hand.

"Sister Katherine, at old St. Malachy's would be very proud of you Finn, the way you shot your hand right up. Please proceed and tell us what you would do."

"Well Chief, I'd try to run down the laundry mark and see where the laundry was that it came from. I'd start by locating the laundry, and then work backwards from there to see if that could lead me to the customer and then see who was working there, or who was working there in the recent past. I'd see if any of the names that come up have any records and then I'd roust them. If that didn't pan out, I'd keep on and interview the whole list of employees," Finn finished and sat down.

"My faith in the squad is *moderately* restored. Oh, Mickey, please stand up. Gentlemen I made sport of Detective Finnegan earlier in this meeting, now I'd like to say, Mickey if you weren't so fuckin' tired from searching every nook and cranny in a 15-block radius of Tower Grove Park, all of what I just said would have been apparent to you too. Great job Mickey! Gentlemen, give him a round of applause." Harrigan led the clapping and walked over, hugged Finnegan and patted him on the back, "Mick go home and get some sleep, take tomorrow and the next day off, I'll clock you in myself. Finnegan's eyes teared up. "Now don't go getting emotional on me,' Harrigan chided.

Harrigan turned from Finnegan and said, "Columbo, since *Navy Brands* is on 'The Hill' and it is populated by your *Eye*talian kinsmen, I want you to lead the restaurant, butcher shop and bakery canvassing investigation out there, take Joe with you.

Columbo smiled and gave the Chief of Detectives an acknowledging tip of his hat.

"The rest of you write down this laundry number and get out there and start running it down. Whoever gets a 'Bingo!' call me straight away, and we'll pull the squad together Johnny-on-the-spot. Otherwise, same time tomorrow lads. Class dismissed."

After the meeting, Finn came up and said, "Chief, I'm glad you praised Mickey in front of everybody, I know he's not the sharpest knife in the drawer, but he's the hardest working policeman in shoe leather. He's real sensitive though. Sometimes your words really hurt him, more than you probably realize."

Harrigan looked over the top of his reading glasses, "I know Finn, sometimes I'm an asshole. It comes with my job."

Finn furrowed his brow and said, *"sometimes?"*

Harrigan scowled, "Eamon, if you and I didn't go back as far as we do, I'd mop up the squad room floor with your big fat ugly Irish puss for that crack. Now get out of here before I do exactly that!"

As Finn cleared the door, Harrigan laughed to himself.

Finn knew him well, maybe too well.

Harrigan returned to writing his notes:

```
Guns located. Smashed up.
Purse and man's coat and wallet,
wedding ring, stickpin and cufflinks
still missing.
Souvenirs not dumped in trash dump.
Still in the perps possession???
Find the souvenirs - find the killers
```

———

Newspaper Clipping – *St. Louis Star,*
March 20, 1931

Married Playboy And "Madame X" Murders May Have Mafia Connection

Frederick L. Kirtschner
Of The Star Staff

The most recent round of rumors swirling in the city's crime circles are putting their money on a Mafia connection to the murder of Pierre Laclede Devereaux and the yet to be identified "Madame X" who was found slain in what has been reliably reported as a compromising position in the rear seat of the playboy shoe executive's car.

Reliable informants and exclusive **Star** resources have confirmed the fact that Mr. Devereaux has been a frequent visitor to area speakeasys, gambling parlors and 'houses' in recent years. Attempts by this reporter to obtain comment from the Devereaux family have been thwarted by a phalanx of attorneys led by Jonathon McCall.

The incident has caused a high level of public embarrassment to the prominent family and its scion, Edmund O. Robertson, who sits on the boards of many prominent St. Louis companies and charitable organizations.

Chief of Detectives, Charles M. Harrigan, discounts the Mafia assertions as pure speculation. "The crime has all the earmarks of an amateur robbery attempt. Professional murderers would not kill their victims in such a public way. They strike fast and silently," Harrigan asserted.

Speculation as to the identity of "Madame X" has fueled the prurient interests of local citizens and her identity and rumors of what her relationship to the late Mr. Devereaux has become the topic of conversation in every corner diner, coffee shop and elegant hotel or private club dining room all across town.

So far, *Star* reporters have been unable to gain access to the Coroner's photos of "Madame X." Coroner Taylor has kept them as part of the news embargo being enforced on the case. He did comment however that the photos were too disturbing to be fit for publication in any newspaper.

———

Late Saturday afternoon – August 16, 2031

Mac stood up and took a long series of body stretches, she was tired of reading. The rain was getting heavier as the day wore on. It was almost 5:00 p.m. and she was still in her robe. She thought, "I'd better get dressed and run out to Schnucks, but it's such a crumby day. When I get back I can put something in the oven for dinner and get back to the Journal, but I need a break, and if tomorrow is nice, well, I think I'll take a drive down Grand to 'Little Bosnia' and see if any of the old haunts that Kirtschner wrote about are still there.

The Compton Heights area had had its ups and downs since its halcyon days of the 1920's. In it's most recent incarnation, the area had made quite a comeback as many of the old homes on Cleveland, Halliday, Shenandoah, Victor, Russell, Folsom, Arsenal, Flad, DeTonty, Compton and Magnolia had been renovated by the 2nd generation of Bosnians whose parents settled in the area when it was in a teetering borderline condition back in the early 21st century.

Initially, there was a lot of friction with the poorest of the blacks who lived in the 'hoods' south of Lafayette Square and east of Jefferson. There was also a bit of intramural European cultural rivalry with the Italians, who still fiercely maintained their ethnic enclave on 'The Hill' But the Bosnians were tough, smart and very hard-working. They took on the task of updating and renovating the once stately old town homes that had fallen into disrepair and neglect in the neighborhoods surrounding Compton Heights' big private streets of Longfellow, Hawthorne and Flora Place, and over the years they brought them back. Today, 'Little Bosnia' and the "Tiffany" area, as the neighborhoods south of I-44 and west of Jefferson became known, enjoyed some of the highest real estate values in the city.

The Bosnian influence also spread south along Grand Avenue from Utah Place all the way down to Meramec Street, then to Bates and finally on to Holly Hills and Carondolet Park in the neighborhoods that were once populated by the 'Scrubby Dutch,' St. Louis' largely blue collar German community that worked at the breweries, tool and die companies and machine shops that supported the automotive, shoe and aircraft industries.

Thoughts about how St. Louis had changed in the 100 years since 1931, got Mac reflecting on her own career. She had grown up in the sprawling hills of Wildwood in Falconhurst, one of far west St. Louis County's most affluent subdivisions, off Wildhorse Creek Road. A graduate of Villa Duchesne, one of St. Louis' four most prestigious 'silver spoon' private schools for Catholic girls, she had attended Smith for undergrad work and got her graduate degree in communications at NYU while she was making her way in the media world in New York City. When her father, Peter C. McGauley, a world renowned pediatric oncologist at St. Louis Children's Hospital, died suddenly, she came back to St. Louis to be close to her manic-depressive mother. Her impressive resume landed her a job at WebKSDK and her hard work and reporting talents rapidly advanced her to the top of the regional news industry.

"It's been a curious road," Mac reflected on her career as she got dressed, "Maybe I should eat out tonight. I don't really feel like screwing around in the rain with a lot of grocery bags. I could grab an early bite at Duff's or Llwellynn's and go grocery shopping afterwards, or, if it's still pouring, I'll just go tomorrow. Who knows, maybe I'll meet some handsome stud in the pub and get 'lucky,' God knows, I could use a little serendipitous lovin'.'"

The one thing she hated about her job was the long and often irregular hours and her 24/7 on-call status that made meeting 'normal men' and developing a relationship tough. Her so-called 'celebrity' status also meant she attracted the wrong kind of men; it seemed like her life had been a succession of star stuck immature man-boys, media stalker creeps or egoist professional men looking to put a celebrity notch on the handle of their trusty sexgun.

"Well, my baby, how does Mama look," she asked *Rojo* as she brushed her hair and looked at her reflection in the full length mirror, "Well, look at you girl! If I was a nice handsome, gainfully employed, upstanding man, who liked long talks by the fireplace and loved to take walks in the rain, I'd would certainly want to fuck me."

"*Sheeesh*...I sound like one of those pathetic *Yahoogle Meet Your Soulmate* ads," Mac went in to the bathroom and took a 'just-in-case' 24-hour contraceptive pill, spritzed a mist of perfume on her neck, belly and wrists and said, "I'll be back, don't wait up, and please *Rojo* be a good boy and stay off my bed! If I do get 'lucky' I don't want to have 'Mr. Right for Tonight' see one of your icky yellow hairballs! It could ruin the moment."

"Bye-bye baby boy," she said as she closed the condo door.

Mac decided to go to Duff's, the hearty home-cooked comfort food there was more appealing to her than Llwellynn's pub grub. It took her about 5-minutes to navigate the ride down Waterman to Kingshighway and then she jogged north for about 50 feet and turned right into the alley between the Racquet Club and Hortense Place. The alley led straight up to Euclid and came out less than 10 yards from Duff's. When she looked out onto Euclid, she saw an open parking spot right in front of Kopperman's Deli. She zipped across the street and pulled into the spot. Finding a spot this fast and this close could almost qualify as a miracle. She wasn't sure if it was the early hour or the day long rain that had kept the crowd away, but she knew that parking on Euclid doesn't get any better than this. She got out of the car and pressed her key's barcode against the parking meter sensor and held it there until the meter maxed out at 4 hours for $10.50. The rain was cold for August, but not coming down too hard, as she made her way down the sidewalk and into Duff's vestibule. She peered inside and saw that the bar's side booths were all still open and the bar itself had just a few patrons yakking away at one end. The dining room side had just a few early-eater older couples at the very front window tables. Mac walked up to the bar and took a seat on one of the few stools with a low wooden back. She noticed that there was a new bartender on duty. Hmmm, I haven't seen him before. He's kind of cute. Mac took out her wallet and pulled a $50.00 from inside. As she glanced back, the bartender was now bending over and restocking the cooler in a pair of tight gabardine slacks. She thought, "Mmmmm, what a nice set of buns, I wonder what the rest of his package looks like?"

A moment later, he was in front of her wiping off the bar, "Here, Miss let me tidy up for you. What's your pleasure on this *uncheery kinda dreary* late afternoon or early evening, depending on how you look at it?" His smile was very pleasant and his face was handsome. Dark complexion, with dark grey green eyes and high cheekbones, he was a real mixture she thought.

"Miss, what can I get you?" he asked again.

"I'm sorry, I'm a little distracted today," Mac smiled back, "How about an Irish Coffee to take the nip out of the air and the chill out of my bones."

"Spoken like a fair colleen," he laughed, "That sounds like some of the blarney one of my ancestors might have spouted. Do you want fresh whipped cream on top?" She scrunched up her nose made her 'no way' face. He asked, "Do you prefer Jameson's, Paddy's or Bushmill's?"

"Never Bushmill's that's Protestant whiskey, put a shot of Jameson in...that's real *Catholic* Irish whiskey," she laughed. She wondered about his reference to his ancestors, was he talking Irish here? He looks pretty dark, black curly hair and all. Well, he could be from the Black Irish, the descendants of the Spanish sailors who washed up in Ireland after the English sank the Armada back in 1588. They intermarried with the fair-skinned colleens in southeast Ireland and produced a breed of dark-haired, dark-skinned, black-eyed people with legendary taste for lusty living and loving.

"Here you go, one *Catholic* Irish Coffee."

"My name is Mary, but everybody calls me Mac..."

"Call me Chip, I recognize you from the news, Miss McGauley, are you slumming tonight or do you live in the neighborhood?" he asked.

Mac didn't know quite how to react, "I'd hardly consider Duff's slumming."

"I didn't mean anything by it, just a figure of speech. Are you expecting someone?"

"No, I'm dining alone tonight."

"Want to eat here at the bar? Same menu as in the dining room, only in here, you get me to entertain you and keep you company," Chip smiled warmly.

"Well, how can I refuse such a nice offer from such a handsome man? But, how will you keep me company when the bar fills up? I don't want you to feed me and then leave me sitting here all alone and unattended," she flirted.

"That cuts both ways, what if some rich lawyer or a Cardinal baseball player walks in, you might toss me in the can like yesterday's webNewsfax," he flirted back, "I'll tell you what, you can keep the score on attentiveness. If you or I feel unattended at any time, you can just put a hash mark on this pad," he slid a pad and pencil from the back bar in front of her, "and we'll make it up to each other later."

"How?" she asked.

He leaned over the bar and whispered, "The marks we put on this pad will be how many kisses and hugs we can collect from each other when I get off at 9:30 tonight."

She feigned proper indignation, "Well Chip I stepped right into that one. I certainly have to give you an A+ for chutzpah, but we hardly know each other."

"Can you think of a better way to get really well acquainted? Here's a mark to get you started," he made a hash mark on the pad and laughed as he went down the bar to tend to another customer.

She sipped on her Irish coffee and thought; maybe Chip could be 'Mr. Right for Tonight'? God, he does have a cute tight butt. Her mind mulled over all the possibilities …maybe he was a dark-haired, dark-skinned, black-eyed, black Irish lad with legendary taste for lusty living and loving. It sure looks like it would be fun to find out. And what the hell, if he is a dud in the sack, in the morning a girl can always say, 'Goodbye Mr. Chip.'

The corny pun made her smile. She thought, *I might just have to see how this works out.*

XXIV

Mac decided to take Chip up on his offer and eat at the bar. She ordered the lamb stew, which was always great at Duff's. It was hearty fare with big chunks of carrots, braised white potatoes pan fried 'til the outside was crispy and then cut in quarters, lots of onions and savory chunks of lamb that had been marinated in, as the menu described it, *'Duff's ancient meat crock concoction.'*

In the interest of keeping her wits about her, she switched from Irish Coffees to *Kalibur*, the non-alcoholic beer from Guinness, when her meal came. The lamb stew was delicious and very filling. All during the course of her meal, Chip kept up a delightful running conversation with her. As the bar filled up, he occasionally raced by to put a hash mark on the pad. And if her glass went empty, she would catch his eye and put another mark on the page. It was a fun flirtation that made the evening go by very fast. As the bar clock edged toward 9:15, she started to get really cold feet, I don't want him to think I'm some kind of tramp that flops into bed with every man that comes along. Maybe I should leave him the $50.00 and just slip out. Then her other voice would say, "If I was that hunky male stud, I'd would certainly want to fuck me!"

The white angel sitting on her right shoulder lost the carnal debate to the crimson devil sitting on her left one. She decided to sit tight and moist, for the time being and wait to see what 9:30 p.m. brought.

"Hey, how're we doing?" Chip asked as he looked at the pad, "Wow! how many marks are there?"

"Fifty three, but who's counting," she smiled and flipped her hair back off her forehead. All night long she'd been sizing him up. She figured he was between 25 and 30. He was fairly well built, but not an iron pumping gym-freak Adonis wanna-be or a neighborhood pretty boy. Clean-shaven was a plus and he had an easy way about him and a smile that was, well, kind of boyishly irresistible.

"Well Mac, I'll have to ring you out now, 'cause at 9:31 I'm out that door. Where will you be?" he asked coyly.

"I'll be in my Lexus out front...and my motor will be running."

"It'll save time if you have your car engine turned on too,"

Chip winked, picked up the $50.00 and went toward the cash register.

"Keep the change Chip," she called as she slid off the stool and went toward the door.

It's not too late, her white angel whispered.

Oh yes it is, she thought.

A few minutes later, he came out of Duff's front door and dashed through the rain toward the Lexus with the flashing emergency blinkers, double-parked about 20 feet south on Euclid. "Nice ride," Chip said as he slid into the shotgun seat, "are you sure it's okay for a humble bartender to be in here?"

"Should I be worried?" she asked.

"No M'am, my mother raised decent and respectable sons. She taught me and my brothers, - *and yes, there are two more like me* – to treat every woman like she was the Queen of Sheba."

"Well, do you have any suggestions, or should we just sit here in the rain until we get a ticket ?" Mac asked.

"How about this – if it doesn't sound too much like what the spider said to the fly, how'd'ya like to drive me back to my place? It's just up the block on Taylor. Let me take a speed shower and splash on something that doesn't smell like beer, smoke and fried food and I'll take you out to Blueberry Hill and we can listen to whatever band is playing, throw back a few beers and get to know each other. The evening's still young." Chip suggested.

"Did you flirt with me just so you wouldn't have to walk home in the rain?" Mac asked.

"Well, that was reason number 33," Chip admitted, "C'mon, let's go, you're safe with me."

Mac was intrigued. He seemed so comfortable in his own skin. He was funny and nice. And, he was so refreshingly unimpressed by her job and really easy to talk with.

"Okay, lead Mac on Duff," she laughed and wondered if her bad Macbeth pun registered or was over his head.

"To Dunsinane Hill doth we come…or is it, *go?*," he winked back.

Two-minutes later they arrived at *Convent Gardens* at the corner of Pershing and North Taylor, the old 9-story apartment building built just prior to the Great Depression of 1929, had gone condo back in the 2007. The property was named to reflect the fact that when it was built, it overlooked the high-walled rose gardens across the street that were tended by the Madames of the Sacred Heart, who ran City House Academy, a high school for Catholic girls and Madame Sophie Barat Hall, a prep school for boys on that block.

"Pull around the side and you can park in the garage, there's always an open spot next to mine. Mr. McLeod, one of the old guys in the building had his car taken away about 3-months ago, after he plowed into four or five other cars in the Cathedral parking lot."

Mac parked and followed Chip from the garage, though the backdoor of the building and into a small lobby. They rode the elevator up to the seventh floor. He led her down the hall to his door, 70_, there was a space were a number had gone AWOL.

"Here we are 705, better know as 'seven-*oh where's the five?*'"

"Where is the five," she asked.

"I have no idea," he turned the lock, opened the door and switched on the front hall light, "It was missing when I moved in three years ago. I've been meaning to replace it." He moved down the short hall and into an eat-in kitchen decorated with a kitchen table and chairs that were early Goodwill or vintage garage sale.

"There's beer in the fridge and I think there are some chips in the cabinet. I'm going to jump in the shower. Make yourself comfortable in the living room. I'll be back in 10 minutes. No longer, I promise." Chip vanished down the hall and left Mac standing in the kitchen a bit astonished.

"Well, he seems to lack a little bit of grace and finesse in the hospitality department," she thought. She looked in the refrigerator and found a bottle of Heineken behind a carry out pizza box from *Rossino's* and an assortment of carry-out Chinese cartons, half-eaten tubs of chili from *Steak 'n Shake* and various packages of deli meats and salami. Out of morbid curiosity, she opened the freezer, to find only a frosted over box of White Castle hamburgers. *Yeech.* Well, at least this proves he is a bachelor without a steady girlfriend!

Mac walked out into the hallway and around the corner into his living room. It was furnished in the same style as the kitchen. It had two well-worn upholstered chairs, a prehistoric butler's table and a sagging couch that had to date back to the late 20th Century. She picked up the remote and turned on his ancient Panasonic. She mused, now there's a brand you don't see anymore. Everyone today has a Chinon HHDL, the Chinese holographic hi-def laser multimedia player that drove Panasonic out of the residential electronics market. She looked around the room and noticed that there was a stack of law books on top of the small desk by the front window. Is he a lawyer, or law student? She walked over and her heart jumped when she saw what was lying on the desk behind them.

On the desk was new 9mm.Glock in a leather holster and resting next to it, a St. Louis Police Department badge number 8336. Mac was now thoroughly confused, "Bartender, lawyer, cop...*who is this guy?*"

"I'll be right out, just getting dressed," Chip called from down the hall.

"Say Chip, do you do anything for a living, besides bartending?" she called back.

"Yeah, I'm the CEO of Anheuser-Busch In-Bev, I only tend bar to keep tabs on consumer trends in beer drinking. And in my spare time, I'm an interior decorator," he hollered back, "Why do you ask?"

"I saw your badge...and your gun. It is *your* badge and gun...*isn't it.*" Oh shit, she thought, maybe I should've kept my big mouth shut. What if this guy is some kind of crazy... like a cop impersonator...*or worse?*"

Chip emerged from the bedroom combing his damp hair, "Yes, they're mine. Does it bother you that I'm a cop?"

"No, I like cops," she answered.

Chip added, "I just tend bar to pick up some extra cash, and I've applied to the Washington U. Law School, and if I'm accepted, I plan to quit the force and go to school fulltime and tend bar in my time off to make ends meet."

"How long have you been a cop? She asked.

Lessee, I joined after getting out of Mizzou in '22, so it's been 9 years...going on ten."

"What made you want to be a cop?" Mac asked as she mentally ran the math, he was 30, no 31. Gee, I'm a cradle-robbing older woman!

"Being a cop is a family tradition; my great grandfather, grandfather and dad...as well as a boatload of assorted uncles and goofy cousins have all been on the force. We go way back to the days of the Paddy Wagon," he said as he slipped his tanned bare feet into an old pair of sad looking Weejuns.

"Do you have any ID on you? How do I know you're not a fake cop, who preys on innocent young girls?" she crossed her arms in *faux* indignation.

Chip pulled out his wallet and tossed a 360-degree holographic identification card on the butler's table in front of her. "Is this official proof enough, Ms. Investigative Reporter?"

Mac picked up the card emblazoned with a gold badge and the Seal of the City of St. Louis. She almost gasped aloud when she saw the name next to his slowly revolving 3D photo.

Sergeant Charles M. Harrigan, IV
Forensic Investigation Unit
St. Louis Metropolitan Police Department
Bureau Of Detectives, Central District Police Plaza
Tucker Boulevard and Clark Street
Badge Number 8336
CMHIV@slmpd.org

"What's wrong? You look funny? Is my picture that scary," Chip asked.

"No, just a bit of gas...lamb stew can do that," she laughed. *"Oh my God, can he be the great grandson of 'Iron Charlie' Harrigan? This is too weird,"* she thought. Then her mind flashed back to something Fred Kirtschner had written early on in his journal.

In St. Louis, it's all connected.

They drove out Delmar to Blueberry Hill, the eclectic bar and tribute to Rock 'N Roll, beer and darts that had been created by the late urban entrepreneur Joe Edwards. They parked on the corner and as the rain picked up, ran down the sidewalk over the bronze stars set in the St. Louis Walk of Fame.

"Damn, there's no band until 11:30 p.m.," Chip noted as they shook off the raindrops inside the bar's doorway. "Well, can I interest you in a pitcher of *Bud Supreme* and some darts?"

"Sure, but I'll beat you," she said coolly.

"Oh really, so what are you like the Robin Hood or William Tell of darts?" he asked.

"I grew up playing darts in the rec room with my brother and his friends, let's just say I'm no novice."

One pitcher and three games later, Chip said, "It's a good thing I don't have a fragile ego." She had trounced him in every match by a wide margin.

"Mac smiled, "C'mon big boy, the loser gets to buy me a skewer of braised shrimp and a nitecap."

They moved from the first floor dart room into a booth in the bar and placed their orders. The beer and shrimp came out fast and on the other side of the bar wall they could hear the jazz combo warming up with an old Keb Mo song, *Everybody Be Yoself.*

"Do you like jazz," she asked.

"MmmHmm," he mumbled indicating that the hot shrimp in his mouth made it hard to speak at the moment.

She was wondering if he was going to make a move. "So what's next Mr. Excitement?"

Chip wiped his mouth and said, "I don't want you to be offended by what I'm about to say, okay?"

Oh boy, here comes the proposition. Mac said, "You cannot offend me unless I accept the offense. Speak your mind."

"Okay, Mac...I have had a great time tonight. And I really like you. And we are both adults right?" She nodded in affirmation, and he continued, "Well I'd like to see where this might go, and I don't want you to see me as some guy who is just trying to get into your knickers. Although, that is a worthy objective, I'm sure," he laughed, "And, I'd hope that you don't see me as just some boy-toy. I really have enjoyed tonight and rather than ruin it by having some spur of the moment, heat of passion, bang-the-wall, tear-up the-sheets and roll-on-the-floor 'til the neighbors call the cops sex, I'd like to suggest that you take me home and save cashing in those hash marks until we know each other a little better." He reached into his pocket and unfolded the hash marked sheet that she had left on the bar. "You keep this, there is no expiration date on it. If you ever decide to redeem it, nothing would make me happier, but it would be your call, yours entirely," he reached over to hand her the note.

She reached out and clasped her hand over his, sandwiching the note in between. "I have another idea," she said.

"What's that?" Chip asked, as he prepared to take a sip of beer

"How would you like to come back to my place for a night cap and I'll show you my blindfold and whip collection?"

Chip almost shot beer through his nose. Mac smiled back and thought, *you're not getting away from me so easily Charles Michael...interesting men like you don't come along every day.*

"Well whadd'ya say?" she asked

"Are you sure?" he asked again.

"Yes, but I'm just kidding about the blindfold and whips," Mac grimaced sheepishly,

"I do have whipped cream, orange-scented bubble bath and warming gel though."

"Are you *really* sure?" he smiled and stared deep into her eyes.

Mac leaned across the table and whispered, "Chip, please tell me you're not gay…"

Chip's eyes widened in shock at her inference, "Not! Definitely, not! Lead on MacMuff, I'll show you who's *not* gay," he whispered back.

"Let me get the check and we're on our way."

———

Sunday morning August 17, 2031

The smell of bacon sizzlin' mixed with the aroma of fresh coffee always lured her out of bed, even as a young girl. Mac rolled over lazily and half opened one eye to check the clock, 8:11 a.m. The soft morning light was filtering through her window sheers and she felt the sensation of a thick rumpled terrycloth towel under her butt. She felt under it and found the damp remains of a large sticky wet spot. Her hand felt further behind her to see if "Mr. Right for Tonight' was still there. The bed was cold, she rolled over to find 'his' side empty. Her heart started to sink when her brain asked, *"Who's cooking the bacon."* She slid out of bed and made her way through the piles of his quickly discarded clothes and her underwear that was littering the bedroom floor. Grabbing her robe from the hook behind the bathroom door, she wrapped her body, quickly brushed her teeth and made her way down the hall to the kitchen. She peeked around the corner and saw him cooking away clad only in his striped boxers. The frying pan atop her Viking was sizzling and popping, her coffee maker was perking, she could see that he had already made toast and placed it under the infra-red light on the Viking's warming shelf. Four eggs stood at the ready, resting on a kitchen towel he had folded neatly on top of the slate gray granite counter. Am I dreaming...*he can cook too!*

She padded up behind him in her bare feet and put her arms around his waist and hugged him, "Good morning Charles Michael." He was surprised by the sudden embrace and turned to see her. He was smiling and said, "How are you this morning, you wildcat? And say, how did you know my middle name was Michael?"

"Just a wild guess," she said as she bit his nipple and ran her hands ran down his well-muscled back. As they passed over the hollow of his back just above his round firm buttocks, he winced.

"What's wrong?" she turned him around and saw four scabbed over scratches in his skin. She immediately recognized them as cat scratches.

"I think your cat thought I was hurting you last night because she jumped on my back and caught me in the middle of a down stroke, and when I was coming back up, she dug her claws in and launched off of me," he laughed. "It's nothing... we've already made up," He gestured at *Rojo* who was sitting in the sun on the east window sill

"Oh my God, *Rojo* is a bad, bad, very bad cat...she is also a de-balled he, by the way. Let me get some peroxide and clean that up before you get an infection," Mac said as she ran down the hall to the medicine cabinet. She returned in a moment with cotton balls and a bottle of Walgreen's peroxide.

"I thought you had slipped out and left me all alone until I smelled this wonderful breakfast cooking, you are so sweet," she kissed his neck from behind as she cleaned the scratch sites.

"I'm on from 11 to 7 today, but I wanted to cook breakfast for you and serve it to you in bed before I had to shove off."

"I had a *great* time last night...a really great time in every way," she hugged him, "Thanks for being such an uninhibited lover. I don't want to know how, where or with whom you learned to thrill a woman like you do, I just want you to know that I appreciated it!" Mac blushed a bit.

He hugged her and looked down into her eyes, "I think we might have used up all 53 hash marks last night. But, who was counting? I just hope the walls here are thick and the neighbor's are deaf."

"I didn't worry about the walls or the neighbors, but, you were so, ah...shall we say, *vigorous*, I was more concerned about you punching a hole in my air mattress," she teased. "Let's eat and I'll drive you back to your apartment after we take a shower."

As she enjoyed her breakfast gazing at him, Mac wondered if she should tell him about the journal she was reading and ask if *'Iron Charlie'* was his great grandfather. Nah, that'll keep for another day, I'll bring it up after I find out how the whole thing comes out. Who knows, maybe his ancestor will turn out to be the hero of the story...that would be a nice surprise for me to tell him about.

"Ready for your shower, Chip? I give really terrific hot, soapy sudsy showers," she got up and took his hand and led him down the hall. She dropped her robe and knelt down on her sheepskin bathroom rug and rolled off his boxers. "Well, lookey here, who's this just waking up? Why, it's one-eyed Willy, who gave me chilly thrillys, when I tickle him like this does Chip feel silly?" Mac looked up, smiled and then showed her appreciation for the night, the breakfast...and for her hope of things to come.

XXVI

Mac came back to her condo whistling, she had dropped Chip off and given him a long goodbye kiss. Then she completed her shopping at Schnucks' *Culinaria*, the new gourmet grocery store at the corner of Maryland and Kingshighway. For years a store on that corner had been operated by Jack Straub's family and it catered to the tastes and whims of the Central West End's elite and to the famous guests staying in the venerable *grande dame* of all St. Louis hotels, The Chase Park Plaza Hotel just across Maryland.

As she unpacked and stowed her groceries, she thought about the curious web that synchronicity was weaving around her. She smiled when she thought about Chip, although a twinge of parochial school girl guilt still made her feel a bit uneasy about the spontaneous bungee jump she made into the sheets with him last night...it being their *'first date'* and all.

Well, he'll either call me for a real date *or not*...can't worry about it. Maybe he will turn out to be just another *'Mr. Right for Tonight.'* The work week ahead was looming and she had a full plate of stories to deal with and several community relations appearances scheduled at noontimes next week. It was going to be an action-packed week with little time to get back to the journal that was lying on the table beside her chair in the bay window.

She decided to forego cooking and took a bowl of cut up Granny Smiths and some dried apricots with her into the living room. She curled up in the chair with *Rojo* behind her on the headrest purring loudly as Abyssians love to do. With a big bottle of Crystal Springs water and a bowl of fruit within easy reach, she settled back and opened the old reporter's journal to the place she had left off.

———

KIRTSCHNER'S JOURNAL ENTRY:
EW/1H/2H/HS

Alcott and Dext checked with me every day to find out what Schu my snitch had to say and if it jibbed with the inside track information that was coming to me every morning after the detective squad meeting from Harrigan. So far, things were syncing up pretty well.

For days, the new developments were scant. EOR had battened down the hatches and put a phalanx of high-priced attorneys between the world and his family. Devereaux had been cremated and interred at Valhalla in a very private ceremony. Reporters and a throng of curious on-lookers were stopped at the cemetery gates. Photographers were frustrated by the black draped windows in the hearse and the tightly drawn rear curtains in the short procession of chauffer-driven Cadillacs, Packards and Pierce-Arrows that followed.

Pierre Laclede Devereaux may have been laid to rest, but as long as Madame X's body lay unidentified and unclaimed on a cold slab at city morgue, our Publisher was determined to keep the heat on the story by stoking the fire by any means possible. The *Star* was still running 6-column above-the-fold stories every day. The headline writers were cut loose and the front page started read like reports from a marathon event:

Day 3: **City Elite Shocked By Pierre Devereaux Murder**

Day 4: **Married Playboy And 'Madame X' Slain In His Madame X**

Day 5: **Identity Of Murdered 'Madame X' Remains Mystery**

Day 6: **Why Were They In Tower Grove At Midnight?**

Day 7: **On 7ᵗʰ Day Police Can't Rest As Public Pressure Mounts**

Day 8: Murder Victim Devereaux Laid To Rest
Day 9: 'Madame X' Still Lies In Morgue Body Unidentified

Alcott especially liked referring to the yet to be identified slain woman as *'Madame X,'* because the model name of the custom-built Cadillac, was a Madame X model with coachwork by Fleetwood.' Readers must have loved it too. The *Star's* circulation jumped by over 9,000 daily and 17,000 on Sunday and moved us ahead of the PD for the first time. Advertising revenue picked up nicely too as the smarter advertiser's realized that the *Star* was being picked up by thousands more St. Louisans everyday and, because the story was moving so fast, the *Star* had no time to raise its advertising line rates to reflect the skyrocketing circulation levels. Buying the *Star* became an advertiser's bargain!

"Fred, you're doing a great job, keep it up, but let's get a fresh angle. We need a new intriguing wrinkle, a compelling twist. We can't keep beating on poor old Pierre Devereaux; he's already a dead and cremated horse. But the mystery woman, *'Madame X in the Madame X,'* - her identity, her story... that's a murder mystery and a society sex scandal...and that combination sells papers," Alcott pounded his hand on his desk.

Then Dexter had an idea, "I heard the autopsy photos are too gory, totally unprintable, but if we could get our hands on one showing the woman's face, we could have George Lewis make a pen and ink sketch and run it with a headline like, *'The Face of Madame X Revealed.'* We could even offer a $250 reward to anyone who knows her identity. The whole town will become part of the investigative team."

"Dext, that's brilliant! Absolutely brilliant! Fred, do you think your snitch could pull it off? If he could get us a photo showing the murdered woman's face and a copy of the latest coroner's report, we would put another 10,000 on our daily circulation, like that" Alcott snapped his fingers, "I'll bet we could do another 30,000 on Sunday."

I was pretty much spent from practically working 'round the clock for the past several days, I had even been sleeping at the paper overnight on a cot in the pressmen's locker room. As a result, my enthusiasm for Dexter's latest idea was somewhat subdued. "All I can do is *try*, but it is getting pretty risky for him. He's already very jittery about being discovered," I said.

"Tell him not to worry; this place is air tight, only you, Dext and me know who he is. Try this too, tell him there's $200 in it for him, *if* he can get it to you by noon tomorrow," Alcott suggested, "Greed makes the world go round, and St. Louis is no exception."

So, I made the call and the drop was arranged, but the predictably frightened Schu extracted another $100 first. He knew he had a good game running, and he also knew that it could run out at any time. All I had to do now was sit and wait for the call from the chili parlor.

It came hours sooner than expected. When I answered my phone, the familiar voice said, "O.T. Hodges, chili order is ready."

I grabbed my coat and went over to Arnold Dexter's office and leaned in his doorway, "Dext, it's ready and waiting." I turned and started to leave, but Dext said, "Fred I'll pick it up, I'm going out anyway. You stay on the lead story for tomorrow and make the *'Who is Madame X' and the Star reward* angle really sing. You own this story Fred, this is a career-maker if ever there was one."

He patted me on the back and said, "I'll be back in 15 minutes.

Newspaper Clipping – *St. Louis Star,
March 20, 1931*

City Elite Shocked By Murder Of Pierre Laclede Devereaux

Frederick L. Kirtschner
Of The Star Staff

Mystery continues to whirl around the murder mayhem in Tower Grove Park.

The *Star* has learned that 15 to 20 shots were fired in the assault that took the life of socially prominent St. Louisan, Pierre Laclede Devereaux, son-in-law of Continental Shoe Company president, Edmund O. Robertson and husband of former Veiled Prophet special maid of honor, Ada Robertson Devereaux.

The Devereaux and Robertson families have not been available to comment on the tragic and mysterious circumstances surrounding the murder of the shoe executive and the female victim who has become known as "Madame X."

Reliable *Star* sources reported that the company believed that Mr. Devereaux had departed from St. Louis earlier this week on a sales trip to New York City. Calls by this reporter to the New York Athletic Club and the Missouri Athletic Club here revealed that Mr. Devereaux had not made his trip arrangements as believed.

Coroner Taylor released a preliminary report that indicated that the male victim had been struck by 12 shots and the female victim by one. Chief of Detectives Harrigan refused to speculate as to motive, but did confirm that various pieces of jewelry and personal property belonging to the victims had been removed from the car.

Chief Gordon Strickland urged the citizenry to remain calm and to co-operate with the police as the investigation moves forward. Strickland said, "I do not believe that this is the start of a crime wave, but rather an isolated incident such as a robbery that went terribly wrong. Residents of the area and the entire city can be assured that we will not rest until the murder or murderers are apprehended and brought to justice. I have every confidence in Chief of Detective Harrigan and his elite detective bureau."

Funeral services for Mr. Devereaux have not been announced. Attorney Jonathon McCall, acting as spokesman for the family did say that the services would be strictly private.

Newspaper Clipping – *St. Louis Star,*
March 23, 1931

Pierre Laclede Devereaux Laid To Rest

Frederick L. Kirtschner
Of The Star Staff

The gates of Valhalla Cemetery were blocked today by private security guards to prevent reporters and curious onlookers from witnessing the interment of slain shoe company executive Pierre Laclede Devereaux.

A long line of 17 limousines with tightly drawn curtains followed the Donnelly Mortuary hearse into Valhalla at 10:30 this morning. The ceremony lasted only 45 minutes as the cortege left the grounds under the same tight ring of privacy and security at 11:15 a.m.

The police investigation has thus far produced few new leads, although an exclusive *Star* source near the case reports that the search for evidence continues apace within the park and within the surrounding neighborhoods.

Edmund O. Robertson, who has been publicly quiet since the murder of his son-in-law and "Madame X" was revealed, has not been inactive. Reportedly, he is calling the Mayor's office and the Police Chief on a daily basis insisting on faster action and demanding results. Pressure from his friends has been more public and equally insistent that the police use every means at their disposal to rapidly solve the case.

Chief Of Detectives Charles M. Harrigan would not confirm rumors that he was under severe pressure, but simply noted that the investigation is progressing along several fronts and that all leads are being followed up. He urged the public to be patient and to allow the detective bureau to do its job without undue interference or criticism.

The *Star* has dedicated a special team of investigators to assist this reporter in the coverage of this story.

Managing Editor, Gordon P. Alcott announced today.

KIRTSCHNER'S JOURNAL ENTRY: 1H/2H/HS

Canvassing the commercial laundries in town proved to be a more daunting task than initially imagined. The big laundries; West End, E.B. Halloran, Purity Clean, Dutch Girl and Excelsior-Leader had hundreds of customers and they often shared parts of the largest commercial accounts or did subcontract work for each other and for the major hospitals. The sad fact was, aprons that are laundry marked initially for one account often end up at other accounts and get switched around within the laundry network. So an apron marked by West End for St. Mary's Hospital cafeteria on Clayton Road, could find its way into the supply of aprons delivered to the Courtesy Sandwich Shop way up on North Grand at St. Louis Avenue or to Miss Hulling's downtown. Plain white aprons without business trademarks simply floated around in the universe of all plain white aprons. Only the smaller neighborhood laundries that did not contract with other laundries or have shared commercial accounts had any real chance of actually getting back the same aprons they send out.

Almost a week had dragged by as the squad made the rounds and visited every laundry at every shift. So far they had come up empty. Then, one day while out canvassing the bakeries, butcher shops and restaurants on 'The Hill'," Louie Columbo had an idea.

Nick Correnti's Correnti Cleaners at Arsenal and Watson on the southwest edge of 'The Hill' was a small independent, Mom & Pop commercial and residential laundry. Lou Columbo had attended St. Ambrose and played soccer with Nick's son, Sal Correnti, so the call had a social side to it as well as an investigative facet.

"Hey Sal!" Lou called as he and Joe came into the shop's customer waiting area, "have you got a minute?"

"Hey yourself, Luigi Columbo, how's your papa?," old man Correnti called from his desk just inside the shop's back room door, "I haven't seen him at a *Sons of Garibaldi* meeting or down at *Rose's* for Saturday bocce in weeks. Has he been sick?"

"C'mon back Lou and talk loud, Dad can't hear so well," Sal waved for him and Culhane to join him in the shirt pressing area where he was repairing an *Ironrite* steam-pressing machine.

Lou paused at Mr. Correnti's desk which was piled high with unfiled papers, "Mr. Correnti, this is my partner Sergeant Joe Culhane, and thanks for asking about Papa. But he died about two and a half years ago."

"Oh Luigi, I'm so sorry, I knew that. But, I forget. Hell I'm just getting too damn old, I can't remember a damn thing anymore," the old man felt very embarrassed.

"Mr. Correnti, it's not a problem. It happens all the time. Excuse me, but we've got to see Sal about some official police business," Lou confided.

"You gonna arrest him?" the old man asked.

"Oh no, nothing like that Mr. Correnti, Sal is a good, hard working boy, we just need to ask him a few questions about a laundry mark."

"That's good, I thought you might be here about the whiskey he's selling out of the cellar," the old man said as he returned to reading *Il Pensiero*, 'The Hill's' weekly Italian language newspaper.

"Please don't ask Papa anymore questions." Sal rolled his eyes, "Lou, tell me, how can I help you? Whatever you need you got it."

Columbo showed him the laundry number and Sal said, "I think that's one of our codes, yeah, I'm sure it is. Let me look it up. Sal went to his account book and flipped through the pages until he came to the first three letter prefix. Yeah, here it is 584-022829-A. 584 is the Gagliardi house account code and 02-28-29 means it was first marked out on February 28th of '29. The 'A' means it's a standard non-trademarked garden variety white waiter's apron."

"Which Gagliardi's got it? The one at Grand and Washington, or the one on 'The Hill' or the new joint out on Debalivere Strip?" Louie quizzed him.

Sal said, "That I can't tell you, but it's definitely from the Gagliardi laundry lot."

You're absolutely sure?" Culhane asked.

"I'm 95% positive, this a Correnti code – if I could see the apron itself up close, I'd be 100% certain."

"Thanks Sal. Have you got a private phone around here that I could use?"

Columbo asked.

"Sure, c'mon upstairs to my office, you can use my phone," Sal volunteered, and led them up the steep and rickety stairway to his private office.

"Sal I'm going to have to ask you to wait outside and let us make the call in privacy," Lou asked.

"No problem, just close the door behind you when you're done, I gotta go down and make sure Dad isn't yelling at the help. If I leave him alone for longer than five minutes he start's yelling at the coons," Sal left and went back down the steep narrow stairway.

Joe Culhane sat on the end of the desk as Lou dialed the Chief of Detectives' direct line.

"Harrigan here," he barked as he picked up.

"Chief it's me, Lou. I'm here with Joe at Correnti's Cleaners out on Arsenal.

And we have a 'Bingo!'

"Where did the apron come from?"

"Gagliardi's."

There was a long pause and then Harrigan erupted, "Jesus *Haitch* Christ! Get right over to the 7th, I'll meet you in Jeremiah's office in a half hour. And, pick up a sandwich for me at Volpi's on the way. Bring me a salami, proscuitto and coppa on hard crusty bread with gorgonzola and pepperocinis. Hell, just tell 'em 'with the works," Harrigan hung up the phone without even so much as a goodbye or a kiss my ass.

Joe asked, "Was he happy?"

"Deliriously happy," Columbo replied, "C'mon, we gotta pick up a sandwich at Volpi's for him and then hotfoot it over to the 7th to meet with him and O'Connell. And we gotta be there in 30 minutes. Let's hope the line at Volpi's is short today. The last thing we need to do is be late."

"He was happy, wasn't he?" Joe badgered, "He's been under a lotta pressure from the top so this news has got to make him happy, right?"

"Yeah, like I said, he's *deliriously happy*," Columbo replied.

As Harrigan drove west out Market Street to Grand Avenue and turned south toward the 7th, he wondered aloud, "Could I have this thing figured all wrong? Maybe, it is an Italian job after all? What a fucking mess that would be...the last thing I need right now is to lock horns with Carmine Gagliardi too. I've got the Mayor and Chief Strickland on my ass, the city elites are all riled up and raising hell, EOR is calling the Mayor several times a day demanding progress, the newspapers keep hammering on the story, Jeremiah's at his wits end, and now this! The deal we worked out with Carmine after he eliminated *'The Green Ones'* - his competition from New Orleans, has worked out so well for everyone. Carmine has kept a lid on all Wop crime activity outside 'The Hill', and we've turned a blind eye to the way he conducts business in his own neighborhood. But this bullshit could blow the lid off our cozy little Armistice."

As he roared past the smiling *bas relief* bottle of *Pinky Pevely* on the façade of the Pevely Dairy at Grand and Choteau, he repeatedly slammed his fist on the LaSalle's steering wheel, and cursed, "Jesus *Haitch* Christ!"

"Iron Charlie" was about 180 degrees due south of *'deliriously happy.'*

KIRTSCHNER'S JOURNAL ENTRY:
EW/1H/2H/HS

It was everything I could do to keep my eyes open as I was finishing my draft of the next day's lead story. Eddie the copy boy brought me some more coffee and was waiting at my elbow, ready to run my story to Alcott for approval and then straight down to the linotype operators in the composing room. That's when Arnold Dexter came waltzing back through the newsroom."

"Did you get it?" I asked.

Dext stopped at my desk and told me, "Yeah, it was ready and waiting. I ran it up to George and told him to get started on the line drawing right away and to keep his door closed and not to let anybody see it. He'll call me as soon as it's ready and I'll retrieve it along with the original photo and walk it down to the engraver. It won't get out of my sight after that."

"What does she look like," I asked.

"Well, coroner's photographs are never very flattering, to say the least. Of course, having half your head blown off and having brains and blood matted in your hair is not a good look for anyone. But, if you can get past that, she looks like the kind of girl that you might meet in any neighborhood shop or drugstore. I told George to use his artistic imagination to make her look normal and not to just replicate the coroner's photo. Even an ink drawing of her face in death is quite grotesque and greatly distorted from what she probably looked like when she went out for her last evening. He told me he'd do his best and have it ready just before press time," Dexter concluded.

"It would really help me finish this piece if I could write a line or two about her looks when she was alive," I said.

"Don't worry about it, I'll handle the photo's cutline, you wrap up your piece and give it to Eddie, and then, go home and get some sleep in your own bed. I don't want you sleeping on a cot downstairs tonight. Believe it or not, The *Star* can get this edition out without you. And besides, you are no good to anyone if you are exhausted, least of all me. No arguments, turn in the story then head home and hit the sack, that's an order," Dexter smiled and squeezed my shoulder, "you can meet *'Madame X'* like everybody else, when the paper hits your porch, okay?"

"Okay," I was tired and Dext was right, sleep would do me good. I typed -30- to end the story, handed it to Eddie and headed for home.

"Well, it's about time," Harrigan growled as Columbo and Joe joined him and O'Connell in the 7th District commander's office.

"Sorry Chief, but I figured it was better to show up 10 minutes late *with* your sandwich than to be on time without it," Columbo volunteered as he handed the sandwich over. Harrigan looked at him and grudgingly nodded in agreement, "Long line at Volpi's?"

"We hit there just as the 2nd shift was coming in from Scullin Steel," Joe replied.

"I've already given Jeremiah the rundown, what I need you to help us with Luigi is a bit of Italian strategy. I know that Gagliardi can be Machiavellian in the way he thinks and works. And, I while I want to proceed apace, I also want to do it carefully," Harrigan said.

"Who's *Mike E. Vellian*," Joe asked.

Columbo said, "He's a secret adviser to Gagliardi, he lives in Italy."

"Oh, no wonder I never ran into him," Joe said.

Harrigan looked at him incredulously and thought, his brother really did get all the fucking brains in the family.

"Lou, how would you approach, Carmine?" O'Connell asked, "that's what the Chief and I are talking about."

Columbo began, "Well I think you're on the right track by really thinking this one through. Carmine can be very emotional and if you hit him the wrong way it can take a bad turn and never come back. He's a volatile Sicilian, and not a sweet-natured Milanese lover like me."

"Lou, Luigi, Louis! We all know that you are the greatest cocksman since Casanova, but in the interest of time, can we skip the recounting of your more than ample amorous attributes and get to the substantive part of the discussion," Harrigan said as he unwrapped his sandwich, "I'll eat and listen, you talk."

"Sorry Chief, here's my way of thinking. First of all, all we know right now is that the arrows seem to be pointing toward some kind of connection in the Italian community.

"Columbo began to tick of his list:

1. The apron the smashed guns were wrapped up in is from *Correnti's*.
2. It has a laundry code linking it to one of Gagliardi's *legitimate* cafeterias – there's one on 'The Hill', one on Washington, west of Grand and the new one out on the DeBallivere Strip.
3. Gagliardi has a lot of workers in his restaurants that have criminal pasts.
4. *Navy Brands* trash dump, where the apron was found is on the edge of 'The Hill'
5. Tower Grove Park is also on the edge of 'The Hill' – just two blocks east.
6. Gagliardi runs some 'speaks' in the immediate area, it's possible that the victim's were at one of them before they went and got themselves killed.
7. It's possible the killers were there too, and followed them to the park
8. Gagliardi could be of great service to everyone, if he could make a few discreet inquires and see if anyone may have seen or heard anything that can help solve these terrible murders.

"That's what we know and it is all purely circumstantial.

"Now, if we rush in, badges-in-hand and confront Gagliardi in one of his places and start tossing around accusations, inferences, innuendos and the like; or worse yet, roughing up some of his people, that is a recipe for disaster. Any attempt to publicly embarrass him or confront him in any way, no matter how slight the encounter, will cause Carmine to react very badly. He'll become extremely angry and very defensive. All leads will dry up. Any co-operation from people in the neighborhood will stop. He'll close the gates and pull up the drawbridge like the Doge of Venice. *La familia Italiano* will close tighter than a steel fist.

"I think the way to handle this is very privately and very diplomatically. No offense Chief, but Gagliardi knows that you are in thick with *The King Of Kerry* and that would not sit well with him. If Joe and I went to see him, he'd peg Joe as Tom's brother in a heartbeat and he'd see me like a kind of low level turncoat, not worthy of being dealt with by a man of his stature. Sicilians are very big on building their stature in the community. It's all about personal image and inspiring fear and respect.

"If it was me, I'd try to set up a private and confidential, one-on-one meeting in a neutral place with Major O'Connell dressed in his street clothes instead of his uniform. I'd suggest someplace, like the Old Cathedral, St. Pius the Tenth, or a Convent Chapel, someplace where it will be safe, private, neutral and totally secret. It's also hard for Sicilians to get loud and emotional inside a holy place too.

"Then, I'd start by asking for his help."

"*Ask for his help?* That'll be the fucking day," Joe was incensed, "why the fuck would we..."

"Joe, shut up," Harrigan snapped and motioned with sandwich in hand for Columbo to continue.

"Yes, I'd *ask* for his help," Columbo repeated as he shot a glare at Joe, "I'd tell him that there is a situation that could cause both the Italian community and the police to come into conflict. I'd tell him that we want to avoid that at all costs. I'd tell him exactly what we know, point-by-point. I would assure him that the police do **NOT** suggest that he or anyone in his organization are behind the murders and I'd tell him why we believe that.

"I'd also speculate with him and suggest that the killers might have passed through his restaurants as employees, but firmly state, that we know, that he cannot be expected to know the actions of or be held in anyway responsible for every *Tomaso, Ricardo* or *Arrigo*, that carries a plate of pasta for him...

"Tomaso Ricardo *who?*" Joe interrupted hotly, "Talk American willya fer chrissake?".

"Sorry, Joe, that's *Tom. Dick and Harry*, to you," Lou laughed, "I'd also make it abundantly clear that you, Major O'Connell, as the ranking officer in the 7th District are speaking for the entire department when you ask him to make some discreet inquiries into the matter. Let him know that you respect his position of leadership in the Italian community and do not want in any way to impugn his reputation or cause him or the community any problems on account of some people, who *may* have crossed the line of mutual arrangements and longstanding relationships that are beneficial to every one. I'd give him my private line number and ask him to call at anytime on a strictly one-on-one confidential basis to discuss this or any matter of mutual concern or interest. I'd thank him, shake his hand look him squarely in the eye and mean every word of it. That's exactly how I'd play it," Columbo concluded.

"What do you think?" Jeremiah asked Harrigan.

Harrigan wiped off his mouth, eased out a garlic and salami belch and said, "Lads, I think we have heard the wisdom of Solomon. Luigi, if Jeremiah is willing to take on this task, can you call Gagliardi and set it up?"

"Yes, I think I can do that," Columbo nodded.

"Jeremiah?" Harrigan looked over at him and waited for his answer.

Without hesitation, O'Connell replied, "Tell him I'll meet him any time at any place of his choosing that is, *what did you say, Louis?*, 'safe, private, neutral and....'"

"And *totally secret*," Columbo added.

"Just tell him the nature of the meeting is *very urgent*...so the sooner it happens, the better, at his convenience, of course." Harrigan underscored, "All right let's get to it."

The meeting broke up. Columbo went alone to see if he could catch Gagliardi at his restaurant on 'The Hill.' O'Connell went back to work reviewing the District's dailies and Harrigan drove Joe back to headquarters.

"Joe, I have a special little job for you. One that's perfectly suited for a man with your lack of scruples and keen powers of observation," Harrigan continued, "We have a rat in our midst, some low life cop, who's become a snitch for the *Star* newspaper. I want you to keep your eye out for any shenanigans, anything odd, anybody with new found wealth. Anybody who's whoring around more or placing more bets than usual. If you see or hear anything that is even remotely suspicious bring it to me."

"So you want me to be your secret adviser, kinda like that Mike E. Vellian," Joe was happy to be honored by the assignment and he appreciatively smiled at the Chief.

Harrigan looked at Joe and laughed, "Yeah Joe, just like Mike E. Vellian."

KIRTSCHNER'S JOURNAL ENTRY: HS/2H

The bells above the front door of Dennis Brenahanny's furniture store jingled to announce the first customer of the day. Brenahanny had just opened up on Tuesday, and he was alone in the store. An elderly Negro man in a well-worn suit made his way slowly through the furniture displayed on the first floor and came up to the customer service office in the center of the room.

"What can I help you with this morning?" Brenahanny asked as he looked over the top of his glasses. He remained seated behind his desk until he saw the old Negro take the rubber band off a wad of cash, then he got up and came over wearing an ear-to-ear grin as phony as a three-dollar bill.

The old man said, "My friend told me that a man with a powerful thirst for knowledge might find a chapter or two of thirst quenching wisdom in here."

"Yes sir, that is possible if you can afford $2.00 a quart," Brenahanny replied.

The Negro peeled off a five dollar bill and said, "I'd like one chapter of rye and one of bourbon, if you please, sir."

"Just a moment," Brenahanny disappeared into the back room and went down to the cellar to get the bottles. He reemerged about 3-minutes later with a full paper sack. But the old man was nowhere in sight.

"Hey buddy, are you still here?" Brenahanny called as he walked toward the front door. "Now where did he go?"

"Hello Dennis darling,'" a voice from behind startled him. He turned to see Tom Culhane seated in a tall wingback chair four rows of furniture back that he had just rushed by.

As Brenahanny walked toward Culhane, he passed a big over stuffed chair and casually dropped the sack of hootch on to the seat. "Mr. Culhane, what brings you out on such a fine morning," he asked nervously.

"I'm looking for some new furniture, I'm thinking of outfitting a couple of furnished apartments in some property I own over on Ashland Avenue," Culhane replied.

"Well sir, you have come to the right place, as you know, we specialize in financing the sale of entire suits of furniture for any room in the house," Brenahanny spieled on, "Why we can sell you a complete living room suit, bedroom suit and kitchen suit for under $200. And, we have delivery and set-up at no additional charge."

"Don't trouble yourself about the free delivery, Dennis, I brought my own movers." Brenahanny turned to see Fred Washington and five of the biggest niggers he ever saw, dressed in blue-grey coveralls with a kelly green shamrock and the words: *Fitzsimmon's Cartage* embroidered on them, get up from where they had been hiding on the couches around the showroom.

"How's the quality of your goods?" Culhane inquired as he squeezed the padding on the chair's arms, "What's inside? Is it horsehair or wool batting or cotton or cellulose? Is the wood on your tables solid or veneer?"

"It's all spelled out on the tags, Mr. Culhane," Brenahanny said, "Let me show you."

The King of Kerry stood up and his powerful hand dug into Brenahanny's shoulder and stopped him dead in his tracks. "Let me have my working men look into it for us. After all Dennis, we're in management, aren't we?" Culhane smiled.

"Fred will you and your lads please see what's inside these high quality chairs and couches? And while you're at it, see if the wood used on the dining room and bedroom *suites* is solid or just cheap veneer," Culhane instructed.

With that, Fred and his men pulled pocket knives, straight razors and hand axes out of their deep coverall pockets. Fred took the first slice with a straight razor and opened a couch from one end to the other. He ripped open the 5-foot long slash with his powerful hands and pulled out huge tufts of the stuffing. "Looks like cotton batting in this one, Mr. Tom," Fred reported.

"Cotton batting, that's good Dennis," Culhane commented, "It should sit comfortably."

Brenahanny looked on, frozen stone still in horror as the Fred and his men slashed and chopped wildly through every piece of furniture within arm's reach. Finally he could endure no more, "Stop, please in the name of sweet Jesus! For the love of God, please stop! I'll be ruined! Please Mr. Culhane, please, please make 'em stop!" Brenahanny was shaking, sobbing and groveling before him on the floor.

After a few more minutes of unbridled mayhem, Culhane called for his wrecking crew to stop and waved for them to come over to join him in a circle around the uncontrollably weeping and shuddering Brenahanny.

"Hand me that package on the chair willya Fred?" *The King* asked. Culhane opened the paper sack Brenahanny had tried to slough off. "Dennis, I believe you dropped this. Oh my goodness, now, what have we here? Fred, will you look at this." Culhane asked, "Is this whiskey or furniture polish?"

"I'm not sure Mr. Tom," Fred answered.

"Well there's only one way to find out. And that's to have an expert on furniture polish and whiskey to taste it. Pick him up," *The King* yelled.

Two of the sweating Negroes jerked the quivering sobbing Brenahanny to his feet and Fred handed Culhane a bottle of *Watkin's Ultra Sheen* liquid furniture polish off the display rack behind the sales counter. Culhane was amused by the irony of the slogan on the bottle, *"People with fine taste prefer Watkins for that tasteful shine!"*

"I'll bet Mr. Brenahanny can tell us which is which. I hear he's an expert on whiskey and furniture polish. Here Dennis, *'to your continued good health and prosperity.'* Have a *tasteful* swig," Culhane handed him the furniture polish.

"Please Mr. Culhane, please," Dennis was sobbing and shaking.

"Drink it," Culhane yelled as he whipped out his .38, "Or I'll put your fucking brains on that wall across the room." Brenahanny accepted the polish bottle and took a small sip.

"Drink it all down, every fuckin' *tasteful* drop," Culhane whispered in Dennis' ear as cocked his pistol and pressed it against the side of Brenahanny's head. Brenahanny closed his eyes and choked down the entire bottle.

Next, Culhane pulled the cork on the quart of rot-gut rye and handed it to Brenahanny. "Now drink this one down," he ordered.

Brenahanny began drinking and got about a third of the way through it when he dropped to his knees and began violently convulsing and projectile vomiting. His puke splashed on to *The King's* highly polished shoes and all over the cuffs of his tailor-made suit. The freshly enraged Culhane, who was holding the full bourbon bottle, smashed it with all of his might over the top of Dennis' bobbing and puking head. Whiskey, shattered glass and blood flew everywhere as Brenahanny hit the floor face first, further splattering the large puddle of his own hot vomit.

"Whip 'em out and hose him off," Culhane ordered. Fred and the other Negroes unbuttoned their flys, pulled out their uncircumcised black horse cocks and began pissing all over Brenahanny and on all the slashed furniture in his showroom.

"Pick him up," Culhane ordered, "Put him in that chair." Two of Fred's men picked Dennis up and threw him into a living room chair that had been slashed to pieces. Brenahanny was a bloody mess from having the quart bottle full of bourbon smashed over the top of his skull; he was bleeding profusely from the deep gashes in his head, he was barely conscious, still heaving, convulsing and puking. He reeked of whiskey, furniture polish and piss.

"Dennis, what did you learn today?" Culhane asked the pitiful shaking wretch. "Well, let me tell you what I think you should have learned. First of all, it's pronounced *suite* of furniture, not *suit* of furniture, you illiterate moron. Next, you should have learned that mixing whiskey and furniture polish is a very bad idea. That's why I don't sell furniture polish, that's *your* business.

"You should also have learned that you shouldn't be selling whiskey, because that's *my* business. And, hopefully you learned that if you do have a relapse in judgment and decide to sell whiskey, that that ill advised action on your part takes money away from me, my family and my business associates, and that makes us *a tad unhappy.*

"Did you learn those valuable lessons today Mr. Brenahanny?" Culhane waited for an answer, "Dennis, I can't hear you. Has the cat got your tongue?"

Brenahanny mumbled something unintelligible and tried to nod his head in the affirmative.

"Dennis, I'll take that as a '*Yes*'," Culhane said, "Now there's just one final lesson for you to commit to memory. I have to be absolutely, positively sure that you never forget what you learned here today. We covered a lot of topics in this private tutorial session, and I want to be certain that you remember all the teaching points I've made today. And, I want you to remember them with every step you take for the rest of your miserable fucking life. So here is my *final point*."

With that, Culhane whirled around and used a roundhouse swing of his powerful right arm to ram the full length of an 8-inch *Polar Wave* ice pick straight through the front of Brenahanny's right kneecap and deep into the thigh bone behind it. You could hear his scream two counties away.

As Fred and the other Negroes cleaned out the store's cash box and register drawer, Tom pressed a nickel into the screaming Brenahanny's palm and said, "Here's a nickel. You can do one of two things with it. You can call the factory and order some new crap and start all over *or* you can call the cops and see if you can make them give a shit."

On his way out the front door, Culhane turned the sign from the side that read;

OPEN
Please Come In
to the side that read;
CLOSED
Please Come Back Tomorrow.

KIRTSCHNER'S JOURNAL ENTRY: 1H/2H/HS

With the remedial educational meeting at Brenahanny's furniture store behind them, Fred Washington and his colored muscle split off from *The King of Kerry* and returned to the Fitzsimmon's Cartage Company warehouse off Biddle to clean up and have a little meeting of their own.

The men were talking as they changed out of their grey-blue mover's coveralls and hosed Dennis' puke and blood off each other in the garage. One of the men said, "I can tell yo'all one thing fo' sure, I ain't never gonna go and ever piss off that *King of Kerry*, that mutherfucker will mess you up somethin' terrible."

"That's the truth, that man will put a serious hurt on anybody who fucks with him. Shit did you see the way he spiked that ice pick, you could hear that po' man's knee cap crack right in half. It sounded like a snapping tree limb."

"I heard that *The King* once cut off one man's dick off and then made his partner suck on it before he blew both their heads off."

"Mmmm, mmmm mmmm, he is one red-headed-freckle-faced-white-assed Irish Devil, thas' fo' sure."

"How did Fred get in so tight with his evil ass?"

Calhoun, the oldest of the group said, "I heared folks say *The King* caught Fred stealing food from outta his restaurant cellar when he was just a punk kid. And when he went to whip on his black ass, Fred fought back at him. They say *The King* beat him half to death, before his Mama heard him holler'n and came runnin' down the alley and saved him. Turns out *The King* know'd the Mama because she was a cook or cleaning woman from someplace in the neighborhood. When Mr. Tom found out that Fred was just stealing food out of his cellar 'cause the family was so fuckin' poor they was practically starvin', he felt bad for wailing on the kid.

"After that, *The King* gave Fred a job and kinda raised him up like the daddy he never had. Least, that's the story what I've hear'd tell of."

Fred came bounding into the garage and yelled, "C'mon you niggers quit fuckin' around on my time and get your lazy black asses over here."

"Mr. Fred, you're starting to sound like a white man!" Calhoun called out and they all started laughing. When the group had gathered round and settled down, Fred began, "Cal, that was a great performance you put in at the furniture store this morning as old man shuffle-along. You're a regular, Steppin' Fetchit."

Calhoun stood up, turned and faced the group and took a deep formal bow and said, "I thank you kind sir." The rest of the men clapped, whistled and cat called.

Fred settled them down again and continued, "Here's what I need you all to do right away, and without delay. Put your ears to the ground in the barber shops, the 'speaks,' in all the restaurant and hotel kitchens and in the catering companies. Talk to all, and I mean *all* of the colored workers in Devereaux's shoe factories and at their main office too. Talk to the neighborhood gossips in the AME churches. Talk to the maids, janitors, dock hands, cooks and chauffeurs. Talk to the colored Madams too, see if they are running any colored pussy over to those exclusive white male stag party circles. See what you can find out about the Robertsons, Devereauxs and any other white folks that are close to them.

"Maurice, you and Cedric will work the backside of the easy streets for me. I'm going over to Cottage Avenue to personally pay a little social call on the Devereaux's help,

Mr. Bee and Miss Willie Henderson.

"Okay, let's get out there and see what we can learn. Talk to everybody, listen to everybody and pay close attention to every little thing. Spread a little free whiskey around to loosen up tongues, if you have to, *but don't break the bank*," Fred cautioned.

The Big Nigger ran his organization in the same firm, hands-on manner and with the same ruthless efficiency that his mentor and father figure, *The King Of Kerry*, had taught him so well over the years.

Later that night, Fred Washington's big *Buick* sedan pulled up in front of 2313 Cottage Avenue, he parked his car and walked up the sidewalk through the neatly mown lawn lined with low trimmed hedges and small flower beds. He rang the doorbell.

When Bee Henderson opened the door, he was unpleasantly surprised to see the biggest of the black bootleggers standing under his porch light; he knew that *The Big Nigger* didn't make social house calls unless there was an important reason. Bee feared that something bad was up, "Please come in Mr. Washington."

Fred respectfully took off his hat and walked into the living room. "You have a lovely home Mr. Henderson. I was hoping to have a quiet word with you and your wife, is she here," Fred inquired.

"No sir, she has been staying over at the big house since Mrs. Devereaux is needing special help, what with the killing and all the commotion and all," Bee replied, "How can I help you."

Fred asked, "May I sit down?"

"Oh yes sir, of course, please sit here," Bee gestured to the large armchair beside the couch.

Bee sat on the couch, leaned forward and put his fingers together and rested his arms on his knees. *I hope this will keep me from shaking he thought.*

Sensing his nervousness, Fred said, "Mr. Henderson, I want you to relax. Neither you nor your wife have anything to fear from me or from the police either, for that matter."

Bee breathed an audible sigh of relief, "This is all so upsetting to us, we're just common working folk and we don't know what to do, we're just caught up in all the commotion."

"I understand. Let me tell you how you can be of great service and help to me," Fred continued as Bee looked at him in rapt attention, "When Mr. Devereaux was killed, the police found two cases of whiskey in the trunk of his car. They traced that whiskey back to me and I traced it back to you. *See how that works?*"

"Yes sir," I did bought that whiskey from your man Mr. Maurice Oliver just the day before Mr. Pierre was killed. I put the whiskey in the trunk, because after I drop him off at work and go to run his errands...along the way, I drops off a bottle here and a bottle there, I just makes an extra 25-cents a bottle off the maids and gardeners and janitors in the neighborhood, and Mr. Maurice said that was all right," he added a bit defensively. "But this time, Mr. Pierre went and took the car himself and I didn't have no time to git the whiskey out first."

"I know all that and you have done nothing wrong. If the cops ask you any more about the whiskey, just play dumb, shrug your shoulders and tell 'em you bought it in the alley from some hustler and tell them you don't know him or anything about where he got it. Trust me, it won't go any further than that. If they haven't asked you about it yet, they may never ask you about it," Fred reassured him.

"The whiskey's not the reason I'm here anyway. I'm here because the cops were going to sweat you and your wife in a most unpleasant way, when a, *shall we say*, 'powerful friend' intervened and persuaded them that we might learn more from you and your wife if we approached the matter in a quiet and totally off-the-record manner. *Do you agree?*" Fred asked politely.

"Yes, Mr. Washington and I appreciate it. I really do. Willie is not in the best of health and if the cops put her through the wringer, I'm afraid she'd have a heart attack," Bee was truly thankful that the situation had been avoided.

"How can I help you? Just name it. Ask any questions, if I know the answer, I'll tell it. If I don't know it I'll tell you who does."

Fred Washington pulled out a monogrammed silver cigarette case from his inside suit pocket, "Do you smoke?" he popped the spring-latched top and offered Bee a *Cavalier.*

"Thanks I do," Bee replied and Fred lit their cigarettes.

"Bee, I'm going to lean back, enjoy this smoke and listen to whatever you have to say, and I can stay here all night. We have plenty of cigarettes, I have whiskey in my car and I'm in no rush. I just want you to tell me everything you know about what goes on in public and behind all the closed doors at 43 Washington Terrace. And, I mean *everything*, and, you can be sure of this. You have my word of honor that whatever I learn here tonight will never be attributed to you. Everything you tell me is strictly off-the-record. No one will ever know it came from you. *Are we clear on that important point?*" Fred looked for a sign of confirmation.

Bee quickly nodded, "Yes sir, where should I begin?"

"Start at the beginning. I want to know every little detail."

"Do you need a pencil and some paper to write on?' Bee asked.

Fred's face lit up as his trademark smile spread across it, "In my line of work, the less you write down, the better," he lightly tapped his temple, "I have an excellent memory."

Bee settled back on his couch, rested his elbow on its doily-covered arm and took a deep drag on his *Cavalier* and began relating what he knew.

———

Newspaper Clipping – *St. Louis Globe-Democrat*, March 28, 1931

A Cup Of Joe with Joe

Your morning coffee column with Joe Leonard

Thugs Vandalize Neighborhood Furniture Store – Furniture retailer Dennis Brenahanny was injured in an assault and robbery in his north side store on Union Boulevard at Natural Bridge Avenue earlier this week. A gang of thugs knocked him out, robbed his cash box and vandalized his store before fleeing. "It all happened so fast, I didn't get a good look at any of them," Brenahanny reported to police.

Morning Joe says, "Let's put more beat cops out on the street!

KIRTSCHNER'S JOURNAL ENTRY: 1H/2H

Columbo walked into Gagliardi's on Daggett on 'The Hill' and the place was empty in that dead period after lunch and before the after work drinkers and the early diners begin to arrive. The restaurant was beautiful, a white octagonal tile floor accented the long ebony bar, it's huge backbar mirrors reflected the image of the elegant pillared dining room with it's murals of Italian scenes, frescos and fountains.

A lone bartender was getting ready for the evening when Columbo startled him, "Paulo, is Mr. Gagliardi here?"

"Oh Luigi, you made my heart jump, yeah, the Boss, he's in the dining room at the back table with Carlo and Armando. You want me to tell him you're here?"

"Yes, please announce me and ask him if he has a moment to see me in private," Columbo responded.

Paulo left and went into the dining room and passed out of view, a few minutes later, Paulo, Carlo and Armando came into the bar. "The Boss told me to send you right in, he's in the back booth," Armando said as he took a seat at the bar, "he also said to have Carlo pat you down and to leave any guns or knives out here on the bar. *Capice?*

Columbo raised his arms as Carlo patted him down and removed his service revolver. "He's clean, no knives and guns on his calves."

"Okay, go on in," Armando gestured.

Columbo crossed the room and approached the *Big Dago*, the 6'3" balding, 325 lb. fat man seated in the last booth. He was eating from a plate piled high with steaming *carbonara.*

"Luigi, come and join me, can I get you some *Chianti* and *carbonara,* or *Pinot Grigio* and *fettuccini* with some *langoustines?* Whadd'ya like?" Carmine Gagliardi asked.

Chianti sounds great and the *carbonara* looks and smells wonderful," Luigi said as he sat down.

"Tony! Hey Tony!" Gagliardi yelled toward the *la cuchina,* "Bring my friend Mr. Columbo here some *Chianti,* a big plate of *carbonara* and some hard bread, with fresh shaved *Romano* and olive oil too."

"What brings the white sheep of 'The Hill' to see the black sheep?" Carmine asked as he rolled his next forkful of *carbonara* using the big serving spoon.

"I'm here on behalf of the Department…"

"I didn't think you dropped in to buy a raffle ticket for *The Son's Of Garibaldi* raffle this coming Saturday, although that can be easily arranged," Carmine stuffed in a huge mouthful of *carbonara* and washed it down with a half a glass of *Chianti.*

The waiter brought Luigi's food and wine, he thanked him and continued, "The Department needs your help, Major Jeremiah O'Connell has been selected by Chief Strickland to represent the force. And, I have been sent to ask you to meet with him alone in a place and at a time of your choosing and, at your earliest possible convenience."

Columbo took in a forkful of *carbonara* and waited for Gagliardi to answer.

"Do you like it?" Carmine pointed his fork at the *carbonara*.

"Yes, its different, but *delicioso*."

Carmine wiped his mouth with a big red napkin, "It's my own recipe, I use thin strips of red pepper *Coppa*, I call it the 'poor man's *proscuitto.*' That's the little difference that makes the big difference. *Coppa* has *soooo* much more flavor than *proscuitto*, it's also cheaper and much more *robusto*, eh?"

Luigi nodded and took a sip of *Chianti*.

"What's this meeting about? How do I know it's not a set up?" Gagliardi took another big drink of *vino*.

"It's not a set up. We need your help and we need it very discreetly," Columbo said.

"It's about the park murders, isn't it. You think me and my boys are mixed up in that?"

Carmine put a little edge in his voice.

"As a matter of fact, we all believe that you and your boys had absolutely nothing to do with it. And that opinion is held - *to a man*, including Chief Strickland, Chief of Detectives Harrigan and Major O'Connell and for what it's worth, by me too."

"So why the meeting? What do you think I can do?"

Columbo replied, "We think you can help us find the killers and keep the peace that we've all enjoyed since *The Green Ones* and *Eagan's Rats* have gone away."

"Tell me what you've got so far," Carmine stuffed another overloaded forkful of pasta in his mouth.

Columbo hesitated, "I'm sorry, but briefing you is supposed to be Major O'Connell's job..."

Carmine interrupted, "Luigi, you tell me *now*, or there is no possibility of any meeting.

You understand?"

Columbo was stopped cold, he composed his thoughts and said, "You ask a lot, Mr. Gagliardi, but I know you are a man of honor. Can I count on your complete confidence? If my bosses ever find out, I would be done."

Gaglairdi nodded and that was good enough for Columbo.

"Okay, here's what we've got...and it is all very circumstantial. Let me emphasize, once again that *we are not accusing you or any of your men of being involved*, but we think it could be someone who has passed through your employ in one of the restaurants, cafeterias or 'speaks,' that's why we need your help in a very quiet and totally secret way."

"I see. I hire a lot of people, but, you're right too, I don't know every time they cut a fart, take a shit or kill a guy," Gagliardi shrugged his shoulders, "How could I?"

"That is exactly our belief, but we are hoping that you could tell us – *quietly and strictly off-the-record* – who has worked for you since February 1928," Columbo said.

"That might be possible, but if it does turn out to be one of my boys, *by some off chance*, I have to handle the punishment. I'd have to make an example to maintain discipline. Can that be arranged as a condition for the meeting?" Carmine asked.

"I think it can be arranged, but I'll have to confirm it with my bosses, you understand" Columbo added.

Carmine shook hands with Columbo, "Okay, you have my respect and my personal pledge, now, what have the cops got? I've been following the story in the papers, but it looks like they haven't got a fucking thing except two stiffs so far."

Columbo repeated his litany of known factors for Carmine's benefit.

1. The apron the smashed guns the killer or killers used were wrapped up in it from *Correnti's.*
2. It has a laundry code that links it to one of Mr. Gagliardi's *legitimate* restaurants or cafeterias – there's one on 'The Hill', one on Washington, west of Grand and the new one out on the DeBallivere Strip.
3. Mr. Gagliardi has a lot of workers in his restaurants that have criminal pasts.
4. *Navy Brands* trash dump, where the apron was found is on the edge of 'The Hill'
5. Tower Grove Park is also on the edge of 'The Hill' – just two blocks east and south
6. Mr. Gagliardi runs some high class 'speaks' in the immediate area, it's possible that the victim's were at one of them before they went and got themselves killed.
7. It's possible the killers were there too, and followed them to the park
8. Mr.Gagliardi could be of great service to everyone, if he could make a few discreet inquires and see if anyone may have seen or heard anything that can help solve these terrible murders.

Gagliardi listened attentively and mulled over all the information and the meeting request as Luigi finished every last noodle on his plate of *carbonara.*

Finally, Carmine spoke, "Okay, I got the picture. Tell O'Connell to be standing on the corner of Grand and Meramec in factory worker clothes three days from now at 7:00 am and I'll pick him up. If he's there, he needs to come with the arrangement I asked for. **Or, no deal and no meeting**. You want some more *Chianti?* I do. Hey Paulo! Paulo bring us some more wine."

A half a bottle of Chianti later, Luigi Columbo placed a call to Chief Of Detectives Harrigan and then one to Major O'Connell. He told them both of Carmine's conditions and terms. Both said, "Tell him he has a deal."

Luigi was feeling just a bit tipsy as he hung up the phone and said, "Mr.Gagliardi, you have a deal."

"Here," have some more *Chianti*, Carmine poured two full glasses and said, "Luigi there's just one more thing?"

"What's that?"

Gagliardi reached inside his coat and Columbo's eyes instantly widened in fear.

"How many tickets would you like for *The Son's Of Garibaldi* raffle?

A whole book of ten is just a dollar and you can win half the pot, it's a 50-50 raffle to benefit our college scholarship fund. *Be generous*," Carmine urged him.

"Jesus, I thought you were pulling out a gun! I'll take three books," Columbo relaxed.

"If I did pull a gun, how many would you buy?" Carmine asked.

Then he and Columbo both laughed and clinked their wine glasses together.

"If I don't win, I hope you do Mr. Gagliardi."

Carmine finished his glass of *Chianti* in one long drink and said, "My cousin Pasquale Poncerolli is pulling the winning ticket, *and for his sake*, I hope I win too."

———◆———

KIRTSCHNER'S JOURNAL ENTRY:
EW/1H/2H/HS

I had slept more soundly than I had since the night before the murders. The ensuing 20-hour days at the office, the fitful nights on the rickety cot in the pressmen's locker room and the short catnaps stolen on the couch in the Managing Editor's conference room had left me on the verge of complete exhaustion. I was glad that Arnold Dexter had ordered me home. To be honest, I barely remembered getting undressed and I had no recollection of my head even denting the pillow the prior afternoon.

I was still yawning with every breath at 12:23 p.m. the next day when I finally got up and stumbled downstairs to put on a pot of coffee. As the *Old Judge* coffee perked away, I went out onto the front porch and brought in three morning *Globe Democrats* and three *St. Louis Stars* that had collected on the front stoop in my absence.

I lay them on his kitchen table in a pile and prepared some bacon and eggs. I made toast and buttered it, put the eggs and bacon on my plate, poured myself a cup of coffee and sat down. I started by sorting through the stack of unread papers until I found the most recent edition of the *Star*. *I wonder how the story came out.* I unfolded it and snapped open the front page to reveal the headline: **FACE OF MURDERED "MADAME X" REVEALED**. When I looked down at George's line drawing and my entire body was swept over by a feeling of disbelief, the bone chilling cold of grief and the sudden sensation to vomit. I jumped up and began dry heaving into the kitchen sink.

I heaved up some vile yellow bile and stomach acid and then with my throat and mouth still burning, I collapsed and sank down onto the linoleum floor sobbing uncontrollably, "Oh *Jesus no, no please God, no. Please Jesus...please no!*"

———◆———

Newspaper Clipping – *St. Louis Star*, March 25, 1931

THIS IS THE FACE OF 'MADAME X' STAR OFFERS $250.00 REWARD

Frederick L. Kirtschner
Of The Star Staff

The artist's sketch below is a *Star* exclusive. The drawing was made from autopsy photos taken at the City Morgue by the Corner's office. Exercising its First Amendment rights, the *Star* will not identify the exclusive source of these photos, but assures its readers that Managing Editor Gordon P. Alcott and Assistant Managing Editor Arnold Dexter have substantiated the veracity of the photographs.

If you have any information regarding the identity of "Madame X" please call OLive 3456, the *Star's* special reward phone number. The *Star* will pay $250.00 to the first person to successfully identify "Madame X" the young woman slain in a hail of bullets in the back seat of shoe tycoon, Pierre Laclede Devereaux's custom-built Cadillac on March 16, 1931 in a Tower Grove Park lover's lane.

Chief of Detectives Charles M. Harrigan hailed the Star's initiative as a fine example of civic spirit designed to aid the intensive investigation underway by the St. Louis Police Department's elite detective bureau.

PHOTO CUTLINE:
Madame X, do you know her? Is she a neighbor, a co-worker, a friend or just an unfortunate stranger passing through St. Louis?

The woman is described in the preliminary Coroner's report as: **Jane Doe** White female, 18-25 years of age, 108 lbs., 5' 0" tall, with crescent birthmark ¾ " by 2" on left inner thigh. Blonde hair (dyed) natural hair color: brunette, green eyes. Red manicured finger nails and toe nails. The female victim was hit by a total of one (1) fatal shot. One (1).32 caliber round was recovered from the remains of the right posterior lobe of the victim's brain.

Gordon P. Alcott, *Star* Managing Editor commented, "The *Star* is committed to helping Chief Harrigan and his squad bring the murderer to justice and will spare no time, effort or expense in pursuit of that goal.

The King of Kerry was waiting impatiently in his office above the *Celtic Room* for Fred to arrive with the news of his visit to the Henderson's. Harrigan had already called twice this morning for an update and Culhane was growing a bit weary of his badgering.

Suddenly his office door flew open and a wild-eyed boy in his early 20's came through the door with pump shotgun in hand. "Who the fuck are you?" *The King* bellowed.

"Sit down and shut up and keep your hands flat on your desk," the shaking kid ordered.

"I'm asking **again**, who are you and how did you get up here?" *The King* was not cowed by the jumpy kid.

"I'm Matt Brenahanny and you, you son-of-a-bitch you crippled and almost killed my Dad. Now, I'm gonna kill you, you mother fucker, but first you're gonna suffer like you made him suffer."

"Now listen to me laddy, there's been some sort of terrible misunderstanding here, are you looking for *Tom Culhane?*" *The King* asked calmly.

"Yeah, I am...*ain't you him?*" the young Brennahanny asked. The floor behind him creaked as the door of the ante-room opened, "No that's him," Culhane pointed to the right of the kid. The kid pivoted around, pumped the shotgun to fill the chamber and fired. The blast caught Mamie in mid-stride and hurled her little body and the tray of sandwiches she was carrying across the hallway and out into the landing's corner, where she came to rest seated with her legs spread wide and her back against the wall. She looked down in disbelief like a wounded Raggedy Ann doll at the gapping hole in her belly that was leaking out bowels and dark red blood.

The kid was tossed suddenly forward into the wall and door jamb by the two shots that tore through his left shoulder and shattered his elbow. Culhane had come up firing with his old service .45 that he pulled from his middle desk drawer.

Culhane crossed the office and kicked the shotgun across the ante-room and stepped over the moaning kid to get to Mamie out in the hallway. She stared wide-eyed into space cupping her oozing guts in her hands. She looked up at *The King* and said, "Tommy, who is he??...he's killed me." Her head dropped down on her chest and he felt her neck... *there was no pulse.*

The badly wounded kid was crawling across the floor trying to reach the shotgun when Culhane came up behind him and kicked him in the balls. "You fucking asshole you killed Mamie!" *The King* knelt over him and opened a *Camillus* knife pulled from his vest pocket. He jammed the knife blade deep into the kid's bellybutton and cut him open all the way up to the bottom of his rib cage. Culhane reached inside and pulled the kid's living guts and organs out with his bare hands. He was yelling like a madman, "If you come to kill me, you'd better fucking kill me before I get my hands on you." The kid screamed hellacious screams and his body bounced around on the floor in mind-maddening pain as Culhane ripped at his innards.

Matt Hellman and Fred Washington raced up the stairs and burst into the hallway and the ante-room with guns drawn, but it was all over but the dying. *The King* came back to Mamie's lifeless body; his shirt was sopping wet crimson and arms were awash in blood up to the elbows. He knelt down next to her and lovingly pulled Mamie close and began to rock her in his arms. Then through his tears, he looked up at Fred and said, "Round up your meanest niggers and kill every fucking Brenahanny, every man, woman and child." Fred looked at him in horror. "Do it now Fred, I want them all dead before sunset today."

"Do you want me to kill this one," Hellman asked as he stood over the writhing disemboweled kid.

"No, let him die as slow as he pleases. I want to enjoy it," Culhane said as he continued to gently rock Mamie's limp body in his arms and caress her long red hair. He watched stoically as the goggle-eyed young man convulsed and twitched erratically in his final death throes.

Fred looked at Matt Hellman, at the dying kid and back at Mamie and *The King*. Then he ran down the stairs toward the other men, who had come running toward all the shooting. "Everything is under control, Matt's upstairs, Tom's fine, but Mamie's dead...and we shot and killed the murdering bastard who did it," Fred reported as he reached the knot of people clustered at the bottom of the stairwell. "Call Joe Culhane at the Central District and tell him to get over here right away. Go man do it now!" Fred went out to the dining room's phone booth, dropped in a nickel and dialed Calhoun, "Cal, get all the men together at the warehouse, we have a rat's nest to clean out. I'll be there in 25 minutes."

The Brenahanny home was a 3-story pale yellow brick town home at 5475 Kensington, a block or so west of Kingshighway and north of Delmar. There were five children living there from 12 to 20, three girls and two boys, along with their parents, Dennis and Margaret, and Dennis' 72 year-old mother Nora.

Cal and his men came in through the unlocked back kitchen door from the alley and went quickly through the house rounding up all the Brenahanny's and herded them into the basement fruit cellar, a windowless room under the poured concrete front porch. The terrified family was all huddled together in the dark dank room, praying, crying and holding on to each other when Fred's men shot them to death with 12-gauge sawed-off shotguns. It was all over in less than a minute.

The men poured coal oil and kerosene over the bodies and all down the basement stairs as went back upstairs to the kitchen. They all left except Fred and piled into the back of the unmarked panel truck parked in the alley. Seconds later Fred came out and got in the truck cab on the passenger's side. Cal shifted into gear and the undistinguished truck drove down the alley at an unhurried pace and then turned north. By the time they reached Natural Bridge several blocks to the north, Fred looked back to see billows of thick, dark black smoke rising from the raging inferno. He could hear fire engine sirens way off in the distance.

He hung his head down and began to cry. He had done a lot of bad things in his life at *The King's* behest, but the things he did today in the Brenahanny cellar, had destroyed the last piece of human decency that was left in his heart. He bit his lip and wept bitterly for the loss of his own immortal soul.

KIRTSCHNER'S JOURNAL ENTRY:
EW/1H/2H/HS

I had pulled myself together enough to call her home number several times. Her phone rang off the hook, as I sat listening in silent shock at the phone table in my downstairs hallway.

I had even called her workplace earlier, but no one at Southside National bank was concerned in the least. She had taken a week's vacation to go to Hot Springs, Arkansas. Her supervisor was under the impression that she was going there with a new beau, someone she was 'head over heels' and just ga-ga about. I did not ask the supervisor if she had seen the drawing of *'Madame X'* in the paper. Maybe it was just my overwrought and overworked imagination that made me think that the likeness on page one was the supposedly vacationing female bank employee.

I felt like I was going mad. That's when I decided to call Joe Culhane to see if Joe could get me into the morgue for a look at the female victim's body. That was the only way I could be sure. Culhane was not there when I called because the squad room had emptied out on account of some shooting at *The Celtic Room*. I wondered if *The King* was dead, maybe I should go there...or maybe this would be a perfect opportunity to slip into the morgue during all the distraction that would result from a shooting at *The King Of Kerry's* lair. I pulled on my coat and headed downtown. Maybe Schu could get me into the examining room, hell; I'd only need 5-minutes?

———◆———

The King Of Kerry sat stark naked on a pile of towels, slumped down in the leather chair behind his desk. Matt and Joe were busy washing all the blood off him and rinsing and wringing out the bloody cloths in an odd assembly of commercial kitchen soup pots and wash basins hastily gathered from the bedrooms upstairs and now arrayed on the office floor.

"Tom you gotta get out of town, "Joe urged.

"He's right Tom," Harrigan agreed, "Let us clean up the mess here. You get on the next train to New Orleans and the next steamer to Havana. I'm advising you to go there and stay there until all this blows over. We'll make sure Mamie has a fitting funeral, there is nothing more you can do for her here, and she'd be the first to want you out of harm's way. You know that..."

"That's no lie," Matt chimed in.

Culhane was very quiet and almost comatose from shock and grief. Finally he spoke, "I didn't know it was her coming in, I thought it was Fred. Fred would never have gotten himself gut shot, we'd've made short work of that fucking punk," Culhane took one last look at the dead kid, who was now wrapped in a blood-soaked shroud and being carried downstairs by the ambulance drivers.

"Tom, listen to me," Harrigan asked, "Do you know anything about a fire this afternoon at this Brenahanny home? The whole Brenahanny house burnt up. The neighbors think the entire family might have perished inside too. I talked to the Engine Company Battalion Chief and he told me the fire looked suspicious. But, the whole building burned up and everything collapsed into the cellar. It'll be days before they can sift through the debris to see if anyone was inside," Harrigan added.

"All I know is that it sounds like a terrible tragedy. But, if it's true, at least they're all together in hell now," Culhane's icy eyes stared at the far wall.

"Here's the way the official report of this incident will read, it'll go something like this; one of Brenahanny's no-account sons died of gunshot wounds inflicted by your watchmen while he was burglarizing the premises. Sadly, he had already murdered poor Mamie, who must've walked in and surprised him.

"What we don't need, I'm thinking, is some smart ass reporter nosing around and starting to put two-and-two together trying to connect the unrelated coincidences, that tragically befell this unfortunate family, to you or your colleagues," Harrigan speculated.

Joe continued, "Havana is beautiful this time of the year, especially at the *El Presidente*."

Harrigan continued, "I sent Eamon to the house to fetch fresh clothes from Mary Clare for you. We burned up your bloody clothes in the ash pit already. When you get dressed, why don't you let Joe and Finn take you home, pack you up and then take you to catch the *City of New Orleans*.

"You're right as always, Charles Michael," Culhane agreed.

"Get some sun, drink some rum, play cards and relax...I'll wire you when it's safe to come home. And, Thomas Edward, while you're relaxing down there, maybe you could pick up a few boxes of *Cubano* cigars for me. I'm running kinda low," Harrigan remarked as he used the cigar cutter on *The King's* desk to neatly snip the end off a *Filipe Montoya*. Harrigan closed his eyes as he passed the cigar below his nostrils and inhaled the rich aroma of the hand-rolled full tobacco leafs, "I'd offer you one too, Thomas Edward, but this is the last one of these beauties in my possession."

———◆———

Newspaper Clipping – *St. Louis Post-Dispatch*, March 30, 1931

Watchman Kills Burglar Who Killed Housekeeper

Post-Dispatch Reporter
Harry H. Nelson

Matt Hellman, a watchman at *The Celtic Room Restaurant* at Grand and Dodier responded to a shot fired in the upstairs business office yesterday shortly before noon. Hellman, first to arrive on the scene found the lifeless body of Mamie O'Halloran, 46, the housekeeper on the upstairs landing. Miss O'Halloran, who lived in the apartment adjoining the business office, apparently surprised the burglar who was ransacking the business office where the day's cash receipts were kept.

Matt Hellman opened fire on the burglar who was trying to flee with the contents of the cash box kept in the owner's desk. The burglar was identified as Matthew Brenahanny 22 of 5475 Kensington Avenue was pronounced dead at the scene.

Chief Of Detectives Charles M. Harrigan speculated that, "Ms. O'Halloran must have walked in and caught Brenahanny in the act. Ms. O'Halloran was killed by a single shotgun blast to the abdomen. She was walking toward the gunman, not running away. Amateur thieves often panic when startled during the commission of a crime and that's when innocent people get killed."

Police have taken the matter under investigation, but no charges are anticipated against Mr. Hellman. Business owner Thomas E. Culhane was out of the country at the time of the crime and could not be reached for comment.

At first, Schu was uncomfortable as a whore at Midnight Mass, but $50 in *Star* cash was courage enough to persuade him to lead this reporter though the lower level labyrinth that connected the Central District's basement to the lower level of the City Morgue. "Let's make it snappy, it's in, take a quick look and right back out. We can't get caught down here. I'll lose my job and my teeth. Got it?" Schu emphasized.

I didn't answer.

"Got it?" Schu said as he poked me in the chest.

I was annoyed when I replied, "Yeah, I *got it.*"

The two of us slipped into the darkened autopsy room and Schu flashed his light on the paper identification tabs that was inserted into the small black metal frames above the handles on each of the drawers that held a body. He walked down the rows until he found the tab insert marked, *'Madame X.'*

"Here she is," Schu said as he pulled open the chilled drawer, "Get over here and take a good look, one is all you're gonna get. Make it quick."

I moved in as Schu pulled the sheet back to reveal the murdered woman's face, he shined his high-beam flash light squarely on it. The woman's skin was a pale bluish-white. It was badly discolored from death, from the loss of blood and from the trauma that resulted from the gapping gunshot wound in the side of her skull. Her lips were sewn shut, tightly pursed and dehydrated. The moving flashlight cast eerie shadows across her nose and dark sunken eyes.

"Seen enuf?" Schu asked. I nodded, even with the body in this highly distressed state there was no mistake. *It was her.*

Schu quickly re-covered the face, closed the drawer and led me out of the morgue's autopsy room and back through the twisting underground hallway.

"I gotta get back before I'm missed. Follow this hall to the right and you'll come out in the basement of the Police Academy. There's a door to the immediate right that will let you out into the garage. Then walk through the big garage door that's always open and you'll be out on 12th Street and no one will be the wiser. *Are you okay?*" Schu asked.

"Yeah, I'm fine," I mumbled as I slowly wandered off down the hall.

Schu had a creepy feeling about the whole thing. His sixth sense told him something was wrong, *very wrong.*

He was right.

KIRTSCHNER'S JOURNAL ENTRY: 1H/2H/OF

Jeremiah O'Connell was nothing if he was not lucky. And, the harder he worked the luckier he got. Harrigan had asked him to handle the first official follow up interview with Mrs. Devereaux and the staff at her home. O'Connell waited for nearly a week after the victim's body had been cremated and interred at Valhalla. He wanted to give Ada and her family time to grieve and to give them some time to come to terms with the scandalous and embarrassing circumstances that surrounded her husband's death.

While he was doing the decent thing and allowing some time to pass, Jeremiah had asked his wife, a former college research librarian to dig into Mrs. Devereaux's past to see what could be learned about her and her family.

Major O'Connell had his eye set squarely on the chair occupied by Chief of Police Strickland and he had carefully planned every adroit career move since he joined the force. He was not about to make any missteps now.

Navigating the tricky waters around the Pierre Laclede Devereaux murder case would require careful diplomacy and tremendous public and interdepartmental political tact so as not to offend or incur the wrath of his colleagues in the police department or EOR and his powerful cadre of society friends who called a lot of the shots in St. Louis.

The day of the mayhem at *The Celtic Room* and the subsequent carnage on Kensington Avenue, began very quietly for Jeremiah, he was contemplating his upcoming meeting with Gagliardi. Columbo had stopped by the evening prior on Harrigan's orders to brief him personally and even brought him a pair of workman's coveralls and a cap to wear to the rendezvous.

He was enjoying his morning coffee at his desk and reading over the notes his wife had gleaned from her sources and neatly organized and typed up for him.

———————

Facts About Ada Robertson Devereaux

Born: To Edmund Oscar Robertson of St. Louis and Swan Lucille (nee) Masterson of New Orleans, Louisiana. Born in St. Louis, May 25, 1903. Age 28.

Education: Mary Institute College Preparatory School, St. Louis, Missouri Stephen's College, Columbia, Missouri, B.A. Fine Arts

Society Debut: Veiled Prophet Ball, 1923, Special Maid of Honor

Married: Pierre Laclede Devereaux, St. Louis Cathedral, July 12, 1925

No children from union to date

Siblings: Sister, Edith Swan Robertson, born January 12, 1908, age 23 Graduate of Mary Institute and Connecticut College For Women, B.A. in French

Society Debut: VP Ball, 1928, Special Maid of Honor
Newspaper Mentions: All I could find was the typical information: Her parents make a lot more news than she does, particularly her father. I was able to locate, in the *Society News,* her birth and wedding announcements, stories about charitable foundation work and some theatrical reviews from her college days at Stephens. (I have put all the clippings in the attached envelope) I found nothing unusual or extraordinary; she is by all appearances a well-educated and socially prominent woman of refined character with a sense of social responsibility who is active in community charitable affairs. Hope this is helpful.

All my Love,
Kathleen

———◆———

    Jeremiah opened the envelope and fanned out the newspaper clips on his desk. He read through each one of them and his wife was right, this lady was leading a life of upper class privilege and societal responsibility by all accounts. Then one small age-yellowed clip from the *Columbia Missourian* made his blood run cold.

———◆———

    Ms. Ada Robertson stunned the audience last night at *The Stephens College Theatre* with her hair-raising portrayal of *Lady Macbeth* in the timeless Shakespearian classic. The third year fine arts and theatre major from St.

Louis literally seized and possessed the very soul and essence of the demonic character, segueing with remarkable ease from cajoling spouse to cunning plotter and grief stricken murderess. Her ability to make her body tremble and to cause rivers of tears flow at will added a startling realism to her emotionally charged performance. Bravo! Miss Robertson, Bravo!

———◆———

O'Connell's mind flashed back to the parlor on Washington Terrace when tears and mascara streaked down Ada's face. He recalled how she was completely inconsolable, sobbing and trembling from head to toe.

Jeremiah wondered if he had witnessed a *tour de force* solo performance.

———◆———

Newspaper Clipping – *St.Louis Post-Dispatch*, March 31, 1931

Raging Inferno Destroys Family Residence On Kensington Avenue

Post-Dispatch Reporter
Harry H. Nelson

The home of Mr. and Mrs. Dennis Brenahanny was destroyed by fire late yesterday afternoon. The 3-story residence at 5475 Kensington was engulfed in a 5-alarm inferno that originated in the basement, possibly by the ignition of a 100 gallon heating oil storage tank.

The 6 known residents of the home are missing and presumed dead. Battalion Chief Gary T. Bingham said that it would be several days before the Fire Department could make a definitive determination as to the cause of the fire. The fact that the 3-story brick building collapsed into the cellar has complicated investigators trying to sort through tons of wet and smoldering debris.

Two other bizarre incidents of misfortune have also befallen the Brenahanny family in recent days. Kensington Avenue owner and resident Dennis Brenahanny had recently been in the news because his furniture store was robbed and vandalized, and his twenty-two year old son Matt was shot to death just hours before on the same day as the fire, in a thwarted burglary attempt.

At this juncture, police have no evidence to make any connection between these three incidents.

This reporter wonders if this is the *"Bad Luck of the Irish?"*

KIRTSCHNER'S JOURNAL ENTRY: EW/1H

I stood in the doorway of Gordon Alcott's office and solemnly announced, "I have to see you." Alcott was alarmed by the sight before him. This reporter's sallow look, disheveled appearance and drooping posture was shocking, I must have looked as though I was carrying the very weight of the world on me. Alcott buzzed Arnold Dexter and said, "Dext c'mere right now."

Alcott closed his door and took me by my arm to steady me. "Fred come and sit down here on the couch," Alcott beckoned, "Do you want some water? A shot? What's the matter man?" Alcott asked as Dext stepped through the side door from the adjoining conference room.

I sat very still. My unshaven face and sad dark circled eyes made me look very old, sick and tired. After a few moments, my lower lip began to tremble and tears welled up in my eyes.

I looked up at Alcott and Dext and said, "I know who '*Madame X*' is."

"Who is she man?" Alcott asked as he quickly knelt down on one knee next to me and leaned in on the couch arm to hear better.

"She's my *sister...*" I sobbed as I buried my head in my hands and began to weep from the darkest depths of my soul in a low and mournful tone.

Alcott looked at Arnold Dexter in speechless shock. Dexter, walked back two steps and literally dropped his full weight into an armchair and said "Holy Mother of God, Fred I'm so sorry."

For the next hour, there was little that Alcott or Arnold could do to console the sobbing wretch curled up in a fetal position on the couch. Wave after wave of heart and gut wrenching emotions swept over me. My so-called big story, my career making front page by-lined expose of money, murder and sex had turned into a horrific and soul wrenching personal nightmare of proportions unfathomable by the two onlooking newspaper executives.

Finally, I collapsed into a deep narcoleptic sleep; my exhausted psyche apparently unable to endure another moment of conscious horror and inescapable guilt and grief. Alcott placed a topcoat from his closet over me and silently motioned for Dext to follow him into the conference room. Then he softly closed the door behind them.

"This is a twisting tornado we're inside of now Dext. I need you to help me think this through, will you?" Alcott asked as he poured a himself a stiff bourbon, "Want one?" Dext nodded, '*Yes,*' and the two men sat down at the conference table and took a big swig of whiskey. It burned all the way down.

"We've got either a blessing or a bomb in our laps," Alcott stated. "Which is it?"

Dexter looked back and shook his head, "What are our choices? We have to come clean with the facts."

Alcott leaned over and whispered, "Do we? I'm not so sure."

KIRTSCHNER'S JOURNAL ENTRY: 2H

The train to New Orleans pulled out on time and rumbled southward through the early golden dusk on the red-reflecting rails that wound gracefully through the fertile river bottoms and the rolling hills of Eastern Missouri. The route roughly following the wide, deep, fast coursing channel cut through the ancient river bluffs in the heartland by the mighty Mississippi. Towns swept past his sleeper window. Crystal City, Herculaneum, Cape Girardeau, Ste. Genevieve then, at West Memphis, Arkansas, it crossed the river and pulled into Memphis to take on passengers, coal, water and a new crew of conductors, porters, colliers, fireman, brakemen and an engineer.

The King of Kerry got off, walked through the station and hailed a cab at the main entrance. He went directly to the Peabody Hotel where he rented a 4th floor suite. He paid cash in advance for two weeks. Once settled in his room, he withdrew a list of phone numbers from his wallet and had the hotel operator connect him to a local number.

"Hello," a soft woman's voice answered.

"Clovis, it's Tom. I'm in town and I need to see you," He said.

"*Fred!* What's happened to Fred," the suddenly frantic voice asked.

"Clovis, get a hold of yourself, nothing has happened to Fred. He is fine, perfectly fine. It's me that needs to see you," Culhane replied.

"Where are you?"

He looked at the key on the nightstand; I'm in room 401 at the Peabody."

Clovis laughed, "That's mighty tall cotton for shanty Irish like you. Give me an hour or so and I can be there. 401, right?"

"All right Honey, see you when you get here, bye-bye baby," Culhane hung up the phone and began to unpack. The suite had two-bedrooms, two baths and an elegant parlor and dining room with fine Flemish tapestries on opposing walls. The large two-story windows on the far wall overlooked the Peabody's famous fountain and the ducks that frolicked there.

"Well, make yourself comfortable, Thomas Edward, you're going to be here for a while, and at $35.00 a night, you might as well enjoy it."

While waiting for his guest to arrive, Culhane had the operator call Harrigan in St. Louis.

"Charles Michael, I'm in Memphis at the Peabody in four-oh-one if you need me."

"I kinda figured as much when you agreed to leave town so easily. Does anyone else know you're there? Do you want me to tell Joe?" Harrigan asked.

"Tell Joe? Why don't you just call the *Globe* and the *Post* and the *Star* and have 'em print it on the front page?" Culhane actually laughed, "No, I don't want you to tell Joe or anyone. I gotta run I'm expecting a guest momentarily."

"Say hello to Clovis for me, and give her my very best. And, Thomas Edward, stay out of trouble while you're down there, your still a mighty big fish, but not in the Memphis pond," Harrigan cautioned as he hung up

The Peabody Hotel was the crown jewel of Memphis hotels and it was as segregated and as lily white as any hotel you could find in the South. Colored guests were not allowed, and even colored visitors coming to see to registered white guests were never permitted inside and the negro house staff used segregated stairs and elevators to move about the hotel in the performance of their duties. A few high profile negroes like LeRoi Campbell, the lavishly uniformed lead doorman and Andrew Williams, the lead bellman and Walker Burdett, who managed the elevator operators and their crews were the only exceptions. They set the subservient *"Yasah"* and *"Nosah"* tone for the Peabody.

That's why when he opened the back door of the chauffeur-driven Lincoln that pulled right up to the hotel's front door, LeRoi Campbell was taken aback to find Miss Clovis Washington in the back seat.

"Pull up that jaw and close your mouth LeRoi, you don't know me today," Clovis said as she swept past him and through the Peabody's highly polished revolving doors. She walked proudly and deliberately across the elegant lobby. Male heads turned in admiration and female heads in envy of the beautiful woman in the impeccably-tailored red blazer, rippling white silk blouse and pleated navy blue skirt that swished ever so alluringly with each step. Blue and white high-heeled spectator-style shoes accented her long shapely legs. She paused at the elevator bank waiting for a door to open. One of the white men seated nearby on a lobby couch nudged his colleague and audibly remarked, "My Lord, she makes me want to enlist in the Navy."

Clovis smiled at the flirty comment, entered the elevator and told the operator, "Four please," she checked her make-up in the mirrored infinity wall of the elevator and looked at her light olive Creole complexion. Her skin was fair and flawless, what the colored folks called 'high yellow' and she could pass for white anywhere, even here in the all white enclave reverently called *The Great White Lady*' by everyone who wasn't great or white.

Culhane answered the knock on his suite's door and opened it to find Clovis standing at an oblique angle with one hand on her hip and her gaze fixed squarely on him.

"May I help you Ma'm?" he asked.

Clovis brushed past him and walked into the sitting room between the bedrooms; she turned back on her heel to face him and re-posed in the same defiant stance she struck in the hall.

"Ma'm may I help you?" *The King* said trying to stifle a laugh.

"You might be able to help me. If you know where I can find that freckle-assed Irishman who is the Daddy of my baby."

Culhane recoiled in false indignation, "Why Madam, I believe you have come to the right place." He opened his arms and said, "Give us a hug Clovis Lucille!"

She flew into his arms and embraced him and kissed him wildly and warmly on his, cheeks, neck and lips, "Oh Thomas Edward, it is so good to see you, but you made my heart jump out of my chest when you called. I was scared to death that something had happened to Fred."

"Our boy is fine, as a matter of fact, he couldn't be better. How could he be otherwise, with his Mama's fine looks and with my wit, brains and charm?" Tom asked.

"Still the modest one I see," Clovis laughed and said, "Are you going to stand there all day or are you going to offer a thirsty lady a drink?"

"Where are my manners?" Tom asked. "Still a bourbon lady?" Clovis gestured back with three horizontal fingers. "I remember,'3-over-ice-that's-mighty-nice,' isn't that what you always said?" Culhane asked as he opened his suitcase and pulled out a bottle of 12-year old bonded bourbon.

"It's been quite a while since we've been all alone like this. I think the last time was in Havana," Clovis commented as she looked around the elegant suite, "What else do you remember?"

Culhane smiled back at her and said, "I remember that you are unforgettable." He handed her the bourbon and took her hand and led her over to the large heavily cushioned floral chintz couch.

"C'mon, sit here and tell me all what you've been up to," Tom said as he noticed her Celtic hearts wedding ring, "You still wear it...*I'm surprised*."

"Never take it off, the love of my life gave it to me," Clovis squeezed his hand tightly.

Clovis took off her blazer and slipped out of her shoes and she curled up on the couch beside him with his strong arm around her shoulders. "Talk to me Clovie, I need to hear your voice," he whispered as he kissed the back of her neck. A cascade of tingly goose bumps swept down her neck, over her shoulders, down her back and over her breasts making her peanut-sized nipples rise in automatic response. "Damn Tom, you can still make me quiver and shiver like when I was a girl of 20."

They spent the next few hours on the couch, catching up, laughing, nuzzling and even crying together over what happened to Mamie. Clovis wanted to know all about the clan's latest shenanigans, she was really curious about how his "Irish twins," Harry and Rosemary, were doing, she wanted to know what Mary Clare was up to and could not get enough details about Fred and how he was getting along in the world.

She asked questions about Fred's amorous adventures too, but *The King* refused to answer and simply evaded her questions by saying that there are some things that grown sons never share with their Mammas. Drink glasses were refilled a few times as the old lovers reconnected, in many ways it was like the old times they used to spend together in the bedroom of his tiny apartment above the first taproom that Tom ran over on Cass Avenue up in the old Hyde Park neighborhood. Clovie had moved to St. Louis after the World's Fair like so many women looking for better wages than what they could earn down South. Her light skin and refined Creole features helped her find work in the *Society Laundry* on Newstead and Finney. Tom met her there when he dropped off and picked up his weekly bachelor bundle. One day, he asked her if she'd like to earn some extra money on the weekends, doing some housekeeping for him. She needed the money so she started coming over early every other Saturday and cleaning his apartment. It was all very innocent at first, but after a few months, the relationship evolved to a warm but platonic friendship. Tom was never an educated man in the formal sense of the word, but he loved to read and he read anything and everything. Politics, history, sports, classics, philosophy and all the business books he could lay his hands on, he devoured them, sitting in the living room for hours on end. One day Clovis, showed an interest in what he was reading and he began to lend her books. When she came to clean and dust and tidy up, they would talk about what she was reading and their minds connected. It was an odd union, he was the son of nearly illiterate and heavily bigoted Irish immigrants and she was the daughter from a line of slaves and French shopkeepers. Yet, somehow they found a magical almost mystical connection in the pages of the books and in the ideas they shared. One day, overcome by the passion of their youth, they fell spontaneously into his bed and spent the rest of the weekend making Fred Washington.

"What's worrying you Tom?" Clovie asked, "I've seen you in a black dog mood before, but never like this."

"I know this is going to sound crazy, but all my life I've never had a single thought of me dying. Not once, not even in France when the Huns were fighting us hand-to-hand with bayonets and bare fists. Not even during the street wars between Eagan's Rats and the Cuckoos. Not even when I had to fight within the Purple gang to secure my own place and business areas. I never feared death, never even thought of death. I watched my friends and enemies die, I saw my wife die and I sent many an errant lad to his final reward personally. But when I held Mamie in my arms and smelled her blood spilling out in my lap, I realized for the first time in my life that I was going to die too. Clovie, that realization, as obvious as it may be to everyone else, just became a reality in my life, and it has me scared to death," Culhane confided with tear-filled eyes.

Clovie got up and said, "I'm going in that bedroom and when I call you, I want you to come in, but not a moment before. She vanished into the larger of the two boudoirs and closed the frosted French doors behind her.

Culhane sat alone sipping on his whiskey and feeling full of sadness, remorse and even a twinge of guilt as he reflected back on the savagery of the last few days. He actually felt remorse for having the whole Brenahanny clan killed. He thought, a line that's lasted through the eons to nineteen hundred and thirty-one should not have come to such an awful end. Then he heard Clovie call him.

"I wonder what she's up to?"

The sight that greeted his eyes swept him back more than 25-years, she was lying nude in the center of the huge canopied bed with her hands on her knees and pile of pillows propping her lovely body up from behind. As he came closer she spread her legs and said, "As I recall, you once had a taste for *pussy les francais.*"

Culhane stripped off all his clothes and crawled into bed and began softly kissing and twirling his talented tongue around the tiny sentry guarding her *Gate of Heaven*.

Moonlight in Memphis looks pretty much like moonlight anywhere, but on this particularly orgasmic evening the moonlight filtering through the featherweight gauze sheers into the suite took on an almost ethereal and angelic nature as it bathed her shapely nude body. Tom lay below her now and she sat straddle-legged over him. She had made him weak from the past hours of on and off again, frenzied and friendly lovemaking. She had gratified him in every way she knew how, and now it was time to share a well-deserved cigarette. She had returned to the disheveled bed just moments before with a large ashtray that she place on his red-flushed stomach. She put two *Old Golds* between her lips and lit them both from a single match. *"Here you go,"* she whispered as she handed him a cigarette and inhaled deeply on her own. *"How do you feel? Your eyes look awfully sleepy, teddy bear,"* she cooed playfully as she softly pinched his nipples.

"I'm feeling really dreamy…are you hungry?" he asked.

"Not right now, I just had a *'snack',*" Clovie said as she reached behind and softly squeezed his scrotum, "but maybe in a little while we can get room service to bring us something, but right now I'm fine. But I'm looking at a man and wondering if I was fine for him."

"Fine? You are better than fine…way, way, way better," he smiled.

"Mmmm, I'm glad you still like the way I make love to you my baby." She felt a weak pulsing sensation beneath her wet pink bottom that was resting atop his shriveled manhood, and said, "My taste is all French, but…" she skillfully rotated her hips in a circular motion and pressed her wetness down on him, "but my motion and emotion is all African!"

Culhane beamed as he took the cigarette out of her mouth. He snuffed out his and hers in the ashtray and set it on the nightstand. Then he pulled her close and tightly cupped her soft buttocks in his powerful hands and kissed her like he kissed her in his tiny upstairs bedroom so many years before.

When dawned rolled around, she awakened to the sound of his voice in the other room. When he came back in she said, "What'cha doing honey?"

"I just ordered up breakfast for two and the morning papers," he smiled coyly as he slid his ruddy naked body alongside hers.

"Tom do you ever think that folks like us could live a normal life as man and wife?" Clovie asked. Tom rubbed his pale freckled hand down the full length of her torso and over her beautiful smooth thigh. "Not in our lifetime Sheba," He always called her Sheba or Queenie after they made love, "Too many taboos, too many bigoted pricks and hoity-toity blue nose prigs, they would never understand. To them black is black and white is white and race-mixing makes 'em very nervous. It threatens their own views and notions about the way things ought to be. Some people like to be on top. They get used to it. The Brits on top of the Irish, whites on top of colored folks, cowboys on top of Indians, hell baby it's just the way the world is."

"How are you doing cash wise?" He asked, clumsily changing the subject.

"Well, you send me $50 grand a year, Fred sends me $12 grand, my legitimate businesses: the catering company, laundry, barber shops and beauty parlors net another $50 grand, my small loans another $40 to $50 thou., and I still keep one "house' full of girls over in West, Memphis, for old times sake... and that is the most profitable of all, "Clovie laughed, "Tom, I even have a white cleaning woman."

"Damn Sheba, I knew you were sitting on a million dollars the first day I laid eyes on you," he rolled her over and playfully slapped her sweet caramel-colored butt.

Clovie quickly pulled her knees up under her stomach and pushed her ass high in the air, "I think we've got time for one brisk ride around the track before breakfast gets here if his majesty, *The King of Kerry* can still mount up?"

"Once around? Hell Sheba, let's make it a steeplechase like *The Irish Derby!*"

KIRTSCHNER'S JOURNAL ENTRY: 1H/2H

O'Connell looked at his pocket watch it was 7:03 a.m. He looked north on Grand Avenue, then south. The morning traffic was heavy and the crowd waiting for the streetcars was filled with the normal array of Southsiders on their way to work. Jeremiah was feeling a little odd in the work clothes Columbo had provided. He hoped that no beat cop on patrol would recognize him. That would be an embarrassment he'd never live down. He was also thinking about the theatrical review from the *Columbia Missourian*. He had not shared that tidbit of information with Harrigan as yet, although he planned to do so. He knew it was better to wait because of the ruckus at *The Celtic Room*. The newspapers were already busy trying to connect the Brenahanny store vandalism and robbery with the family house fire and the 'burglary' and killing of Matt Brenahanny in *The King of Kerry's* office. Even the usually cop-friendly Fire Department was giving the police an arm's length treatment as their own arson investigators dug through the pile of smoldering wet debris in the cellar of what was once the Brenahanny residence. No one seemed to be buying the story that Culhane was out of town at the time of the burglary and that his watchmen had caught the kid rifling his office and killed him in a shoot out. Then latest news also reported that Matt Brenahanny's body had been accidentally cremated prior to an autopsy at the City Crematorium behind Malcom Bliss Mental Hospital. That caused the *Post- Dispatch* editorial writers to wax eloquently about police incompetence at best, and corruption at worst. Jeremiah knew that Harrigan had his hands full. If there was a silver lining in the storm clouds surrounding the force, it was the fact that the Brenahanny incidents had taken the *'Madame X'* story off page one, at least temporarily.

Jeremiah was looking west across Grand toward *Al Smith's* and wondering where Gagliardi was when he heard a horn honk twice from the alley. *"Hey buddy, let's go."*

O'Connell had to look twice to believe his eyes. It was Carmine Gagliardi, *The Big Dago* himself, dressed like a day laborer driving the truck. Jeremiah walked the 30-feet to the alley and got into the front seat. The truck was a non-descript delivery truck with faded white block lettering on the side: St. Louis Catholic Supply.

"This is quite a disguise Mr.Gagliardi," Jeremiah commented.

"Please call me Carmine, Major O'Connell. I've heard a lot of good things about you," Gagliardi pulled out on to Meremac Street, crossed Grand Avenue and headed east toward South Broadway.

"And, I've heard a lot about you too. Are you taking me to the Workhouse?" O'Connell inquired as the City Workhouse for short time offenders serving under 6-months jail time was located dead ahead at Meremac and Broadway.

Carmine looked at O'Connell and then burst out laughing, "I didn't know police Majors were so funny, I'm gonna have to start paling around with you."

The truck moved past St. Anthony of Padua Church and continued east on Meremac passing by the 3-block long, northern perimeter cast-iron topped stonewall fence that defined the boundaries of the 18-acre Maryville College for Catholic Women. As the truck approached the corner of Meremac and Nebraska on the southeast edge of the campus, Carmine made a hard right through the tall stone pillars with the overarching ornate ironwork that formed the main entrance to the college campus. The truck went up the driveway past the 5-story main building with its commanding center tower and 12-foot gold cross atop its dome's pinnacle. The truck rambled down the road that circled the campus and pulled in and parked behind a small hillock that formed the backside of a rock-walled prayer grotto that contained a statue of *Our Lady Of Fatima* flanked by sheltered banks of votive candles burning on the left and right sides of the Virgin Mother's statue.

"Well, let's get out and have a talk," Carmine said as he turned off the old Ford's engine, "This is a quiet place to come and talk. The votive lights are my gift to the nuns," he said as he opened the back doors and took out a cardboard box and placed it inside a concealed wooden storage bin behind the tiered banks of flickering lights.

"Okay Major O'Connell, let's talk about how can we help each other?" Gagliardi, leaned back on the grotto's rough stonewall and lit up a *Parodi*.

O'Connell led off by thanking him for the meeting and then proceeded through the very same litany of information that Columbo had covered with him a few days earlier. Gagliardi puffed on his dark crooked Italian cigar and asked questions from time to time, never letting on that everything Jeremiah was telling him was something he already knew.

"Major, you are aware of my conditions?"

"Yes, if any of the men in your organization are involved," O'Connell hastened to add, "which we believe is highly unlikely; you will handle the 'discipline.'"

"Is Harrigan in agreement?" Carmine asked.

"Yes, you have my word of honor on it." O'Connell looked him square in the eye.

"Honor and respect are two things we Sicilians prize. We do not pledge our honor casually, and respect is earned by loyalty and maintaining honor in all of one's dealings. I have heard that Jeremiah O'Connell keeps his word," Carmine approved of the man standing before him and extended his hand to shake on the deal.

"You said, *'how can we help each other'* – I have told you how you can help us, how can we help you?" O'Connell asked as he shook the mob leader's hand.

Carmine was impressed, "You are a good listener. I like that. I wish my own men paid as much attention when I talk to them," Carmine laughed. "Here's how you can help me and yourself at the same time. There is a man, a very ambitious and dangerous man that the police need to keep an eye on. His name is John Joseph Vitale, you 'Mick's' know him a little bit because he grew up in the Sicilian section of north St. Louis, not too far from your own Kerry Patch. 'Johnny V' is now a 22-year old punk, a low level thief, but he has big plans and he is becoming a problem for me and my north side associates, especially my young cousin, Mikey Palazzolo. As respectable businessmen, we'd like to see *"Iron Charlie"* take a special interest in young Mr. Vitale's activities. It would be possible for the department to learn in advance about his criminal activities and then to cause him to become... *ahhh*, what is the word I'm searching for..."

"Arrested," O'Connell volunteered.

"Well, that wasn't the exact word I was thinking of…the word I had in mind was, *deceased*. But I'll settle for *'arrested,'* because if 'Johnny V' goes to Jeff City, I can make sure it's a one way trip," Carmine explained.

"Give me a few days to nose around; I'll call your man Columbo, if I find or hear of anything. You know I like that guy, I hope you appreciate what a fine person he is. He's the future of Italians in St. Louis, law abiding, hard working, smart, educated and running clean businesses. At least that's my dream. C'mon, Major I'll drop you off back at the corner; I trust you can figure out how to get back to Grand and Magnolia from Grand and Meremac."

O'Connell flashed his call box key, "I've got a car standing by to pick me up whenever I call."

Carmine surprised him by kneeling down and lighting a new candle as a traditional prayer request. He said a short prayer, when he rose, he made the sign of the cross and then he put some cash in the offering box "Mind if I ask you what you prayed for when you lit the candle?" O'Connell asked.

"I was praying for *'deceased'* instead of *'arrested,'*" Carmine laughed.

KIRTSCHNER'S JOURNAL ENTRY: 1H

Harrigan's idyllic life had turned in to a nightmarish hell as events had gathered like an unpredicted storm that were about to swamp his boat. The elites of the City outraged by the Devereaux killing and spurred on by EOR were beating on the Mayor, the Mayor passed the pressure down the line to the Chief of Police and he channeled the torrent of anger directly into *Iron Charlie's* lap.

True to his word, Harrigan had turned into a devil from the 4th level of hell and he was prodding, poking and scorching the asses of every detective in the bureau on a daily if not hourly basis. Then the Brenahanny mess blew up, and Harrigan finds himself tidying up after his cousin's loss of all judgment and sanity. Even the normally docile press had suddenly grown a set of shiny new brass balls in light of all the public mayhem and thanks to the circulation war the *Star* had kicked off.

It was a bloody mess all the way around, with no sign of any relief in sight. He sat in his office contemplating his next moves and wondering how it could get any worse when his phone rang.

"Harrigan, what is it," he snapped.

"This is Gordon Alcott. We have a complicated situation developing over here and we need to meet with you right away," the managing editor's voice was cold and somber.

"At the *Star*?" Harrigan clarified.

"Yes, just as soon as you can get here, come straightaway to my conference room," Alcott replied.

Harrigan hung up and headed out the door, as he left he called, "Schu I'm heading over to the *Star*, something's come up." That announcement caused rivulets of sweat to run down the middle of Emil Schumacher's back and an ominous queasy feeling gripped the pit of his stomach. Was he about to be ratted out?

Alcott and Dexter briefed Harrigan on the news Fred Kirtschner had blurted out just a few hours before. Harrigan sat back with his hands in his pockets and said, "Well gentlemen, what do you plan to do with that news?"

"Actually, here's how we propose that *you* plan to handle the news," Dexter commented. Harrigan looked puzzled at the suggestion.

"Here's how we see it working, Our story will be that after consulting with the Chief of Detectives, who is managing the case, we will agree to sit on the news in a total press embargo, so as not to jeopardize your ongoing police investigation," Alcott began, "With the killer or killers still at large, we believe that you are right in your contention that revealing the identity of '*Madame X*' at this time may cause the perpetrator or perpetrators to flee this jurisdiction."

"Will Kirtschner go along with it?" Harrigan asked.

"Fred is in a very fragile and emotionally and physically exhausted state right now, I suspect he's near madness with shock and grief. He would like to protect his sister's reputation and spare his family any embarrassment. I have spoken to him about the arrangements, and if you will help us accomplish them, he will abide by our wishes," Alcott stressed, "But, he has a few conditions."

"What does he want?" Harrigan asked as he lit up a cigar.

"First of all, his sister is not expected back at work for a few days. We propose to have a wire sent to her boss from Hot Springs, Arkansas announcing her resignation. Her boss thinks she's having a honeymoon rehearsal, so she'll probably think she's just run off with her lover.

"Next, we will never run the drawing of her again. So far, we've had over 400 phone calls come in from people who think they know who she is. We will turn those names over to you and your men can go through the motions of checking out the leads.

"Fred and his late sister were not terribly close and there are no other immediate family members living here in St. Louis. Fred has agreed to let us, the *Star* that is, assist in her private internment in Calvary under her own name, Mary Elizabeth Kirtschner.

Alcott continued, "We'll need your assistance to have a substitute 'Madame X' cremated in order to pass Fred's sister's body over to a friendly embalmer like Finan or Donnelly. After the recent accidental cremation of Matt Brenahanny, I wouldn't suspect that it would be hard to accomplish another 'accident'," Alcott arched his eyebrow.

"So far I have heard nothing impossible, please continue," Harrigan said as he sat in phlegmatic silence, completely devoid of any expression.

"Here comes the hard part," Dexter interjected.

"Let's hear it," Harrigan took a long draw on his cigar and blew a thick lazy smoke ring across the table.

Alcott said, "If we don't do what he's asking, I'm afraid he might go off the deep end." Harrigan leaned in and gestured with his fingers and open palms for Alcott to give him the rest of the conditions.

"Fred wants to follow the story through to the bitter end. He wants to be inside the squad with Joe Culhane every hour until the killer or killers are found. He wants to be there when they are apprehended and he wants to ultimately see justice done," Alcott finished.

Dexter chimed in, "We can take him off the front page assignment and give him this as a special assignment with no daily duties here and no writing assignments of any kind. If you can manage to give him the appearance of working alongside the squad, no one will get embarrassed, not the late sister, not Fred, not the police and not the *Star*. His deal with us is simple, in return, he and we and the police will all agree to forever keep the true identity of *'Madame X'* secret even throughout any criminal trial or public proceedings. As far as anyone would know, she would have only a *'Jane Doe'* identity in the official records. Her official cremation would close the case on her identity forever.

"I have convinced Kirtschner that this is all within the realm of possibility ***with your help.*** I think it is obvious to you, to us and even to Fred that his sister was not the target. She was just in the wrong place at the wrong time. So, if you make the case against Pierre Devereaux's killers, there will be no reason to drag her name and her reputation into the limelight and through the mud. Fred's very adamant about protecting her reputation and identity," Alcott shrugged.

"And, his own good name to boot," Harrigan rubbed his chin and said, "If I could make all that happen, I'd need to have the *Star* do a few things to accommodate my agenda."

"Name them," Alcott urged.

"First of all, Fred Kirtschner will have to sign a legal document that I will have drafted to indemnify me and my men and the entire department and to expressly forbid any reporting of events that he may witness. If he ever breaks that covenant and goes public, his sister's identity will be posted on every street corner. And I won't use her First Communion picture; I'll post the photo that shows Pierre's prick in her mouth."

"Next, I want to walk out of here with your cop snitch's name in my pocket.

"And finally, I get six wishes from the *Star* just like the Genie in Aladdin's lamp," Harrigan grinned.

"Aladdin's Genie only granted 3-wishes, he didn't get any for himself," Alcott corrected him.

"You're missing my point dumb fuck," Harrigan laughed, "In my version of the story the Genie gets six fucking magic wishes from the *Star*. And, I get to call in those magic wishes whenever I need 'em, and the *Star* will grant 'em, no questions asked and no ifs, ands or buts about it."

"Now why would we agree to a deal like that? It's far too open ended," the insulted Alcott blustered. Dexter looked at the vein rapidly swelling up on Alcott's neck, in their 20-years of side-by-side association, no one had ever dared to utter a curse word in his presence, much less call Gordon Philpott Alcott a 'dumb fuck.' Dexter was sure he had felt a seismic tremor.

"Well let me explain to you why you'll want to grant me six magic wishes," Harrigan smiled, "If you don't, I'll walk out of here and call the Publisher at the *Post-Dispatch* and tell him the whole sordid story of how the *Star's* lead reporter's sister is *'Madame X'* and how you two fucking geniuses tried to bribe me to cover it up so that the *Star* could continue it's circulation war and you could keep on bribing police officer's for inside information and paying cop snitches to leak official documents and photographs. I would explain how I played along until I had enough solid evidence to take the whole matter to Chief Strickland and then to the public. That would create quite a fuss in the community, don'tcha think? I'll bet by the time your fellow journalists got done with you two fucking chumps that neither one of you could even get a job delivering newspapers," Harrigan played all his trumps.

"You are an unscrupulous, ruthless and cunning son-of-a-bitch, Mr. Harrigan," the red-faced Alcott was completely flustered.

"And those are my good points," *Iron Charlie* stared straight back into Alcott's eyes,

"Now, do we have a deal or don't we? Make up your fucking mind, I haven't got all day."

"We have a deal Mr. Harrigan...a deal with the devil," Alcott and Harrigan shook hands as Arnold Dexter looked on in the stark realization that Harrigan could make him and Alcott and the *Star* dance like puppets on his strings from that day forward.

"I'll have that snitch's name now," Harrigan held out his hand. Alcott scribbled the name on a piece of paper and handed it to Harrigan. The Chief Of Detectives folded it into his pocket without even so much as a fleeting glance.

"Send Kirtschner around to my office at 11:30 a.m. sharp in the morning.

Have a nice day, gentlemen," Harrigan bade farewell.

"Well Gordon that went extremely well," Dext said cynically.

The normally unflappable Alcott stared sputtering and red-faced at Arnold Dexter. Then he calmly got up from the conference room table and walked into his office slamming the heavy oak door full force behind him. From the inner recesses of the Managing Editor's office the entire floor heard an earsplitting, *"Fuuuuuuuuuuuuuck!"*

Harrigan got on the down elevator whistling the *Gary Owen.*

Ahhh, things were looking up after all.

———

XXXVIII

The research department at WebKSDK was on the 5th floor of the *Yahoogle* building at 10th and Market, its tall windows overlook the block-wide green space parkway that runs through the middle of downtown from the eastside of the Old Federal Courts building for four long blocks down to the Old Courthouse where the Dred Scott decision was handed down before the Civil War. The parkway immediately across the street is the site of the rusted Serra Sculpture, Emily Pulitzer's controversial artistic gift to the City. In recent years, sculptures by local artist and Mickey Mouse memorabilia collector of international renown, Ernest Trova also dotted spaces in the winding paths throughout the parkway. The local citizen's referred to the eclectic outdoor art collection as "The Travesties and Trovasties."

When Mac arrived at work, she had a list of tasks for "Liz the Lez" Leonard to work on."Liz, can you do a deep dive on the archival information in this list for me?" Mac asked politely.

"By when?" Liz whined.

"How about by the end of the day, I'm on a deadline," Mac cajoled.

"Sure, why not, I was just sitting here working my fourth sudoku of the day and sipping on a Starbucks, *I have absolutely nothing else to do*," Liz said sarcastically as she gestured in a sweeping motion over a desk piled high with papers and reference materials waiting for pick-up by the sports, news, media sales and community relations staff.

"This is going to cut into my midmorning naptime you know," Liz replied cynically, "Lemme see the list. But let me warn you, *honey lamb*, I'm into archive retrieval...not archeological digging." Then Liz looked over the list, sighing audibly as she read.

Need Biographies and newspaper clippings for period 1920 to 1960 on:

Chief of Detectives Charles M. Harrigan	Carmine Gagliardi
Eamon Oscar Robertson	Ada Robertson Devereaux
Pierre Laclede Devereaux	Major Jeremiah O'Connell
Frederick Washington	Thomas Edward Culhane
Fred Kirtschner	Gordon P. Alcott
Arnold Dexter	Dennis Brenahanny
Robert Emmett Hannegan	Madame X

Please keyword search **all** newspaper files from 1920 to 1960.

Liz looked up and said, "Sure, I can have this finished by the end of the day...the end of the day three days after I retire... and I'm only 43.'

Mac bit her tongue, she knew for a fact the old dyke had shaved off at least 10 years.

"Mac, this is a lot of work. And most of it is not digitally archived, of that I'm sure. In all likelihood, I could spend the better part of a week on this and still come up virtually empty. Our files here and the ones over in the Main Library, Missouri Historical Society and at the three Universities and in City Hall records that are available for on-line searching through *Yahoogle* tend to be from 1960 forward. Nobody has spent time digitizing the old newspaper files from before that era. Especially the files of newspapers that went under before the *Globe-Democrat* and *The Post-Dispatch* reached the JOA. Frankly, you'd be better off going over the *The Mercantile Library* and looking through their old microfiche files. We are a member of *The Merc*, and they have research assistants who will look up any file for you for about $25 to $30 a file. If you give me a departmental charge number or a job P.O., I can set it up for you," Liz promised.

"Great, here's my budget ID number, just swipe it into the system and put a rush on this if you will, I'd really appreciate it." Mac was happy to get things moving. When she returned to her office, a message was waiting in her VM.

"Hi Mac, it's Chip. I'm sorry I missed you, but here's the reason for my call. I'd like to invite you to dinner on next Friday. I know you work the late news, and I'm not sure what time you get off work. But I'm flexible, I hope you'll accept my offer, but if Friday doesn't work for you, let me know when you would be available. Assuming, of course, that you are interested in going out. If you're not interested, I'll understand. I'm going out on an assignment now, so I'll be out of touch. If you're good to go email me at either one of these addresses: CMHIV@stlpd.org or CMHIV@yahoogle.com."

Mac was about to hang up when she heard the rest of Chip's message.

"If I don't hear from you I'll jump off the Bill Clinton Bridge and then you'll have to cover the story of the despondent detective driven to death dive in dating despair by news diva. How's that for alliteration. Please email me and save my life. Bye-bye!"

Mac emailed him immediately.

Friday is great for me! My tiny, cute, petite fanny will clear the door at 11:30 pm. Let's have a late dinner or an early breakfast. I'm off all day Saturday, how about you? Call me when you get a chance. Mac

Mac worked through the day keeping her appointments, attending the news staff meeting and then prepared for the 6pm news, the 8pm update and the 10pm evening news. When she returned to her office she was surprised to see her desk, chair and floor covered with the plastic interoffice mail baskets overflowing with stacks of envelopes from *The Mercantile Library*. St. Louis's venerable, members-only privately-operated commercial library had certainly lived up to his reputation as the definitive source of in-depth information from the halcyon days of 19th and early 20th St. Louis.

Each envelope was neatly labeled with the names she had provided to Liz, with an additional notation on the source of the material inside. On top was the copy of an invoice carefully enumerating each file and the name of the publication from whence it came. The invoice total was: $1710.00 to copy 57 individual files plus $55.00 delivery, plus $342.00 (20% same day rush charge). Grand Total: $2107.00.

"Holy Shit!" Mac exclaimed, "I'm screwed when this bill hits Etzkorn's desk."

Bob "Scrooge McEtzkorn" Etzkorn was the penurious WebKSDK News Director, and he was the cheapest man who ever walked in shoe leather, with the possible exception of the legendary skinflint Bob Wayland the longtime CBS O&O executive, who actually deducted money from his news staff's paychecks for coffee, pens and pencils.

Mac rehearsed her speech, "Etz, my instincts on this story are right... there is a great special feature series in this century old murder. You know what an incestuous village St. Louis is. You know how fascinated people are with St. Louis family scandals. I think that it can be a big audience building promotion that we could run during ratings sweep."

Then she envisioned Etzkorn's beady little eyes and how they would squint in reaction to the bill and her rationale for incurring the cost, and then she knew that her initial instincts were right. *"I'm screwed when this bill hits Etzkorn's desk."*

She buzzed Studio Tech Services and asked if some of the IATSE crew could come up and help her with a personal favor. The cameramen and stage hands were all her buddies and she had built a warm personal relationship with each one of them on a firm foundation of home-baked chocolate-chip cookies and her famous triple-lemon layered birthday cakes, so calling in a favor to help her get the files down to her car would not be an issue.

A few minutes later, she pointed her loaded car due west, its back seat, front seat and trunk filled with *'The Merc'* files. She looked at the reflection of the heap of documents in the backseat in her rearview mirror and thought, *"I'm totally screwed when this bill hits Etzkorn's desk. Totally!"*

"News gods don't fail me now!" she prayed aloud.

KIRTSCHNER'S JOURNAL ENTRY: 1H/2H

Fred Washington had been busy cleaning up the mess surrounding the Brenahanny killings. The old panel truck had been cut up and scrapped in the Fitzsimmons' garage and the parts already melted down at Granite City Steel. The weapons were disassembled and tossed into the Mississippi north of Chain of Rocks and each man on the 'wrecking crew' was given $1000.00 for living expenses and to buy a train ticket out of town to points unknown with specific orders to get lost and stay lost until the word came down that it was safe to return. Each man carried a different phone number that he was to call every Sunday morning to check in.

Just when things had begun to calm down for him, Fred got the call from Harrigan, *"Mr. Fred,"* Harrigan played his *faux* respect card, "We need to get together and talk about what you've picked up from the Henderson's and the rest of the colored folks in the neighborhood. My leads are drying up and we need to make sure that no stone is left unturned."

"Where do you want to meet, Mr. Charles?" Fred asked.

"I was thinking breakfast at Miss Hulling's at 7:30 tomorrow. Okay?"

"Can we make it 8:30 am?" Fred asked.

"Sure *7:30 am* will be fine, see you there," Harrigan emphasized as he hung up.

"7:30 a.m., is the middle of the night for me, but sho'nuf Mr. Charles, I can kiss your arrogant white police ass," Fred thought. "7:30 am at Miss Hulling's it is. And knowing that cheap prick I'll end up picking up the check."

Miss Hulling's cafeteria-side opened for breakfast at 6:00 am seven days a week and there was usually a line of regulars waiting for the cashier to throw the latch and open up.

When Fred arrived, *'Iron Charlie'* was already through his third cup of coffee at the corner table with Alderman Cornelius Wenzel. Harrigan saw Fred come in and said, "My man's here Corny, I'll catch up with you later about the ticket mix-up, just tell Billy I'll handle it and not to worry." Harrigan shook hands and crossed the room to meet Fred at the tray station. Even though St. Louis was in the Midwest and not in the deep South, it was still very unusual for a black man to eat in a public dining room like Miss Hulling's that was considered to be a 'white establishment.' As Harrigan greeted Fred, he looked at the cashier and said, "It's all right Leonard, Mr. Washington is with me."

The two men went through the cafeteria line and loaded up on scrambled eggs, sausages, bacon and toast. "Fred," Harrigan whispered, "Would you mind getting this, I'm a little short on C-A-S-H until I can get over to Cass Bank later?"

"No problem, I'm on *The King's* expense account today," Fred counted out the cost.

Paid the cashier, picked up his tray and joined Harrigan in the last high-backed booth where the server had just finished bringing the juice over and pouring their coffee.

The caffeine from his prior meeting with Corny must have kicked in because Harrigan was rattling off comments without so much as a taking a breath, "Thanks for meeting me so early, I appreciate it because after I leave here I've got to update Chief Strickland, then it's down to the morning squad meeting and then I need to drive over to the 7th and brief Jeremiah at lunch on your findings because he's got an interview with the grieving widow this afternoon, her father and his lawyers'll be there too. Have you heard from *The King*," Harrigan asked in a frenetic topic jump?

"Not a word," Fred replied honestly, "I assume he'll wire me when he get's settled in at the *El Presidente*."

"Well Fred what have you got for me? I'm all ears."

"Mr. Charles, it seems that there is a lot of unhappiness going on in that house. Once I got Mr. Henderson loosened up with a little Dewar's he proved to be very informative. It seems that there has been a lot of tension building between the wife and the deceased husband for well-over a year. Apparently it erupted into open fighting about a month ago when the husband moved out of the bedroom he shared with his wife and took up sleeping in the guest room on the third floor. Henderson also reported that there were many nights when he didn't come home at all. His excuse was that he got involved in a poker game and drank too much so he'd stay over at The Racquet Club in one of the guest rooms on the third floor or sleep it off on a daybed down in the basement steam room."

"You said, that was *'his excuse'* what was he really up to?" Harrigan probed.

"Well, apparently he had a love nest somewhere on the south side. Henderson had never driven him there, but he had overheard him talking about it in the car with one of his drinking buddies, but he couldn't remember who it was. Bee also suspects that it was the home of the lady who was killed with him, '*Madame X.*' It seems that Pierre's wife also overheard him calling her from the den and even listened in on phone extension in her bedroom. Henderson told me that his wife, Willie, had walked in on her and was shushed up so her voice wasn't heard by the husband and his lady friend. Henderson said his wife told him that Mrs. Devereaux was so furious after that call that she moved him out of their bedroom that same day.

"Anything else?" Harrigan finished mopping his plate with the last piece of toast and leaned back to enjoy his coffee.

"Plenty more, Henderson said that Pierre and his father-in-law were real thick, lots more so than most folks knew, they are like cattin' around buddies. Seems old EOR has a taste for the young ladies too, especially colored ladies. My associates who talked with other colored help on the '*Easy Streets*' said that some of the men of the neighborhood liked to carry on at a place over on Buckingham, at the residence of one Percy "Perky" Leicester, he's some kind of doctor and by all accounts a playboy with all kinds of connections – female, male, opium, reefer, heroin – he's pretty much a one man *Rexall*. The old man and the late Pierre both liked to avail themselves of his hospitality."

"Hmmm…now isn't that interesting," Harrigan mused.

"Now, I haven't spoken directly to Henderson's wife as yet. Willie has been staying over at the big house since the murder to help with all the extra doings surrounding the funeral and all the visitors calling to pay their respects," Fred concluded.

"*Respects*,' considering the circumstances of Pierre's unscheduled departure to the celestial plane, it's kind of an ironic use of the term isn't it?" Harrigan suggested.

Harrigan was pleased with what Fred had learned thus far. "Good job Fred, this new information throws some fresh light on the case. Keep your ears open and see if you can get Willie or Bee...you know who I mean, *the wife*, to sit down with you and see what else you can learn from her. I suspect she doesn't tell her husband everything. What wife does?"

"That cut's both ways," Fred pointed out, "And, by the by, Bee is the man and Willie is the woman. It's a little confusing."

"Right you are!" Harrigan smiled, "C'mon Fred let's both get off our butts and get to work. I'll bet you have a full day ahead of you too, especially with *The King* in Cuba.

If you do hear from him, please, *gently remind him* about my impending cigar shortage."

Fred Washington reached into his pocket and pulled out a wad of cash.

"No, no, no, here, let me get the tip," Harrigan pulled out a handful of change and then left a dime next to his coffee cup.

"Are you sure you don't need to make change?" Washington joked.

"No, a whole dime is fine," Harrigan said seriously.

Fred thought, *"What a cheap prick."*

KIRTSCHNER'S JOURNAL ENTRY: EW/1H

The morning update with Chief Strickland and the squad meeting both concluded as scheduled and Harrigan had briefed his men on some of the information gleaned from Fred Washington's work. Since there was still no break in the case, he sent them back out once again to shake up the crime community and to look into Perky Leicester's activities. Harrigan was also convinced that sooner or later, the killers would do something stupid; a slip of the tongue when drinking, pawning Devereaux's stolen jewelry or even bragging about getting away with murder. It was just a matter of time…and Harrigan hoped he could catch the killers before time and patience ran out upstairs and over at City Hall.

I arrived at 11:30 a.m. as Alcott and Dext had directed me to. Emil Schumacher, was stunned to see me. I was drawn, gaunt and poorly shaven, the dark circles under my eyes must have made me look like I had not been to bed in a month. My snitch Schu was becoming increasingly nervous as he escorted me to Harrigan's office where I was greeted by *'Iron Charlie'* and invited to have a comfortable seat. Harrigan thanked Schu and asked him to hold all incoming calls unless it was the Mayor, Strickland or O'Connell, then he closed his office door and drew the blinds. All this behind the doors hocus pocus made Schumacher extremely uncomfortable.

"I understand you have a legal document you want me to sign," I began.

Harrigan came over and sat on the edge of his desk and stared coldly into my eyes. "Now listen to me and listen good because I'm only going to say this once. First off, I'm sorry that your sister got killed. It was terrible and I make no judgments about her. Second, you work for two idiots. Third, I know there is a snitch in here who's feeding you inside information. By the way, Mr. Kirtschner do you know that it is a crime to bribe a policeman? I could lock your ass up and sweat you until the snitch's name came out, but I haven't the time or the inclination right now. Fourth, I have a nasty double homicide to solve and if you fuck up my investigation in any way, I promise on all that is holy that I'll personally put a .38 right through your forehead. Are we clear on that?" Harrigan asked.

"Clear as a bell," I replied, "What about the document Dext told me about?"

"Fred how fucking stupid do you think I am to put in writing what I talked with your two moron bosses about? I'd have to have a head full of rocks to do that, and since I don't, we're just going to let them think you signed an indemnification document,' Harrigan answered, "Fred, I'm your best chance of catching your sister's killers and believe me I want those son-of-a-bitches just as bad as you do. For me it's professional for you it's personal, I get that. And I can't blame you for wanting to be fully in the hunt. I'd want the same thing if they'd have killed my sister. But, here's our solemn covenant, you can come along and be with me and Joe on one condition. *You can never report anything about me and my men, I expressly forbid any reporting of events about this case that you may witness or otherwise learn of.* If you ever break that covenant, it will be the last living act you will make on this earth. Are we clear on that?" Harrigan asked.

I nodded in agreement, "I won't be any trouble at all and anything I can do to help...*anything*...I will do it. You can count on me. I give you my solemn word on it," I promised.

"You're also going to hear some dirty and ugly things said about your late sister, just remember no personal offense is intended because none of the men will know her real identity and relationship to you. It's just the way frustrated and angry men will talk. You will have to maintain your objective composure, emotional detachment and poise at all times. If I see you so much as flinch, waffle or waiver, our deal is over on the spot and I will call an immediate press conference that will sink your sister's reputation, your own career, Alcott's, Arnold's and possibly the *Star* itself. This is not a threat; this is exactly what will happen if anyone fucks with me or my investigation. Are we clear on that?"

I nodded in concurrence.

"As of this moment, no one knows the true identity of 'Madame X' besides me, Alcott, Arnold and you...and as far as I'm concerned that's three people too many. There is one more I'll have to bring into the circle and that's Jeremiah O'Connell, you'll meet him at lunch today," Harrigan asked, "Do you have any questions?"

"None," I said .

"Then let's go meet Major O'Connell for lunch and I'll catch you both up on everything I know at the same time," Harrigan paused, "Are you packing a gun?"

"No, I don't even own one," I replied.

"Good, keep it that way, I don't want you getting any *'revenge'* notions rolling around in your skull. This is 100% my show, leave the law enforcement to me, are we clear on that?" Harrigan asked.

I had enough badgering. "Look, I said I was clear about three times, let's get past my reliability and get back to finding the killers," I said as I extended my hand, "We have a deal, I won't break my promise. Do whatever you have to do, I don't care what it takes. I just want to see justice done for her sake."

Harrigan shook my hand and said, "Good, then we'll speak no more of this – but, never tell Joe Culhane about our covenant or *'Madame X's'* true identity. He cannot keep a confidence and he is a man of somewhat – *shall we say* - diminished intellectual capacity. Trust me on that."

———————

The Pelican was not too crowded when Harrigan and I arrived. Harrigan led me through the main dining room and then up the side stairs to the 2nd floor where Jeremiah was waiting in a small private dining room with the plaque on the door that read *Pier 43*. *The Pelican* was a landmark on the corner of Grand and Shenandoah and just a few blocks north of the 7th at Grand and Magnolia. Harrigan and Jeremiah often met here, either as a duo or with *The King,* who lived just a block to the north on Hawthorne.

After Harrigan introduced me to O'Connell, he asked, "Have you ever had the turtle soup here? It is fantastic and it is rumored that they still serve it with a shot of sherry for their best customers." I said I had not tried the legendary Pelican house specialty so Harrigan ordered a full tureen and three bowls for the group. Then, he dove right into the details and brought Jeremiah completely up to speed. O'Connell was understandably shocked at the news about my sister and he expressed his condolences to me in a most gracious and gentlemanly manner. Harrigan's news about the inside shenanigans Fred Washington uncovered through the negroes working at the Devereaux house and the friction between the husband and wife was a logical jumping off point for O'Connell who started by sharing the theatrical clipping with Fred and Charles Michael. He aired his suspicions about the sincerity of the tears shed by the widow Devereaux, and the news from Fred Washington only added to his mounting suspicion level. Then he told me and Harrigan about the bizarre meeting with Carmine Gagliardi and his *quid pro quo* request that Harrigan take a special interest in one Mr. Johnny Vitale. The conversation continued for nearly 90 minutes over lunch.

"At 4:00 pm I'm meeting with Mrs.Devereaux, her father and an attorney named Jonathon McCall. I've heard he is a very shrewd attorney. I plan to be very careful because of all the concerns the Chief and the Mayor have," O'Connell stated, "As Charles Michael and I have agreed, my role is to be the 'good cop.' His role is to be himself."

Harrigan arched his eyebrow and said, "I'll take that as a complement, Jeremiah. But you'll still need to ask her some probing questions. See how much she'll open up or if the lawyer tries to keep her from talking. If the lawyer and her father try to prevent you from getting information to aid in the investigation, that won't jibe too well with EOR's public outcry for a solution to the case. If the family clams up, I think we'll have hit a raw nerve."

O'Connell outlined his questions and the group refined and added to the list. Ironically, I was very helpful because of my skill as a reporter. I knew how to ask a seemingly innocent question that could come at an issue in an unexpected and often oblique way that had the effect of throwing the interviewed person into an unguarded stream of consciousness conversation where surprising tidbits of information often spilled out.

O'Connell was quick to pick up on the value of this technique.

Harrigan allowed as how he and I were going to visit his late sister's home at 4645 Tennessee Avenue after lunch to see if they could uncover any connections to Pierre Devereaux there. After that Harrigan and I would meet with Fr. Jimmy Johnson at Finan's Funeral Parlor to make the final arrangements to inter my murdered sister.

It all been arranged for a private ceremony at Calvary.

"Any news on the Brenahanny case," Jeremiah asked, "I heard from the Battalion Chief Bingham that arson was suspected."

'All I know is *nothing*" Harrigan answered, "The Fire Department is still digging through all the wet smoldering debris, brick walls and the slate roof that collapsed into the cellar. So far as I know, no Brenahanny has reappeared. The whole family, except for the son who was killed in the botched burglary, has simply vanished in a puff of smoke."

Jeremiah speculated, "Or in a blazing inferno." Harrigan just shrugged his shoulders.

"Good luck in your interview, let's talk tonight or in the morning before the briefing.

Fred and I are going to head over to his sister's home and see what we can find there," Harrigan got up from the table and made his good byes.

As they drove off in opposite directions, Jeremiah, me and Charles Michael all wondered what secrets would be learned at the mansion on Washington Terrace and in the modest bungalow on Tennessee Avenue.

If only the walls could talk.

———◆———

KIRTSCHNER'S JOURNAL ENTRY: 1H/HS

Lou Columbo was finishing off his lunch when the telephone rang, "Luigi, I may have something for your friend O'Connell." It was Carmine.

"Yes sir, what is it?"

"It might be nothing and it might be something, Anyway, in checking around, I found out that one of my best waiters, Mario Rizzo has not been into work in about a week. That is very unusual, because Mario is very reliable, even the kinda guy who comes in early and stays late. He's always looking for more hours. Carlo my manager thought he must be very sick, but when he called to see how he was doing, Mario told him that he was quitting his job and moving to Florida to go into a business with his brother Sal. Now that doesn't ring true to me, because Salvatore is a punk and a two-bit horse-player, and a poor one at that. When I checked with our book, I found out that Sal had been laying off some pretty heavy bets lately, losing as usual, but paying off in cash with no problems. *That's not the Sal we know.* Neither one of these guys has the sense to come in out of the rain, so how are they going to afford to move to Florida, open up and run a business? And where is the money coming from? Savings on a waiter's salary and tips? Did Sal have a lucky streak at *Fairmont?* Not in our book. Look into it, like I said, 'it might be nothing and it might be something."

"Thank you Mr. Gagliardi, I'll look into it right away. Goodbye sir."

"Ciao Luigi, take care of yourself," *The Big Dago* hung up.

A few minutes later Eamon O'Meara, Joe Culhane and Mickey Finnegan came through the squad room doors with big self-satisfied grins on their mugs. "Hey Pisano, we got a tip from the Christ-killing Jews up at Levine's that we need to run by you," Culhane called across the room.

The Levine Hat Company on Washington Avenue was located in the heart of the bustling St. Louis shoe and garment district and was famous for their fine hats and the famous *"Sixth Street Roll,"* the distinctive deep brim pressing that was very popular in certain crime circles. Every Levine Hat from the prestigious banker's Hamburg, to summer straw skimmers and hats for businessmen and union leaders all came with a small hat owner's identification card inside each Levine headband.

The card read: **LIKE HELL IT'S YOURS!** The owner's name appeared immediately below and it saved a lot of arguments and more than one man's life in a dark 'speak' where all hats on a hook look alike after a few drinks.

"Whaddya need," Columbo asked?

"Listen to this, Solly Abrams, our favorite little Hebrew pal up at Levine told us that two of your *Eye*talian countrymen came in yesterday and bought 7 hats a piece, that's 14 fucking hats, and that these gentlemen were also wearing new $50 suits and brand new Allen Edmund shoes," Finn reported, "We wondered if you might know these prosperous lads."

"Wait a minute! Don't tell me their names, let me see if I can read your minds," Columbo put his palms up and closed his eyes, stretched out his arms and slowly rotated his extended hands in small circles, "Wait, wait, *shhhh...shhh*...yes it's coming through...I'm getting two names...I'm getting the names...*Sal and Mario*...yes, it's Sal and Mario Rizzo," Columbo exclaimed as he snapped his eyes open to see the shocked looks of disbelief on the faces of his *Welcoming Committee* pals.

"How did you do that?" Finn asked.

"Yeah?" was all the dumbstruck Mickey could muster.

"I used my Machiavellian powers," Columbo laughed.

"Mike E. Vellian is a guy that lives in Italy, he knows everything," Joe Culhane confidently explained to the confused Mickey and Finn, "I know all about him."

"Hey Schu, where's the Chief," O'Meara asked?

Emil didn't look up from his paperwork, "I think he went to the 7th to meet with Jeremiah and he took Culhane's little newspaper buddy with him."

"Kirtschner?" Culhane asked.

"That's the one," Schu replied.

Finn asked, "Louie, should we call the Chief now or wait 'til tomorrow?"

Columbo thought for a moment, "Let me make a few discreet inquiries, then we can find out where the Rizzos are and what they've been up to in addition to shopping, I don't think we can arrest them for buying hats. Why don't we fan out and make some very quiet inquiries about these lads, but I really mean very quiet inquiries, no strong arm stuff. If they are the killers and they get wind of us, they might take it on the lam before we can pull together a case on them. Let's move fast and then tomorrow at the squad meeting we can give Harrigan a more complete picture. Does that make sense to youse?"

O'Meara, Culhane and Mickey all agreed. "Louie, I'll go with you," Joe volunteered, "I'd like to learn some more of them Mike E. Vellian techniques. The way I see it, being able to read minds could come in pretty handy."

"Some minds are easier than others Joe," Columbo said dryly.

———

KIRTSCHNER'S JOURNAL ENTRY: 1H/2H

Major O'Connell arrived punctually and was greeted by Willie Henderson and escorted to the library where EOR, McCall and Mrs. Devereaux were waiting. "Care for some refreshment, Major?" Ada inquired as she greeted her guest; she was impeccably attired as a widow in mourning, wearing an elegant floor length black dress with a flowing train and intricate black bead work on its bodice and long sleeves.

"I've just come from a late lunch, so I'm fine, M'am. Good day Mr. Robertson and you must be Mr. McCall; I'm pleased to make your acquaintance."

"Likewise Major, your reputation has preceded you," McCall replied as they shook hands.

"Willie, please bring us all some tea and bring a setting for the Major too should he change his mind. Please Major O'Connell, won't you make yourself comfortable. I'm sorry that this meeting was delayed, but I needed time alone to absorb the shock of everything that happened," Ada spoke softly in almost a whispered voice.

Jeremiah spoke in a soft measured tone in his finest diplomatic style, "That's quite understandable M'am and the department appreciates you meeting with me today. My purpose here is to help advance the investigation by interviewing you first and then in short order, we'll interview the rest of the family and the house staff. Another group has already interviewed the staff at Mr. Devereaux's office and we are trying to be as discreet and yet as thorough as possible because of the serious nature and the brutality of the crime. As long as the killer or killers remain at large, all citizens are in potential danger.

O'Connell continued, "I'm glad you have legal counsel present, which is always advisable. I am hoping, however, that you will be completely candid and open with me and fully answer every question. Arguably, some of the questions will be difficult and perhaps even painful, but they must be asked. I also want you to know that I take no pleasure in the asking and will try to be as concise and considerate as humanly possible."

"I appreciate that," Ada said, "Shall we begin?"

"Not quite," O'Connell turned to EOR who had been seated quietly on the couch, "Mr. Robertson, I can appreciate you wanting to be here to support your daughter, however, my questions will also involve matters of privacy between a husband and a wife, and the presence of the father may inhibit Mrs. Devereaux's responses. Mr. McCall can remain because he's kind of like a priest in the confessional, his client relationship with Mrs. Devereaux is privileged, so he can be here to represent her and she can speak freely in front of him knowing full well that he will protect the confidentiality of what is said."

EOR, leaned forward in indignation and said, "Are you telling me to leave?"

"No sir, I'm *asking you* to make my job here and your daughter's ability to speak freely easier by removing your presence during the questioning. I can't tell you to leave, but I'm asking you, as politely and as reasonably as I know how, to let me speak privately to Mrs. Devereaux only in the presence of her counsel," Jeremiah stressed firmly but politely.

"It's a reasonable request, Edmund," McCall commented, "If Ada is in agreement."

"Daddy I'll be fine," she leaned over and kissed her father's cheek and patted his hand.

He didn't like it one bit, but EOR reluctantly complied and left the library, "Jonathon, call me back in as soon as this is finished," he glared at O'Connell as he passed by.

"Thank you Mrs. Devereaux, I appreciate the confidence," Jeremiah said.

"I actually think it will be easier on Daddy if he doesn't have to sit here and listen," Ada agreed, "Shall we begin now?"

"Yes M'am. Can you describe your relationship with your husband?"

"Well," she sighed, "Ours was not a perfect marriage, although to all outside appearances, we both tried to make it seem so. We had our ups and downs like most couples, but Pierre also had a *grande* weakness. He had all the Gallic passions for *liberte, fraternite, equalite*...plus *l'amour*. He was always an attentive and loving husband, but he was still French to the core of his male essence and he loved the chase. He was a hopeless flirt and seducer. I put up with his dalliances because I knew that they were just that, dalliances, trivial meaningless affairs. They meant nothing to him. I was the love of his life and I believed, right or wrong, that he would outgrow his innate drives in time."

"Thank you for being so forthcoming," Jeremiah continued, "You have no children from the union. Is that correct?"

"Sadly no," she wiped her eyes, "We had conceived a son, but I lost him. I miscarried in my 6th month. That was about 4-months ago, since then Pierre and I had been trying, but conceiving again has proved difficult for me."

"I understand, my wife Kathleen and I lost two unborns of our own before she was able to carry one to term. Now we have three, all healthy thank God," he said empathetically. Ada smiled and nodded in acknowledgement. Jeremiah continued, "This is the drawing of the woman who was killed too, do you recognize her?"

"No, I have no idea who the so-called *'Madame X'* is, and I've studied her picture for hours, not so much looking to see if I could place her face, but to try to understand what attracted Pierre to her. When a wife comes face-to-face with the 'other woman,' she feels, or at least I felt, a sense of anger and inadequacy. What was wrong with me? How did I let Pierre down? What could she do for him that he could not find in our bed? I know it sounds crass and vulgar, but satisfying her husband's needs is something that defines a wife's sense of self-worth and esteem as a lover and life partner. It's all wrapped up together, at least it is for me. It makes you question your worth as a woman and a wife to some degree. Even now as I see this sketch, I have mixed emotions, I don't hate her, I'm sorry she was killed, but I also wonder what she and Pierre had said to each other. What were their last words and thoughts? It's all so sad...so tragic," Ada replied.

"Was there anything special about your husband's wedding ring?"

"No, it was just a plain gold band. It was simple and tasteful and 18k gold, if I recall."

"What about his cufflinks and stick pin?"

'Those were quite unique, one-of-a-kind, I gave them to Pierre last Christmas. I commissioned them at Elleard B. Heffern. I had them custom made in 18k white gold and platinum. The cufflinks had his monogram on them and featured a small diamond inset in a recessed gold star etching, each diamond was about a 1/4 carat I think, and the stickpin was a full carat in a platinum and white gold setting. Have they been recovered," Ada asked?

"No, the killers took them and his suit coat, which we are assuming contained his wallet. The woman also had no purse with her, so it looks like the killers grabbed what they could and ran," O'Connell theorized.

"It must have been a robbery, Pierre would have put up a fuss, he was feisty…that's probably when the shooting started," Ada speculated.

"Perhaps, it's one of the avenues we're pursuing. Did your husband have any other vices? Gambling, opium, heroin or anything, was he an alcoholic?"

"No, Pierre was very physically fit, he played squash with Daddy once – sometimes twice a week, he loved fly fishing, played polo and loved to duck and deer hunt out at *The Wings*."

"*The Wings?*" O'Connell was puzzled.

"*The Wings of St. Denis*, it's our family farm and hunting lodge in St. Denis, its out near Pond and Labadie. Daddy built a home out there about three years ago, he plans to retire there some day, but in the meantime it's our hunting retreat," Ada explained.

"Sounds beautiful. This is a hard question, but I have to ask it," Jeremiah said.

"Go ahead Major, I have no secrets."

"Do you or any others stand to gain financially from Mr. Devereaux's death?"

"Yes, I will inherit all of Pierre's property and assets, Jonathon how much is that," she asked?

"In round numbers, about $4.5 million, give or take $100,000.00," the attorney replied.

"Any insurance?"

"Yes, Mr. Devereaux had two policies on his life, one for $500,000 and one for $1,000,000. The beneficiary on the first policy is Mrs. Devereaux and the beneficiary on the second policy is Continental Shoe, it is designed to allow the company to repurchase Mr. Devereaux's stock in the event of his death," McCall noted.

"When were these policies issued? *Approximately* will do, if you don't have the precise dates with you," Jeremiah said.

McCall answered, "The company policy was underwritten in 1929 and the policy for Ada was taken out by Mr. Devereaux in 1927, I believe, but, I'll have to check to be sure. That second policy also has an accidental death rider, that boosts the death benefit disbursement to $1,000,000, but it remains to be seen if the policy issuer, *Mutual of New England,* will consider the circumstances of his death to be 'accidental.' We may have to file suit to press the issue once all the circumstances surrounding the murders are determined."

"Mrs. Devereaux is there anyone you can think of who might have had a motive to kill your husband?"

"No, Pierre had his faults, but he was very likeable and I can't think of anyone who would want to kill him," She wiped the tears that had welled up in her eyes.

"This is my last question, were you and Mr. Devereaux living together as husband and wife at the time of his death?"

She burst into tears, "I'm sorry to say that Pierre and I had a fight and that I asked him to move in to the guest room just few days before he was killed. I feel terrible about it. It was all so stupid. We were fighting over household expenses, Pierre was angry that I had bought a new silver service from *Mermod, Jaccard and King.* He blew up at me and I lost my temper and told him I was sick of his financial excesses with his friends, playing poker to all hours at The Racquet Club and losing God only knows how much money. It was all so stupid and it was my entire fault for withdrawing my comfort and affection from him," she said as she lowered her head and wiped her eyes.

"He died without me ever holding him in my arms again," she lowered her head deeper into her hands and sobbed softly.

"Major, *please*...I think Mrs. Devereaux has been more than co-operative," McCall implored.

Jeremiah thanked them for the time, apologized to Mrs. Devereaux for having to ask the painful questions and then took his leave from her home. As he walked toward the car, he said to himself, *"She's clever...and she's lying."*

———

KIRTSCHNER'S JOURNAL ENTRY: EW/1H/2H/OF

I led Harrigan through the narrow gangway that separated the houses on Tennessee Avenue. I opened the backyard gate and walked toward the detached garage on the alley. "My sister keeps a spare door key over the garage door in case she gets locked out or if I need to get in when she's away." I reached over the inside garage door jamb and felt along it until I found the key on the small key chain with the brass fob. "Here it is."

A few moments later we opened the back door and entered the kitchen. The square brick one-story bungalow was typical of the look-alike or cookie-cutter homes in the neighborhood. Walking from back to front there was the kitchen, then a long rifle-shot hall leading to a tiny front foyer with an upright piano and a small coat closet. Off the hall on the right side was the large bedroom. Further up the hall was the bathroom, the basement door was opposite the bathroom door on the left side, then a small left-hall bedroom was situated across from a small dining room and the connected living room. The front of the home had a small brick porch made of white stone steps and trimmed in a band white tiles about three feet high that defined the porch and the *fascia* of the house above the white foundation stones and the red brick that went all the way up to the roofline. The white tile border ran across the porch and around the corners of the front of the house, for a distance of about two feet into each of the gangways. A decorative white tile motif in the shape of diamonds accented the roof line just below the copper gutters.

It was a neat and tidy home with a small front lawn between the house and the sidewalk then another patch of lawn between the sidewalk and the stone curb that edged the brick paved street.

At first every thing looked normal, then I said, "Someone's been here since Mary Elizabeth was killed."

"How can you be sure of that?" Harrigan asked.

"I know my sister, she was one of those 'a place for everything and everything in its place' people. She would never have left her dresser looking like this. I pointed to the open jewelry box with its contents spilling out and to the empty *Tiffany* ring box on the dresser surface.

"She could not afford anything but costume jewelry, so where did the *Tiffany* ring box come from? Was the ring on her finger the night she died?

Harrigan speculated, "It came from Devereaux, I'll bet." Harrigan looked around and opened the closet door, the clothes had all been pushed to one side and the top shelf was in disarray with hat boxes open and lids on the floor of the closet. "Looks like somebody was in here too...looking for a stash of cash or more loot maybe," he said.

Harrigan and I checked the rest of the house and it had definitely been searched but not vandalized. The burglars, whoever they were, were not in a hurry. I noted that my sister's check ledger was missing from the secretary in the living room. The thieves took only a few things that were easy to carry and easy to turn into cash.

After about a half hour, we locked up and left by the back door, as we went back through the gangway out to the front of the house, we were greeted by a man with a double-barreled shotgun.

"Just stop right where you are and put your hands up. There's no use in running this time, 'cause I've got my gun with me and I know how to use it. I've already called the police and they'll be here any minute."

"Mister, let me identify myself, I'm Chief of Detectives Charles Harrigan and this is Mister Fred Kirtschner the brother of the lady who lives here," Harrigan started to reach for his badge.

"Put your hand up pal or I'll blow a hole in you so help me God."

Harrigan put his hand back up and stood still. About five minutes later two cars from the Carondolet District arrived and made their way through the crowd of neighbors that had gathered. Sergeant Kevin Kelly was first to see Harrigan with his hands up, *"Holy Jesus! What have we here?"*

"Kelly will you tell this fuckin' moron who I am!" Harrigan was hot.

"Put your gun down sir, I'm afraid you just made a citizen's arrest on the Chief Of Detectives of the City Of St. Louis," Kelly placed his hands on the shotgun barrel and lowered it away from Harrigan.

"I'm sorry, I thought it was the guys that I chased off the other night. I'm sorry, I was just looking out for Mary's place while she was on vacation. I'm Lester Lawrence and I live right next door."

Harrigan, with surprising composure said, "No troubles Mr. Lawrence, but tell me about the guys you ran off the other night."

"Well it was dark when I saw them come out of Mary's back yard. I was pulling my car in the garage when they came out of her back gate into the alley. They had a car parked behind her garage. I yelled, "Hey! Who are you and what are you doing over there."

Before I could get over there, the two Dagos were in the car and lickety-split off down the alley without even turning on their headlights," Lawrence said as he slapped his hands.

"Did you see the license plate," Harrigan asked, "And what makes you think they were Wops?"

"No, it happened pretty fast, but they were Dagos all right, they cussed at me in Italian and broken English, called me some bad names for busting up their plans. I'll bet they were pretty sore. I figured they were gonna break in. But when I checked Mary's place, front and back and cellar doors and all the windas, it was still locked up tight, so they mustn't have got in."

"Did you call the police?" Harrigan asked.

"No sir, I didn't figure there was anything to report except trespassing since nothing was amiss, I just figured it was over, until I looked out my kitchen winda and saw you two inside her house. That's when I grabbed my gun and told Estelle to call the police while I went over and got the drop on you. Am I in trouble?" Lawrence asked.

"No Mr. Lawrence, not this time, but do me a favor, if you ever see anything suspicious over here again, just call the police and leave the law enforcement work to the police professionals. Agreed?"

"Yessir! And thank you sir, I'm awful sorry I pointed my gun at you."

"Not half as sorry as I am," Harrigan said, because he knew the news of this incident would surely beat him back to the Central District. The entire force was going to have a good laugh at his expense.

"C'mon Fred, let's call it a day. Maybe Jeremiah had more luck than we did."

KIRTSCHNER'S JOURNAL ENTRY: 1H/EW/OF

By the time the morning briefing rolled around, Jeremiah had already called Harrigan and filled him in on the widow Devereaux interview. "We need to get Fred Washington to talk to her maid, we have to have Willie Henderson corroborate her husband's version of the story," O'Connell urged, "And the sooner the better."

Harrigan handled the matter as soon as the two concluded the information swap on the previous day's activities. Fred Washigton promised to get over to see Willie that morning and see what he could find out and report back to O'Connell with whatever he learned.

As Harrigan entered the squad room, every man stood up and applauded the Chief. "What's all this about?" he asked.

"I take it you haven't seen the *Globe-Democrat* this morning, eh Chief," O'Meara asked as he tossed the front page on the table. Harrigan looked down and read the headline.

Chief Of Detectives Held At Gunpoint.

"Sounds like Wyatt Earp got the drop on you Chief," Culhane laughed.

"Will everyone who thinks this is funny please raise his hand," Harrigan smiled and leaned against the wall and crossed his arms. The silence in the squad room would have made a cloistered monastery seem raucous.

"That's good, because anyone who thinks it's funny can start looking for a new job," Harrigan was red-faced and everyone knew that he wasn't kidding.

"Awright, sit down and make your reports," he barked.

Columbo stood up and said, Chief, we might have something here that came up independently from two sources yesterday afternoon and three more last night. Detectives, O'Meara, Culhane and Finnegan ran down several sets of sources and my contacts in the Italian community also confirmed the information."

"It was downright Mike E. Vellian," Culhane chimed in.

"Let's hear it," Harrigan said, as he looked at Joe in utter chagrin.

"It seems that two brothers, Salvatore and Mario Rizzo have come into some sudden good fortune. Mario was until quite recently a waiter in the employ of the restaurateur, Carmine Gagliardi. Mario's brother Sal is a man of questionable moral character and aside from doing a little strong arm work for the 'vigs' and winning an occasional race bet, he has no apparent or visible means of support. Mario has recently quit his job and told his former employer, Mr. Gagliardi that he and Sal are planning a move to Florida to open a business of an undetermined nature.

"What makes this suspicious is the fact that up until the last few weeks, neither man had two nickels to rub together. Now they are shopping in Washington Avenue tailor shops, sporting $50 suits and Allen Edmund Shoes and get this, they each bought seven hats – seven hats a piece – at Levine's no less."

"Now what would two dumb Dago brothers without a half a brain between them have need for 14 hats for," Harrigan said, "That's a real head scratcher."

"That's what we thought too Chief," Finn broke in, "But Louie pointed out that shopping isn't a crime, so we fanned out last night to see what else we could pick up on these two."

"*And...*" Harrigan gestured with both hands for them to proceed.

O'Meara spoke first, "It seems that Sal, they call him '*Dago Sal*' has been seen in the best 'speaks' either here or in East St. Louis every night for the past week, with one or two ladies in tow each night. We checked it out very quietly and discovered that he's also rented a two-bedroom suite for $22.00 a night on the 8th floor at the Statler Hotel, where he's been taking his lady friends for after hours play. He starts out every night in the Statler restaurant before he heads out for the evening." Finnegan added, "My cousin, Eddie Brennan is the night desk man down there. He also told me Sal paid cash when he came in and is paid up for another week, so it looks like he might be getting ready to head to Florida when his stay runs out."

"What about the other Wop, Mario," Harrigan asked?

"He's living in a rented flat out on the northeast corner of Marconi and Shaw catty-corner from *The Sons Of Garibaldi Hall*. As far as we can tell, he only goes outside to walk his dog and get a paper. He's like a recluse. We called the 7th and we now have the house surveiled in case Mario makes a sudden move."

"Luigi, does O'Connell know about this Gagliardi-Rizzo-waiter connection," Harrigan asked?

"No Chief, we wanted to tell you all the stuff we had first," Columbo replied.

"Great work lads! Finn, Joe, Mickey and Luigi, I'm proud of the work you men have done. Now, Luigi call Major O'Connell right now and fill him in on all the rest. Then join me in my office with the rest of *The Welcoming Committee* for a little discussion," Harrigan said as he looked across the squad room at Fred Kirtschner and winked.

About fifteen minutes later *The Welcoming Committee* gathered in Harrigan's office. He began barking orders, "Tonight we need to pay a little visit on *'Dago Sal'* at the Statler. Mickey you get over there this afternoon and slip your cousin a five and get me a pass key to Rizzo's suite. Finn, I want you to round up *'The Mad Russian,'* we might have some heavy lifting to do before the night's over. Luigi, you go get Coleen and Arlene Shea from *The Celtic Room* and tell them to get all dolled up in their most tit showing dresses, I want Rizzo to be able to look down their blouses and see their pubic hair! And have them in the Statler Restaurant by 7:00 pm."

Finn knew that there was real dirty work ahead when the Chief wanted uniformed Sergeant Ivan Tazerek, a.k.a. *"The Mad Russian"* to be there. Ivan was 6'5" tall and weighed in the neighborhood of 275 lbs. and he was solid muscle, the man could bench press 350 lbs. without breaking a sweat and he was without any qualification whatsoever, a real *'knuckle-dragger'*, one of the meanest and dumbest Neanderthals ever to put on the uniform of the St. Louis Police Department. *"Iron Charlie"* liked to use him in especially difficult cases because he would crush a man's testicles with his bare hands and laugh while he did it. Finn figured that Charles Michael must be planning to put the squeeze on Dago Sal.

It was Willie's first day off since the murder and she was glad to be home with Bee, at least she was until the door bell rang and Fred Washington came calling. Fred came in and gathered the Hendersons together in their living room and he recounted his earlier conversation with Bee. It seems that Bee had neglected to tell Willie anything about it and she was none to pleased to hear about what she had overheard Mrs. Devereaux say, being repeated, especially from the lips of a bootlegger. Willie was a churchwoman in the New Harmony A.M.E church and she did not hold with her husband's side-business as a distributor of the "devil's spirit," as she called whiskey.

"Mrs. Henderson, I understand your loyalty to Mrs. Devereaux, but I have to have you confirm what your husband told me. Is it true that you interrupted Mrs. Devereaux listening to her husband talking on the phone to his lady friend. Mr. Henderson told me that you walked in on her and she shushed you up so your voice wasn't heard by the husband and his lady friend. Bee also told me that Mrs. Devereaux was so furious after that call that she moved him out of their bedroom that same day. Is that true," Washington asked?

If looks could have killed, Bee Henderson would have been dropped on the spot by Willie's glare. "It's true," she said tersely.

"Now, Mrs. Henderson, it is important for you to understand that you must tell me everything you know, because if you don't tell me, I won't be able to protect you from the police and they don't care how they get information from colored folks. Please Mrs. Henderson, spare yourself and your husband any unpleasantness," Washington pleaded.

Willie Henderson glared at her husband and then let out a deep sigh of resignation and probably of deep relief. "Here's what I know. Mr. Pierre was an awful lowlife Jezebel-chasing pig. He was terrible to Miss Ada and how that woman stood it I'll never know. I used to sit with her as she'd cry on her bed. He broke her heart so many times. But she loved him, she even forgave him for givin' her the syphilis that caused her to have the baby taken. Even after that, she still loved him until the day she came home and caught him in bed with her sister Edith."

"Good Lord woman, you never told me any of that," Bee jumped up.

"Sit down you old fool, I don't tell you half what I know, and the fact that this man is sitting here is reason enough to explain why I don't and why I won't" Willie scolded.

"You mean that Devereaux brought home syphilis from his whorin' around, gave it to his wife and that caused her to miscarry a baby?" Fred was surprised.

"Yes, but it was no miscarriage, I helped Doctor Leicester, who did it up in her bedroom. I was there, I ain't proud of it and I don't think it was right her being a Christian woman and all, but Miss Ada was not gonna bring no brain-damaged *'syph baby'* into the world. So, I helped her when she asked me to," Willie pulled a hankie out of her sleeve and wiped a tear away.

"And, then I'm supposed to believe that just a few weeks later she catches her own sister in bed with Devereaux? This is totally unbelievable," Washington shook his head.

"Believe it!" Willie stressed her words as she looked Fred dead in the eyes, "Mrs. Devereaux arrived home early from some charity or hospital meeting and walked in on them in her own bedroom naked as jaybirds and mating like jungle animals. It was a terrible scene that I had to clean up afterwards. Miss Ada broke every lamp and every stick of furniture and mirror in that room. Her naked sister locked herself in the bathroom and Pierre had to wrestle Miss Ada to the floor and roll her up in a blanket to keep her from killing them all. It was after that day that she and her sister never talked again and Mr. Pierre was sent packing, first to The Racquet Club and then later to the upstairs guest room a few days later after Mr. Robertson made some kinda peace between them all. Miss Ada deserved a lot better than what she got, but I think even now she still loves him, just the other night she was holding his wedding

ring in her hand and crying something awful. As far as he goes, I sure hope he's burning in Hell...that's where he belongs... *with his back broken!*"

Fred Washington listened attentively to other rambling details, but none of them pointed to the killers. After about an hour, he said goodbye and left. As he walked down the sidewalk to his car, he could hear Willie ranting and raving at Bee.

It wasn't going to be a happy homecoming after all.

———◆———

XXXXV

"Hi Mac," Chip greeted her as she came into the station lobby.

"Been waiting for me long?" she asked.

"Just all my life..." he smiled and gave her a kiss on the cheek.

"You are a smooth one Mr. Harrigan, I'll give you that. Did you bring your car or are we taking mine?"

"It's the gift of gab and I come by it honestly," he laughed, "I had one of the boys drop me off and I caught the end of your news feature on the embezzlement in the Ladue School District, what was that guy, Sneeden thinking?" Chip asked.

"I don't think he was thinking at all," Mac pressed the button for the garage elevator, and called to the security guard, "Goodnight Condoleeza, have a good weekend."

"You too Ms. McGauley, and don't do nuthin' with that handsome man that I wouldn't do," Condi called as the elevator door closed.

Once inside the elevator, Mac planted a big wet one on her date and ran her hand across his chest, "Mmmmm...Chip you are such a good kisser...I could eat you up. Where are you taking us for dinner, you sexy man?

"I have midnight reservation at *Chef Matt's* in the new Hyatt-Westin in Union Station, it's supposed to be fantastic from food to wine to late night jazz."

"Sounds perfect," she tossed him the keys, "Here you drive while I fix my make-up."

"*You wear make up!* I'm shocked!"

Chef Matt's was the only *Amer-Asian Renaissance* restaurant in the United States to been awarded a *FiveStar* rating by The Food Network's *Elite Chefs Of The World* panel, and the review had made the place so difficult to get into that the reservation list was 6-months long.

"How did you manage to get reservations here," Mac asked as they arrived at the *Maitre'd's* station?

"I have friends in high places...and low places...and in-between places, guess which one helped me work this bit of magic for you?"

"Good evening Mr. Harrigan and Ms. McGauley, follow me please your table is waiting." The *Maitre'd* led them to table on the mezzanine level overlooking the main dining room below with it's black and yellow checkerboard dance floor and jazz combo. "*Chef Matt* selected this table for you himself and asked me to have Eduoard attend to all your needs this evening, here is the wine list, please select any vintage you like compliments of the house."

"Thank you very much, and please tell *Chef Matt* that he is too kind," Chip said.

"I think you can tell him yourself," the *Maitre'd* gestured behind Chip to an approaching figure in a heavily starched canary yellow Chef's jacket, black checked pants and a tall heavily starched Chef's hat.

"Hello cousin," the gargantuan man embraced Chip who had risen to greet him, "Introduce me to this heavenly creature that you have tricked into being your date." Chef Matt leaned over and kissed Mac on the cheek and whispered, "If he doesn't treat you like the Queen of Sheba, you let me know and I'll cut off his tail with a carving knife.

"Eduoard, bring us a bottle of Dom 2025 to get their meal off to a festive start, the lobster bisque is heavenly, *as always,* and if you like seafood, I am baking a Dover Sole ginger-almandine that will make you think you've died and gone to heaven.

"I got to run and welcome my guests at the Chef's Private Table. I have the new owners of the Cardinals here tonight celebrating their $3.7 billion dollar acquisition. I hope they have money enough left over to pay for their dinner after spending all that dough on the team. If I can get loose later, I'll swing by and have a nightcap with you. Nice to meet you Ms. McGauley, and Charlie my boy, you have done well grasshopper. *Bon Appetit!*

Mac asked, "Wow is he always like that?"

"Only when he's awake, you've actually seen him in a serene mood tonight, as a kid he was totally-wired all the time. He always talks a mile-a-minute and you can rarely get a word in edgewise. But, he is a helluva chef and I hear that he is an absolute tyrant and perfectionist of manic proportions in the kitchen," Chip reported.

"And he's your cousin," Mac asked?

"Yep, he's a Culhane descendant on his mother's side. They broke the mold when they made him," Chip replied.

"I'm curious about your family Chip, especially its long police tradition, how's all that come about?"

"Do you really want to know?" Chip asked, "I think it's kind of boring."

"Police work, boring? I wouldn't think so…" Mac looked intentionally puzzled.

"It all came out of economic necessity actually; the Irish couldn't get decent jobs when our people first came here. They had no education, no formal schooling. But they could swing nightsticks and break skulls, so police work became their on-ramp to the American Dream. My namesake, the original Charles Michael Harrigan was the son of beat cop who joined the force and rose to the rank of Chief of Detectives. He was known as *"Iron Charlie"* back in the day."

"Sounds like one tough hombre," Mac nodded.

"Well in his day, you didn't read people their Miranda Rights and due process was still kind of a fuzzy law enforcement concept. In his day it was a very mean and hard world. You'd be surprised to know that about half my ancestral cousins were cops and other half were into bootlegging, lone sharking and gambling and God only knows what else. Our family tree is full of colorful characters on both sides of the law.

"Today, there is just boring me in the cop business, all the rest have moved on to run places like this, develop real estate in Arizona and Colorado or run liquor and beer distributorships around the country. Ever heard of Kerry Importing Companies USA?

It's headquartered in Chicago now, you can look it up. That Fortune 1000 company can trace its roots back to St. Louis during the Prohibition days when Chef Matt's great-great-grandfather, Thomas Edward Culhane, *The King Of Kerry Patch* was St. Louis' leading lawbreaker and my great-great-grandfather, his first cousin, *"Iron Charlie"* Harrigan was St. Louis' most feared cop. Kind of ironic isn't it."

"Fascinating, especially to me, I love history," Mac encouraged him to continue.

"Rumor has it that the African-American gentleman who runs Kerry Importing in Chicago today is descended from an illicit union between Tom Culhane and a black woman called the "Queen of Sheba" that he took up with back in the 1920's. Some of the family stories say he even dilly-dallied around with the famous black ingénue and dancer Josephine Baker.

Interracial dating was taboo behavior in those days," Chip stopped, "Our family is very big on legends, tales and history, and 99% of the history is probably B.S. People and stories get bigger with each telling, that's what my grandmother always said."

"It sounds like Mr. Culhane was ahead of his time, at least he was open to racial equality," Mac noted.

"That's one way of looking at it I suppose," Chip raised his glass of champagne and proposed a toast, "Here's to continually improving the Harrigan breed!"

"I'll drink to that," Mac smiled, "Maybe we can get started on it after dinner and dancing tonight!"

"Let's order!" Chip urged, "I think I'm going the high protein route, might come in handy later!"

Mac whispered seductively, "Don't eat too much Mr. Harrigan, I want you to save plenty of room for a nice, warm and *oh so* delicious '*dessert*' back at my place."

"Mmmm, sounds delicious, will I get to lick the bowl?"

"I'm hoping you will," Mac blushed and smiled coyly.

———

KIRTSCHNER'S JOURNAL ENTRY: EW/1H/2H/HS

At 7:30 pm on the dot, the polished brass elevator doors opened into the Statler Hotel lobby and the dapper Sal Rizzo bounded out and walked cockily across the lobby toward the restaurant. Seated inside in a booth along the far wall were the Shea sisters, Colleen and Arlene, two of *The King's* finest 'hostesses.' They were sipping gin martinis from coffee cups and waiting for their mark to arrive. When Sal Rizzo entered the room the girls gave him the 'once over' twice and smiled, giggled and whispered to each other and then waved a little come hither wave at him.

Sal said, "Nick, give me a cup of coffee like the ladies over there are having. He waited for his 'coffee' and walked over and said, "I couldn't help noticing that you two ladies were having a lot of fun, are you waiting for someone?"

Colleen squeezed her ample cleavage together and cooed, "We might be waiting for a nice man like you to buy us dinner, we're in St. Louis for training at Southwestern Bell all week and we're on a very limited expense account."

Arlene patted the booth seat and said, "Why don't you sit in here between us Mr. Valentino? We might be short on cash, but when it comes to having fun, the sky's the limit."

Arlene scooted over to make room for Sal to slide in between her and Colleen. "Where are you girls from," he asked?

"Arkansas, we're up from Little Rock and Searcy, and we've been so bored all week. We have two roommates upstairs who are tight-assed Baptists from Sikeston and all they want to do is study, read the Bible and go to bed early. We'd like to have some fun up here in the big city," Coleen said.

"I am all about having fun, especially with lovely ladies," Sal oozed, "Why don't we grab some dinner here and then I'll take you two dolls out on the town."

"Ohh, that sounds great, but we can't go out with a total stranger," Arlene protested.

"Well let me fix that, my name is Salvatore Rizzo, but all my friends call me Sal."

"*Sal-va-tore* is that *Eye*-talian?" the tipsy Colleen said as she ran her hand up his thigh, "I've heard so much about *Eye*-talian men. They're supposed to be so romantic."

"Is that true, Mr. Valentino?" Arlene asked as she ran her hand up his other thigh.

Sal could feel a bulge swelling in his slacks, "Ladies, I can assure you that whatever you have heard about Italian men it is not even *half-true*, do you know that just one Italian man can easily please two women at the same time?" Sal flirted.

"Colleen, do you think that's true?" Arlene asked.

"I don't know, maybe Salvatore is just bragging."

"There's only one way you can be sure, ladies" Sal stated.

"And what's that?" Colleen cooed.

"Come up to my suite and let me show you firsthand what I can do for the two of you."

"Why Mr. Rizzo, what kind of girls do you think we are?"

Sal reached under the table and ran his hands up their smooth thighs past their garter belts and touched the damp crotches of their silk panties, "Why, I think you're both kind of excited by the possibility of discovering what an Italian lover with many talents like me can do for you. Should we eat here, or skip dinner and go upstairs and eat?"

Coleen reached over and squeezed the stiffening bulge in Sal's trousers, "What's for dinner upstairs, do I feel a sausage in my future?"

"Yes you do, and it's a spicy Italian sausage called a *Salsiticcia*, they named it after me cause its so big, hot and juicy…I think you'll find it especially enjoyable it when it slides in between some soft white buns," Sal was grinning and pouring it on thick.

The two ladies looked at each other and winked and giggled, then Arlene reached down and retrieved Sal's rubbing hand from her crotch and said, *"Lead on Mr. Valentino."*

Sal smiled wryly as he paid the check and thought, "Sal you are too-two-too lucky this is going to be a *ménage a twat.*"

KIRTSCHNER'S JOURNAL ENTRY: 1H/2H/EW/HS

The key opened the door to the suite and the gentlemanly Sal held the door open and said, "Ladies first." Colleen and Arlene walked in to the suite's living room, "*Ohh...*this is much nicer than our room, what's in there?"

"This is the bedroom," Sal reached inside to turn on the light switch when he suddenly lurched backwards for a split second and then went flying forward as he was jerked off his feet into the darkened bedroom. His body smashed face first into the headboard knocking him senseless.

Harrigan stepped out of the darkened bathroom and handed the girls an envelope, "Thank you ladies, have a nice evening." He let them out and bolted the door and walked into the bedroom. The table lamp beside the bed was now turned on and Sal Rizzo was slowly regaining consciousness, his nose was bleeding profusely and he had no idea what had happened to him. Ivan, Finn, Mickey and Joe stood around the bed where the dazed Rizzo was trying to regain focus. Ivan had grabbed his arm when he reached in to turn on the light and arm whip-tossed him full force into the headboard and shattered the mahogany center panel with Rizzo's face.

"Hello Mr. Rizzo, how are you this fine evening," Harrigan asked, "are you enjoying your stay here at the Statler?"

The dazed Rizzo looked around in total disorientation wiping the blood from his mouth, "Who are you? What did I ever do to you?"

Harrigan spoke, "Let's get the rules straight Salvatore, we'll ask all the questions and you'll give all the answers." Harrigan reached over and pulled the diamond stick pin out of Sal's blood spattered tie, "Now what have we here, why it's a lovely diamond stick pin. Where did you get it Mr. Rizzo?"

"I don't know, I don't remember..."

Harrigan jammed the stickpin's point through Rizzo's right cheek, "Does this prick your memory?"

"Jesus are you fucking crazy?" Rizzo cried as he jumped back in pain from the hole just punched in his cheek.

"No, I'm perfectly sane, I just don't like lying Wop bastards like you, now where did you get it?"

"I won it in a poker game," Rizzo mumbled holding his punctured cheek.

"Poker game? And where did this poker game take place?"

"At the Mayfair with a bunch of guys in town from Cleveland," Sal sputtered.

Harrigan jammed the stickpin deep into Sal's bicep, "I think you're lying!"

"Oooowww fuck! I'm not lying, I swear to God, I'm not lying," Sal was crying.

Harrigan jammed the bent stick pin into Sal's scrotum, "Stop lying to me!"

"Owwwww, Jesus...Jesus...Jesus," Sal rolled over in acute pain and cupped his punctured testicle.

"I'm glad to see you're on a first name basis with our Lord and Savior, but I haven't got all night to turn you into a praying pin-cushion," Harrigan gestured to Finn, "Open the window, let's give Mr. Rizzo some fresh air, maybe that will clear his head and refresh his memory."

Finn opened the left side bedroom window. Harrigan gestured to Ivan, "Ivan give the man some air will you please."

The Mad Russian jerked Rizzo off the bed and took him over to the open window and pushed his head and torso outside. "Oh he needs much more air than that, Ivan," Harrigan gestured again and Tazerek pushed Rizzo out over the window sill and grabbed the hyperventilating Sal by his ankles, swinging him out into the night air eight floors above the pavement.

Harrigan opened the right side bedroom window and leaned outside, "How's that Sal, is the fresh air helping your memory?"

"Please in the name of Jesus, bring me back in, please I'll tell you whatever you want to know, just bring me back inside," Rizzo was whimpering in terror and begging for his life.

"Jesus, what's that smell?" Harrigan asked.

"He shit himself," Ivan rotated the free swinging Sal so Harrigan could see the river of shit flowing northward like the Nile up the middle of Sal's inverted back and out his shirt collar and onto his chin.

"Sal, see where lying gets you, now you've made a terrible mess in your brand new suit, do you feel like coming clean now," Harrigan could not resist the pun.

"Yes, just pull me inside for the love of Jesus," Sal begged, "Please in the name of Christ and Holy Mother Mary, I'm begging you...please..."

"I'll tell you what Sal...you tell me what I want to know before Ivan here get's tired and I'll do better than bring you back in, I'll release you. I'm not interested in catching some dumb, low level, low life Wop prick like you, I want the man who put you up to it," Harrigan offered.

"Up to what?? Tell me '*up to what*'?" Sal begged pitifully through his tears.

"Sal you know what I want to know, I want to know who hired you to kill Pierre Devereaux."

Ivan recoiled from the smell of the human stench dangling below him as Sal released another gurgling round of watery defecation in reaction to Harrigan's last question.

"Sweet Jesus, please bring me in I'll tell you everything," Sal begged.

"Sal, you're in no position to negotiate, and I think Ivan's getting tired. Tired of listening to your bullshit and tired of smelling your Wop shit, you'd better start talking," Harrigan urged.

With that, Ivan released one of Sal's ankles and let him swing crazily to one side. Sal screamed and clawed for the wall trying to get an upside-down grip in the tuck pointing.

"Ivan, how long before your last arm gives out," Harrigan asked?

"Maybe a minute, maybe two…I'm getting real tired of smelling this shit," Ivan droned.

"Sal it's now or never," Harrigan stated with an air of finality.

"Okay, okay, okay, we got $15,000 upfront to do the job from a guy named Reynolds. He gave us the money all in cash."

"Who's '*us*' and who's '*Reynolds*'?" Harrigan pressed.

"*Us*' is me and my brother Mario, and I don't know Reynolds's first name I swear to Christ I don't. Mario knows it. Mario knows him from the restaurant. I swear on the Sacred Heart of Jesus, that's the truth," Sal was hanging very still now, so as not to wear Ivan's arm out by wiggling around.

"One more question Sal," Harrigan asked, "Why did you kill the girl."

"We got tired of waiting...."

"What!" Harrigan was shocked, "What do you mean '*you got tired of waiting*'?"

"It was getting late and we were going to follow them and when he dropped her off, we were gonna kill him. We had followed them before and he always dropped her off at her place, but that night they stopped in the park and it was getting on toward midnight so we figured '*what the fuck*' kill 'em both, no extra charge."

"What was the big hurry? Do you turn into a fucking pumpkin at midnight or what?"

"No we was just tired and wanted to get it done and go home to bed."

"Why did you take his jewelry?" Harrigan pressed him again.

"Mario told me we had to get his jewelry to prove that we did the job, he said he had to give the guy's wedding ring to Reynolds to get the rest of the money."

"How much more money?"

Sal sputtered as he spit blood and watery shit from his mouth, "Another 15-grand."

Harrigan whistled in admiration, "$30,000, that's ten year's of cop's pay, not bad for two minutes work? Where's the rest of the jewelry and the money, we only found $2000 in cash in your closet here?"

"I got a grand in my pocket and Mario has the rest at his place..." Sal was crying softly now, and he was trembling in stark terror, emotionally drained and totally exhausted.

"Reach in your pocket, get the thou' and hand over to me, its evidence" Harrigan instructed.

Sal reached into his pocket and pulled out a soggy diarrhea-soaked wad of bills and as Ivan slowly raised him up, with trembling hand he passed the wad over to Harrigan who was leaning out the adjoining window.

Harrigan handed the wad back inside to Finn and said, "Go rinse the shit off."

"Please, in the name of Jesus, I've told you everything… please…please…" he sobbed pathetically.

"All right Ivan, you can release him, Mr. Rizzo is free to go."

"Release him?" Ivan was confused and looking for clarification.

"Yes Ivan, I said, *'Let Mr. Rizzo go!'* He's as free as a bird. Let's hope he can fly like one," Harrigan said as he gestured to Ivan by opening his clenched fist, Ivan swung the dangling Dago away from the building and released his grip on Sal's ankle. That momentum sent the screaming man flying out away from the building and then arcing down. The boys crowded by the other windows in the suite watched Sal flail his arms and legs wildly in the air until his head and right shoulder clipped the fire hydrant and tumble-tossed parts of his skull and his limp body out into the street like a sack of potatoes.

"I'm glad you finally said, *'Let him go,'* I wasn't sure how much longer I could have kept from dropping him," Taz said sincerely.

"You did well Taz, take tomorrow off with pay, I'll handle it for you.

All right men let's get down stairs and call in this terrible 'Hit and Run.'"

Joe Culhane was puzzled, *"Hit and run?"*

"Yeah Joseph Patrick, it's a 'hit and run.' Didn't you see his head hit the fire hydrant and his brains and body run out into the street. And, did you hear the funny sound he made? *'Dago Wop!'* when they hit the ground from up this high," Harrigan laughed.

I could not believe what I had just witnessed from the vantage point where Harrigan had left me and Luigi Columbo in the parked police car up the block. I was suddenly very sick, the puke and bile came roaring up so fast I barely had time to throw open the door before the projectile vomit shot through my nostrils and mouth and into the gutter.

Within minutes, the whole front sidewalk of the Statler Hotel was filled with people who had emptied out of the hotel to see what all the sirens and the commotion was about. Finn O'Meara was talking to Bill Caulfield, the rookie beat cop who was first on the scene. Finn was explaining how he and Chief Harrigan were driving by when a vehicle going the other way smashed into the pedestrian now lying in the street and then sped off toward the Eads Bridge. Finn said, "We stopped to help the poor man, I tended to him and the Chief went inside to call it in."

"Excuse me, I saw the whole thing," a short balding man said as he pushed into the conversation. "Just a minute sir, let me finish with this officer," Finn turned his back on the man and spoke quietly to the beat cop, "Bill, why don't you ride in the ambulance down to the morgue and I'll stay here and take care of the detective work, if you get embroiled with taking statements from these confused citizens, you won't be getting off at 11:00 p.m. tonight, you'll be here filling out reports until 3 o'clock tomorrow afternoon."

"Thanks Finn, I appreciate you handling it," the young cop left and felt relieved to have escaped all the tedious report writing.

"Now sir, how can I help you?"

"I saw the dead man get thrown from that window way up there," he said as he pointed to the 8th floor suite.

"Really? Come with me please, Chief of Detectives Harrigan will want to talk to you personally since you're an eyewitness." Finn walked the fat businessman over to the curb where Harrigan was talking to Finnegan.

"Chief, we have an eyewitness here," Finn signaled with his eyes that the man had actually seen the Dago toss.

"Yes sir, I'm Chief of Detectives Charles Michael Harrigan *and you are?*"

"I'm John Fosse from Milwaukee."

"Detective O'Meara tells me that you saw what happened here tonight. Can you tell me exactly what you saw, and don't leave anything out," Harrigan urged him?

"I was coming back to the hotel after dinner and I saw some man up there in that window hanging out, it looked like a big man was holding him by his legs and another man was leaning out of that other window right next to him. I couldn't hear what was going on then all of a sudden just like that the man comes flying down and hits the fire plug and the bounce throws him *'Hurley burl tippety gale'* head over heels out into the street like a rag doll with pieces of brain and skull flying everywhere. I haven't seen body parts fly like that since the bombardment during the *St. Mihiel* offensive."

"Could you see the faces of the men up there?" Harrigan asked as he screened his eyes and looked up at the 8th floor windows.

"No, I could only make out their silhouettes, all the light was behind them, you see."

"Well Mr. Foster, how long can you stay here in St. Louis?" Harrigan asked.

"It's *Fosse*," he corrected, "And I'm going back to Milwaukee tomorrow morning."

"Oh no sir, you're an eyewitness to what by your own account is a capital murder, and I'd even go so far as to say that you might have witnessed a *Mafia* murder. I'm afraid; we'll have to put you in protective custody as a material witness," Harrigan stated with the authority befitting the Chief Of Detectives.

"How long will that take? I have a job and a family," Fosse stuttered

"Hard to tell, it could be a week and it could be six months, it depends on the Grand Jury's schedule. And believe me,

Mr. Fosse, if this was a *Mafia* murder and those men find out that you, an eyewitness, saw them, you won't be safe in Milwaukee. But I can almost certainly guarantee your safety here in St. Louis as a guest of the department. And, don't worry about the cost, all of your expenses up to $2.50 a day will be paid by the city. Of course, you won't be staying in as nice a hotel as the Statler, but your room will be clean and comfortable," Harrigan continued, "Now, if you'll be kind enough to accompany detective Finnegan, he'll take your statement in the lobby, in the meantime, we can get started making all the arrangements to try and keep you safe from harm.

"Mickey write this man's statement down and be sure to get it all word for word, we may need it as a sworn affidavit at the trial if anything unfortunate should happen to him before he can testify," Harrigan said, "Go with officer Finnegan, Mr. Fosse and thank you for stepping forward to do your civic duty. Not many people would be willing to take the time off work and away from their family, let alone put their own life in peril to see this thing through to its final legal conclusion."

Finnegan led the wide-eyed balding fat man from Milwaukee away into the Statler lobby and the once eager eyewitness now looked somewhat shaken and very unnerved by the crime he had just witnessed and by what he had just had explained to him by the kindly policeman.

O'Meara laughed and said, "Chief, what do you think he's gonna tell Finnegan."

"Five bucks says he's gonna tell him he has amnesia," Harrigan winked, "C'mon Eamon, let's go get the other end of the Rizzo bookends, there is no time like the present especially since we're three grand to the good and our interrogations are going so well."

XXXXVIII

Mac rolled over and came up on her elbows and looked at Chip, "You are the best lover any girl could ever dream of," she said as she leaned in and bit his nipple.

"And you are insatiable," Chip winced at her pleasure bite.

"Is that bad?" Mac asked.

"No that's good…as a matter of fact, *'insatiable'* is an excellent quality in a comely young lass with a soft freckled ass," Chip rhymed and rolled over and put his arm around her and slapped her butt.

"You don't think my ass is too big, I do," Mac declared, "I think it's getting bigger each day from all the sitting I do."

"It's not too big, it's perfect for me. Trust me on that love."

"Is 'Mr. Happy Harrigan' down for the count?" Mac reached down and flipped Chip's flaccid penis from side-to-side slapping it on his thighs.

"Give the old soldier a few minutes and I'm sure he'll be able to get up for reveille," Chip suggested as he wondered, *I've already cum three times, what is she expecting?*

"Maybe it would help if the barracks bugler gave him some encouragement," Mac said as she dove down open-mouthed and engulfed his manhood.

"You are insatiable, and God I love that about you," Chip felt a shudder and then relaxed to let Mac work her mouth's magic. He glanced at the alarm clock and it was 6:30 a.m., they had been making love since 2:30 a.m. and she was as still as fresh and eager as the first time. Damn, what an uninhibited and sexually voracious woman...he thought as waves of intense pleasure rippled up from deep behind his bellybutton. Within moments he erupted like Vesuvius. She never missed a stroke, and drank his essence all in and kept on relentlessly driving him to new and higher levels of intense pleasure. Finally, he reached down and pulled her head up onto his stomach, "Oh my God, Mac, Mac, Mac stop, stop...the whole world is spinning," he moaned. Mac softly squeezed his tender aching balls and said, "I love spinning your world Mr. Harrigan...I love spinning it." She kissed his warm stomach and fell asleep to the steady rhythm of his deep breathing.

Chip lay there in the dark, quiet and contemplative. Mac had made his world spin in more ways than she realized. He stroked her sleeping head and whispered softly, "Will you be my Queen of Sheba?"

———◆———

KIRTSCHNER'S JOURNAL ENTRY: 1H/2H/EW

Columbo pulled the car around in the alley four doors east of Mario Rizzo's home.

Harrigan turned to address me, O'Meara and Joe Culhane in the back seat. "Kirtschner, you stay here out of the line of fire, if Mario puts up a fuss, I don't want you getting shot. Joe, you and Finn go around to the front of the house and let the surveillance officer know that we're going in, then start ringing the doorbell and yelling, *'Open up Police!'* that'll wake up Mario.

Harrigan continued, "Now one of three things will happen next. *One,* he'll answer the door and let you in, all peaceable like. *Two,* he'll make a break for it out the back and try to get to his car in the garage, or beat it on foot into the darkness of the alley. He' won't jump out a side window into a gangway, he'd be boxed in there, and he won't waste time goin' down and out the cellar. *Or, three,* he'll come out gun blazing and try to make a break for it out the front. He'll try to blast your asses off and make a run for it, *although*, I doubt if he'll try that since he'll probably be expecting a lot of cops will be waiting for him.

"On the other hand, I've seen panicky people do really some stupid stuff. So, keep yourselves covered up," Harrigan instructed Finn and Joe, "Luigi and I will be waiting in the backyard and if Mario comes out the back, we'll take him down, but I want him alive. Are we clear?"

"Clear Chief," They responded.

"Luigi, did you call Mr. Gagliardi and let him know we were coming here?" Columbo shook his head, *Yes*. "Okay, let's get it over with," Harrigan opened the door and drew his .38.

A few moments later Mario Rizzo jumped up in the darkness of his bedroom, his peaceful sleep rudely interrupted by the doorbell and the loud banging on his front sash. He could hear Joe and Finn yelling, *"Open up! Open up Rizzo! It's the Police! Open up!"*

Mario stumbled out of bed and made his way into the darkened hallway, he was dressed only in his shorts as he made his way to the front door. When he reached the front of the house, he flipped on the light inside the tiny entry hall. He was still rubbing the sleep from his eyes when he unlatched and opened the front door. Finn came flying through first and threw the bleary-eyed Rizzo in to the wall and then slammed him down onto the hall runner face first. Culhane came in next gun drawn and said, "Is there anyone else in here?"

"No just me, I'm alone," Mario said, "I swear Sal's not here.

"That much we know," Finn commented.

Culhane waved at the surveillance officer who was parked across the street and yelled, "We got it handled, you can head back to the 7th!" Then he closed the door and said, "Finn, bring him back to the kitchen and I'll let the Chief and Columbo in."

Mario was seated on a kitchen chair when Columbo and Harrigan came in. Harrigan walked right over and jerked Rizzo up by his hair. "Do you know why we're here?" Harrigan snarled.

Mario was shaking something terrible and he knew that the game was up. He nodded, *Yes.*

Okay, now Mario, we can do this the easy way or the hard way. It's up to you. Your late brother – the recently deceased Sal decided to do it the hard way and his brains got splattered all over 9th Street tonight. I hope you're smarter than he was," Harrigan sneered, "See this stickpin, I took it out of Sal's tie earlier this evening. Do you know where he got it?"

The abrupt delivery of the news about Sal's death shook him to his core, his face contorted in peculiarly anguished smirk, then Mario looked at the bent pin and started to cry, "We took it off the dead guy."

"What dead guy?" Harrigan asked.

"The guy we shot in the park." Mario was shaking heavily.

"Mario, I'm glad to see you're not a liar like Sal, I hate liars..." Harrigan paused,

"Who did the shooting?"

"We both did," he sobbed, "Sal shot the girl and the man first. And then I finished him off," Mario whimpered.

"What gun were you shooting?"

Mario answered, "I had a .25...Sal had a .32"

"Who paid you to do it?" Harrigan asked quietly.

"Reynolds gave us $15,000 grand in advance and another $15,000 when I handed over the wedding ring to him," Mario choked out the words."

"Reynolds...does he have a first name?" Harrigan intoned sarcastically.

"Sumner...Sumner Reynolds, he's a guy I know from the restaurant.

Harrigan looked quickly at Columbo and was obviously surprised, "You said, *Sumner Reynolds* paid you the cash? *'30 thou'!*"

"Yeah, he asked me if I knew of any Pisanos in the gangs, who wanted to earn some easy money for making a problem go away. I said. 'How much' and he said, '30 thou' – hell, I'd shoot Hoover for 30 thou'. I got Sal to help me. Reynolds gave us the name of the guy and told us where to find him. He even gave us a sheet outlining his daily habits and haunts. Reynolds said we could kill him anytime that worked best. He gave us 15 thou' down and 15 thou' when the guy was dead,' Mario paused, "It was easy money, you know. Do you know how long it would take a waiter to earn 15 thou'? That was my cut."

Harrigan asked, "Where's the money now?

"It's in the garage in the back of the bottom workbench shelf behind my tool box."

"Go get it Lou and bring it in here," Harrigan ordered.

"Where's the rest of the loot?"

"It's all in the box, his cufflinks and wallet, the woman's purse and the checkbook we took from her house. We went there a few days later to see if she had any money or jewelry that we could pinch, but all we found was cheap junk and a check book with $300 bucks in it. We were going to clean it out before we blew town," Mario confessed.

Harrigan pulled up a chair turned it around backwards to face Mario and straddled it with his arms resting on the chair back. "Tell me about this guy Reynolds."

"What's to tell? He had a problem that he needed eliminated and he paid us 30 thou' to kill the guy. That's it," Mario stated.

"No Mario, there has to be much more to it than that. Sumner Reynolds is an ex-cop, a lush, he doesn't have 30 cents let alone 30 thou'," Harrigan observed, "So, who paid him to pay you? Tell me that Mario that's what I really want to know."

"I don't know, I swear I don't know...please believe me I'm telling you everything I know...I swear to Christ I am," Mario pleaded.

"I believe you Mario, do you know what's going to happen now?"

"I'm going to jail and I'll probably get the gas chamber."

"That might not be necessary, you see, it was Sal who killed the girl and Mr. Pierre Devereaux. You actually shot a dead man and put two slugs into the car's back seat. You didn't really kill anyone. Sal did all the killing...now, if you'll come completely clean, I might be able to help you with the judge and you'd plead to an assault and robbery rap and be in and out in 10 years. How does that sound?" Harrigan smiled.

"Sir, I swear I'm telling you the truth, that's all I know, I swear," Mario's eyes welled up and tears ran down his cheeks, "You've got to believe me."

"I believe you Mario. Luigi here is going to take you with Finn and Joe to see the Night Court Municipal Judge now, you can make a plea and then the judge will enter it and you'll be locked up to await trial."

"Thank you, thank you." Mario wept as he was overcome with mixed waves of fear, grief, remorse and relief.

Harrigan gestured to Columbo to follow him into the dining room. He opened the box to find $24,500 in cash, the balance left after the brothers' downtown shopping trip and Sal's hotel and whore expenses. They also found Pierre Laclede Devereaux's empty wallet, his monogrammed diamond cufflinks, Mary Elizabeth Kirtschner's purse, wallet, house keys and check ledger. Harrigan counted out $5000, folded it in half and handed it to Columbo.

Then he gave Luigi his marching orders, "When you drop off Mr. Rizzo, give this to Carmine for *The Son's Of Garibaldi*, it's blood money, so tell him to put it to charitable use." Harrigan put the $3000 he took off Sal Rizzo into the box with the remaining $19,500 and tucked it under his arm...*$22,500, was not a bad take for one night.*

Harrigan left and took me with him in Mario's 'impounded' car and drove back to the Central District. Luigi drove as Finn and Joe flanked Mario in the backseat of the police car. It only went three blocks south and then turned into the alley behind the Odorizzi Meat Company on Macklind Avenue.

"What're we doing here?" Mario asked sensing that something might be wrong.

"We have to pick up a package for the boys back at the stationhouse, it'll just take a minute, let's go," Finn pulled Mario from the backseat and Joe took his other arm as they followed Columbo into the back room of the packing house.

Once inside, Mario knew that he had been tricked because Carmine Gagliardi was waiting there with Paulo, Carlo and Armando from 'The Hill' restaurant and three other men in white aprons who were working in the shop making sausage.

Columbo spoke quietly to Carmine and handed him the $5000, then he signaled to Finn, who viciously cracked Mario across the back of his head with a blackjack sending him straight to the floor. Finn rained on a few more blows to make sure Mario was out cold. Then Finn, Joe and Columbo bid farewell to Carmine and his associates and left. As they drove back to the Central District, Joe Culhane asked, "What's going to happen to Mario?"

"They're gonna make sausage out of him. It's a traditional Machiavellian way to get rid of loose ends," Columbo half-joked.

Joe burst out laughing, "Yeah, right...Luigi you're killing me with this Mike E. Vellian *Eye*talian bullshit."

Columbo and Finn laughed at Joe, too.

Mario was barely starting to regain consciousness when Carlo and Armando lifted him to his feet. Paulo slipped a clothesline over his head and garroted him as Carmine puffed on his *Parodi* and looked on at the bug-eyed man kicking and writhing in his dance of death.

Two hours later Mario's body had been bled out, dismembered and butchered into softball-sized meat chunks and ground up into a mixture of Italian spiced pork, beef intestines and trimmings. The mixture along with No. 3 coarse ground Mario was stuffed into natural sausage casings and packed in boxes stencil labeled:

Fresh Ground Sausage
Customer: St. Louis City Jail
Original Family Recipe
Odorizzi Sausage Company
St. Louis, Missouri

Mario's decapitated head, hands and feet, broken bones and offal left over from his de-boning were placed in a waxed butcher's box and tossed into the coke smelter at Scullin Steel during the shift change. By next month, Mario's molecules would be part of a Ford fender, steel boiler plating or a bridge girder. Mario's penis and testicles were put in an alcohol-filled quart canning jar and shown around the organization as a graphic lesson of what happens to those who step out of the bounds set by *The Big Dago*.

Carmine Gagliardi had his $5000 tribute. Order and discipline had been maintained. Promises were kept, Respect had been given. It seems there is Honor among thieves, after all.

One could even argue that justice...and Mario were served.

KIRTSCHNER'S JOURNAL ENTRY: EW

Back in his office, Harrigan stowed the box of cash and loot in his closet and locked it.

He knew it would be safe there since he had the only key. I sat across from his desk and waited in numbed and stunned silence for Harrigan to offer some kind of explanation for what had transpired.

Harrigan sat down, lit up a cigar and began looking at the notes on his desk. He must have sensed that I was staring at him, so he looked up.

"What?" he asked incredulously.

"What? I'll tell you *'what'* I spoke up, "What was throwing that man out the hotel window all about. It looked like murder to me. That's *'what'*!"

"Whoa, whoa, just hold your fucking horses Kirtschner! Nobody got tossed out a window. True, we did hang Sal out the window to scare him into talking, but he was the one who was thrashing around so much, he pulled out of the man's grip that was holding him," Harrigan said, "And that poor man who couldn't hold on to that squirming Dago bastard, well, he's beside himself with grief and heartsick that Sal slipped from his grasp. I had to give him some days off to regain his composure."

"Bullshit!" I blurted, "You probably beat up and scared that poor man witless and then threw him to his death."

Harrigan erupted in anger, leapt up and came around his desk and grabbed me by my tie and jerked me bolt upright. The veins on his neck were bulging as he pulled me nose to nose.

"Listen to me Freddy boy, you may not agree with my methods, but I get results. And since you weren't in the room, just where do you get off telling me what happened up there? For all you know, the law of gravity might have been the law that dispensed justice tonight. By the by laddie, that criminal asshole was the one who blew your cocksucking sister's brains all over Devereaux's backseat."

'Iron Charlie' threw me back down into the chair, "If you so ever as much as open your mouth and start accusing me or my men about something that you don't know about for *absolute-fucking-sure*, I'll throw you, Alcott and Dexter to the wolves. Just try me boy," Harrigan said as he jabbed his fat forefinger deeply into my chest.

"Now get the fuck outta my sight, and don't come 'round unless I call you," Harrigan pulled me up by my arm, opened the door of his office and shoved me out into the squad room and slammed the door behind me.

"Schu!!" Harrigan yelled, "Get your fat ass in here! *Now!*"

Schumacher was physically shaken by what he had just overheard and witnessed, but he went in to Harrigan's lair anyway.

"Yes, Chief?" he held his breath expecting the worst.

"Get me the address of our former associate, detective Sergeant Sumner Reynolds...and I mean get it today, not someday!"

Schumacher quickly left the office and headed for the file room. He was relieved,

"God damn, I thought Kirtschner had ratted me out."

Back in his office Harrigan looked at the paper Alcott had given him. On it was the snitch's name in pencil block letters: *Schumacher.*

Harrigan put a red X through it and slid it under his desk blotter. *'Iron Charlie'* would deal with Sgt. Schumacher in his own sweet time.

Next door at the morgue, the night attendant was replacing the name tags on the refrigerated drawers that held the bodies. If Fred Kirtschner had been there, the irony would certainly have struck him as the name tag *'Madame X'* was replaced with one that read: *Rizzo, Salvatore.* The killer now lay on the same cold metal that just a few hours before had held one of his victims.

About 25 minutes later, Schu returned to Harrigan's office with the manila folder from the detective bureau's personnel file room. The name on it read: *Reynolds, Sumner J., Sergeant*

"Here you go Chief, need anything else?"

"No Emil, thanks...well, maybe some coffee...if there's any on the hot plate," Harrigan replied as he took the folder.

"I'll make a fresh pot, no trouble at all," Schu said as he closed the door and left.

Harrigan opened the file and saw Reynolds photo and his Dismissal Proceedings Report from the Board Of Police Commissioners and the Internal Affairs Department. Sumner Reynolds had managed to reach the rank of Sgt. Of Detectives, but his binge drinking, petty thievery and excessive public brutality had created too much of a stir even in a town where police brutality was considered business as usual.

In October 1929, he was dismissed from the force in disgrace and stripped of his pension in his own personal *Black Friday*. Harrigan had thrown Reynolds to the wolves, and he had taken pleasure in doing it.

Harrigan flipped through the manila file folder and found Reynolds last address:

3432 Eads Avenue. Harrigan knew the street well. It was named after James B. Eads, who designed the first bridge across the Mississippi, and the street ran east to west from Nebraska almost to Grand. The 3400 block was between St. Vincent on the north and Henrietta on the south where Eads Avenue dead-ended behind *The Wyman School* and the famous *Gallaudet Institute For The Deaf*.

Harrigan stretched out on his couch and continued to read the reports, no sense going home now he thought. I'll just sack out here and then after the morning briefing, we'll go pay a little call on my old pal Sumner Reynolds.

Down the hall in the empty traffic clerk's office, Schumacher was busy dialing Reynolds at his home. But, there was no answer. The phone was ringing off the hook.

"Pick it up you asshole...c'mon Sumner, sober up and pick it up," Schu whispered to himself. After four attempts, he gave up. *"Fuck it...I tried to warn you,"* Schu hung up and returned to the squad room and took Harrigan a fresh cup of hot coffee, just the way he liked it with two sugars with heavy cream.

At 3432 Eads, the phone now lay silent in the eerie stillness of the darkened house and Sumner Reynolds, its lone occupant did not stir.

———

KIRTSCHNER'S JOURNAL ENTRY: 1H/2H

"Wake up Charles Michael," O'Connell said as he slapped the soles of the sleeping Chief of Detectives feet. Harrigan came instantly awake on his office couch and asked the intruding Jeremiah, "What the hell's going on?"

O'Connell pulled up a chair and leaned into whisper to the shoeless Harrigan, who was now sitting up on the couch rubbing his eyes, "Charles Michael, have you lost your mind?"

"What the hell time is it," Harrigan asked?

"It's 8:15 a.m.," Jeremiah answered, "are you awake enough to understand me?"

"Yeah, I'm awake, what's all the fuss," he asked?

"The fuss is the Rizzo brothers. That's the fuss. What were you thinking?"

"Calm down Jeremiah, tell me what have you heard?"

"I heard you tossed Sal out of the 8th story at the Statler Hotel and then picked up Mario and he hasn't been seen since. What is going on?" O'Connell was clearly upset.

"And just who's babbling all these fairy tales?" Harrigan asked as he got up and stretched.

"My surveillance officer reported that Joe Culhane and other members of this squad picked up Mario last night. When I called Joe this morning to find out what went down, he confirmed that Mario's house was visited and then asked me if I had heard about Sal Rizzo?" O'Connell replied, "He told me about the so-called 'hit and run' at the Statler.

Jesus, Charles Michael, if this gets out?"

"Jeremiah, it won't get out. I'll talk to 'Slow Joe' and make sure he keeps his maw shut."

"Where's Mario?"

"You'll have to ask your close personal friend Mr. Gagliardi that question. We kept our deal with *The Big Dago*, so I suspect you can light two votive candles, one for each Rizzo rat the next time you and your pal Carmine get together at the Virgin Mother's grotto,"

Harrigan put on his shoes and opened his desk drawer to retrieve his shaving kit, "I'm going over to the academy gym and clean up, why don't'cha join me for a steam and let me fill you in?"

As the two walked down the stairs to the tunnel connecting the Central District to the Police Academy next door O'Connell asked, "Have you talked with Fred Washington?"

"No, not yet, I told him to call you with any news he got from the colored maid. Did he?'

Harrigan asked.

"Yes he called me, and when I tell you what Washington picked up from Mrs. Devereaux's maid, you're not going to believe what was going on in that house," O'Connell shook his head.

"Nothing will surprise me, there's just as much weird shit going on in the big houses on the easy streets as in the bedrooms above *The Celtic Room*...and sometimes the very same men are involved, only the pussy has changed," Harrigan noted cynically.

"Speaking of *The Celtic Room*, have you heard from your cousin the Cuban vacationer." Jeremiah asked?

"Not a peep...*not a peep*," Harrigan lied.

———◆———

During the steam, shower and shave, Jeremiah filled Harrigan in on the story Willie Henderson had told Washington. And, Harrigan gave O'Connell *most* of the details on Sal, Mario and Sumner Reynolds. He did, however, conveniently omit the tedious financial details about the amount of the money the Rizzo's had received and the recovery of same. He saw no point in needlessly burdening Jeremiah's mind with the economic mathematics of the case.

Harrigan mulled it all over and then said, "Jeremiah, you need to bring the Hendersons in today and get separate written statements from both the man and the woman.

'Take 'em down to the 7th and make nice with the coloreds. But, if you get any guff at all from them, call me and I'll come out throw the fear of God *and me* into them. I'll scare 'em both white if I have to. But get their statements now and swear them to secrecy, tell 'em they'll loose their jobs if they let Mrs. Devereaux or anybody else on to what we know.

"And what are you going to do today?" O'Connell asked.

"A visit to one Sumner Reynolds is on the top of my list, right after the squad meeting.

I'm also going to send Eamon out to get a statement from that Doctor what's his name?

Lester Percy?"

"Percy Leicester," Jeremiah corrected, "He's an English 'Lester' it's spelled...

L-e-i-c-e-s-t-e-r."

"Any way you spell it, he's a fucking English baby-killer... give his address to Finn, willya? We'll need to get a statement from that prick to corroborate the nigger maid's story about killing the unborn Devereaux baby," Harrigan bristled, "I might just arrest and sweat his pompous English ass just for the sport of it. Killing babies is against the law. Maybe he'd like to have his license revoked and to get to spend twenty to life dispensing aspirin to the rest of the cons in Jeff City. I half hope he decides to fuck with Finn."

"Let me handle Dr. Leicester, Finn's too heavy-handed, and we don't need another body in the morgue. This is best left to me, along with the Hendersons since they are both connected," Jeremiah calmly suggested.

Harrigan was still clearly annoyed, but he agreed, "Fine, you handle it."

———

The morning briefing went as planned; Harrigan intercepted Joe, Eamon, Mickey and Columbo beforehand and told them all to keep their mouths shut about the Rizzo Brothers — even within the squad and especially within the department at large. Harrigan made it eminently clear to 'Slow Joe' that he was unhappy about his spilling the beans to Jeremiah. He emphatically underscored the fact that he and only he would break any news about the Rizzos and that he would do it at a time of his choosing.

"Look, this case is a long way from being solved, so far we only flushed out two low level rats, the people behind them are the one's Jeremiah and me are after, and I swear to Christ, if anybody – *are you paying attention Joseph Patrick Culhane?*- if anybody fucks up my investigation, I will fire them…and then kill 'em. Am I clear," Harrigan asked?

The men nodded and awaited their orders for the day.

"Louie, Finn and Mickey, I want you to come with me to visit Sumner Reynolds. Joe, I want you to take three uniformed men of your choosing back over to Mario's place and go through the house very carefully and I mean with a fine tooth comb. Don't tear the place all apart and make mess either… go through it very methodically, room-by-room, drawer-by-drawer…upstairs, in the cellar, in the attic, in the crawl space and out in the garage. I want you to look for any evidence that can connect Mario and Sal to Reynolds or to the people behind him. Look for money, cancelled checks, appointment books, calendars, notes and so forth. Catalog it all and bring it back here for my review," Harrigan instructed. " Any questions? Good, let's get going."

———

The house at 3432 Eads was typical of the middle class homes of the area. It sat on a broad lot with a nice front lawn. It was a two-story single family made of brick with a slate roof, it was one of the nicer homes on this block of single family homes and 2-family flats. Sumner Reynolds' car was parked out front under the street lamp when Harrigan and company pulled up.

"Mickey and Finn go round the back, Lou and I will ring the bell and see if our man is home, "Harrigan ordered, "Now, remember this is a friendly visit, were not carrying a search or arrest warrant, so let's show some respect and courtesy for our former brother officer…unless of course, he decides to play it differently."

Harrigan waited for Mickey and Finn to get in position, and then he and Columbo went up the white stone stairs and rang the doorbell. Harrigan pressed it several times and it didn't ring. Then he rapped loudly on the frosted glass in the front door with his large signet ring. He waited and there was no response.

"Try the door," Harrigan told Columbo.

Louie pressed the thumb pad and the door unlatched and swung open. Columbo stuck his head inside and immediately recoiled gagging. Then the odor hit Harrigan's nostrils, it was the unmistakable cloying sickening stench of rotting flesh.

"Jesus Christ," Harrigan gasped as he pulled a handkerchief from his pocket to cover his mouth. He reached inside the door and pressed the buttons on the light switch to turn on the hall lights, nothing happened. The switch was dead. Harrigan stepped over a pile of mail strewn across the floor below the mail slot and went into the living room and pulled the chain on the floor lamp. There was no power. Harrigan went back out on to the front porch and handed his suit coat to the still gagging Louie Columbo. "Take off your jacket and put it in the car with mine, we'll probably have to burn it anyway, we'll never get the stench out...and Louie get some flashlights out of the car and come back right away. I'm going through the house and out the back door – I'm gonna open as many first floor windows as I can along the way, to see if we can get some air in here." Harrigan was not easily affected by death, but the smell reeking from inside meant that someone or something had been dead...for a very long time.

A few minutes later Columbo joined Harrigan, Mickey and Finn in the backyard.

"Lads, there's no corpse on the first floor, and there's no point in everyone getting sick, so I'm going upstairs and check it out, Harrigan said. "Finn, take the car to the nearest call box and get some people over here from the Coroner's Office as soon as possible. The rest of you wait here."

Harrigan returned inside, turned on his flashlight and ascended the stairs to the second floor, he stopped briefly to open a small stained glass window on the landing. He stuck his head out the window and took one last deep breath of fresh air, then he made his way into the upstairs hall. He tried the light switch at the top of the stairs, but to no avail. The stench was now overwhelming, much stronger than on the first floor. As Harrigan made his way down the hall, he shined his light into the bedrooms, they were empty and in good order. There was no sign of any violence. Then he paused at the bathroom door and pushed it in. As the door swung wide and it's glass door knob hit the tile wall, Harrigan's flashlight illuminated a sight like none he had ever seen in his life. The hardened cop recoiled and threw up in the hallway and then ran to the back of the house and threw open the upstairs window and stuck his head outside.

"Jesus Christ, Chief!!" Mickey saw him first. Harrigan was hanging out the upstairs window leaning far over the sill and violently vomiting into the yard below.

Inside the darkened bathroom the badly decomposed body of Sumner Reynolds sat in an evaporating tub half full of reeking bathwater and dissolving human flesh, rotting and ruptured by the escape of trapped gasses and fecal disgorgement. The upper part of Reynolds' body that was not submerged in the cesspool of liquefying intestines, stomach, torso and legs, was swollen and rotting with a black and bluish hue around the sunken open yellow-mucus coated eyes and gaping mouth filled with wiggling maggots.

Harrigan made his way downstairs and out into the backyard, he was still gagging and vomiting and his stomach was cramped from spasms. He told his men to stay out of the house and to not let anyone in until the coroner arrived.

About 2-hours later, after the Coroner's team had arrived, Harrigan and his men got a preliminary report from the lead examiner on the scene. "It looks like the victim accidentally electrocuted himself with a space heater. We found a

Heat-A-Lator rotating coil heater in the tub. It was still plugged in, that's what blew the fuses. We had to scoop and ladle the body out in globs and pieces because it fell apart when we started to move it. The whole bottom was just a pile of putrid sloughed off skin and rotting intestines. Even the skin on the feet came off. We have it all in sealed autopsy cans to take downtown. Before we go and clear the scene for investigation, we're washing down the tub and the room with ammonia and vinegar to get most of the residual flesh out," the examiner reported, "but you'll never get the smell out, this house will have to be condemned and torn down.

"How long was he dead," Harrigan asked?

"Hard to tell, but judging from the part of his body that was above water, I'd guess between 3 and 4 weeks, maybe a little more. It's a really ugly mess...you might see something like this once every ten years. I'm surprised the mailman or the neighbors didn't report it. He was really a stinker. *Who found him?*"

Harrigan raised a lone finger to signify that he was the one.

"Oh, man, I'm sorry Chief, that was a helluva sight to walk in on."

"Thanks," Harrigan said.

"Lou, please collect the mail. The earliest unopened letter's postmark will give us an approximate date of death. Then call Jeremiah and have him put some uniformed officers on guard here around the clock for the next few days. Let's get some big fans over here and let them blow all day and all night to get as much stink get out of here before we have to go in and search the place. I'm going home now and get cleaned up. Finn, drive me willya?" Harrigan asked. It was pretty obvious that the Chief was still shaken and sickened by the awful sight.

On the ride to his house, Harrigan was uncharacteristically silent. His mind was mulling over the last two days events. He wondered, with the Rizzos dead and now Reynolds, would the investigation hit a dead end. He was really worried for the first time in his long career and thought, *I need some help here.*

And, there was only one man who he felt might be able to help.

KIRTSCHNER'S JOURNAL ENTRY: 1H/2H/OF

Schumacher read the report from the Coroner's Inquest on his coffee break in the empty clerk's office. The report was inconclusive as to the cause of death of the four children and three adults whose remains were found burnt beyond recognition under three floors of debris in the cellar of the Brenahanny residence.

The Fire Department Report which was attached, listed the cause of the fire as *Suspicious,* but stopped short of *Arson* because Brenahanny had kept a 100 gallon heating oil tank in the cellar and the cause of ignition was indeterminable. The destruction caused by the five-alarm inferno was so widespread that drawing a conclusive cause was nigh unto impossible.

Schu neatly refolded the documents and placed them back in the envelope and returned them to Harrigan's mail slot in the squad room. So far, Schu had felt that he had dodged the bullet of detection and now that the investigation was winding down and Kirtschner was being controlled by Harrigan, he felt his best course of action was no further action. He wasn't sticking his head out any further, for love or money.

When the report came in about Reynolds' death, Schu decided that the time might be right for him to take a vacation and get out of town until all the dust had settled. He had two weeks coming, so he made up a cock and bull story about an ailing sister in Ohio and got the Watch Commander to let him take immediate leave without the customary two weeks scheduling notice.

Schu left the building and headed for home at the end of his shift. It had been a good run, he had made a little over two thou' and it was time to take his money off the table and cut his risks to zero. *Or so he thought.*

Meanwhile, Jeremiah had the Hendersons picked up and brought down to the station, and, with a police stenographer present, he had them repeat what they had told Fred Washington.

While unwilling to cooperate at first out of fear of losing their jobs, they finally relented when Jeremiah assured them that if they did not cooperate with him that he would have to turn them over to Chief of Detectives Harrigan. The Hendersons knew of *'Iron Charlie's'* reputation for ruthlessness in the Negro community and they quickly came clean. Jeremiah had his sworn affidavits from two material witnesses.

In short order, Dr. Percy Leicester arrived at the station and was confronted by Jeremiah with the Hendersons' statements; he readily admitted that EOR had called him to help out his daughter who was in "trouble." 'Perky' also stated that he had confirmed the diagnosis of 'Cupid's Curse,' late stage syphilis and the onset of brain deteriorating general paresis, which he had corroborated with Mrs. Devereaux's OB-Gyn prior to agreeing to terminate her pregnancy.

In his professional opinion, Leicester believed that the baby she was carrying had already contracted syphilis and that if carried to term that it would be in all likelihood born with severe mental and physical deficiencies and it would not survive to adulthood under the even the best of care conditions.

He also carefully spelled out that facts and concluded that Ada herself was also condemned to a slow and agonizing death sentence. The progression of the venereal disease she had contracted from Pierre would in all probability terminate her life before the end of the decade. He also allowed as how EOR had paid him $15,000 to keep the whole thing quiet.

Jeremiah felt that they now had a motive, but the connection between the Rizzos and Reynolds did not as yet directly implicate or connect EOR or Mrs.Devereaux in the murders. But, he was confident that Harrigan would make Reynolds sing and arrests would follow in short order.

Later that day, when Jeremiah learned of Reynolds death, his heart sank. It could be a complete dead end. Why did Harrigan jump the gun with Sal and Mario? He wondered if Mario was still alive. Maybe a call to Carmine could get him back in police custody.

He called Columbo to ask him about the prospects of calling Carmine to intercede for Mario.

Columbo said, "Save the nickel."

Newspaper Clipping – *St.Louis Post-Dispatch*, April 10, 1931

Too Many Suspicious Coincidences In Three Brenahanny Police Cases

Post-Dispatch Reporter
Harry H. Nelson

On March 30th the home of Mr. and Mrs. Dennis Brenahanny was destroyed by fire and six family members perished in the inferno. Earlier the very same day, their son, Matt Brenahanny 22, was shot and killed in an alleged burglary in *The Celtic Room* business office. And, just days earlier, the Brenahanny Furniture Store at Natural Bridge and Union was robbed and vandalized and owner Dennis Brenahanny was assaulted.

Are "Coincidences" Linked To Bootlegging Rivalry?

The 3-story Brenahanny residence at 5475 Kensington was engulfed in a 5-alarm inferno that originated in the basement, possibly by the ignition of a 100 gallon heating oil storage tank. The St. Louis Fire Department investigation listed the nature of the fire as *"Suspicious"* but stopped short of an *"Arson"* assessment.

Battalion Chief Gary T. Bingham said that the Fire Department could not make a definitive determination as to the cause of the fire. The fact that the 3-story brick building collapsed into the cellar complicated investigators trying to sort through tons of wet and smoldering debris.

The two other bizarre incidents of misfortune that also befell the Brenahanny family have been further obscured by the so-called accidental cremation of the body of Matt Brenahanny. Spokesman for the Coroner's office reported that young Brenahanny's body had been placed in a mis-labeled autopsy storage unit and that it had been sent to the City Crematorium prematurely.

Reliable *Post-Dispatch* sources have reported that his father, Dennis Brenahanny had been selling bootleg whiskey out of his store and that this may have provoked violent actions by associates of Thomas E. Culhane, proprietor of *The Celtic Room*. Culhane is a figure frequently mentioned in connection with alleged illegal liquor distribution and other criminal activities in St. Louis.

The Post Dispatch is calling on the Circuit Attorney William J. Geekie to initiate a special investigation into these horrific incidents. We also urge Chief Gordon C. Strickland to appoint a special lead investigator to replace Chief Of Detectives Charles M. Harrigan, who is related to Thomas E. Culhane owner of *The Celtic Room*. Detective Joseph P. Culhane of the detective bureau is also a brother of Thomas E. Culhane.

Three coincidences and an accidental cremation of a shooting victim prior to an autopsy stretch the boundaries of Police Department integrity and credibility beyond the breaking point. The St. Louis Police Department cannot let these incidents simply be swept under the carpet. The Brenahanny family and the citizens of St. Louis deserve a thorough investigation into these matters.

Mac closed the old Kirtschner Journal and looked around her condo's floor at the spread out, open files and aging news clips from the Mercantile Library. As a reporter, she was engrossed by the amount of detail and the compelling nature of the story. She was also shocked and appalled to realize that Chip was from the same blood line as *"Iron Charlie."*

How was that possible? Was Chip really that different from his thug ancestor or did the same latent tendencies for domination, brute violence and criminal malfeasance lurk in his DNA too?

Mac sat there and sipped on her bottled water and wondered if she should share the story with Chip? How would he react? Should she tell him now? Or when she'd finished and had reached a determination on what to do with it? Would telling the story of his grandfather destroy the love that was seeming to blossom between them.

She'd have to tell him before anything aired, she realized, *God, I could never blindside him with this.*

In the ensuing weeks, she and Chip had been spending more and more time together. The great sex was always there, but it was giving way to a deeper than physical connection and mutual attraction. They were making the migration from spontaneous passion in the pure pursuit of pleasure to the *'what if'* discussions that precede the planning progression leading up to that tricky intersection where two lovers decide to take the prenuptial plunge or to begin the painful segue of separation.

Mac's attraction to Chip had grown deeper as she got to know him over dinners, movies and of course, the inevitable pillow talk. He had even said the *"I love you"* phrase that is the precursor to the end of bachelorhood. At first, she had dismissed it as his post-orgasm babbling, but his recent emails, surprise e-cards and unexpected flowers arriving at webKSDK had set her heart aflutter and the newsroom buzzing.

Mac wanted everything to work out and hoped that her *Mr. Right for Tonight* would morph into *Mr. Right for a Lifetime*. She also wondered why the old reporter's Journal had dropped in her lap. She asked herself if meeting and falling in love with Harrigan's great-great grandson was part of some synchronous karmic dance that she didn't understand and of which he remained blissfully unaware.

It gave her a headache thinking about it. At one point, she contemplated tossing the files and the Journal into the fireplace and burning up all the bad *juju* that was unfolding with each new page. She even contemplated paying The Mercantile Library research fees herself and telling her boss 'Scrooge McEtzkorn' that there was nothing to her intuitive hunch about the story. But, she knew in her heart of hearts that he'd smell a rat in either scenario, especially if she volunteered to pay The Merc bill. That would set off alarm bells in his head for sure. If Etzkorn knew anything about reporters, he knew that they were penurious misers...the cheapest S.O.B.s on the planet with the possible exception of Etzkorn himself.

Her mind whirled around in tornadic circles as she wondered what bizarre twist the story would take next. And, what would it mean for her and Chip? For now, she decided to keep it all to herself and see where the fates took her.

She got up and put on a pot of coffee, changed into her pajamas, brushed and flossed and returned to the kitchen to fill up her coffee cup.

Another long night of reading and revelations lay ahead.

KIRTSCHNER'S JOURNAL ENTRY: 1H/2H

Harrigan had a fitful night, sleep eluded him and he ended up sitting in his kitchen all night smoking cigars and running over all the details in his mind. The possibility of having his case collapse around him was unnerving; perhaps his reach had finally exceeded his grasp with the premature disposal of the Rizzos and the unanticipated and apparently accidental death of the sot Reynolds.

How would he explain his way out of all that? What if Kirtschner wouldn't play along? What if Schumacher and Kirtschner went to Chief Strickland? What if the Rizzo blood money in his office closet came to light? What if the Matt Brenahanny shooting cover-up and the fire at the family home blew up in his puss?

Harrigan played a number of scenarios out in his mind and it they all ended like a Greek Tragedy where he was killed in Act III and his body was dragged through the streets and impaled outside the city gates as a cautionary lesson to other law enforcement officers. Finally, as 8:00 a.m. rolled around, he decided to make the call to the one man who might be able to help him.

"Hello," a soft and refined woman's voice answered.

"Is Thomas Edward there?" Harrigan asked.

"Is this Charles Michael?" Clovie asked, "This is Clovie, I was expecting room service to call back."

"It's me Clovie, is the love of *our* lives handy?"

"Let me get him, he's just shaving." Clovie set the receiver down and went to fetch *The King,* who was standing still wet and naked shaving before a steaming washbasin.

"Charles Michael, to what do I owe the honor?" Culhane asked as he returned to the living room of the suite wrapped in a towel.

"Thomas Edward, I can't go into every detail, but is there any way you can meet with me in person – *right away* - with Jeremiah and Fred? And I'm even thinking we may need to pull in a friendly judge too."

"Sounds like you've painted yourself into a corner, Charles Michael," Culhane speculated.

"More than that, I'm afraid…I can really use your good counsel and your help."

"That's what blood is for. I'll catch the next train back to St. Louis. You round up Fred and Jeremiah and I'll call Judge Slack. Let's set up an enclave at the castle the day after tomorrow at 10:30 in the morning. Bring all your dirty laundry and let's sort it out. *Fair enough?*" Culhane asked.

"I couldn't ask for more, thank you cousin, and please give my very best to Clovie."

"I will, and I'll see you soon," *The King* hung up.

"*Trouble?*" Clovie asked.

Culhane smiled, "It seems so, sounds like Charles Michael has caught his cock *and his balls* in a laundry ringer."

"When are you leaving?" Colvie asked wistfully.

"I'll have to be heading back on the night train," Tom replied.

"Well, that doesn't leave us much time..." Clovie embraced him, rubbed her hands over his wet body and kissed his chest.

Culhane picked her up in his arms and carried her into the bedroom, he threw the damp towel aside and rolled into bed next to her, "Clovie, if we had eternity and a day, we'd still never have enough time to be makin' love."

The large *Emerson* floor fans whirled 'round the clock blowing the stench of death out of Reynolds' house. Finally, the air was barely bearable for detectives to enter if they were wearing heavy surgical masks. Columbo had drawn the short straw and he lead the team that went thought the house from top to bottom. Harrigan had issued almost the same orders as he had for the search of Mario's home.

"Don't tear the place all apart and make mess of it either... go through it very methodically, room-by-room, drawer-by-drawer...upstairs, in the cellar, in the attic, in the crawl spaces, in his car and out in the garage. I want you to look for any evidence that can connect Mario and Sal to Reynolds or to the people behind them. Look for money, cancelled checks, appointment books, calendars, notes and so forth.

Then Harrigan underscored a very critical and important point, "The most important thing we can find is the wedding ring that Sal twisted off Pierre's broken finger. If Reynolds still had it in his possession at the time of his death, it means that the transaction hasn't been completed. If he doesn't have it, it means that whoever paid the money is now in possession of it. Finding that ring will link them to the murder, no doubt about it."

The detective crew worked their way through Reynolds home from top to bottom. No ring was found, but two items of note were brought back to the station and to Chief Harrigan's attention.

"Did you find the ring?" Harrigan asked.

"Just a ring of rotted flesh around the tub," Columbo replied, "But, Chief, we did find Reynolds' bank account at Southside National Bank, and his passbook showed that he deposited $20,000 in cash beginning in the period three weeks before the murders until four weeks ago. A total of four cash deposits of $5,000 each were made," Columbo reported, "And we found his badge and his identification card too."

"*His badge?* How did he still have his badge?" Harrigan was surprised because Reynolds lost his badge when the department discharged him.

"Not his police badge," Columbo said as he tossed a small brass badge and the leather identification folder to which it was pinned on to the Chief's desk. The badge read: ***Continental Shoe Company 101***, and the Identification card read:

Sumner Reynolds
Chief Of Watchmen
Continental Shoe Company
St. Louis, Missouri

"Well, now isn't that an interesting development?" Harrigan said as he raised his eyebrows, "This means that Reynolds is the missing link, now all we have to do is connect him and the money in his bank account to the Robertson's and we're got ourselves an extremely strong, albeit circumstantial case.

"Did you find anything else?" Harrigan asked.

"We're still rifling through all the papers in his desk and in the upstairs bedroom closets, but there is a lot of crap stuffed in shoe boxes to look at. Reynolds was not a very tidy or organized. It'll still take us a few days, but we thought you'd want to see this stuff right away, Chief," Columbo said.

"Good work, keep digging, " Harrigan urged, "And Louie, take a fucking shower and change your clothes before you come up here again, the dead man's stink is hanging on to your clothes. You might want to help yourself to some of Sal's and Mario's new suits, since they won't be needin' 'em any longer... and, you're going to have to burn anything you wear into that death house," Harrigan suggested.

Columbo was nonplussed at the idea of trading in clothes permeated with the stench of death from one dead man for clothes owned by two recently deceased brother Pisano's, nonetheless he said, "Thanks Chief that's a good idea, I appreciate you thinking of me."

Harrigan smiled, "I'm always happiest when looking out for my men, Luigi. Now, get outta here before smellin' you makes me start puking again. Go on, hurry on now!"

———◆———

KIRTSCHNER'S JOURNAL ENTRY: 1H/2H

The overnight train from Memphis pulled into Union Station the following morning, right on time and Fred Washington and the one-armed chauffer Matt Hellman were waiting at trackside for *The King*.

"I was surprised to find out that you never went to Cuba," Fred said as he took *The King's* monogrammed belting leather grip from his hand.

"Well, *'Welcome Home* to you too my dear Mr. Washington," Culhane replied sarcastically, "And how was your trip?"

"I'm sorry Mr. Thomas, how was your trip?"

"It was fine, and where I go and what I do and who I tell is my business and no one else's," Culhane scolded.

"Yes, sir, I'm sorry," Fred replied.

"Forget it, I have," Culhane said, "Now have all the arrangements been made?"

"Yes sir, everyone will be at the house at 10:30," Fred said.

"Excellent, let's get home, I'm tired from all my traveling. And, Fred, has there been any news on the Brenahanny Coroner's Inquest Report? I'm beginning to wonder if the seed money I so liberally sprinkled around before I left town has borne any fruit as yet," Culhane wondered aloud.

"No word that I've heard of, maybe Mr. Charles will know?" he answered.

"Remind me to make inquiry into that matter tomorrow," Culhane instructed, "That'll be time enough."

At 10:15, Harrigan's black LaSalle pulled into the driveway of the castle at 34 Hawthorne Place and parked next to Fred Washington's *Buick* sedan in the rear brick-paved courtyard. Within a few moments, Major Jeremiah O'Connell, Chief of Detectives Charles Harrigan and Judge Francis X. Slack entered the rear of the house. Mary Clare greeted them and said, "Tom and Fred are waiting for you in his library."

Culhane rose to greet his guests, "Welcome gentlemen, Jeremiah, Charles Michael good to see you," he crossed the room and shook the hands of the short balding former Bostonian, Judge Francis Xavier Slack of the St. Louis Circuit Court.

"And a special welcome to you Francis Xavier, thank you for accepting my invitation to join us. I have a feeling that we'll be in need of a dose of your judicial wisdom before this day is out. Please make yourselves comfortable. There's coffee and Jameson's on the sideboard, help yourselves," Culhane gestured to the beverages.

Harrigan began by stating, "It is very important that we lay all our cards on the table and that we can speak freely knowing that whatever is said here stays in the room. Agreed?"

Everyone nodded in ascent and Culhane asked Harrigan to bring everyone up to date since he was the one who called the meeting.

The only person who had not been involved up to this point was Judge Slack. Francis Xavier or 'FX' as Culhane liked to call him, was a longtime St. Louis attorney, who had represented *The King* and many of his legal businesses before moving to the bench. The two were lifelong friends and had known each other since they played soccer together at old St. Malachy's. Slack was a Bostonian by birth, whose father and mother migrated from South Boston to Kerry Patch when old man Slack got a job as an AFL union organizer in St. Louis as part of the old railroadmen's boilermakers local. FX was a bright kid who used his brains and his grit and gristle to earn a scholarship to college and law school, as well as, his stripes in St. Louis legal circles. He was also an astute politician, who knew how to walk on the very thin razor's edge between the legal and illegal, between his friends in law enforcement and as he liked to say, his friends who took *'a more liberal interpretation of legal rules and regulations.'* He was a master craftsman when it came to making deals and his sage advice was often sought by *The King* and by the finest legal minds in Missouri.

Harrigan walked everyone carefully through the sequence of events beginning with the discovery of the murder victims all the way up to the discovery of Sumner Reynolds connection to Continental Shoe and the Rizzos.

Judge Slack and Culhane listened quietly and patiently as Harrigan explained in excruciating detail how the investigation had proceeded and how it now looked like a dead end with the death of Sumner Reynolds. Sure, there was $20,000 in Reynolds account, but so far, there was no way to connect it back to the syphilitic widow or EOR because the all deposits had been made in cash.

Harrigan and Jeremiah were both clearly frustrated, but for very different reasons. Jeremiah was frustrated by Harrigan's premature dispatching of the Rizzos before he had closed the loop by arresting Reynolds and sweating him to reveal the source of the murder money.

Harrigan was frustrated by Jeremiah's finger-pointing criticism of his methods in dealing with the Rizzos and by his political pussy-footing around, which 'Iron Charlie' judged to be a lot of ass covering designed to protect his career and aspirations to succeed Chief Strickland.

Jeremiah summed it all up, "When it's all said and done, we're at a dead end without the victim's wedding ring, Rizzo said the victim's jewelry was taken to prove that the job was done and to prove that they did it. According to Mario, they gave the wedding ring to Reynolds, the middleman who hired the killers. We did find Pierre's stick pin and cufflinks, in Mario's garage, but not his wedding ring. So, I'm guessing that Reynolds already gave it to the person or persons, who ordered the killings, and that's how the Rizzos got paid and that's where the $20,000 in Reynolds bank account came from. But, I'm also guessing that Devereaux's wedding ring is long gone, tossed in the river or melted down by now."

Harrigan noted, "We can connect all the links in the chain except the final one."

Fred Washington, who had been sitting silently on the side window seat taking it all in finally spoke up, "I'm not so sure about that."

"What do you mean," Harrigan asked?

"Well, something just jogged in my mind; I never thought it was important until now.

But, back when I was questioning Willie the maid she said, '...Mr. Robertson made some kinda peace between Ada, Pierre and the sister he was caught fucking.'

Well, she didn't exactly put it that way Fred admitted, but she did go on to say, "Miss Ada deserved a lot better than what she got, but I think even now she still loves him, just the other night *she was holding his wedding ring in her hand and crying something awful.* As far as he goes, I sure hope he's burning in Hell...that's where he belongs...with his back broken."

Harrigan leapt to his feet, "Are you sure?"

Fred nodded, "I remember that because of the way that church lady wanted to see Pierre burning in hell. For being a God fearing woman, she had no mercy in her heart for him. None."

"If Fred is right, then Ada has the wedding ring. All we need to do is get a search warrant and go over to the Devereaux house and find the ring and make the arrest," Jeremiah was elated.

Judge Slack, looked up and said, "It might not be that simple."

"Why?" asked Harrigan.

"Well, Charles Michael, how do you propose to prove that the wedding ring in question was actually taken off the dead man's finger by his killers and then given to Sumner Reynolds and redeemed for cash by the people who ordered the murder for hire?" Judge Slack added, "If I was defending Ada Robertson and her father, EOR, I'd have the case dismissed in 10 minutes."

"But Sal Rizzo admitted to taking the wedding ring and we found the rest of the jewelry in Mario's garage and Mario admitted giving the wedding ring to Reynolds," Harrigan was making his case.

"Fine," FX said, "Let's call the Rizzo brothers and Reynolds to the witness stand.

Oh, oh, there's a slight problem...dead men make terrible witnesses.

"I'm afraid you can't make the case. It's all circumstantial. And, going up against a prestigious community leader, powerful business executive and socially prominent man like Edmund O. Robertson and his widowed daughter armed with a lot of speculation and a bag of hearsay from *in absentia* thugs and a deceased drunk isn't going to get past the Grand Jury. And frankly, Charles Michael, no wet behind the ears district attorney in his right mind would even consider bringing it up for a Grand Jury determination," Slack folded his hands on his stomach and stared back at the Chief of Detectives.

Jeremiah put his head in his hands, "This is going to bring us all down if we go after them. Everything will come out and we'll all be ruined."

A stony silence of despair settled over the group as Harrigan and Jeremiah contemplated the wisdom of Judge Slack's advice. The ticking of the grandfather clock in the corner of the library was the loudest sound in the room until *The King of Kerry* broke the silence.

The King softly spoke, I once told my brother, "Joseph, don't'cha know that you don't win poker with cards, you win poker with balls. It's just like real life."

Harrigan, O'Connell, Washington and Judge Slack all looked at the smiling face of *The King of Kerry* and wondered what was so amusing about the *non sequitur* he just uttered.

Then, before they could ask for further explanation, Culhane asked them all a thought stopping question, *"Where's the profit?"*

"Where's the profit?"

KIRTSCHNER'S JOURNAL ENTRY: 1H/2H

"Where's the profit?" Harrigan was flummoxed, "What the hell are you talking about dear cousin? I'm completely asea."

Tom Culhane got out of his desk chair, extended his arms to their full span and panoramically gestured at the library walls as he rotated 360-degrees.

"Gentlemen, what do you see here?" he asked.

Harrigan was quick to speak, "I see books, after all Thomas Edward, we are in your library."

"Look closer and think deeper," Culhane urged.

Jeremiah said, "I think I get your drift, are you saying, *'don't judge a book by its cover?'"*

The King of Kerry walked over to the bay window and drew back the heavy draperies to let in more light and said, "Where is the illumination…where is the light in all of this dark business? *Where's the profit?"*

Harrigan was growing more frustrated by the second, "Thomas, I'm lost in all this intellectualizin' can you tell me where you're going…and explain it to me like I was two years old."

"I'll do better than that," *The King* said, "I'll explain it to you and draw you a picture just like I was explaining it to my own dear brother, 'Slow Joe.' "

The reference to 'Slow Joe' brought a gale of laughter from the somber men. It was a welcome relief in the pall of unspoken tension and frustrations that was clouding the groups' thinking.

The King sat back in his Chesterfield leather chair and continued, "History gets written by the daring, not by the meek and timid. These shelves are filled with the stories of those who dared to win and those who when confronted with adversity simply folded, knuckled under and gave up.

"Have you ever heard the story of the Gordian Knot?" Culhane looked a round waiting for a response. Judge Slack said, "Yes, I kind of remember it was about a king who had a problem to do with untying a knot, but that's about all I can recall."

"It is about Alexander the Great, he came upon a chariot that had a huge knot tied all around its yoke. The legend had it that whoever could loose the Gordian Knot would conquer the world. Many kings and princes had tried to untie the knot, but it was so big, so complicated and so tightly knotted that it resisted all attempts until Alexander came along."

"How did he untie the knot?" O'Connell asked.

"He didn't **untie** it. He paid attention to the clue given in the legend which stated, '*whoever could **loose** the Gordian Knot would conquer the world.*' Loosing the knot did not say, *untie* it. So Alexander took out his sword and cut through the Gordian Knot with one strong decisive and totally unexpected blow.

"And that gentlemen, is precisely what we must do. We can't unravel all of these knotted up events in any way that benefits any of us. So we have to cut through with one strong, daring and unanticipated blow. But before we do it, I'll ask you all the question once again, *"Where's the profit?"*

"Tom, I've known you man and boy for over 40-years," FX stated, "And you've always been way ahead of the rest of us in the brains and thinking department, so do us all a favor and spare us the thinking part and get right to the explaining part."

Culhane laughed and said. "Okay, to find out where the profit is, you have to start with another question." Everyone groaned and begged him to get on with it.

"Patience lads, think this through with me. Of all the people we've talked about today, who has the most money?"

"EOR, no doubt about it," FX stated with certainty.

Culhane asked, "Now, who stands to gain the most money?"

Jeremiah spoke up, "Mrs. Devereaux stands to inherit Pierre's estate at about $4.5 million and she'll get another $500,000 on her policy, maybe a $1 million if the insurance company pays it off as an accidental death."

"Oh yeah," O'Connell continued and there's another policy, one for $1,000,000 owned by Continental Shoe, to repurchase Mr. Devereaux's stock. So that dough would flow her way too."

"Add it up...I'm getting $1.5 million to $2 million in insurance dough, check my math, willya," Culhane asked.

"Now the next question," Culhane turned to Harrigan, "If you got syphilis from your husband and it cost you the life of your baby, and eventually, your own; what would you do?"

"I kill the son-of-a-bitch," Harrigan said.

"Now, suppose this same syphilitic son-of-a-bitch was banging your sister too, do you think she might get the syph as well?" Culhane asked, "How would you feel about that?"

"I'd kill the fucker twice if I could!" Harrigan concluded.

"Follow along now," Culhane leaned in and sketched four circles on a piece of paper.

Here is Pierre, the syphilis spreading S.O.B., this circle is his loving and long-suffering wife Ada." Harrigan put a dot inside her circle, "And here is the unborn baby. This circle is the sister Pierre seduced and probably gave her the gift of *Cupid's Curse* too...and this last circle is EOR.

"Now," Culhane drew a dotted line from EOR to another circle, "And this is Sumner Reynolds, ex-cop, fulltime sot and go between to these two morons," Harrigan drew two more small circles, "The recently deceased Rizzo rats."

Then, with a sweeping arc, Culhane drew a bold line from the Rizzos to Pierre's circle and a small circle he drew next to it, "This is *Madame X*...a lady who was next in line to get Pierre's little gift for women. She was just in the wrong place at the wrong time practicing her amorous feminine skills.

"Now, gentlemen, look at the picture and tell me, *Where's the profit?*"

"Well, there is no profit in getting syphilis no matter how much money you stand to inherit, so I'd have to say only EOR stands to profit, everyone else is either dead or most likely already under a death sentence from the disease," FX pronounced.

"It's hard to find a hero or a heroine in this mess, isn't it FX?" Culhane cracked, "So the challenge for us is *not to untie* the mess in the pursuit of justice. Our challenge is to see that we get the money *loose* and let God's own justice work itself out in time's due course.

"I have a plan, but it will take a daring, swift and unexpected stroke. Would you like to hear how we're going to loose the Gordian Knot and get $1.5 to $2 million? *And, if we do it right,* we can tap into a river of '*Shoe Town*' gold that'll flow like an annuity into many worthy coffers for years to come."

"Now, one final question…who else knows everything that we know? Nobody, right? Only we know what we know." Culhane clapped his hands together, "That's our advantage,"

LVI

Friday night late dinners, Saturday morning breakfasts in bed and lazy Sundays spent just lolling around her condo or being out together had become the routine for Mac and Chip over the last few months. This weekend was no exception. Chip met Mac at the station when she got off and they were going out to dinner. Mac had insisted some months before that they alternate paying for dinner, since she didn't want Chip paying for everything out of his cop and bartender salaries, especially since he was trying to rack up some cash for law school.

"Hi honey," he kissed her as she came into the lobby, "I've got a surprise for dinner in store for you tonight. Someplace you've never been before."

"But isn't it my turn," she mock protested.

"No arguments, just put yourself in my capable hands," Chip asked.

"I'd love to Mr. Harrigan, but doesn't that usually happen *after* dinner?" she joked.

"You are a *very* naughty girl…and I love that about you," Chip smiled, "Let me drive so I can surprise you."

As they pulled out of the garage, Chip handed her a small satin sleep mask, "Here put this on and no peeking!"

"Am I being kidnapped, held for ransom? This is exciting… are you going to tied me up too or do I get handcuffed?" Mac asked.

"I might handcuff you later…but if you keep asking so many questions, I'm going to put some duct tape over your mouth right now," Chip threatened.

Mac put on the silver satin mask and decided to be quiet and listen to the ambient sounds and see if she could sense were they were going judging by the street noise, lefts and rights, time between turns and speed. She decided to play the game as if it were for real. Then she had a weirdly chilling thought, *"I hope he isn't taking me to Tower Grove Park."*

Chip made it hard for her by turning on the Sirius stereo surround sound. The powerful BBO, Bose Bang and Olufson, speakers blared out the neo-retro-rock hit *Who Shot Obama, Mama?* by *Dick Chainie and The Dead Presidents.* That sound effectively drowned out all outside audio clues to their current location.

Mac estimated that about 20-minutes had passed since they left the station. The non-stop speed of the car indicated that they were on a highway within two to three minutes after leaving the station so they could be on I-64 east or west, I-44 southwest, I-55 south or north or I-70 east or north. The big intercity, trans-Mississippi interstate interchange and the Bill Clinton Bridge was just 3 blocks from the station. When that occurred to her, she realized that she could be headed in any direction.

Chip asked, "Are you peeking?"

"No, I'm in total visual sensory deprivation," Mac admitted.

"Well, we're almost there," Chip announced as Mac felt the car slow down and brake to a stop. It waited, like for a light to change. Then Chip turned the car right. Mac silently counted one thousand-one, one thousand-two..."

At one thousand and fifty five the car turned right again and then slowed and pulled to a stop. Chip put the car in reverse and swung to the right as he backed up. Mac thought, he's parallel parking.

"Okay, now stay put and leave the sleep mask on, I'm coming over to get you and I'll lead you into the surprise dinner location," Chip was very strict, "No cheating and no peeking, okay?"

Mac said, "Lead on McDuff!"

Harrigan exited the car, came around and opened her door and helped her out. "Take my arm and just walk with me," Chip was laughing.

"What's so funny?" Mac was a little worried about this surprise.

She felt her feet walking on hard pavement for about fifteen steps. Then Chip said, "Okay stand right here." Mac heard a door open and then Chip said, "Step up one step." Mac complied and felt the surface under her feet change as her heels clicked on wood and then a few steps later on carpet as Chip steered her to the right.

"Are you ready?" Chip asked.

"As I'll ever be," Mac replied.

Chip lifted off her mask and 35 Harrigan's yelled, "Surprise!"

Mac was shocked, she had never met Chip's family and now she was standing in someone's living room surrounded by his entire clan. A handsome woman in her late 50's came up and said, "Welcome to the House of Harrigan, I'm Helen, Chip's mother and this is his Dad, Charlie. We've heard so much about you Miss McGauley and Chip insisted on making you the guest of honor at his birthday party."

His birthday party! Mac was stunned and she looked at Chip who was beaming back at her. His brothers and cousins came to her and introduced themselves in rapid fire order. "Oh my God!, I'll never remember who's who" she protested, "This is...this is...overwhelming."

"Don't worry, after a few drinks they won't remember who they are either, just call 'em Harrigan or Pug Ugly...whatever works for you," Chip's Dad said, "C'mon let me fix you a drink... Chip says you're partial to Jameson's. Me too!" he smiled and confessed.

Mac followed Chip's Dad into the knotty pine paneled room off the living room where a bar had been set up. The walls of the room were covered with family photos from every era. Mac was looking around to see if there were any baby pictures of Chip.

Mac's heart skipped a beat when she came to the small cluster of framed photos showing Chip's grandfather's unsmiling face, *Iron Charlie* was in various group shots with the notables of his day. Mayor Raymond R. Tucker, Senator Stuart Symington and President Harry S Truman, Chief Jeremiah O'Connell, a very young Prosecuting Attorney, who later became George McGovern's shortime Vice Presidential running mate and longtime Missouri Senator, Tom Eagleton. There was even a suprising photo of the Officers Of The Ancient Order of Hibernians where he was seated next to *The King of Kerry.*

Two things immediately stuck her about *Iron Charlie's* countenance in every photo. First of all in every shot he was clutching his ubiquitous cigar and second, it was his eyes. From beneath the furrowed brow on his expressionless face they stared directly at the camera lens and ultimately at the photo's viewer. They stared at her across the decades focused and like cold shark eyes. Mac wondered what thoughts might have been lurking in his mind when each of the photos was taken?

"That's quite a rogues' gallery," Chip's Dad noted as he broke her concentration and handed her a Jameson's on the rocks in a heavy cut-crystal Waterford tumbler, "Drink up darlin' here's to seeing lots more of you. Chip's been going and on endlessly about you. And, since we see you on iTV all the time, we kinda feel like we already know you."

The secret dinner location turned out to be Chip's birthday party at his parent's home in St. Louis Hills on Donovan Avenue, just across the street from Francis Park. He had insisted that it start late and hold off on the real celebrating until he could bring home the girl he'd been rambling on about for months.

When Mac got Chip aside, she whispered in his ear, "I'm going to kill you...I'm so unprepared."

"There is no way to prepare you for meeting the clan Harrigan...it's best just to throw you into the deep end and go from there...*trust me they all already love you*...but not as much as I do," Chip kissed her cheek.

The Harrigan party rolled on 'til well past 3 a.m. and stories flowed like the Mississippi as one brother, sister-in-law and cousin rose to toast the birthday boy and regale his lady friend with an embarrassing story about Chip's misspent youth. When Chip and Mac said their goodbyes, the last of the revelers were still going strong and doing shots in the kitchen as they fried up an O'Brien's Breakfast - a mess of sausage, red potatoes, onions and eggs.

"Well, what did you think?" Chip asked as they got in the car and pulled away.

Mac looked back and said, "They are quite a collection of... "Characters..." Chip injected.

Mac said, "I was about to say, '*lovely people.*' But, why all the secrecy?

"I was afraid that a sophisticated, well-educated West County lady like yourself might be wary of going into a home full of wild Irishmen of the cop persuasion," Chip joked, "Besides, I wanted to surprise them as much as you."

"What do you mean," Mac was puzzled by the remark.

"Well I told them I was bringing home the girl I was going to ask to marry me. I just wanted them to know what they were getting into...and I wanted you to know too."

"Wait a minute, you told your entire family that you were going to ask me to marry you before you asked me?" Mac was stunned, "Well of all the nerve."

"Right, but don't worry, you passed with flying colors," Chip smiled.

"Well that's a relief," Mac shot back, "When were you planning on asking me?

And, what if I say, *No!*"

Chip pulled over to the curb and put the car in park. He reached in his jacket pocket and when he pulled out his hand, he opened his palm to reveal a small Kelly green box. "How about now...will you marry me and be my Queen of Sheba?"

Mac opened the box to see a 1-carat diamond mounted in between two Celtic hearts in a white gold and platinum setting. She was very quiet and solemn as he slipped it on her finger. Then she looked back at Chip and her eyes welled up.

"Does that mean *Yes* or *No?*" He asked.

Mac threw her arms around him and said, "It means Yes... Oh Chip it means, *Yes!*"

———————

The ride back to her condo and the ass-pinching race up the stairs was just a prelude to the unbridled lovemaking session that lasted until well past noon when the two exhausted lovers collapsed into each others arms.

As Mac drifted off to sleep spooned up in front of Chip with his powerful right arm around her, she thought of so many things. *Mrs. Charles Michael Harrigan IV*…hmmm, that has a nice ring to it.

She reached down and pinched her own butt and whispered, "It's not a dream…*it's a dream come true*."

And no nightmares from dark and distant days would ever change that she vowed.

———◆———

KIRTSCHNER'S JOURNAL ENTRY: 1H/2H

Ada Elizabeth Robertson Devereaux returned home from the Muny Opera. Her evening's companions saw her in safely and then left for their own homes on the surrounding stately streets. Ada went upstairs and entered her bedroom. She turned on the table lamp and immediately noticed that the recessed wall panel above her dressing table was slid completely to one side and the concealed wall safe behind it was wide open. *My God! I've been robbed!* She rushed over and reached inside to retrieve her jewelry box. She opened it and was relieved to find that everything was still inside. *What were they after if not this?* Then she panicked and reached back into the safe and felt around to see if the small envelope she had secreted behind the jewelry box was still there. Her hand felt nothing but the safe's felt lining and she groped even more feverishly hoping it was in the back corner.

"Looking for this, Mrs. Devereaux."

Ada's heart leapt almost out of her chest as she spun around sending a shower of crystal perfume bottles flying onto the bedroom carpet. She could see the silhouette of a man standing in the shadows behind her daybed on the far side of the half illumined room.

"My God, who are you? You're frightening me."

The figure stepped into the light and said, "I'm the man who's holding your late husband's wedding ring. *To Pierre Love Forever, Ada*...that's a touching sentiment," Harrigan read from inside the gold band.

Ada stood trembling in stark terror as the onlooker watched an involuntary shower of urine spray from between her legs and run in rivulets down both her thighs, calves and onto her feet and the carpet.

"I'm sorry, I didn't mean to scare the piss out of you, Mrs. Devereaux," he said.

Let me re-introduce myself. We've met once before, I'm Chief Of Detectives Charles Michael Harrigan and this is my associate, Mr. Thomas Culhane. On that cue, *The King Of Kerry* stepped out of her darkened bathroom.

Culhane tossed her a bath towel and said, "Wipe your piss off and sit down and shut up."

Ada did as instructed and then she folded the towel, placed it under her wet bottom and sat down on the dressing table's chair. *"What do you want.?"*

"The truth, Mrs. Devereaux. We want the truth...*and $2 million dollars*," Culhane said.

"Actually Charles Michael wants the truth, all I really care about is the $2 million in insurance money that you stand to collect for killing your husband."

"That's absurd," Ada blustered, "Why I'd never..."

Culhane yelled, "I said shut the fuck up!"

"Look, Mrs. Devereaux, before you get all huffy and put your royal knickers all in a twist, you'd better see what we've got on you and your dear old Dad," Harrigan injected.

Harrigan reached in his pocket and pulled out a fistful of official looking envelopes,

"Let me enumerate what I have here for your education and edification:

1. This is a sworn statement from Mr. Salvatore Rizzo that attests to the fact that he and his brother Mario shot and killed Mr. Devereaux and his girlfriend.

2. This is a sworn statement from Mr. Sumner Reynolds that attests to the fact that he hired the Rizzo brothers to kill your husband on behalf of you and dear old Dad.

3. This is Mr. Reynolds statement that confirms that the very same wedding ring we found in your safe tonight was taken from your dead husband's finger and given by Mario Rizzo to him and that he subsequently gave it to you and Daddy before the final installment in the murder for hire money was paid.

4. This is an affidavit from Dr. Percy Leicester attesting to the fact that he performed an abortion on you in this bedroom.

5. This is a corroborating statement from Mrs. Willie Henderson who assisted him.

6. This is the report from your physician attesting to his diagnosis of syphilis.

7. This is Mrs. Henderson's sworn statement about the events surrounding Mr. Devereaux and your sister Edith that also transpired on these very sheets.

8. Finally, this is the proper Search Warrant for these premises executed by Judge Francis X. Slack of the St. Louis Circuit Court.

The envelopes were all neatly labeled and laid out on Ada's bed one by one. Then Harrigan walked over and handed Ada the Search Warrant signed by Judge Slack "We have it all Mrs. Devereaux," Harrigan concluded.

"That said," Culhane injected, "We're not unsympathetic to your situation. After all, getting syphilis from your husband is bad, losing a baby because of it is even worse, but having him give the syph to your own sister by fucking her right here in your bedroom on your own marriage bed, well that's a killing offense, at least in my book," Culhane said.

"What do you want me to do..." Ada asked.

"Call your Daddy and tell him to go outside and get into the car that's waiting out front.

There's a nice colored gentleman waiting to bring him here," Harrigan instructed.

Ada did as she was told and then hung up to await EOR's arrival.

"Care for a cigarette?" Culhane offered her an *Old Gold*.

"Thanks, I could use one...and I could use a drink too."

"What's your pleasure?"

"Scotch, you'll find a bottle of Dewar's in the bathroom linen closet on the 3rd shelf behind the towels," Ada took a deep drag and blew a smoke ring at the ceiling, "In a way, I'm glad this is all over."

"Oh it's not over...at least not yet," Culhane corrected.

"Can I wash up before my Father gets here?" Ada asked expecting a common courtesy.

"No you can't, we want Daddy to smell your piss and know just how scared you are," Culhane snapped.

———

About 35 minutes passed until EOR arrived. He bounded up the stairs with Fred Washington right behind him. He burst into the bedroom and went immediately to Ada's side. "What is the meaning of this outrage?" EOR glared at Harrigan and said, "I'll have your fucking badge."

"Robertson, why don't you have a seat and join your daughter in a game of shut the fuck up," Culhane said.

"And just who are you?" EOR stood his ground.

"I'm your worst fucking nightmare or your newest best friend; it kinda depends on how our conversation goes."

"I said, *who are you!*" EOR was not used to being ignored.

"I'm Thomas Edward Culhane, now sit down and shut your fucking mouth or I'll have the *Big Nigger* here shut it for you," Culhane took his coat off and threw it on the bed. His .38 in the shoulder holster was now clearly visible. It had a calming effect on EOR.

"Charles Michael, show this pompous asshole the Search Warrant and tell him what we have on him and his fucking Special Maid Of Honor from the Court of Love and Beauty," Culhane glared at EOR.

EOR put his arm around Ada and said, "Have you no respect for a widow?"

"As a matter of fact, we don't," said Harrigan and here's why. He grabbed the Search Warrant back from EOR's hand and displayed the eight envelopes on the bed as he repeated the litany.

Confronted with the display of evidence, EOR's demeanor shifted from the antagonistic autocrat to the negotiating businessman, "Okay, are we under arrest? Or do you and Mr. Culhane have another arrangement in mind," he asked.

"Mr. Robertson, we are not entirely unsympathetic of your situation, but we can't have citizens killing people in public parks and then collecting insurance money to profit from it, now can we?" Harrigan asked.

"Look, do you seriously think we had Pierre killed for the insurance money. That's just plain stupid. We don't need any more money. We have more money than you'll ever dream about!" EOR was angry…and as Culhane predicted, angry men will make mistakes.

"Oh, I don't know about that, *I'm a pretty big dreamer,*" Culhane laughed.

"Pierre deserved to die. He gave both my daughters a syphilis death sentence. He killed my grandson. He killed my bloodline. He killed my legacy," EOR was erratically rambling.

"We might agree with that, but another innocent woman also got killed, why was that?"

"She was just a cheap little flirt, a teller at the bank. She saw Pierre's account balances and I think she thought she could whore her way into his bank account. I'm on the Board at Southside and I exposed her after Reynolds trailed her and Pierre to their love nest. She was to be fired and would have been when she came back from vacation. She was just in the wrong place at the wrong time."

"None of that alters or justifies the fact that she's dead. And the last time I looked, sucking the cock of a philandering asshole like Pierre was not a killing offense," Harrigan emphasized, "So don't try to peddle your holier than thou Brahmin bullshit out here on main street."

"Is there any accommodation that we might reach," EOR asked.

Culhane thought, *"Here is the moment when we play the 'pride and joy' card."*

Harrigan was very stern, "There may be an accommodation, but it will be entirely on our terms. No exceptions, No haggling, No negotiating. You have to agree to every detail or we'll haul your ass and your daughter's ass up before the Grand Jury faster than you can say, *'Jack Robinson.'*"

Culhane laughed, "Frankly I'd like to see that, dragging the high and mighty Robertson name through the bloody, muddy streets would be fun to watch, but it wouldn't be too good for Continental Shoe sales would it? I can just imagine the great Edmond O. Robertson on trial with all the syphilis testimony and bloody murder news spilling out on every front page in the country. That'd also set a lot of tongues a waggin' at St. Louis Country Club I'll bet."

"Look, obviously you two are ready to make some sort of deal to make all of this go away. I'm ready too. Just tell me what it will take," EOR seemed resigned.

"Listen close and say, '*I agree*,' after you hear each condition," Culhane instructed, "Pay close attention this is the law enforcement and justice dispensing part of our discussion."

Harrigan began to read the list of conditions,

1. There can be no profit from the killings.
   "*I agree*"
2. The entire proceeds from the insurance $1.5 or $2 million will be disbursed as we specify.
   "*I agree*"
3. You and your daughters must leave the City of St. Louis and never set foot inside the City Limits again.
   "*I agree*"
4. In addition to the $2 million in insurance payments, you will pay out another $10 million over the next 10 years at a rate of $1 million a year from your own personal funds as we specify..
   There was a long pause and then Robertson sighed and said, "*I agree*."
5. You will withdraw your financial support from the Prohibitionist efforts "*I agree*"
6. You will immediately contribute $500,000 to the Missouri Democratic Party and another $500,000 to the National Democratic Party to help FDR get elected.
   "*I agree*"
7. Willie and Bee Henderson will receive an immediate lump sum retirement payment of $150,000 from the Devereaux estate.
   "*I agree*"

Harrigan concluded, "In return, the official story will be that Pierre Laclede Devereaux and an unidentified woman were slain by Salvatore and Mario Rizzo, two petty criminals during a robbery attempt. We'll tidy up all the loose ends like Sumner Reynolds and Dr. Leicester and the case will be officially closed. You will make a statement about how grateful you are to the Police Department and then you and your daughters can retire from public life to live out your remaining days in all the comforts that God sees fit to give you. Now here is the list of who gets the $1.5 to $2.0 from the insurance death benefits."

EOR looked at the list.

From Insurance: $1.5 Million level

Sons Of Garibaldi Italian Benevolent Association - $100,000

The Ancient Order of Hibernians - $1,000,000

The St. Louis Police Department Widows and Orphans Fund - $200,000

Fr. Dempsey's Charities - $ 200,000

If payout is $2.0 million

$500,000 to establish College Scholarship Fund for sons and daughters of police families

From Personal Funds:

FDR Election Fund - $500,000

Missouri Democratic Party - $500,000

The Hendersons - $150,000

Kerry Investments - $1,000,000 per year through 1941

EOR looked up at Culhane and Harrigan and said, *"This is nothing but absolute extortion."*

"Yes it is," Culhane noted, "And today, we Irish have elevated it to a fine art form."

"We'll expect to see $3.65 million deposited in this account by a week from today."

Culhane handed him an account number at Cass Bank. "That shouldn't be a problem for a man who just moments ago said, '*We don't need any more money. We have more money than you'll ever dream about!*' "

"Here's something for you to dream about in the meantime, Mr. Robertson. If the money isn't there as agreed, we will give your daughter and you six columns of Front Page Grand Jury indictment news. That'll give her a whole new set of reasons to piss in her panties," *The King Of Kerry* concluded.

"Oh, and I'll be hanging on to all of these documents and to the wedding ring we obtained here today with this Search Warrant. You know, I always said that if we found the wedding ring we'd find the killers. Have a nice evening," Harrigan picked up his hat and left the room.

"Since you've just become my very silent and *ever to remain so*, business partner, I'll be in touch from time to time too," Culhane said as he put his suit coat back on, "It's been a pleasure doing business with you Mr. Robertson. Mrs. Devereaux, you may change your panties now. Fred, let's go."

Harrigan, Washington and Culhane left by the side door and walked down the street to where Culhane had parked. The three men got into the car and looked at each other and burst out laughing, they had just secured over $13 million in cash commitments from EOR and Ada. And they had done it with empty envelopes, a dummied up warrant, non-existent affidavits from dead men, the help of a colored maid, an abortionist doctor, a safecracker and two and a half great big sets of Irish balls!

They had cut the Gordian Knot in one bold unexpected stroke.

The article in the *St. Louis Star* three days after EOR had deposited the $3.65 million read as follows:

DEVEREAUX MURDER SOLVED BY RELENTLESS POLICE WORK

By Fredrick Kirtschner
of The Star Staff

The St. Louis Police Department today largely concluded the investigation into one of the most shocking double homicides in St. Louis history. Social lion and Continental Shoe Company executive Pierre Laclede Devereaux and a yet to be identified woman who were murdered in Tower Grove Park on March 16, 1931. In the ensuing months, a squad of detectives led by Charles Michael Harrigan pursued an investigation that concluded with the apprehension of Salvatore Rizzo 39, of St. Louis.

Salvatore Rizzo and his brother Mario Rizzo 42 were identified by tips from reliable police sources as probable suspects after a spending spree and loose talk about the crime. Salvatore Rizzo confessed to his role in the hold-up before attempting to escape from police custody at the Statler Hotel. Rizzo asked to use the bathroom in his hotel suite and then used the opportunity to flee into an adjoining bedroom. When police officers broke down the bedroom door and rushed in, the escaping Rizzo panicked and fell to his death while trying to make his way along the 8th story ledge to a nearby fire escape.

Chief Of Detectives Charles M. Harrigan enforced a news embargo on Salvatore Rizzo's death and confession until members of the elite detective squad could arrest his brother Mario Rizzo at his home on Shaw Avenue. Mario Rizzo managed to elude police and has apparently fled the city. Detectives did recover evidence linking the other Rizzo brother to the crime. Evidence recovered at Mario Rizzo's home included Mr. Devereaux's diamond stickpin and monogrammed jewelry, his wallet and topcoat.

Reliable sources within the department believe that Mario Rizzo might have been tipped by his brother just minutes before the police arrested Salvatore Rizzo in his Statler Hotel suite. This reporter's sources believe that Mario Rizzo has fled to Miami, Florida or possibly to Havana, Cuba.

Edmund O. Robertson, president of Continental Shoe Company and spokesman for his widowed daughter Mrs. Ada R. Devereaux and the family expressed their gratitude to the Police Department and especially to Major Jeremiah O'Connell of the 7th District and Chief of Detectives Harrigan for the expeditious manner in which they pursued the case. "It was a fine example of rigorous and professional police work which is a hallmark of the Metropolitan Police Department under Chief Strickland's leadership," Robertson said.

The Robertson family and Continental Shoe also announced that the entire proceeds from Mr. Devereaux's insurance policies would be donated to worthy charities and civic booster groups in the community.

Chief of Detective Harrigan has vowed to continue the pursuit of Mario Rizzo and to keep the case open until Rizzo can be brought to justice.

———

Newspaper Clipping – *St. Louis Globe-Democrat*, June 25, 1931

A Cup Of Joe with Joe

Your morning coffee column with Joe Leonard

Final Chapter In Tower Grove Park Murders? – It all seems a little too tidy to your breakfast companion. Pierre L. Devereaux is laid to rest. Salvatore Rizzo falls to his death while attempting to escape from police custody and his accomplice brother, Mario Rizzo vanishes into thin air. Police recover crime scene evidence in Rizzo home and everyone lives happily ever after.

Morning Joe says, "What about Madame X? Who was she? The case will never be closed as far as I'm concerned as long as that *"participle"* is left dangling!"

———◆———

The King of Kerry was congratulated by his cadre of colleagues at a sumptuous private dinner at the Hibernian Hall. It was a night of cigars, fine wine, fine food and celebrating and no one was happier than Robert Emmitt Hannegan, who had just received two checks for $500,000 each. The election of FDR and the career of Harry S Truman took a big upturn that night.

"It's an ill wind that doesn't blow someone some good," Culhane said, "Let's hope this wind blows FDR all the way into the White House."

When Charles Michael Harrigan joined the party a few minutes later, Culhane rose to his feet and said, "Let's give a proper tribute to the new President-elect of the Ancient Order of Hibernians. Gentlemen join me in a song. Culhane led

the group in his finest baritone rendition of the Irish tune...
Harrigan! That's me!

> *H-A-double R - I –G-A-N spells Harrigan,*
> *Harrigan!*
> *Proud of all the Irish blood that's in him*

A century later, one hundred years to the very day and hour, in a moment of universal sychronicity that Carl Gustav Jung and Brendan Francis Behan might have reveled in, the McGauley-Harrigan wedding guests finished singing the traditional second chorus of the Harrigan family theme song.

> *Devil a man can say a word agin him...*
> *H-A -double R -I –G-A-N - you see,*
> *It's a name that shame never has been connected with*
> *Harrigan that's me!*

All the groomsmen crowded around Chip in a half-circle ready to assist if needed, as he reached under his bride's wedding gown and tickled her thigh in his 'search' for her garter. After Mac flashed him her, *"get on with it look,"* he pulled off his bride's garter and tossed it high in the air toward the cluster of horny bachelors leaping and howling on the other side of the dance floor.

Then Mac stood up and turned with her back to the crowd of yet to be married maidens and tossed her bouquet over her shoulder. A crowd of screaming single women leapt high and her special maid of honor, and her best friend since freshman year at Villa Duchesne emerged victorious...and Mary Alice Gagliardi never looked happier.

Mac and Chip joined his groomsman cousin, Tommy Culhane, who was now sporting Mac's garter on his sleeve as he asked Mary Alice to join him in a traditional dance for the newlyweds and the couple with the hopeful hearts who caught the bouquet and garter.

As Mac and Chip glided around the dance floor, she smiled and remembered what Fred Kirtschner had so prophetically written in his Journal,

"In St. Louis it's all connected."

LVII

Loose ends and unmade beds from Mac's
Yahoogle searches and other Archival Records:

Emil Schumacher purportedly took his own life in his garage. Single pistol shot through the roof of the mouth into the brain with his own service revolver. July 14, 1932.

Fred Washington moved to Chicago after Repeal in 1932. He ran the Chicago Kerry Great Lakes Enterprises and became prominent liquor distributor in Chicago, Joliet, Gary and Cleveland. He was active in the NAACP, Black media enterprises and National Democratic politics. Died in 1986.

Clovis Lucille Washington, the Queen Of Sheba closed her Memphis businesses moved to Chicago with son Fred in 1941 and lived the life of a happy grandmother.

She frequently visited her special friend in St. Louis. Died of old age in 1974.

Isadore Cohen became the operational head of Thomas Edward Culhane's Kerry Midwest Enterprises in Missouri, downstate Illinois, Indianapolis and the Quad Cities. Was the longtime CFO and financial architect of what became Kerry Importing Companies USA, a Fortune 1000 company. Now run by **Frederick Thomas Culhane Washington III**. (aka: "TC" for *Top Cat*)

Joe Culhane, retired from the force in 1933 and joined Kerry Midwest Distributing as a sales manager until he retired and moved to Bull Shoals, Arkansas. Died in his sleep in 1977.

Luigi Columbo, left the police department and became a successful real estate executive and served as alderman from 'The Hill' until his death in 1982.

Carmine Gaglairdi, killed in a hail of bullets on the steps of St. Ambrose Church after attending 6 a.m. mass allegedly murdered by Johnny Vitale, 1938

Eamon 'Finn" O'Meara, enlisted after Pearl Harbor, Sergeant, USMC died on Iwo Jima. Awarded *The Navy Cross* posthumously.

Mickey Finnegan, retired from the force and died peacefully in his sleep in 1964.

Sean Corrigan, retired from the force, tragically killed with his wife Emily in an automobile accident on their way to Florida for vacation in 1963.

Ada Robertson Devereaux, died from unknown causes at her family's hunting estate in St. Denis, Missouri in 1949.

Edith Swan Robertson, died from unknown causes in seclusion at her family's western estate in Palm Desert, California in 1951

Edmund O. Robertson, died in Palm Desert, California in 1965 of a heart attack while playing golf with Bob Hope.

Frederick Kirtschner, killed in action in France while serving as war correspondent with the 3rd Army, September 12, 1944.

Gordon Philpott Alcott – retired from the *Star-Times*. Taught Contemporary English Literature at the University Of Michigan. Died in Ann Arbor, Michigan 1961

Arnold "Dext" Dexter – moved to California and worked as the Assistant Managing Editor of the *Sacramento Bee*. Died at his desk in the newsroom of a massive cerebral hemorrhage in 1959.

Percival C. "Perky" Leicester MD– Moved from St. Louis for health reasons in 1932, died in New Orleans in 1953.

Jeremiah O'Connell, became one of the most distinguished Chiefs of Police of the City Of St. Louis. Died peacefully in his sleep in 1972.

Robert Emmitt Hannegan, 1903-1949, one of FDR's earliest supporters, Commissioner of the IRS 1943-1944, Democratic National Committee chairman, 1944-1947, United States Postmaster General 1945-1947, purchased St. Louis Baseball Cardinals with Fred Saigh in 1947. Died suddenly of a massive heart attack in 1949.

Hannegan was an early supporter of Harry S Truman and saved Truman's career in 1940 when he threw his support and the support of "influential St. Louis Democrats" behind Truman in a three way race with Lloyd C. Stark and Maurice M. Milligan, who split the Pendergast machine vote in Kansas City.

Hannegan brokered the deal that put Harry S Truman on the ticket with FDR in 1944.

Judge Francis X. Slack, Prominent attorney, Circuit Court Judge, business associate, confidant and lifelong friend of *The King Of Kerry*, died happily aboard his boat, *Slacken Off Again* in Long Boat Key, Florida in 1968.

Charles Michael Harrigan, *Iron Charlie* – St. Louis' toughest cop retired in 1956 spent his time restoring old cars and occasionally driving his pride and joy, a 1930 Cadillac

Madame X with Fleetwood coachwork in local parades. In the ultimate irony of ironies, the car was always used by subsequent generations to chauffer newly married couples in the family from the church to the reception. Mac rode in the back seat of the same car that *Madame* X had died in 100 years before. As for Charles Michael himself, he was married to the same woman for 47 years, sired 4 sons and 3 daughters.

Died peacefully in his sleep in 1979.

Thomas Edward Culhane, *The King of Kerry* - Died of congestive heart failure just 24-hours shy of 90 years young on October 17, 1972. His funeral wake was held at the Howard Funeral Home on South Grand Avenue in the 16th Ward of The City Of St. Louis and it went on for 3-days and 3-nights. His wake was attended by two sitting U.S. Senators, the daughter of a United States President, (who was representing her father, who was too ill to attend. The King's old friend Harry died the day after Christmas 1972), the sitting governor of Missouri, the mayor of St. Louis, the Fire and Police Chiefs, the prosecuting attorney, many aldermen, the city corner, municipal, state and Federal Judges, icemen, pipe fitters, coal deliverymen, union bosses, rank and file policemen and firemen, Jewish tailors, bartenders, accountants, and a stream of weeping women, whom his sister Mary Clare delicately described as *'Tom's special friends.'*

He had been a widower for over 40-years, but he never lacked for lovely female companionship. More than one person said that he could have been the President Of The United States, if only he had wanted to. But he had too much fun being *The King Of Kerry* and he always had plenty of cash, a new car, many pairs of highly-polished shoes, very fine suits and many stylish hats from Levine's with a **LIKE HELL IT'S YOURS** name tag in the inside of each hatband.

His last living act was a deathbed call to Clovie and Fred Washington to express his love and to wish them well. He left

Fred a long hand written letter with his *Last Will and Testament* that acknowledged Fred as his son and equal heir with Harry and Rosemary. He made sure that his *Queen of Sheba* and her cub were well-taken care of.

Mary Kathleen McGauley Harrigan – retired as webKSDK News Director, to devote her full attention to her family. She locked the Kirtschner Journals and The Mercantile Library archival clippings away in a PODS facility in Maryland Heights. She thinks it might make an interesting story in a hundred years or so. Currently busy nursing her third child, Charles M. Harrigan V, 8 lbs 7 ounces, an Irish Prince, loved, admired and spoiled by his older twin sisters, Helen Rosemary and Mary Anne.

Charles Michael Harrigan IV - Chip, graduated with honors from Washington University School of Law and joined Kerry Importing Company USA in its St. Louis office as an international trade attorney specializing in Chinese markets.

"One hand washes the other..."

The Newspaper Clipping File

Newspaper Clipping – *St. Louis Star,*
March 17, 1931

DOUBLE MURDER IN TOWER GROVE PARK

Frederick L. Kirtschner
Of The Star Staff

The southwest end of Tower Grove Park near Arsenal and Kingshighway was the scene of a grisly double homicide last night. Patrolman Lester C. Batavia of the 7th District was alerted that gunshots had been fired in the park by Mr. and Mrs. Ted Sloboda of 5520 Arsenal Street.

The Slobodas had returned home from bowling and as they were entering their home, they heard a series of gun shots fired from the park. Officer Batavia investigated the scene and found a male and female victim apparently shot to death in the back seat of a late model Cadillac.

A police news embargo was put on the crime scene and details are not as yet forthcoming. Major Jeremiah O'Connell, commander of the 7th District referred all questions to Chief of Detectives Charles Harrigan. He did comment that crime in the 7th District is extremely rare and that the murder has the appearance of a robbery at first examination.

———

EXTRA BULLDOG EDITION
Tower Grove Park Murder Victim May Be Socially Prominent Shoe Executive

Frederick L. Kirtschner
Of The Star Staff

Informed sources to the *Star* have confirmed that the car, in which the Tower Grove Park murder victims were found on the evening of March 16th, is registered to prominent St. Louisan Pierre Laclede Devereaux. Mr. Devereaux is the executive vice president of Continental Shoe Company and the son-in-law of its president Edmund O. Robertson

Major Jeremiah O'Connell, commander of the 7th District could not be reached to confirm the information obtained by this reporter. All inquiries were referred us to Chief of Detectives Charles M. Harrigan who is heading the investigation. Chief Harrigan was also unavailable for comment. However, the *Star* was successful in obtaining a photograph taken at the crime scene. The Missouri license plate visible in the photograph clearly shows that the number is PLD 1764. We are currently awaiting official confirmation from the Missouri Department Of Motor Vehicles on the registration. *Star* sources in Jefferson City have reported that the official DMV records when released through police channels will confirm that the custom-built 1930 Cadillac 'Madame X' with coachwork by Fleetwood will be registered to Mr. Devereaux.

Female Victim's Identity Remains Shrouded In Mystery

As to the identities of the male and female victims found in the car, no official report has been released from the Coroner's Office or from the office of the Chief of Detectives. Speculation is rampant that the male victim may be Mr. Devereaux. *Star* sources confirm these suppositions. However, as the *Star* goes to press, neither the family nor the police have confirmed this widely held conjecture. The female victim also found in the car has not been identified.

Photo Cutline:
Chief of Detectives Charles M. Harrigan and unidentified officers examine the trunk of the car confirmed by exclusive *Star* sources as belonging to Continental Shoe Company executive, Pierre Laclede Devereaux.

———➤———

Newspaper Clipping – *St. Louis Star,*
March 20, 1931

City Elite Shocked By Murder Of Pierre Laclede Devereaux

Frederick L. Kirtschner
Of The Star Staff

Mystery continues to whirl around the murder mayhem in Tower Grove Park.

The *Star* has learned that 15 to 20 shots were fired in the assault that took the life of socially prominent St. Louisan, Pierre Laclede Devereaux, son-in-law of Continental Shoe Company president, Edmund O. Robertson and husband of former Veiled Prophet special maid of honor, Ada Robertson Devereaux.

The Devereaux and Robertson families have not been available to comment on the tragic and mysterious circumstances surrounding the murder of the shoe executive and the female victim who has become known as "Madame X."

Reliable *Star* sources reported that the company believed that Mr. Devereaux had departed from St. Louis earlier this week on a sales trip to New York City. Calls by this reporter to the New York Athletic Club and the Missouri Athletic Club here revealed that Mr. Devereaux had not made his trip arrangements as believed.

Coroner Taylor released a preliminary report that indicated that the male victim had been struck by 12 shots and the female victim by one. Chief of Detectives Harrigan refused to speculate as to motive, but did confirm that various pieces of jewelry and personal property belonging to the victims had been removed from the car.

Chief Gordon Strickland urged the citizenry to remain calm and to co-operate with the police as the investigation moves forward. Strickland said, "I do not believe that this is the start of a crime wave, but rather an isolated incident such as a robbery that went terribly wrong. Residents of the area and the entire city can be assured that we will not rest until the murder or murderers are apprehended and brought to justice. I have ever confidence in Chief of Detective Harrigan and his elite detective bureau."

Funeral services for Mr. Devereaux have not been announced. Attorney Jonathon McCall, acting as spokesman for the family did say that the services would be strictly private.

———————

Newspaper Clipping – *St. Louis Star,*
March 21, 1931

Married Playboy And "Madame X" Murders May Have Mafia Connection

Frederick L. Kirtschner
Of The Star Staff

The most recent round of rumors swirling in the city's crime circles are putting their money on a Mafia connection to the murder of Pierre Laclede Devereaux and the yet to be identified "Madame X" who was found slain in what has been reliably reported as a compromising position in the rear seat of the playboy shoe executive's car.

Reliable informants and exclusive **Star** resources have confirmed the fact that Mr. Devereaux has been a frequent visitor to area speakeasys, gambling parlors and 'houses' in recent years. Attempts by this reporter to obtain comment from the Devereaux family have been thwarted by a phalanx of attorneys led by Jonathon McCall.

The incident has caused a high level of public embarrassment to the prominent family and its scion, Edmund O. Robertson, who sits on the boards of many prominent St. Louis companies and charitable organizations.

Chief of Detectives, Charles M. Harrigan, discounts the Mafia assertions as pure speculation. "The crime has all the earmarks of an amateur robbery attempt. Professional murderers would not kill their victims in such a public way. They strike fast and silently," Harrigan asserted.

Speculation as to the identity of "Madame X" has fueled the prurient interests of local citizens and her identity and rumors of what her relationship to the late Mr. Devereaux has become the topic of conversation in every corner diner, coffee shop and elegant hotel or private club dining room all across town.

So far, *Star* reporters have been unable to gain access to the Coroner's photos of "Madame X."

Coroner Taylor has kept them as part of the news embargo being enforced on the case. He did comment however that the photos were too disturbing to be fit for publication in any newspaper.

—◆—

Newspaper Clipping – *St. Louis Globe-Democrat*, March 20, 1931

A Cup Of Joe with Joe

Your morning coffee column with Joe Leonard

Persuasion is crime prevention – Chief of Detectives Charles M. Harrigan's new crime initiative at Union Station is already paying big dividends. Scuttlebutt from the sages at Wheelchair Willy's shoe shine stand and from around the *Fred Harvey* stools has it that last St. Patrick's Day eve, two known criminal associates of Chicago mobster Al Capone reportedly we're intercepted arriving at Union Station by Chief Harrigan's special crime detail. The two thugs from *The Windy City* ended up heading right back to Chicago after a brief meeting with Harrigan's elite squad. Chief Harrigan commented, "Persuasion is a good form of crime prevention. Our goal is to point out the disadvantages of setting up a crime league in our city. And to see that criminals return home immediately with the message that St. Louis is closed to criminal enterprises."

Morning Joe says, "More free donuts and coffee from *Fred Harvey* and the lovely *Harvey Girls* for our hardworking St. Louis policemen, Eamon O'Meara and Sean Corrigan!"

Newspaper Clipping – *St. Louis Star,*
March 23, 1931

Pierre Laclede Devereaux Laid To Rest

Frederick L. Kirtschner
Of The Star Staff

The gates of Valhalla Cemetery were blocked today by private security guards to prevent reporters and curious onlookers from witnessing the interment of slain shoe company executive Pierre Laclede Devereaux.

A long line of 17 limousines with tightly drawn curtains followed the Donnelly Mortuary hearse into Valhalla at 10:30 this morning. The ceremony lasted only 45 minutes as the cortege left the grounds under the same tight ring of privacy and security at 11:15 a.m.

The police investigation has thus far produced few new leads, although an exclusive *Star* source near the case reports that the search for evidence continues apace within the park and within the surrounding neighborhoods.

Edmund O. Robertson, who has been publicly quiet since the murder of his son-in-law and "Madame X" was revealed, has not been inactive. Reportedly, he is calling the Mayor's office and the Police Chief on a daily basis insisting on faster action and demanding results. Pressure from his friends has been more public and equally insistent that the police use every means at their disposal to rapidly solve the case.

Chief Of Detectives Charles M. Harrigan would not confirm rumors that he was under severe pressure, but simply noted that the investigation is progressing along several fronts and that all leads are being followed up. He urged the public to be patient and to allow the detective bureau to do its job without undue interference or criticism.

The *Star* has dedicated a special team of investigators to assist this reporter in the coverage of this story.

Managing Editor, Gordon P. Alcott announced today.

Newspaper Clipping – *St. Louis Star,*
March 24, 1931

NO REST ON 7ᵀᴴ DAY AS PRESSURE MOUNTS ON POLICE DETECTIVES

Frederick L. Kirtschner
Of The Star Staff

One week has passed since the bullet-riddled body of socially prominent shoe executive Pierre Laclede Devereaux and his presumed paramour "Madame X" were found in Tower Grove Park. Mr. Devereaux was laid to rest in a private ceremony in Valhalla; "Madame X's" body still lies unclaimed and unidentified in the city morgue.

Chief Of Detectives Charles M. Harrigan in a *Star* exclusive intimated that "new and promising leads" had recently surfaced and that the entire detective bureau was running down every lead. Edmund O. Robertson has reportedly continued an unabated behind the scenes campaign with the Mayor, the Board of Alderman and the Chief of Police.

Rumor has it that Robertson is pressing for a new investigative team to replace Chief of Detectives Charles M. Harrigan. When reached for comment in a *Star* exclusive Police Chief Gordon Strickland brushed aside the assertions and said, "The Mayor, the Governor, the Police Board and I have every confidence in the ability of Chief Harrigan and his bureau. Don't believe everything you read in the newspapers."

Who is Madame X?

The seminal question that is rife with innuendo and speculation remains, "Who is Madame X?" and what were she and the late and very married Mr. Devereaux doing in Tower Grove Park at midnight?" So far, the Devereaux Family and Edmund O. Robertson's attorney spokesmen have remained notably mute on this subject. *Star* editors invite letters of comment from out readers.

Newspaper Clipping – *St. Louis Star*, March 25, 1931

THIS IS THE FACE OF 'MADAME X' STAR OFFERS $250.00 REWARD

Frederick L. Kirtschner
Of The Star Staff

The artist's sketch below is a *Star* exclusive. The drawing was made from autopsy photos taken at the City Morgue by the Corner's office. Exercising its First Amendment rights, the *Star* will not identify the exclusive source of these photos, but assures its readers that Managing Editor Gordon P. Alcott and Assistant Managing Editor Arnold Dexter have substantiated the veracity of the photographs.

If you have any information regarding the identity of "Madame X" please call **OL**ive 3456, the *Star's* special reward phone number. The *Star* will pay $250.00 to the first person to successfully identify "Madame X" the young woman slain in a hail of bullets in the back seat of shoe tycoon, Pierre Laclede Devereaux's custom-built Cadillac on March 16, 1931 in a Tower Grove Park lover's lane.

Chief of Detectives Charles M. Harrigan hailed the Star's initiative as a fine example of civic spirit designed to aid the intensive investigation underway by the St. Louis Police Department's elite detective bureau.

PHOTO CUTLINE:
Madame X, do you know her? Is she a neighbor, a co-worker, a friend or just an unfortunate stranger passing through St. Louis?

The woman is described in the preliminary Coroner's report as: **Jane Doe** White female, 18-25 years of age, 108 lbs., 5' 0" tall, with crescent birthmark ¾ " by 2" on left inner thigh. Blonde hair (dyed) natural hair color: brunette, green eyes. Red manicured finger nails and toe nails. The female victim was hit by a total of one (1) fatal shot. One (1).32 caliber round was recovered from the remains of the right posterior lobe of the victim's brain.

Gordon P. Alcott, *Star* Managing Editor commented, "The *Star* is committed to helping Chief Harrigan and his squad bring the murderer to justice and will spare no time, effort or expense in pursuit of that goal.

Newspaper Clipping – *St. Louis Globe-Democrat,* March 26,1931

A Cup Of Joe with Joe

Your morning coffee column with Joe Leonard

Thugs Vandalize Neighborhood Furniture Store – Furniture retailer Dennis Brenahanny was injured in an assault and robbery in his north side store on Union Boulevard at Natural Bridge Avenue earlier this week. A gang of thugs knocked him out, robbed his cash box and vandalized his store before fleeing. "It all happened so fast, I didn't get a good look at any of them," Brenahanny reported to police.

Morning Joe says, "Let's put more beat cops out on the street!

———◆———

Newspaper Clipping – *St. Louis Post-Dispatch*, March 30, 1931

Watchman Kills Burglar Who Killed Housekeeper

Post-Dispatch Reporter
Harry H. Nelson

Matt Hellman, a watchman at *The Celtic Room Restaurant* at Grand and Dodier responded to a shot fired in the upstairs business office yesterday shortly before noon. Hellman, first to arrive on the scene found the lifeless body of Mamie O'Halloran, 46, the housekeeper on the upstairs landing. Miss O'Halloran, who lived in the apartment adjoining the business office, apparently surprised the burglar who was ransacking the business office where the day's cash receipts were kept.

Matt Hellman opened fire on the burglar who was trying to flee with the contents of the cash box kept in the owner's desk. The burglar was identified as Matthew Brenahanny 22 of 5475 Kensington Avenue was pronounced dead at the scene.

Chief Of Detectives Charles M. Harrigan speculated that, "Ms. O'Halloran must have walked in and caught Brenahanny in the act. Ms. O'Halloran was killed by a single shotgun blast to the abdomen. She was walking toward the gunman, not running away. Amateur thieves often panic when startled during the commission of a crime and that's when innocent people get killed."

Police have taken the matter under investigation, but no charges are anticipated against Mr. Hellman. Business owner Thomas E. Culhane was out of the country at the time of the crime and could not be reached for comment.

Newspaper Clipping – *St.Louis Post-Dispatch*, March 31, 1931

Raging Inferno Destroys Family Residence On Kensington Avenue

Post-Dispatch Reporter
Harry H. Nelson

The home of Mr. and Mrs. Dennis Brenahanny was destroyed by fire late yesterday afternoon. The 3-story residence at 5475 Kensington was engulfed in a 5-alarm inferno that originated in the basement, possibly by the ignition of a 100 gallon heating oil storage tank.

The 6 known residents of the home are missing and presumed dead. Battalion Chief Gary T. Bingham said that it would be several days before the Fire Department could make a definitive determination as to the cause of the fire. The fact that the 3-story brick building collapsed into the cellar has complicated investigators trying to sort through tons of wet and smoldering debris.

Two other bizarre incidents of misfortune have also befallen the Brenahanny family in recent days. Kensington Avenue owner and resident Dennis Brenahanny had recently been in the news because his furniture store was robbed and vandalized, and his twenty-two year old son Matt was shot to death just hours before on the same day as the fire in a thwarted burglary attempt.

At this juncture, police have no evidence to make any connection between these three incidents.

This reporter wonders if this is the *"Bad Luck of the Irish?"*

Newspaper Clipping – *St.Louis Post-Dispatch*, April 10, 1931

Too Many Suspicious Coincidences In Three Brenahanny Police Cases

Post-Dispatch Reporter
Harry H. Nelson

On March 30th the home of Mr. and Mrs. Dennis Brenahanny was destroyed by fire and six family members perished in the inferno. Earlier the very same day, their son, Matt Brenahanny 22, was shot and killed in an alleged burglary in *The Celtic Room* business office. And, just days earlier, the Brenahanny Furniture Store at Natural Bridge and Union was robbed and vandalized and owner Dennis Brenahanny was assaulted.

Are "Coincidences" Linked To Bootlegging Rivalry?

The 3-story Brenahanny residence at 5475 Kensington was engulfed in a 5-alarm inferno that originated in the basement, possibly by the ignition of a 100 gallon heating oil storage tank. The St. Louis Fire Department investigation listed the nature of the fire as *"Suspicious"* but stopped short of an *"Arson"* assessment.

Battalion Chief Gary T. Bingham said that the Fire Department could not make a definitive determination as to the cause of the fire. The fact that the 3-story brick building collapsed into the cellar complicated investigators trying to sort through tons of wet and smoldering debris.

The two other bizarre incidents of misfortune that also befell the Brenahanny family have been further obscured by the so-called accidental cremation of the body of Matt Brenahanny. Spokesman for the Coroner's office reported that young Brenahanny's body had been placed in a mis-labeled autopsy storage unit and that it had been sent to the City Crematorium prematurely.

Reliable *Post-Dispatch* sources have reported that his father, Dennis Brenahanny had been selling bootleg whiskey out of his store and that this may have provoked violent actions by associates of Thomas E. Culhane, proprietor of *The Celtic Room*. Culhane is a figure frequently mentioned in connection with alleged illegal liquor distribution and other criminal activities in St. Louis.

The Post Dispatch is calling on the Circuit Attorney William J. Geekie to initiate a special investigation into these horrific incidents. We also urge Chief Gordon C. Strickland to appoint a special lead investigator to replace Chief Of Detectives Charles M. Harrigan, who is related to Thomas E. Culhane owner of *The Celtic Room*. Detective Joseph P. Culhane of the detective bureau is also a brother of Thomas E. Culhane.

Three coincidences and an accidental cremation of a shooting victim prior to an autopsy stretch the boundaries of Police Department integrity and credibility beyond the breaking point. The St. Louis Police Department cannot let these incidents simply be swept under the carpet. The Brenahanny family and the citizens of St. Louis deserve a thorough investigation into these matters.

Newspaper Clipping – *St. Louis Star,*
June 24, 1931

DEVEREAUX MURDER SOLVED BY RELENTLESS POLICE WORK

By Fredrick Kirtschner
of The Star Staff

The St. Louis Police Department today concluded the investigation into one of the most shocking double homicides in St. Louis history. Social lion and Continental Shoe Company executive Pierre Laclede Devereaux and a yet to be identified woman who were murdered in Tower Grove Park on March 16, 1931. In the ensuing months, a squad of detectives led by Charles Michael Harrigan pursued an investigation that concluded with the apprehension of Salvatore Rizzo 39, of St. Louis.

Rizzo and his brother Mario Rizzo 42 were identified by tips from reliable police sources as probable suspects after a spending spree and loose talk about the crime. Salvatore Rizzo confessed to his role in the hold-up before attempting to escape from police custody at the Statler Hotel. Rizzo asked to use the bathroom in his hotel suite and then used the opportunity to flee into an adjoining bedroom. When police officers broke down the bedroom door and rushed in, the escaping Rizzo panicked and fell to his death while trying to make his way along the 8th story ledge to a nearby fire escape.

Chief Of Detectives Charles M. Harrigan enforced a news embargo on Salvatore Rizzo's death and confession until members of the elite detective squad could arrest his brother Mario Rizzo at his home on Shaw Avenue. Mario Rizzo managed to elude police and has apparently fled the city. Detectives did recover evidence linking the other Rizzo brother to the crime. Evidence recovered at Mario Rizzo's home included Mr. Devereaux's diamond stickpin and monogrammed jewelry, his wallet and topcoat.

443

Reliable sources within the department believe that Mario Rizzo might have been tipped by his brother just minutes before the police arrested Salvatore Rizzo in his Statler Hotel suite. This reporter's sources believe that Mario Rizzo has fled to Miami, Florida or possibly to Havana, Cuba.

Edmund O. Robertson, president of Continental Shoe Company and spokesman for his widowed daughter Mrs. Ada R. Devereaux and the family expressed their gratitude to the Police Department and especially to Major Jeremiah O'Connell of the 7th District and Chief of Detectives Harrigan for the expeditious manner in which they pursued the case. "It was a fine example of rigorous and professional police work which is a hallmark of the Metropolitan Police Department under Chief Strickland's leadership," Robertson said.

The Robertson family and Continental Shoe also announced that the entire proceeds from Mr. Devereaux's insurance policies would be donated to worthy charities and civic booster groups in the community.

Chief of Detective Harrigan has vowed to continue the pursuit of Mario Rizzo and to keep the case open until Rizzo can be brought to justice.

——————

Newspaper Clipping – *St. Louis Globe-Democrat*, June 25, 1931

A Cup Of Joe with Joe

Your morning coffee column with Joe Leonard

Final Chapter In Tower Grove Park Murders? – It all seems a little too tidy to your breakfast companion. Pierre L. Devereaux is laid to rest. Salvatore Rizzo falls to his death while attempting to escape from police custody and his accomplice brother, Mario Rizzo vanishes into thin air. Police recover crime scene evidence in Rizzo home and everyone lives happily ever after.

Morning Joe says, "What about Madame X? Who was she? The case will never be closed as far as I'm concerned as long as that *"participle"* is left dangling!"

- 30 -